Grandly Told Tales

Grandly Told Tales

Grandly Told Tales

The Donahues of Solebury

Family, Friends and Enemies Alike

Joseph F. Doherty

Elderberry Press

> Elderberry Press, Inc.
> 1393 Old Homestead Drive
> Oakland, Oregon 97462-9506
> Telephone/Fax: 541.459.6043
> www.elderberrypress.com

Elderberry Press, Inc. books are available from your favorite bookstore, Amazon.com, or from our 24-hour order line: 1.800.431.1579

Library of Congress Control Number: 2005929045

Publisher's Catalog-in-Publication Data
Grandly Told Tales/Joseph F.Doherty
ISBN 1932762248
1. Detective—Fiction. 2. Suspense—Fiction. 3. Police Procedural—Fiction. 4. Cop—Fiction. 5. Literary—Fiction. I. Title.

This book was written, printed and bound in the United States of America.

Elderberry Press, Inc.
1393 Old Homestead Road
Oakland, Oregon 97462
www.elderberrypress.com

They say that the words of one good man
can neutralize a complete textbook of evil.

– Joe Donahue

Acknowledgments

.

With credit to all, a shout of praise to my friends for their vote of confidence and the faith they had in me to pull this book together.

I tip my hat in thanks to those great friends of mine who have been such stalwart buddies and understanding companions while I was writing this book. There is no way that this book could be what it is without them.

First, thanks to Aaron Twer and Reverend Curtis Von Dornheim, two neighbors who labored vigorously over this tome during the initial phases. They made suggestions and gently asked me to change this or that. Eventually this thick-headed Irishman saw the light and the realistic view of what they presented to me. I made the corrections, changed the text and yes, I loved what came out. Thank you both. Guys, I value your friendship more than you will ever know.

John Bagdonas: My critic and ultimate authority on international money matters. John, you filled this mush-head with facts, figures, and tricks of the trade that only the insiders know. Thank you, buddy.

Kathryn Kelly: My wife, lover, confidant, friend, taskmaster and proofreader. "Yes dear, I will do the dishes as soon as I finish this paragraph." Kathryn possesses the strength of "I am Woman" and was my model for the heroine of this story. God, I love you honey! Thank you for who you are.

Kelly Hurley: What can I say; in my view, this girl is the world's best editor. She has taken a manuscript written in crayon and helped me create the best word picture of the mixed up things in my life. Her craftsmanship made this story believable and even readable. The check is in the mail, Kel! With much thanks and my deepest respect: Thank you.

Dave St. John of Elderberry Press has once again listened to my craziness, calmed me down and made the tweaks needed to make this book flow in an easy to read manner. Thank you, Dave.

The front cover artwork is the creation of one of the most gifted free hand artists I have ever had the pleasure of getting to know. Raven O'Keefe, in my mind, ranks right up there with the masters of the craft. Thank you, Raven. You captured the essence of this book and made it come alive.

I told my neighbor and friend Art Steinmark that I was having some technical problems getting my manuscript into PDF format for the printer. Art said, "I can do that for you, Joe" and a ton of concern was lifted from my shoulders. Together we produced the artwork for this book, but it would never have been what it is without Art's craftsmanship and attention to detail. Thank you, Art.

I can't stand deadlines; they drive me nuts. At the eleventh hour, facing an impasse concerning the cover typography, Dee Gammons came to the rescue. Dee is my original editor and webmaster and an all-around great person to know. Visit her website if you get the chance: "Designs by Dee" at www.angelfire.com/in3/deweb. Thanks, Dee; you are the best

Lastly I thank God for my ability to remember facts, names, places, faces and occurrences. I thank Him for the ability to add to the craziness that happened in my life and make it real to the reader yet humorous as well.

Contents

GRANDLY TOLD TALES

CHAPTER ONE

Not Unless You Kiss Me

S o I admit it, I needed a few dollars to make the monthly bills. Retirement income just didn't make it sometimes. The "daily work/daily pay" office just down the street would be open soon and I knew that I would be first in line. Mrs. Grandly always gave me the nicest jobs and so I always greeted her with a big smile. Sometimes I would be a dog walker or house sitter, but the jobs I liked most were the companion positions. These were mostly richer folks just needing someone to talk to them. I usually found these folks to be very interesting, if not a bit sad. As usual, here I was awake at four in the morning with plenty of time to prepare for the day. I took a long hot cleansing shower, shaved, and dressed in some nifty khaki trousers, my nicer slip-on brown loafers and an open-neck light tan, short sleeved shirt. I looked pretty good for an older man, if I did say so myself. I sat to the feast of the morning meal. One poached egg, coffee, orange juice, toast, and half-dozen vitamins and medications to combat the ravages of old age, which for me were mainly due to boredom. Jack was in the cabinet but I told him that I would see him later. Finishing a half can of beer left over from last night, I brushed my teeth and was ready for the adventure of the day.

Mrs. Grandly greeted me warmly and as usual, I sensed her not-so-hidden desires. The longer than necessary handshake, the tiniest yet understood extra squeeze, the depth of her eyeball contact, and her moist lips were not lost on me. I filed this data into my memory bank for further investigation. I always filed and never investigated; for me it was just fun and exciting to consider the possibilities and "trouble!" A special kind of companion job was the offering of the day; a terminally ill man wanted someone to talk to and walk with him a few times today. The pay was good, the job sounded easy, and his nurse would be there in case of an emergency. I took the job. Mrs. Grandly handed me a nylon bag with Velcro straps and told me to give it to the nurse upon my arrival. I was told to bring it back when the day was done, a five-hour job, not too bad for a hundred bucks. Mrs. Grandly said, "Have a nice day, Joe," and I was on my way. It always bothered me when she used my name but I did not know why; someday I would figure that out.

The bus ride across town was uneventful; traffic was light and the passengers few. I got off at the proper stop and found myself in a very affluent part of town. I located the address easily and approached the wrought iron gate centered in the ominous looking black-spiked fence. I went to press the announcement button on the squawk box but I noticed that the wires were hanging free. I looked at it closely and, being that I was an adventurous sort of guy; I touched two wires together figuring that maybe the chimes inside the house would announce my arrival. Sparks crackled telling me that the system was short-circuited and I chuckled at the thought that I probably had just blown a breaker in this guy's fuse box. I nudged the gate with my foot and it opened slowly. Rusted hinges squeaked and I had to shoulder my way in and onto the inlaid weed-laden Belgian block walkway. Passing the untended gardens and untrimmed hedgerows, I made my way to the front door. I knocked on the once majestic doors, which were now dirty, paint-chipped, and faded; I was curious as a cat on a roof. The door opened and a musty aroma smacked me in the face.

The male nurse was a regular sort of guy: open, friendly, and informative. He led me inside with a handshake and a businesslike attitude. The house was gaily decorated but in near total disarray. The nurse told me that the household staff had been let go or had quit months ago. It seemed to me that this guy wanted to die alone amidst the squalor of his splendor. I saw the posters and the ensconced awards and I knew whom I would soon be meeting. The nurse took the bag and told me that this was an AIDS patient with little time left; I cringed. I wanted to bolt right out of there and grab that jug of Jack; this scene was just too depressing even for me and I thought I had seen it all.

We walked into the semi-dark den and there he was sitting on a chair, hands folded under his chin, elbows resting on the mahogany desk; he was emaciated and almost skeletal. He croaked a line from one of his famous songs and he elicited the right response from me; I smiled. He painfully rose from his seat to greet me but did not offer a handshake, for which I was relieved. He merely bowed his head and sadly said, "Welcome to my home." I felt a little better but I knew that this would be the longest five hours of my life.

The nurse gave Mr. Rock and Roll a glass of wine and some marijuana while telling me that none of this mattered any longer. He wanted to go the way he wanted to go, and we were expected to respect his decisions. I couldn't care less. The nurse gave me a quick critique on caring for this poor man but the bottom line was that his disease was not communicable unless body fluids were exchanged. Inwardly I promised myself to not even touch this person. Damn, I wanted a drink, but I would not taste anything in this disease-riddled house.

The sun was shining outside and the temperature was seventy-two; he wanted to go for his walk and my time to shine was at hand. With the help of two gleaming stainless steel canes, he hobbled to the French doors leading to the veranda. I walked with him slowly and cleared any obstacles ahead of him. The three slate stairs down to the walkway posed a real challenge for him so I hesitatingly put my arm around his waist and helped him down. Composing himself and looking down the path of no return, he thanked me for my assistance. Then he smiled; I saw his blackened teeth and taut skin and yet, somehow, I saw his humor as well. He said to me, "Kiss me you fool." I was of course dumbfounded and he laughed as best he could. Finally I let go with a loud "Whew;" we shared a good belly laugh. I liked this man.

He told me of the glamour that once was his life. He told me of the rapid departure of his friends, business associates, and family when his disease became known. He told me that he wanted to hate but sadness was his overriding emotion; he felt little else. I listened but could not relate to the overindulgence that brought him to this horrible station in life. We passed the Olympic-sized swimming pool, but the water was yellow and obviously as sick as its owner was. I thought it to be representative of all the ingested slime of Mr. Rock and Roll's life. I wanted to vomit and I held the tears in check. Somehow, after what was like an eternity passed, we made it back to the house. Thank God that there were no stairs leading to the side door, so getting back inside was not as arduous as when we left via the veranda.

The nurse had made some preparations while we were gone and I saw the IV setup ready to pump up our patient once again. He sat and resigned himself to be an obedient patient helping the nurse with his ministering. IV hooked up, some kind of EKG monitor blipping away, he lowered his head and fell into a welcomed slumber. I was relieved to see this and knew that I had some free time. The nurse and I played a game of chess to kill the time and I found him to be a worthy adversary in the game; then we heard the groan.

The nurse told me that we were now at the worst part of the day as it was time for samples. I was not comfortable wearing the plastic suit with gloves and facemask, but was thankful for it nevertheless. He told me that what we were about to do was not part of my responsibility but an additional five-hundred dollars convinced me that I could get through this; I agreed to lend a hand. We laid him on plastic sheets on the bed and the nurse opened the nylon bag that I had brought with me from Mrs. Grandly. Inside were all kinds of plastic tools, containers, wipes, and medical waste trash bags. We stripped him naked and I could not contain my disgust at his wasted form; I was mortified to see how badly this disease has ravaged his once vibrant body. I tried to remember him as I saw him last in a concert and on television, but surely, I thought, this couldn't be the same man. I saw the embarrassment in his eyes; I saw his apologetic demeanor and then the enema commenced. The nurse took the samples very methodically and much as we tried to afford some dignity to our charge, it was impossible. The urine sample was a bit easier, but drawing blood from collapsed veins proved to be very difficult and painful.

All of the samples, tools, and infected wipes were carefully placed back into the bag and sealed. After the nurse cleaned up our patient, we dressed him and brought him to a comfortable looking couch. He said he was hungry. We unzipped our protective suits and placed them into a large plastic bag. The nurse told me that the suits would be picked up later, as professionals would dispose of them. I was glad to be rid of it.

Eggs Benedict, tea, and toast were the menu of the day, but I passed on it for now; there was no way that I could eat in this scenario. Our patient fell asleep after breakfast and I felt so morbid, I took a nap as well. Kudos to the nurse, this guy had nerves of steel; he watched the news on television while we slept. I had two hours left on my mission but there was nothing to do. Mr. Rock and Roll never woke up. The nurse made the phone call and I was told that I could go home. He thanked me for helping and I knew that in a small way, I was now part of Rock and Roll history.

Mrs. Grandly gave me my check and expressed surprise at the bonus I had earned. She asked how it came about but I did not feel very conversational and let it pass. I went home to my digs, my dog, and my booze. I communed with Jack and replayed the events of the day. "Kiss me you fool!" he said. A tear uncontrollably rolled down my cheek. I called my friend Dr. Ken and made an appointment for a complete medical examination. I kissed Jack as well then called Mrs. Grandly. I told her that never again would I take one of her special jobs; dog walking and Housesitting were more suited to this man, thank you very much. She asked me why and I cried again; I was already half bombed. I wanted to wash it away; I needed to forget, forgive, and get on with my life for whatever it was worth. I saw a willful waste of life and I hated to see it. I put Jack back in his corner and read the book of Ecclesiastics, the King and I. The good king told me to "chase the wind all you like but the grass withers and blows away."

"Yes Mrs. Grandly, Happy Thanksgiving to you as well; now please sign me up for a saner kind of job that will not overtax my sensibilities and compassion." She said that she felt my pain but I thought she was being condescending to me. I let it slide because she had a gig for tomorrow and I needed to do something to forget what I lived through today.

CHAPTER TWO

Top Dog

I was outside sunning my sorry hide up on the roof, talking with my sybarite dog Lucy. The cordless phone rang and I was annoyed. Cranking open a crusted bloodshot eye I looked at my trusty Timex, nine A.M, geesh. Muttering to myself that whoever this was had better have a good reason to be calling me at such an ungodly hour, I unhurriedly pushed the button and answered the call: "Hello, this is Joe, how can I help you?" I said this with my normal, nonsensical faux-business attitude on full tilt. It was my not-so-favorite money pot, Mrs. Grandly, and she had another job for me if I wanted to take it: "Do you want to walk a dog and do some shopping for a retired singer?" I said yes and as usual, the job would pay one hundred dollars for five hours of boredom. I took the job and agreed to be at the address she gave me by noon, and of course I would wear my best winning smile.

I had two hours to acquire a halfway-sane mental attitude and do a refurbishment on my semi-besotted body. Into the shower I went and followed that with a fantastic breakfast of eggs and beer, my favorite "eye opener." I winked into the mirror while shaving and said, "Not bad Joe, you almost look like a normal person." I walked my mutt and even made believe that I cleaned up after her. I couldn't stand those little poop bag deals; too often I made contact with Lucy's morning masterpieces — I just loved that! 10:45 a.m. and I knew I'd better get a move on. I corralled the princess of road kill and locked up as I smiled at Jack and told him that I would see him later for a shakedown cruise. I made a mental note that he was only half full; I congratulated myself for some positive thinking in that I did not see him as being half empty. "Whoopee!" I said to myself; thirty years in construction, a failed marriage, alimony payments up the wazoo, countless sessions with the good mind-bender doctor, and finally I could say that life was on the upswing. A half-full, not half-empty, bottle of poison, yeah, big whoop. I walked down the street to the bus stop.

Fortunately for me, I saw the bubblegum on the bench so I did not sit down as I waited for the bus. Along came one of my neighbors, that grouchy dude in 3A, and he sat right down on the gum. I chuckled under my breath and made believe that he wasn't there. Tough on you, buddy, I thought. That's what you get for being such a pain in the neck with all your constant carping. The bus came and I got on but my neighbor seemed content to just sit there. Maybe he was waiting for some other bus I figured, but then again, I knew him to be a people watcher and perhaps he was just killing time with his little perverted mind game that he loved so well.

At ten minutes to twelve, I arrived at the front gate of this massive fortress of stone, complete with a gigantic iron fence. Just below the intercom button was a small sign that read, Service entrance around the corner. I guessed that was for me so I hoofed it up to the corner and made a left turn to get to the rear of the estate. The walk was long and hot as the sun had come out with a vengeance just for me. Of course I stepped in some dog poop on the way and I was royally upset with the way some people just didn't care. I wiped my shoe off in a puddle and scraped it clean in some grass. I was thankful that it wasn't the other foot, the one with the hole in the sole. Finally I found another smaller gateway and I rang the bell. "Who's there?" I heard from the voice of an apparent Spanish person. She was using a version of the English language that I would never understand. I responded with, "Señor José, the guy to walk the dog and do the shopping." The gate swung open and I made the long trek through the foliage and well-kept lawn to the rear service door. Marilyn Monroe she was not, but she smiled at me and asked me inside. The butler appeared and I was relieved to see a man who could communicate with me in my native tongue, American English.

We had tea at a small table and he signed my form for Mrs. Grandly. He was a nice enough guy and we got along fine. He then outlined my job and it seemed easy enough. I was to walk the family dog and bring back a stool sample for the veterinarian's analysis. Seems el poocho was having some intestinal problems. After that I would be off to the market with a small shopping list and a stop at the liquor store on the way back. I heard some sort of screeching in another room but since Bruno the butler paid no mind to it, neither did I. He was off to get the dog and I awaited our first introduction. Entering the room once again, Bruno had a strong leash attached to a monster of a dog. It was a breed known as a Newfoundland I was told, and she was gentle as could be. Her name was Trixie.

The dog lumbered over to me and lovingly slobbered what I guess you would call a kiss all over my hand. I wondered what they fed this massive beast but then again, in my true-to-form quirkiness, I knew that I would soon find out. The dog must weigh more than a hundred and fifty pounds and looked like a black bear with a Darth Vader mask on its head. Bruno gave me a plastic bag and container for the stool sample and off we went on our adventure. I was told to take the dog off the property and take a lot of time with the walk; Trixie needed the exercise. As the gate shut and locked behind me, the dog seemed to undergo some sort of attitude adjustment.

Tugging was an understatement; this dog was strong as a bull and dragged me along for a merry jaunt down the sidewalk toward a park that I saw in the distance. Just before my arm was torn from its socket, we made it to the park and Trixie had to go. It was almost comical to see this gigantic dog so vulnerable, all scrunched up as she did her daily duty. It never seemed to end but finally there it was a stinking pile of slop lovingly created just for me. I wretched, the stink was unbearable. I put down all my pooper-scooper utensils and leashed Trixie to a strong looking tree. I assumed that the tree would-n't mind holding this four-legged tractor-trailer at bay for a few minutes; I had some work to do.

The only thing that kept me going was thinking of the hundred dollars that I would earn by doing this. Trixie did not appreciate this maneuver very well and, in her throaty baritone voice of chastisement, hinted that she would tell her mistress how well I had not cared for her. I couldn't care less: "Sit there and wait dog, I will be with you soon enough." With great care, I managed to scoop up some of this foul smelling waste matter and get it into the container without mishap. The rest of it could feed the plants I told myself, and then had the thought that I was doing a good thing for mother earth, hooray for me! I was only gone twenty minutes and figured that I should stay out with this massive canine for a little while longer. I thought that if I let her go off the leash I would be in deep doo-doo trying to explain why the family dog went head-to-head with the number eight cross-town bus and wrecked it.

Using better judgment, I left her tethered to the tree for a few minutes more. Trixie sat there and glared at me in hatred and as much as I wanted to ignore her, I started to feel bad for her: "OK, Trixie, let's go for a hike. Pull me anywhere your little heart would care to go." Unhooking her from the tree, she made a beeline for home and I had to jog to protect myself from being dragged face down on the concrete. Although my little Trixie could have battered the gate down with one shot, she seemed content to wait for Conchita, or whatever her name was, to electrically unlock the gate. Trixie took this opportunity to take one more pee and with great luck, she missed my shoe.

This part of my job complete, Bruno took Trixie back into the house and I was relieved to hand him the treasure chest of samples for the vet. I needed a drink! Conchita gave me a Pepsi and I figured that was about all I would get from her. She started to prepare the dog's lunch: burritos, beans, and corn chips. No wonder the dog was in pain, I thought. Bruno came back with a shopping cart and handed me the list. I was told that they had an open account with the supermarket and that they would call ahead with my name. Same thing for the liquor store, all I had to do there was pick up and sign for the order. Out I went with my little cart and I whistled my way back down the walk.

Just before I opened the gate, I looked back toward the house and there on the second floor veranda was whom I assumed to be the mistress of the house. She was a bit far in the distance so I could not really see what she looked like, but there was no mistaking the flowing pink bathrobe that she was almost wearing. She looked voluptuous and top-heavy but I could not stare, so I just walked out and down the street to the stores.

Six blocks of overheated concrete and I nodded at the cute looking au pair pushing a stroller. Some other guy was walking three snarling mutts and I gave them wide berth as I passed by. Passing the park where Trixie had dragged me, I expected to see a government hazardous-materials team set up to remove the glow-in-the-dark stool that she left, but there was no activity to be seen. In my weird imagination, I told myself that the odor of the area kept all the people on the other side of the park. I just walked on by and passed this newly created no-man's land.

At the supermarket I parked the little cart and took one of the store carts to fill the order. Let's see here: orange juice, milk, bread, eggs, and a large size bottle of Rolaids. Seemed easy enough and I set to the task, wondering if I could get my own stuff on their nickel but I perished that evil thought: Well, maybe? Nah, I let it go. Checking out was a snap and I wondered why the heck I needed this gigantic drag-along cart for such a small order. Off to the liquor store I went and I found it easy enough just a half-block down the street. The owner said that he was waiting for me and knew who I was as he recognized the cart. He commenced to plop a case of bourbon into the cart along with six bottles of wine, some cocktail mixers, and four one gallon size jugs of cheap brandy.

Damn, I thought, they should have given me a truck for this order. I wished Trixie were with me; she would have loved to drag this order back to her mistress. I signed the receipt for the guy and started back to the house. The wheels of the cart were showing some wear and were sort of wobbling on the bent axle. Somehow I made it all the way back to the mansion without a mechanical or emotional breakdown and I once again pressed the button for Conchita.

I was dragging the cart up the walkway when I saw the mistress of the house sitting on a rock by the side of the walk. She was dressed the same as she was when I saw her on the veranda but now, close up, she almost caused me some shock. Her overdone lipstick was a smear on cracked lips and the mascara was too black to hide the circles under her eyes. The robe was open far too much for such a decent man as me to look upon, but I looked anyway. She stopped me, took a bottle of booze from the cart, and walked away as she ripped off the screw cap. I watched her walk and she wobbled her way from tree to tree, stopping every now and then to take a long, deep swig from her medicine. By the time she made it to the front steps she was walking just fine and dandy.

Wow, I thought to myself, and thought of Jack waiting for me back home. Bruno was waiting by the rear door; he had seen his boss as well and he could only say that this was normal for her and not to be concerned. He told me that soon she would be auditioning in the living room again and that was the screeching that I had heard before. "Who me, Bruno? No problem buddy; I'm not concerned at all but if I am done here, can I go now?" He offered me a sandwich, which I gratefully accepted, then I took my leave.

The ride to Mrs. Grandly's office was uneventful but I wished it to be over already. Welcoming me into her office, she told me that this client would like it very much if I took this job on a regular basis

24

on a once-a-week schedule. A pay increase was in the offering so I gritted my teeth and accepted this new challenge to my stomach. As she paid me, I noticed the never-to-be-mistaken black label on a bottle of Jack hiding behind a book. I made like I didn't see it and asked Mrs. Grandly if Mr. Grandly had come by to say hello. She batted her eyelashes and with a sly smile told me that there was no Mr. Grandly; that bottle was hers. Gee, I thought, I hadn't noticed that she was watching me as I looked at her stash.

Mrs. Grandly arose from her desk and kicked her office door shut. Taking down the jug, we saluted each other for a fine day's work and we laughed at the silliness of life. On the way out I told her to drop by later tonight if she felt like it, that we could commiserate with my own bottle of make-believe living. I had known her for years, but this was the first time that I actually called her by name: "See ya later, Sandy." I was off to clean up my humble abode and give Lucy a good scolding for pooping on the rug, which I was sure that she had already done.

CHAPTER THREE

History Lesson

Will your parents recognize you when you get home, Private? Thus asked my Marine Corps drill instructor way back in 1962 when we finally graduated boot camp. They had beaten almost fifty pounds off my New York City hoodlum posterior and I was a proud Marine. They told me that I was a lean green killing machine and yeah, I took that home into my heart. I joined the judo club and the wrestling team and took some boxing lessons just for the fun of it.

After about a year of that nonsense and getting far more than my share of lumps and bruises, I let that stuff go and became a half-baked intellectual. I contemplated my navel, considered how many grains of sand there were on all the beaches in the entire world, had another beer, and wasted four years and four months of my life. Not true actually, the Marine Corps took an uninformed, introverted fat kid off the streets of New York City and made him face the reality that he was a man. At the ripe old age of twenty-two, I stood on my feet for the first time in my life. For that I must give thanks to the United

States Marine Corps. Semper Fi.

That was then, this is now. I got married. I became a civilian. Took a job. Tried a different one. Got half an education at night school. Did the cop thing. Went into construction. Punished myself for thirty years. Retired and now I am on my second marriage. I was a man once again, a tad older, not so much wiser, but for sure a lot more tired.

History lesson is over, boys and girls. I hope you enjoyed it. Gosh, oh golly gee, how I would love to leave this little treatise right here and be done with it, but I just cannot. Firstly, you would all wonder just what kind of a nut I really was. Secondly, each of those little sentences above could in their own right be an essay, a book, or a story never to be told or sold. They would, however, remain my secrets for now. Suffice it to say that this "has-been" warrior of old just lived day-to-day without thinking or trying to embellish or glorify the things of the past. Better for me to leave the skeletons in the closet, for when I opened it for viewing, they screamed at me. I can't stand screaming.

My mother used to scream at me.

My father used to scream at me.

My ex-wife used to scream at me.

My drill instructors used to scream at me.

My demons scream at me.

Damn, I hate screaming.

Call me, Mrs. Grandly, and hurry please, for Jack and I are falling in love once again. Homosexual author? Nah, go to the liquor store, look at the shelves, and expand your horizons please. Three days with no shave, half a hangover, and my head was throbbing. I loved the pain and since only the mutt was here with me, I guessed it just didn't make no never mind to anyone on this earth, myself included. Almost out of cigarettes, no more beer, and the TV was busted — what a life. Shock beyond shock, the phone started to ring and broke my reverie like lightning.

Giving the sanest intro I could muster up, I managed to croak out the word, "Hello?" It was Mrs. Grandly and although I was praising God for the call, I played like Mr. Big Guy, kind of aloof, if you know what I mean. It was seven PM and it was really way past the time that she usually calls me. "What's up Mrs. G.?" I said, trying to be Joe Cool. She told me that she had a job for me for tomorrow. She was leaving the office in a few minutes. She wanted to stop by and hand deliver the supplies that I would need for the job and the work/pay slip as well.

Before I could talk her out of this crazy idea, I heard the click on the phone and she was gone. I figured that I had about ten minutes to slam-dunk this hovel into some kind of shape. I opened the windows immediately, kicked the dog up to the roof, and ran the electric shaver over the stubble on my face. A half bottle of Aqua Velva and I was good to go. I draped a semi-clean dishrag over the dishes in the sink and hid the garbage under the counter. Wow! All that in seven minutes; my drill instructor would be proud of me.

I watched as her beat-up Volvo pulled up at the curb. Gee, I thought, one of these days I had to teach her how to drive. She could not park that damn rattletrap to save herself. Well, on the third try she made it, and I watched as she spilled out to the pavement. She was walking a bit wobbly and she had her trusty briefcase with her. I scanned the mansion and saw to my horror that the bed was a mess and my three-day load of dirty skivvies was piled on the floor. I kicked the door shut and that was that. She knocked.

Mrs. G. entered with a phony flair of class, affluence, educational charm, and finesse. She was also bombed off her ass. Her coif needed some work, as did her makeup, but I paid no mind. Surely we looked well suited for each other. Scooping a half-eaten jelly donut off the table, I plopped down my jug of Jack and invited her for some liquid refreshments. Oh good, I thought, as I remembered that I had some munchies to go with our evening tonic. I brought out the can of Planters Peanuts and she was elated. We sat at opposite sides of the table and in all seriousness; she outlined the emergency job that she wanted me to tackle for tomorrow. It had something to do with kids, the zoo, and just some time-wasting exercises. I wasn't listening.

I poured, and then poured another and she gulped heartily. She asked me if I wanted to fool around and I said that I was tired. She said that that was a good thing because she was drunk and would regret it tomorrow if she remembered. I called a cab for her and she was off to the suburbs. I finished off Jack and fell into bed without reading about the job. "I think I hate myself," I muttered just before sleep hit me like a Mack Truck. I fell into the arms of Morpheus with a smile and dreamt naughty dreams of Mrs. G. and me.

Mind-shattering noise in the abode, the alarm clock was clanging like a fire truck and I had wisely put it on the dresser, forcing me to get out of bed. Emergency run to the bathroom and the dog was feeling the same thing. I booted her out and up the stairs to the roof. No milk for the coffee so I toughed it out while reading the job description. At 11 a.m. I was scheduled to take two sniveling brats on a day's outing. It seemed that their single dad wanted them out of his hair for a few hours. I scared myself looking into the mirror and chuckled that I should pick them up just the way I looked right now for laughs.

I called Sandy Grandly and told her that I was on the job and raring to go. She snidely said, "Yeah Joe, sure you are." I looked out of the window and saw that her car was gone. I gave her credit for that; somewhere she must have learned some discipline since she lived all the way up in Yonkers. All things being equal (I hate that meaningless cliché), I felt pretty good and looked ok too.

I stopped at the local coffee shop and had a morning fixer-upper of steak and eggs plus a Bloody Mary. I left the dog locked up on the roof hoping against hope that she would jump over the side and end this crazy symbiotic relationship. I found the place after some difficulty with my Iranian cab driver. He thought I needed a tour of the city as I watched his meter ever increase the fare. Akbar finally let me out and I paid him the twelve-fifty with a scowl.

Nice house, I thought, as I beheld the trappings of an upper middle class income. Knocking on the door, I was relieved to notice no barks from a family pet. I thought I was starting to hate dogs but then again, I was absolutely assured of the fact that cats have no place in this man's life. So if I needed a companion, I would stick with the princess of road-kill.

The man of the house answered and I found a harried-looking guy in an open shirt and needing a shave. He was a bit overweight but so was I, so what's the big deal? Shaking hands, he told me his name was Phil and he was really appreciative that Mrs. Grandly could help him out on such short notice. Seemed he had an important meeting to attend and no babysitter. Five hours would be plenty of time for him if I could manage to keep his kids busy and relatively happy.

I didn't like him. Didn't know why, just something about him bothered me. Oh well, I had been wrong before and the money was ok so I told myself, "Bite the bullet, Joe, and let's get on with life here." His life and even his kids' lives were really none of my business. The kids were great. Two well-dressed smiling pre-teens and I guessed that the boy was twelve and his sister, a blond beauty, about ten or so. Phil signed the pay chit and gave me a hundred dollars to spend on his kids. He told me that Mrs. Grandly had given me a fantastic recommendation and that he trusted her judgment to the max. Wow, I thought to myself, she is some liar!

Anyway, it was off to the zoo and then some rides at the local amusement park, finishing the day with a late lunch wherever they wanted to eat. Phil told me to take his SUV, which was greatly appreciated. The kids were well behaved and had no trouble with the seat belt rule. Parking at the zoo was a snap during the week so we didn't have to walk a zillion miles to get to the turnstiles.

The boy, who was named Ralph, loved the rides on the camels and the ponies, but little Sue wasn't all that interested. She opted for the petting pound where she could cuddle tamed critters of every shape, sort, and stink. I was bored to death but wore my best smile. And then I saw it, the edge of a large black and blue mark just above Sue's knee. Her shorts covered the rest of it, but it got me wondering what had happened. I said nothing but I started to realize that little Sue was a sullen kid.

Three hours of animal smell was enough for my USDA requirement for the next century or so and my sense of smell was overjoyed to once again inhale the exhaust fumes in the parking lot. Off we went to the amusement park. Since Phil asked me not to smoke in front of his kids and I was the obedient servant, I was getting edgy. I bought fifty bucks worth of tickets for the rides and hoped that they would be entertained long enough for me to cop a few drags of my nicotine narcotic. Ralph was like a dynamo: he wanted every ride and he wanted it now. Sue was ok with just tagging along and she said bumper-car rides were her favorite. They begged me to go with them and so I reluctantly wedged myself into one of those brightly colored mini-cars on the electric floor. Ralph proved to be manic in his efforts to crash my little car to smithereens, while Sue just wanted to tool around the oval in a ladylike manner. Ralph granted no quarter and pummeled his sister's vehicle into the wall often. I developed a dislike for little Ralph and I found myself administering some sorely needed discipline to him and his little crash mobile. It was all in fun, right?

After a few repeated rides on that craziness they lost interest and I sighed in relief. Ralph wanted to ride the roller coaster but there was no way that Sue or I would go on it with him, so he went alone. Sue and I waited for her psychotic older brother to finish that ride and we engaged in some small talk. I casually asked about the black and blue mark on her leg. She told me that she fell off her bike but I saw the lie in her eyes; I saw the quivering lower lip and I saw the uncontrolled tear form in the corner of her eye. I dropped the subject, as I knew enough to justify my immediate dislike for daddy dearest, Phil. I wanted to hug her and tell her that I would slay her demons but it was not my place and knew that those kind of emotional displays could and would lead to trouble for me. I was uncomfortable or maybe I was angry, but I became quiet as my mind formulated all kinds of sick scenarios in which this poor kid may be the victim. I lost my zeal to entertain these kids but had to phony out the rest of the time.

Finally loaded into the SUV, we headed off to McDonalds for the promised Big Mac and fries. I allowed them to go in alone as long as they promised to sit at the table in front of the window so that I could see them at all times and they agreed. I sat in the car and they did the right thing and I was happy. Listening to some right-wing conservative talk radio, I puffed on a Lucky Strike. Limbaugh was talking about unreported child abuse and how it was learned behavior, a family trait that, unless interrupted, would perpetuate from generation to generation. I looked at little Ralph as he stole his sister's French fries and I watched as Sue put up no resistance. I thought of my own wacky childhood and my resulting craving to be left alone in this world. I thought of my need to anesthetize my mind in a halfhearted attempt to silence my demons. I wanted better for Sue and yes, if possible, for Ralph as well. It was time to take them home.

His BMW was in the driveway so I parked directly behind it almost bumper to bumper. The house looked quiet and I had a feeling that I was in the enemy camp. The kids barreled out of the car and Ralph yanked open the garage door to get his bike and head out to parts unknown. No problem kid get lost, was my thought. As Sue took my hand and thanked me for a great day, she broke my heart. Phil opened the door, we stepped inside, and Sue went upstairs to her room. She did not run and hug her dad; she did not say anything at all, just disappeared to her safety zone. I smelled marijuana in the house and Phil's eyes were glassy.

I wanted to deck this nerd where he stood. I gave him his receipts and his change and he signed the slip for Mrs. Grandly and so, business done, I made for the door. He stopped me, walked over, and handed me a hundred-dollar gratuity. I saw shame and fear in his eyes but said nothing to him. How noble it would have been to tell him to shove it, how I wished that I needed not sell my integrity to this crumb of a man. As Harry Chapin once sang, "I stuffed the bill in my shirt." I called Sandy and went directly to her office; we needed to talk.

The office door was locked but I saw the light in the transom so I knocked. Listening to the pitter-patter of Sandy walking across the wooden floor, I lit up a Lucky. She locked the door behind us, as we knew that some of her wino clients would be banging on the door for money soon. Tomorrow was payday and they all knew it, so there was no guilt about the silent treatment toward them. We sat at her desk in the inner office. Martha, her secretary, had gone home for the day so she poured some liquid refreshment and we relaxed. I told her my fears for Sue and Ralph. I told her about the smell of grass in Phil's house. I wanted to know if she knew more about them.

She said that Phil was a new client and he visited her office only once. She never met the kids but shared my concern; it seemed that Sandy and I both cherished the same things out of life. To be left alone was foremost on her mind as well as my own. If by chance we were to enjoy a momentary fling of freedom, then good for us, but neither of us wanted an ongoing entanglement. In short, her fears were the same as mine and her history was almost identical as well. We were empathetic toward Sue and Ralph and at this late stage of life we decided to make a difference in any way that we could. We agreed to pay a visit to Phil unannounced, using the premise of lost keys. I was happy to have a co-conspirator, and a witness was a good idea as well. We went out for dinner and decided to "drop by" Phil's house around eight, which we figured, would be around bedtime for the kids.

As Sandy pulled to the curb in front of Phil's house I noticed that she did a superb job of parking. I kept my mouth shut in order to avoid getting slapped "upside the brain-housing group." She shut the Volvo down and we nervously approached the front door. Phil opened the door even before we knocked and he was not all that surprised to see us. With slurred speech, he invited us in and we noticed right away that he had company. He told Sandy that she must be the master of rapid response, as he had only called her office forty-five minutes ago. Sandy was not the master of rapid response but she sure was a quick thinker. She said that she had monitored the call but was unable to answer it at the time and here we were. We guessed that we were invited to his little party, and so we canned the idea of lost keys and decided to play this scene by ear.

Phil was wearing a half-pound of gold-plated junk around his open shirt and he looked like a drunken has-been rock star out to impress everyone. There were about a dozen odd-looking people scattered around the living room or sipping drinks on the back porch. We mingled and let Phil introduce us around to his misfit friends. A poet looking for a publisher, a house painter for the upper class (or so he said), and some guy who told us he was in international banking. I assumed him to be a file clerk but I tried to look impressed nonetheless. Two suit-wearers were on the deck smoking grass. Sandy and I chose not to venture out there and upset their recreational therapy for now.

The ladies were a montage of polyester Victoria's Secret rip-off evening gowns. More than a few were well on their way to tipsyland and we wore our most ingratiating, albeit phony smiles. Finally we were alone by a wall and just before we had a moment to chat, little Sue walked into the room carrying a platter of hors d'oeuvres. My jaw dropped. I felt rage. She seemed to be a different person. She acted coquettish and even wore makeup. Coming over to serve us, she bowed rather sexily and said, "Good evening Mr. Joe, it is good to see you."

Sandy's grip on my arm felt like a steel vise. We both knew that this was a serious, sick, and disastrous place for this child. I asked where Ralph was and she said that he was upstairs playing video games with one of the neighbor's daughters. I didn't want to know any more information; I had to get out of this place and do something to make this right.

We said nothing to Phil, just opened the door and walked out without even a nod to any of the others. We looked up from the driveway and there was loud rock music coming from one of the bedrooms. So much for Ralph and his video games, I guessed. The bedroom lights were not turned on. Sue stared at us from the living room window and I saw the tears and yes, the defiant glare was there as well. We had to turn and walk away. I swore to Sandy that I would find a way to make this right and she said she would be with me all the way. For now though, we decided to find somewhere to sit down and think about all this.

We climbed the stairs to my unimposing little mansion in the sky and Lucy was happy to see us. Sandy said that we should be nice to my little companion and that maybe a little walk in the night air would do all of us some good. Back outside we went and we let Lucy drag us to her favorite dumping and hunting ground. We sat on a park bench and let the dog run free. Who knows, maybe she would find somebody else to care for her better than I; better yet, she could get lost and find fame and fortune over at the local pound.

Sandy said we should call the police or the child abuse center for some advice or intervention. I saw that we had three options: either call the cops, call a buddy of mine to straighten him out in more direct ways, or just forget it and call it the pick of the draw, that's life, and all that. I rationalized that both Sandy and I had come through pretty much the same kind of upbringing. Sandy said, "Yeah Joe, we have, and look at us now, we don't trust anybody and can't find real love." I told Sandy that I had a drinking buddy down in the local cop-shop: he was a detective and I would call him in the morning. We put this whole scene to rest, leashed up the mutt, and slowly walked hand-in-hand back to my apartment.

I awoke early and roused Sandy from a deep sleep. She purred like a kitten and asked when I was bringing her breakfast. I laughed and told her to get dressed and brush her teeth, we were off to the coffee shop and vittles were on me; Impressive, huh? We ate in record time and Sandy was off like a rocket to get to the office in time. I had the rest of the day to play Pope Joe.

I called Barney down at the precinct and he asked me what time it was. "C'mon Barney get over it, you are on the clock now and you are a public servant so give me the pleasure of dropping by your den of iniquity for a little chat." I brought him coffee and donuts, his favorite breakfast after a night of beer and chips. I had known Barney for years, ever since growing up in the Bronx. Although we went our separate ways for long periods of time we always seemed to meet up again back at our favorite watering hole, The Arbor Bar & Grill.

"You look like crap, Barney," I said, to which he responded with an expletive that I would rather let you just think about. It was a slow day in the cop-shop so Barney had the time to listen as I unspun my tale of Phil, Sue, Ralph, Sandy, and me. Barney told me to get a real job. Then he told me it wasn't his department. Then he told me that this stuff happens all the time. Then he told me that he was too busy. Then he ran out of excuses and I laid into him with all the times I had bailed him out of the craziness of our youth. He told me that he would do a little off-the-record investigating on our buddy Phil and see what he could come up with. He asked about the wife in this tale of woe but I was clueless.

In my mind I had done the best I could. I let it go went to the park, slugged down a beer in a bag, and fed the pigeons. When I got back to the apartment, Lucy was in distress so out we went again. I often wondered just what it is that this dog thought I owed her in life; all she did was recycle money. Interesting thought there, I pondered: I bought the food; she ate it and changed it into fertilizer, which replenished the earth and fed the economy to boot. I was indeed a fine upstanding citizen. Well, it was a nice afternoon, so I bought another tallboy and took my seat at the park to watch life go by and the dog chase the squirrel that she never could catch. I did notice the blinking light on the answering machine but I figured that I had had enough drama for today; I would check it when I came back. Phil's extra hundred bucks made it ok for me not to pursue another job with my dandy Sandy Grandly. I started to think about who I was. I was weighing what I thought was morality against the desire to better one's self.

I was thinking of The Sermon on the Mount and how I had acted toward my fellow man. I was thinking of injustice, misery, crime and punishment, and how I fit into the grand spectrum of things. I knew that I was one of those little grains of sand on unnamed beaches scattered the world over. This was déjà vu for me because I remembered that over thirty years ago, I was thinking the same things. What did I do with my time, what difference had I made in this world? In honesty, I knew that I had failed my family, failed myself, failed my country, failed my fellow man, and had failed my God as well.

I knew that so often in the past I had shrugged my shoulders and walked away from situations that I knew I could rectify, so often I had put my own well-being first and thus allowed others to suffer needlessly. It was time for a change. I grow weary of letting the bad guys win. This time I would stand for truth, peace, purity, happiness, and the American way. This time I would be God's little big-mouthed ambassador. This time I would lay down my life (gulp) to set a captive or two free. I went back toward my dungeon to check the voice-mail and feed the dog, the dog that was never satisfied with the menu that I prepared for her.

Barney was waiting for me.

So was Sandy.

Sitting in different cars.

They didn't know each other.

I laughed.

Gee, where did the time go? I thought; it was already two-thirty PM. It was time for some proper introductions, a few laughs, and then maybe some deep thinking on the plans about the Phil/Sue/Ralph issue. We all trudged upstairs to my palace in the bricks, lead paint, and crumbling plaster. Stepping over Woodrow the janitor who was snoring soundly in his urine on the second floor landing, we entered the Joe-ordained nonsensical free zone of life, the place in which I opted to hide from the light of God. Lucy went into attack mode; she didn't like Barney so she peed on the floor.

Barney had the shakes so I gave him an afternoon treatment of my special form of medication. Two aspirin, two cups of black coffee with Jim Beam in them to spark up his medulla, and we were off to the chase. Sandy just shook her head in dismay and asked me if this guy was really a cop. Barney muttered an expletive, called her a bimbo and we all laughed. The team of "Phil Busters not so Anonymous" became a reality. Barney told me that if I would have stayed on the force with him so long ago, I could be just as screwed up as he was. I responded that construction work did the same thing if you let it and I allowed myself to get just as screwy in my own right. Sandy became a bit sullen and said that her ex-husband was a cop. We dropped the subject immediately.

For starters, Barney could not find any documentation on the mother of these children. It seemed that on first glance Phil and his two kids just appeared on the scene two years ago from who knows where. He told us that some of his cohorts were doing a deeper look-see using Phil's social security number. Barney talked the real estate broker out of a lot of information but as yet it had not been checked out. Barney read from his scribbled notes. Phil Fauxmaster, age 38, worked at home as a stockbroker for one of the big houses down on Wall Street. He was fairly successful and had no criminal record with the NYPD. He had a two-year lease on the house they lived in and it was up for renewal next month. So far, according to the real estate people, it seemed that he would be staying put, as he had not informed them of any plans to move out.

The kids went to the local school where Ralph had been in some minor scrapes with other kids. It seemed that he was a bully. Sue was a quiet kid, holding her own with her studies, but definitely an introvert as reported by the guidance counselor. Neither child had a good attendance record. Barney said that he could probably bust Phil on a pot charge but it just was not worth the effort unless he was a major supplier, which he doubted. Further, it would shed some distrust on Phil's part toward his two new friends, Sandy and Joe. We all thought that for now we should not cause him any grief. Maybe, if we found some heavier information, things could shape up and we could get these kids some help and away from him.

Barney smiled. It was four PM and he was now off duty. A quick call to the desk back at the precinct told him that nothing was going on, see ya tomorrow and on and on. "Oh yes," the sergeant said, "you have a message here from Bobby. Bob just said, 'call me.'" Sandy wanted to make a call as well and she checked with Martha, her secretary. All was quiet there, so Sandy poured, I smiled, and Barney moaned. Out came the trusty peanuts and even a few napkins to show some class. I tossed the dog a bone. A knock on the door caused a temporary pause to the festivities. It was Bob, Barney's detective pal; he even flashed me his tin to gain entrance to my humble abode. I was impressed!

Bob Goodman sat and I saw a professional cop. He seemed to be a guy who exuded strength and intelligence coupled with a tenacious attitude to rid the world of criminals and protect the innocent. He told us that the Sarge on the desk made a note of my phone number on the caller ID and did a reverse trace. Bob wanted to see us right away as he was holding a hot potato and here he was. I was starting to worry about my half-full jug of Jack but Bob waved off on the libations. That didn't stop Barney or Sandy so I poured for three and popped the top off the peanuts.

Bob told us that Phil had kidnapped his children from their home where they lived with their mother, Phil's estranged wife. He and his wife were divorced four years ago and he had left Chicago to come here to New York. "It seemed that he went back there two years ago and grabbed the kids off the street on the way home from school," said Bob. The FBI had already been notified, so Bob told us to take a back seat from any further dealings with Phil and his family. The worst part of all of this was that the mother died in an automobile accident soon after Phil took the kids.

She had reported the husband to the FBI but they didn't look into it as well as they should have. She was told to get a lawyer and have him file extradition procedures. Since she passed away, nobody pushed the issue and it kind of dropped off the radar screen. Phil's wife, Carol, had a brother but he was out of the country. Apparently nobody even tried to find him. Phil and his kids fell through the cracks of jurisprudence because of negligent police work. I guess Phil thought he was home free but he did commit a federal crime and crime didn't pay, or so we said.

We batted these facts around the table for a while and came

to realize that in the final analysis, after all the courtroom hoopla, Phil was the natural father and nothing would change. A good lawyer would probably denigrate the mother and prove that from the beginning, Phil should have had the kids and now they would be better off staying with him. Sandy was livid and I wanted to go over and choke Phil just for GP. Poor Barney got loaded after only two drinks and we shuffled him off to the couch. Bob took off to his family and I thought, oh, how I wish I were he.

Sandy and I talked, and in truth, we did our best to laugh at the crazy flip-flops that life can take. I reminded her of the terminal rock star that she had me visit. When I told her that the guy said, "Kiss me you fool!" Sandy cracked up with laughter. The drunken diva story had her in stitches and she told me that I was her best employee and so I always got the problem clients. She asked me how I was doing, like really doing, and I knew that she wanted to get up close and personal. I gave her my usual shrug of the shoulders and a noncommittal answer of, "Same old, same old. You know, like, I'm ok, ya know what I mean?" Our hands touched across the table. White flashes of electricity passed between us. Barney belched; the dog passed gas, and we knocked over the bottle of Jack. We left the apartment and went up to the roof for some air.

Standing by the parapet we looked over our booming metropolis below us. Sandy reminded me of an old television show called The Streets of New York. She asked if I remembered the intro to that show that said, "Eight million people in this city and eight million stories: this is just one of them." I remembered it well and told her that we were just two of those stories. The proverbial "grains of sand on the beach" theme came back to me but I let it go. I took her into my arms and kissed her with true meaning. Perhaps for the first time in my life, I felt comfortable with another person. Sandy wanted the same things out of life that I did and it had nothing to do with confusion, mistrust, pain, or suffering. Both of us were tired of seeing injustice and man's inhumanity to mankind. We wanted to make a difference in this world, a difference that would be a benefit even if for only one other person.

The stars were out in all of their glory and we did not detect the stink of the alley below us. We were elevated to a plane of existence that we welcomed; this indeed was a new thing for both of us. If true inner spirits could manifest themselves into the physical world, then that was what happened. We found peace and acceptance there on that roof, and we wanted to bring it to its next and naturally occurring step of the life cycle.

At that very moment we both saw a shooting star cross the heavens. We smiled and I kissed her again. How comical we would have appeared to a teenager if one happened by, two "senior citizens" in a hot embrace. How little they knew of real life, true love, and mutual respect. "Amazing how this old body can still react," I said to her and in her knowing way, she smiled.

We went downstairs to clean house.

"Rise and shine, Barney blue eyes, it's time to go home." He grumpily arose from the couch and in his crumpled suit; he managed his way down the stairs and down the street, heading for the nearest gin mill. Sandy and I took the dog for a walk in the cool night air. Lucy happily gave us a magnificent work of art and for Sandy's sake, I did the right thing – yuck! We went back to the apartment and that is all you will know about that.

Sandy had to leave as it was nearing ten PM. Her daughter and her new husband were flying in from Germany tomorrow morning and she would be there to meet them and take them to her home in Yonkers. I put away Jack and all the other junk strewn about the apartment, and for some reason, I started to reassess my living conditions. Exhausted, I fell into bed and slept like a baby.

I was banging around the apartment cleaning and polishing my treasures. I even polished my old Marine Corps pewter beer mug. The phone rang. Sounding sober, which was probably the first time in a week and a half, I clearly said hello. It was Sandy. It was noon and I was happy to find that she interrupted my little domestic chores. She was all excited about her daughter and her new husband. She wanted me to meet them: "Meet us at Frangelicos in an hour, ok?" I told her I would be there especially since that stale bagel I ate was all I had eaten so far. Lucy said it was ok for me to go, for which I thanked her profusely, I gave her a yummy and I hit the shower.

I was early; I was always early, and I had no damn idea why I did that. I guessed that having a friend was such a new and good thing for me that I didn't want to do anything to screw it up. Same thing about jobs, I was always early because I thought that maybe somebody was waiting to fire me for any old excuse. Anyway, three Luckies later, I saw the Volvo pull to the curb. Sandy and her look-alike daughter walked arm-in-arm along with a Marine Lieutenant in uniform.

I read his ribbons and was impressed. Sandy greeted me with a ladylike hug and a peck on the cheek. "Joe, this is my daughter Sue and her husband Steve; they just flew in from Germany." Sue was charming and Steve had a grip like iron, just as I expected. Sandy was the perfect icebreaker, telling Steve that I was a brother Marine, her best friend and business associate. I had a real chuckle with that one but I let it slide for now, we would see where that went.

I noticed that Steve had a little trouble calling Sandy Mom, so Sandy graciously told him to call her by her name and not to sweat the small stuff. Big grin from Steve and I was liking this guy already. Frangelicos wasn't crowded and getting a table was easy. I ordered venison with bearnaise sauce, well done if you don't mind. Sue had shrimp Caesar salad with dressing on the side. Sandy wanted beef bourguignonne and Steve wanted a hamburger and fries. Then I knew I liked this guy. Sandy ordered a magnum of Piper Heidseik Brut and the toast was to Sue and Steve, "forever in love, forever in happiness." We had a grand time talking about good times and I knew that Steve wanted to pump me about Vietnam. I could not go there with him and he respected that for now, at least I thought he did.

Sue and Steve went on to tell us that Steve's sister had been killed in a car wreck a year and a half ago and nobody had notified him at the time. He was wondering about his nephew and niece because the mail was returned marked "RTS address unknown." He wanted to find his brother-in-law so he could at least find out what happened, see his nephew and niece, and visit his sister's grave.

He was flying to Illinois in a few days to do some investigating, as the local police were of no help to him on the phone. Sandy and I felt bad for him and offered any help that we could. Sandy told Sue that she was welcome to stay with her if Steve wanted to go alone but since they had a lot to discuss on that issue, no decision was made. I almost offered to go with him because I was a man of leisure, but I held my countenance; I had just met this guy and I didn't want to interfere with his family affairs.

Then it hit me like a ton of bricks. Sandy also became energized and we stared at each other, wondering if this could be true. A few questions from Sandy and me, and we found that all the facts fit. Steve's brother-in-law was named Phil Fauxmaster and he couldn't stand the guy. His sister was Carol and the kids were Ralph and Sue; we were blown away. We told Steve that we might know where the kids were and briefly outlined how we might know. We did not tell him about our fears, nor did we tell him about the way that Phil was raising the children. We had to call Barney and Bob about this to be sure that we were on good legal footing. We knew that the FBI should be notified as well and let all of those legal eagles handle this from here on in.

Two hours later, we had a meeting down at the precinct and everyone was there: Sandy, Steve, Sue, Bob, Barney, two FBI agents, and me. It was a sedate and businesslike meeting. The FBI wanted to grab Phil right away but we all agreed with Bob, who said that an arrest for kidnapping would only be a nuisance for Phil. He would eventually win the case and nothing good would happen for the kids. Bob said a drug bust was better because it would initially make the home an unsafe place for the kids and Phil would then lose custody. That scenario was far better for the kids and maybe it would get Phil some jail time. Steve wanted to bust right in there and take the kids just like I wanted to. But he listened to reason and agreed to do it right, even if it took a few more days. The far-reaching plan was a utopian thought, but one well worth pondering. Sue and Steve wanted to adopt the kids and raise them in a loving home.

The law enforcement guys came up with a sting operation and we all happily agreed to play our parts. Sandy was to call Phil and thank him for the invitation to the party, apologizing for needing to leave early. We would be very interested in any other little get-togethers he might have in the future. We would wear a wire and when something illegal arose, the FBI and the local cops would move in for a clean sweep of any and all persons involved.

Barney looked at me, wondering if this old sot could pull it off, but my steely eyes put that thought to rest in his heart. We then told Steve about the marijuana and how we perceived the emotional manipulation that Phil had imposed on the kids. We had a hard time keeping Steve in his seat. He wanted to go right now to make this right. I didn't blame him. Sue was almost in tears and said that both kids needed therapy and that they would make sure they got it and would have a chance to live this life the way that God intended.

The FBI was comfortable with this plan and said that they would get an open-date warrant for this possible sting/bust operation. The precinct commander and the Assistant District Attorney were also in agreement to the overall plan and general direction that it would take. Sandy and I couldn't wait to bust this cretin and Sandy said that she would make the call right away. Steve and Sue would continue their plans to buy a home here in New York, as Steve had been transferred to the New York City recruitment center as the Executive Officer. The plan was affirmed by all and the meeting adjourned. We agreed to keep the District Attorney and the FBI apprised of all that happened after the phone call.

It was six PM and I was starving. Steve couldn't eat. Sue was emotional and spent her time consoling Steve. Sandy merely picked at her meal but I wolfed it all down. I saw this operation working exactly as planned. Telephone numbers exchanged, we went our separate ways. Steve and Sue went to spend a few days at Sandy's house and

I went back to Lucy, but not Jack.

"Hello, this is Phil Fauxmaster." Sandy said, "Hi Phil, this is Sandy Grandly." The call went off without a hitch and Phil bit, hook, line, and sinker. He told her that he had a little get-together every Friday night and that she and Joe Donahue were more than welcome to come. He did a little word tease and Sandy had to revert to her New York City street-wise jargon. Terms like snow and herb were brought up and Sandy played her hand perfectly.

Phil seemed to be interested in me during the conversation that Sandy recorded. He asked Sandy if I liked "playing with kids." Sandy wanted to puke but gave Phil a titillating chuckle, only saying, "I don't know what Joe likes down deep, but he is pretty broadminded, so let's find out." Phil chuckled knowingly at that one and she made the date. We were to be there Friday night at eight PM. I thought that this was only Monday, and the kids would be subjected to five days of hell. I called Barney. He was out sick but I did manage to get Bob Goodman on the line.

Bob told me that we should not be raising any red flags that might concern Phil, but there were things that could be done for the next few days. I asked him to talk to the guidance counselor at the kids' school but he had already beaten me to the punch; he was on it and had good results. It seemed that Ralph had tried out for the wrestling team a few weeks ago but was rejected due to his being in trouble with the dean. Ralph's bullying had consequences he was told, but in view of the circumstances that now prevailed; they immediately put Ralph on the team.

At the same time, little Sue was asked to join the glee club as the music teacher told her that she had an excellent voice. Both children were excited with these new adventures and the guidance counselor contacted Phil at home. The wrestling team and the glee club both practiced on Tuesday and Thursday evenings and Phil was asked to drive them back to school on those nights. The school would be responsible to bring them back home using the school van after practice was over. Phil was put into a position from which he could not wiggle out. The counselor was adamant that both children needed these outlets to stabilize their emotions.

Phil said that he would cooperate and so both kids were away from Phil for two nights a week. After a meeting with all of the children's teachers, it was agreed that during the remaining three days they would each receive an overabundance of homework that would be "must-do" projects. Phil had no idea about what was happening. I was overjoyed by what Bob told me and I told Steve, Sue, and Sandy what was going down.

Sandy gave me another job on Tuesday evening; I was a rent-a-cop at the supermarket. Lousy pay, boring job, totally uneventful and I couldn't wait for it to be over. On Wednesday, the four of us had dinner together and Steve and I grew closer. On Thursday afternoon, Phil called Sandy at her office and asked her if she had any contacts for some cocaine. Sandy told him that she did, but since she herself didn't use coke, she would introduce him to her friend. He himself would have to do the tasting and the buying; Phil agreed.

Bob and Barney were elated and the FBI agreed to film the drug buy and use an undercover agent to pose as the dealer. The plan worked perfectly. Phil picked up Sandy at her office and drove to the predetermined location to make the buy. The "dealer" was in his car exactly as planned and the tape and the film were rolling. A quick introduction, a handshake, a taste; the passing of the money and drugs were all captured for future evidence. On the way back to Sandy's office, Phil tried to hit on Sandy but she rebuffed him in a polite way.

Listening to the tape later on just made me want to pummel Phil into the dirt. Steve felt the same, as did Sue, Sandy's "bleeding heart" daughter. The police were in constant communication with the school and we were assured that the plan was working perfectly. Phil was called the master of illusion, as all the teachers were falsely impressed with his involvement in the kid's education and general all-around well being. As far as we could tell, the kids were safe from Phil's mental manipulations over them all during the week.

As they said, "Thank God it's Friday." That cliché took on new meaning for all of us. Sandy and I had to attend a meeting with the District Attorney to learn exactly what to say and what not to say. We were not to be seen as entrapping Phil to do anything. They wanted him to sink his own ship and that of anyone else involved in illegal activities. The FBI guys wired us up with listening devices and we were good to go. Steve and Sue would be parked in an unmarked police car two blocks away on a side street with Barney at the wheel. They would hear everything that went on. Barney knew that he could not respond until he was called for and so Steve and Sue were made aware of that fact. The FBI had a "no-knock" warrant and they too were parked nearby with Bob Goodman at the wheel. In a third car were agents from the child protection agency, and they had a psychiatrist and nurse with them.

All the bases were covered. Every contingency was thought of and there were backup plans in effect if anything went awry. I was comfortable with the entire deal but Sandy was on edge; I kissed her. I told her that I loved her. Yes, it was hard for me to say that, but I meant it. Sandy got all teary-eyed and hugged me like there was no tomorrow. We drove to Phil's house and parked at the curb.

The driveway was full of cars and the house was well lit and a bit noisy. Phil let us in and hugged Sandy (I wanted to knock him out right then and there). He shook my hand and offered me a hit on the joint in his hand. Hey, I ain't no prude, and I wanted to make all of this as real as possible to Phil so I took a hit and thanked him. It was early and the guests were not all loosened up yet so we mingled and "made friends."

I recognized one of the municipal court judges sitting in a corner bragging about something or other and I drew closer. I knew that there would be a vacant seat on the bench tomorrow. Phil came by and told me in a gentlemanly way that the people attending the party usually paid two hundred dollars to cover expenses and I missed doing that when we left early the other night. He told me to forget that and just to cover the costs for tonight; I readily agreed. I gave him two hundred dollars of marked money and the noose tightened a little tighter around Phil's neck.

Phil asked Sandy to dance with him and she did so in a very convincing manner. My fist was clenched in my pockets, but I wore a smile and sipped a bit of bourbon. Little Sue handed it to me from her tray. I engaged her in small talk for the sake of the tape recordings. She told me that Ralph was in the kitchen mixing drinks for the guests and she thought this whole thing to be quite grown up. She was wearing a miniskirt and makeup. She looked years older than only ten.

While Sandy danced with the devil, I wandered into the kitchen. I found Ralph sipping on beer and he was bleary-eyed. "Hi ya Ralph, remember me?" He did and called me by name: "Oh yes, you are Mr. Joe, the nice man that took me and my sister to the amusement park and zoo, right?" His words were slurred and I could imagine the pain that Steve and Sue must be feeling right now. I told him not to drink any more, as he might not make it through the night. I said this with a chuckle as if to make it light. He smiled like a man and told me that he was used to it and liked to drink beer every now and then. He told me that his dad didn't object as long as he did what he was supposed to do. Ralph was twelve years old. I heard the song end so I hop-skipped it back into the living room to grab Sandy away from Phil. I was having a hard time hiding my hatred for Phil by now but I bit my tongue, kept on smiling, and tried to be cool.

Sandy was glued to my side for most of the evening. We dropped by the buffet table to grab a sandwich and saw the silver platter with cocaine, a razorblade, and straws set up, all neat and clean. The judge was snorting and offered me some. He said it aloud, "Here buddy, care to snort?" I couldn't help it; I just glared at him as if he were a talking pile of dog crap, which he was. For the sake of the tape, I said to him, "No thanks, Judge Carey."

Two hours of this misery passed and still no busted door that we were praying for at each moment. I could not imagine what more evidence of crime the cops could want, but we held up well and continued this charade to the best of our ability.

I watched the judge drunkenly talk to Phil and they went into the kitchen where Ralph was making drinks. I was alarmed at this and whispered to Sandy that I had to go in there. I gave them about three minutes and then ever so casually; I opened the door and stepped inside. On the kitchen table was a pile of money and the judge was trying to fondle Ralph. Phil just stood there unconcerned. I shouted loud and knew that the others would know what was happening. I pushed Phil aside like a dishrag and dropped the judge to the floor with a left hook to the jaw.

Screams came from the living room as the place exploded with cops and agents of all sorts. I pushed Phil through the door and right into the loving arms of Bob Goodman, who put him in handcuffs right away. I dragged the judge across the floor by his collar and placed him at the feet of the Assistant District Attorney, who promptly read him his rights and cuffed him as well. I walked back inside to talk to Ralph and out of the corner of my eye, I saw that Sandy had little Sue off in a corner and they were hugging.

Ralph was confused. He told me that others had tried to touch him like that as well. So far he had been lucky and never had to finish the act. I thought that the payee probably didn't want to pay Phil the asking price. Ralph, the little big man, started crying and my heart broke. Sandy brought little Sue into the kitchen to get her away from the police activity in the living room and she was crying as well. I wanted to kill Phil, the master of phoniness and the prince of child manipulation and molestation. As we waited, the doctor and nurse came in to chat with the kids. We stayed and waited for Steve and Sue.

Steve and Sue entered through the back door into the kitchen and the kids recognized him. The kids were dumbstruck and couldn't look at Steve; they just sobbed in humiliation and wanted to hide. Steve broke down and told them that it was not their fault and he would be in their lives forever to help them in every way possible. Steve and Sue gave me a big bear hug and thanked me profusely for all that Sandy and I had done. The doctor did a brief examination on both of the kids and found them to be in reasonably good health except for the fact that Ralph had alcohol on his breath. The child welfare agent, after talking with the doctor, told Steve and Sue to take the kids home with them but to bring them in to the office tomorrow for a more in-depth examination and further consultations. Sandy offered Steve the services of a lawyer friend that she had and told them that we would all pitch in to see that they ended up with custody of the kids. After getting some of the kids' clothes, Sandy took the bunch of them out of that place just as quickly as possible. I assured them that I would get a ride home with one of the cops.

I needed to get away from all this depression anyway so I went outside to see what was happening. Barney and Bob were happily talking about the judge, Harold (Harry) Carey. He was known as the criminal's best friend and was always strong for defendants' rights. They were joking about dear old Judge Harry who would stand before a real judge very shortly, Judge Henry Coffin, who was known as "Hang 'em High Henry", was on the bench right now, holding night court. Other than that, I learned that they found a kilo of cocaine and two pounds of marijuana in the house.

Phil was arrested for drug possession with the intent to sell, as well as child endangerment. The FBI was also pressing charges against Phil for kidnapping and interstate flight to avoid prosecution. Phil's boss was not too happy about all this since he was one of the partygoers and had also been arrested for drug possession. There were twenty-two arrests made and Bob and Barney knew that they would get some recognition and maybe a promotion out of all this.

I decided to walk the twenty blocks home. Humidity was high, the clouds low, and the moon had gone on vacation. In the fog, I thought of Jack the Ripper and I thought how much I would have loved to be there to catch that bum before he murdered so many unfortunate people. I thought of all the newest cases that seemingly have escaped proper prosecution and it made me angry. Thoughts of Sandy brought warmth to my heart and broke the morose feelings that I had been having. My mind went to Steve and Sue, then of course to the kids and their future. I saw only good things for all of them. I knew that the bad guys in this life play would suffer their consequences, the consequences they so rightfully deserved. I felt good, so good that I whistled and walked just a little straighter all the way home.

Lucy was waiting for me to come home. She immediately started begging to go out. I didn't even take off my hat and off we went so that she could go pee in the fog. I leaned on a rusty Chevy and lit up a smoke while Lucy explored whatever it was that dogs constantly had to sniff in the soil.

Barney pulled up in his unmarked and rolled down the window to chat a bit. He gave me all sorts of updates on who was detained who got bench warrants, and who would be facing monumental charges. It was interesting, but my thoughts were more for the care and well-being of the kids and that scenario had yet to play out. My other thoughts, thoughts that I could not share with anybody, were about what the future would hold for Sandy and me. It was scary.

Barney saw that I was "lost in space," so he told me that he would be off duty in a half hour and would come by for a few drinks down at the local watering hole. He did not pose it as a question; it was more like an order because he did not wait for an answer. He just rolled up the window and drove away into the souplike fog. I laughed and said to myself, "Well, why not?" I brought the mutt upstairs, told her that I was Crusader Rabbit and she had to be nice to me and not crap on the floor and to keep the hell off my bed. She seemed to nod in acceptance of these orders that she heard a million times, wagged her non-tail, and pointed to the treat locker. I gave her a doggie bone and a dish of fresh water then changed my clothes. For some reason I felt soiled. I put on my cleanest pair of dirty jeans and met Barney downstairs.

Stepping up to the phony oak rail on the bar, Barney ordered two double Jacks and water, no ice. He was radiant. He really enjoyed tonight he said, as this was the first time in a long time that he was able to play cop and be successful at it. He congratulated Sandy and me for what we had done and he was loud mouthed about it. All of his "in-attendance" cop buddies heard the whole story and with each telling, his role became larger and larger. I laughed inside and let him have his glory; he really was a true friend and a great guy.

Tommy McGuinnes was there, my partner from a long time ago, and he saluted me with a wry grin. I looked back at him and acknowledged the greeting but down deep, I remembered him as being a lousy individual who bent the rules to fit his own personal situation. He took graft and it was rumored that he was on the take from some of the local organized hoods as well. Barney didn't like him either and whispered to me that nothing ever stuck to that guy; he was made of Teflon.

Someone wanted me as a partner in a game of billiards and I saw where this night was headed. I played one game and we won, but I did not want to continue. I begged off any more booze with Barney and let him take my place on the billiard table. I made my exit and welcomed the cool air in my face.

I made the bed (now that's a new thing), took off my clothes and lay down wishing for a long and deep sleep. I prayed. Sleep came. The dreams came. Bullets, death, explosions, and screams in the night; it was my recurring nightmare and I bolted upright in bed. I was sweating and had dry mouth. It was 2 a.m. and I sat at my kitchen table just listening to the dog snore. Finally, after rejecting a million things I could do, I went back to bed and made it through the night. I did not take my medications and I did not have a sit-down with old Mr. Jack in the cupboard either. My last thought before falling asleep was actually a question to myself: "Did you really tell Sandy that you loved her?" I could not audibly say the word "yes" but my inner spirit wrote it across my heart in living, blazing color.

The morning sun came across the tenement rooftops like a laser into my little mansion's bedroom window. Birds were chirping and I thought them to be escapees from one of my neighbors' dinner menu of last night. Lucy needed OUT, not later, NOW, daddy please.

I pulled on my jeans and a tee shirt, sneakers, no socks and did my proper dog owner responsibility. I even took a plastic bag with me as I thought that Sandy was looking over my shoulder.

Back home, Lucy ate breakfast. I had my coffee and vitamins. I showered and shaved, much to my chagrin, and put on clean clothes. Then I called a cleaning service to come make my hovel livable. Finally I called Sandy and asked her to meet me for breakfast. She couldn't do it. She had a house full of people and kids. She asked me to come there and I did exactly that. I took a cab all the way to Yonkers and happily paid the twenty-seven dollar tab. As I walked up the driveway, Steve and Sue were coming out with the kids in tow. They had an appointment with Sandy's family physician and they told me that they would rather deal with her than the New York City-appointed doctor. All reports, diagnosis, future treatments, and findings would be forwarded to the proper authorities.

They were sad about how this all had come about, but were assured that the future would bring healing for the kids and love to their home for them. I looked at the kids and they were dressed neatly, but looked a little scared. I tried my "Big Daddy Warbucks/Uncle Remus" trip on them but they weren't buying. I patted Ralph on the shoulder and told him that he was made of the stuff that made Marines. To little Sue I said to be brave and to listen to those who love her. Both of them said yes, but conviction did not resonate from their words. I shook Sue and Steve's hands and wished them God speed. Sandy was at the door waiting for me.

CHAPTER FOUR

So They Say

I t has been said that the words of one good man neutralize a complete textbook of evil. Who said that? I did, just now. I heard myself say'it and I liked it, so I told my wife as well. She repeated it. So then, this newest Joe Donahue neo adage will read as follows: "They say that the words of one good man neutralize a complete textbook of evil." So there now, persons unknown and far and wide can record this new adage of dubious and distinctive wisdom into the tome of great sayings, forever more to be forgotten. My wife Sandy just read this boring-goes-nowhere missive over my shoulder and told me that for sure I was crazy. So what else is new, Sandy, I told you that from the get-go. I started to sing to her, "San-dy Grand-ly Don-a-hue, Doo-dah Doo-dah." Sort of had a musical ring to it didn't it, m'luv? She hit me and, with a smile on her face and a giggle in her voice, she slapped me upside the snot-locker and I cowered like a puppy. I loved when she hit me (wink). I patted her on her posterior, gave her a kiss and she disappeared into the bedroom to finish dressing. Lucy didn't even raise an eyebrow; she was used to this stuff by now. Sandy never hit Lucy and I only scolded her when she needed it, which was hardly ever. My gals stuck together, both of them ruled my life and I loved every moment of it.

Sandy went to work reminding me to stick by the phone in case she had a day-work contract for me to take care of. I agreed and put on my hat to take the dog out for her morning constitutional. When we got back, I put my feet up to read the latest ultra right-wing hardcover about the lady who wanted to be President. I loved reading these things; they got me all hot under the collar and I ended up cussing into the mirror, causing me to laugh at myself and damning those like me, the silent majority. Well anyway, Sandy was gone, the dog was happy for the moment, and I could put my feet up and do as I always did when I was alone: waste time.

The phone rang just as I was getting ready to close my crow foot baby blue eyes. Bob Goodman gave me the latest poop on the criminal proceedings against Phil Fauxmaster and I listened with half an ear. It looked like Steve and Sue would be home free as far as the adoption went. Phil was going into the slammer for a very long time. He had already signed the papers paving the way for an easy transition and it was probably the first noble thing he had ever done in his life. I told him that I would talk to Steve later on this afternoon and would share the good news. I listened to some other "cop shop" talk: Barney was well, made lieutenant, and Bob himself landed a sweetheart job chasing computer bums on the net. I was slated to take the stand this Wednesday, but I already knew that. At all times at least one of us in the family had been at the trial so we were pretty much up to speed on what was going on. "Hey Bob, ya know, what goes around comes around, and this time it was Phil's time to pay the piper." Bob sounded like an echo to me because his response was, "So they say Joe."

Putting on my cute little apron, I set to the task of playing Mr. Mom. I wanted to start with the dishes, but as soon as I walked into the kitchen the princess of road-kill came booming in, wagging her butt and wanting a treat. She always wanted a treat. I always gave her a treat and chastised her later because she was a fat dog. Sometimes I even called her that way: "C'mere, fat dog." And she would come and I would chuckle and so would Sandy. Was this dog abuse? Please don't tell any radio veterinarian talk-show hosts, OK? Yes, dear reader, I really did entertain myself rather well when it was just me and me alone doing the talking. I often told myself that I got no smart answers that way. I finished the dishes, which was no big deal, and then wandered into the living room to model my body in front of the mirror, wearing my skivvies and the apron. Gosh, I'm cute if I sucked in that belly. I did a few Charles Atlas muscle flexes and admired my rippled body that existed only in my imagination. I turned on the radio, tuned in to some soul music and did a little dance for the dog. I think she enjoyed it because she played the tuba just for me. The gas was horrific; I sprayed some freshener, then I ran upstairs.

Sandy called. She had a mission for me to take care of for the business. Snap back to reality time. Since our two-day courtship and third-day marriage, I had become someone I always had been. I reverted back to the Joe of old, the Joe who cared about things. No longer would I give her scant attention. No longer would I look at these jobs as boring or mundane. I was involved in people's lives now and I had a responsibility to tend to their wishes, precisely and professionally. These days I took notes and prepared for every contingency when I went out on a job. Many times if Sandy didn't know the client I would over-prepare, bringing things with me like pepper spray or a stun gun.

One of her more "well to do" clients up in Yorktown Heights had a son who was getting out of prison this afternoon. Nobody was available to make sure that he got from the prison to the house with no side trips. She told the client that she had just the man for the job and I was elected. Sandy told me that I was ugly enough to pull this off without a hitch. I took all the information and told Sandy to assure her client that the job would be taken care of with no snags. Their son should be home by five this afternoon. I called Barney, who called Rikers Island Prison and paved the way for me to gain entrance and pick up this prodigal son of a rich man and escort him home. Barney called back and gave me the lowdown on my charge.

Mario Vincent Lorenzo was the son of the (reported to be) chairman for the Westchester contingent of the "American Sons of the Boot." I always thought the name to be a bit comical, but according to the things that they were involved in, there was nothing comical about them. The kid was busted for assault involving what was reported to be an attempt to shake down a competitive "not-so-legal" enterprise. That attempt resulted in some gunplay and an altercation that landed poor Mario in the slammer for two years. So he paid his debt to society and now he was a free man, rehabilitated, and given a clean slate and a new lease on life. Maybe he would become an altar boy!

Cranking up my new Ford Explorer (life was good for Joe D. lately) I drove down the West Side Highway and tooled on over to Queens to hunt down the viaduct that would take me to depression city. Using my cell phone, I called my nephew Robert who worked there. I hadn't seen him in quite a while and I hoped to see him while I was there. Robert answered and was overjoyed; he said that he would meet me at the front gate. I was early; did I tell you that I was always early for these things?

Rob, now Lieutenant Robert Donahue was talking to the guard at the gate and so, after a quick wave, I parked on the shoulder and dismounted my sturdy steed to greet and hug my nephew. Wow, I thought, this kid was made of steel. He was a bit embarrassed at the display of emotion in front of the guard (who was smiling), but I couldn't care less. We talked of family and things gone by, my kids, who seemed to have forgotten me, and life goes on and all is well, etc., etc.

I followed Rob to the prisoner release center and he left me there in the very capable hands of a lady sergeant who reminded me of a lady wrestler. She glared at me but filled out the paperwork; I signed, and sat down waiting for sweet little Mario to emerge into my loving arms. They brought him to me, all decked out in his New York

City issued $29.95 polyester suit that did not fit. Intimidating little creep of a guy, about twenty-two years old and sporting a nice new scar on his face. He was sullen but tried his wise-guy attitude on me anyway. I wasn't buying. He signed, I signed, and the gates to freedom were opened. We walked to the car and he said nothing, just the way I wanted it. Through the slums and stench of the city we drove. He seemed to relax and enjoy the surroundings, sort of like he was at home here in this depressing environment. What he didn't know was that so was I, and I had a lot more experience than he did with these places.

I took the long way home using the Brooklyn Battery Tunnel into downtown Manhattan. Heading north on East River Drive, I made a left turn on Canal Street heading to Twelfth Avenue, figuring that I would go north from there to the West Side Highway. I purposely let him see Mott Street, where I knew that he and his family played host to all kinds of sotto voce choir practices. Turning the radio down, I let him hear me apply the electric door lock and disengage his side button. I was teasing him and he knew it and he gave me his tough-guy snarl. I laughed and told him that mommy was waiting for him; sorry, no side trips this time. When you get home and we were finished, you could do as you pleased, but for now, we were glued together and where I went, you went. He loosened up and said that he understood and would give me no trouble. I was thankful for that and said, "Good, Mario!" He fell asleep; at least I think he did.

As we headed north I called Steve to update him on what Bob had told me about the adoption. All was well at the home front and he told me that he would call Sandy to let her know that this mission was going down easily so far. I did not tell Steve, nor did I let Mario know that I was aware of the black Chevy that had followed us all the way from Queens.

Barney was one cool cop when he was sober and he had read all my clues. He knew I could not talk freely on the phone so he asked all the questions to which I responded with a yes or a no. Barney told me to take the Major Deegan Expressway to the New York State

Thruway and exit onto the Cross-Westchester Parkway east toward Scarsdale. In about thirty minutes I got to the turnoff, only to be stopped by the Yonkers police department. It was a little DMV registration and license checkpoint. I slowed but the cop stopped me. I handed him my papers while sneaking a look at the faces of the two guys behind me in the Chevy. "All is well Mr. Donahue, have a nice day." I drove off slowly, so I saw the two dudes behind me get out of their car to identify themselves.

My cell phone rang. It was Barney telling me that the two guys behind me were the feds checking up on ME. We laughed but sure enough, just like clockwork they were right behind me again. I passed that mansion where I once tended to that terminally ill rock star and I wondered what ever happened to that steely-eyed male nurse. The house had new paint and the lawn was well tended so I guess it was sold and that chapter of my life was now complete. I felt bad for that guy, but I knew that he had made his own choices in life and he paid the price for them. Such a waste, I thought, but then again, that's who we all were, victims of our appetites, be they good or be they bad. At least, that's what they say.

We were almost home for Mario and we never really got to talk, his choice not mine, so I let him have his thoughts without me to tell him that he was heading to a quickly appearing dead end street. It was four-fifteen PM and true to form I was early. Mario said that I could let him out here and I said no. He replied with a snide, "Yes, Daddy." No gate, so I drove up the driveway to the house. Another one of those stone fortress look-alike monuments to wealth I thought, but I expected nothing less. We got out and I pressed the doorbell but no one answered. Mario and I took a seat on the porch and figured that we would have to wait until five. That was the time that we were expected to arrive. I noticed that Mario was sizing me up. I thought he was wondering if he were powerful enough to teach me a lesson about who was, or was not, the top dog in this scene. I just looked at him with no expression and let him play with his fantasy. I asked him what he would do now that he was free and I regretted asking. I didn't want to know this kid, nor did I want to know his mom and pop. The feds were parked at the curb. The Jaguar pulled into the driveway and Mario's parents (I imagined) got out running and hugging their little wayward son.

Mr. Lorenzo asked me inside to sign the slip of paper for Mrs. Grandly and give me a gratuity. This time I really tried not to accept the tip but he was forceful enough about it. To save each of us the embarrassment, I took the money. On the way out I looked at the three of them and said goodbye. Mario shook my hand and thanked me for the ride. He was smiling but his eyes showed flames. His father was a Two-Ton-Tony Galente look-alike and his mom was a forty-eight year old Barbie Doll. I saw in Mario's eyes that he hated them. I whispered to Mario, "Take care of yourself, stay out of trouble, and go make a life." He nodded and I saw truth for the first time. I felt good and walked away from them with a lilt in my heart and a spring in my step.

What was that new philosophical wisdomlike adage that I had created this morning? Something about good words erasing evil stuff, I couldn't come up with it exactly, but I hoped that thought for Mario anyway.

The federal agents were happy to see me as I drove out of the driveway. They pointed to the end of the block and told me to park around the corner. They wanted to talk to me for a bit. I responded with my worst impression of a sheep and said, "Yes, sir." I got out, they got out, and without handshakes they identified themselves. I looked impressed enough so they took the cold and hard businesslike approach with me. They knew of my involvement with the Fauxmaster case and they knew of my loose association to members of the New York City police department. They wanted to know if Mario had told me anything that may be of interest to them. I had to reply in honesty that he had not. "Ever meet them before?" Nope. "Got another appointment with them?" Nope. "Has your wife dealt with them before in her business or social life?" Not as far as I knew, but I could call her and ask if you like. They told me that it would not be necessary and if they felt they had to know, they would find out in a New York minute. They let me go my merry way but said to me that I did a nice little maneuver on the parkway. I said to them, "What would you do, huh?"

I was near home but I decided to stop by to see Sue and the kids first. Ralph and little Sue were happy to see me and now called me Grandpa. It hurt my ears to hear that. I already was a grandpa to a whole bunch of others that I assumed I would never get to meet. Sue handed me an iced tea and five minutes later Steve came home. They asked me to stay for dinner. They would call Sandy on her cell phone to tell her to come here instead of going home. She said fine, I said fine, they said fine, and we would have an old fashioned family get-together. Steve and I went out on the porch for a sip of brandy and a cigar; this was a welcomed treat for me. Sandy hated the smell of cigars. Steve told me about Bosnia and the terrible things that were and still are happening there. He pried about Vietnam again, but thankfully let it go.

We changed the subject to discuss how the kids were making out with the child shrink. "So far, so good," Steve said and he let me know that little Sue had not been "totally" abused; all was intact. The bruise on her leg had been caused by an adult at one of those parties trying to undress her. This came out after many meetings with the psychologist and little Sue would have some emotional scars to deal with for a long time. I told him that I hated Phil and Steve said he felt the same but noted that "hate hurts the hater." God said to forgive others, but I guess that was a place that neither one of us had yet to arrive at in our spiritual lives. I thought about my little saying from this morning, the one that said the words of a good man erase a book full of evil. I knew that Steve had just done exactly that for my heart.

Sandy came in and she was beaming. She complimented Sue on how great the new house looked and the way the kids were dressed and on and on with all that girly stuff. Steve rolled his eyes, I rolled my eyes, and we sat down to a feast of Virginia baked ham with all the trimmings. After dinner, Steve and I helped the ladies in the kitchen but I played bull in a china shop (on purpose) so they shuffled me out of there and told me to play with the kids. The phone rang and Sue grabbed it, saying hello. It was Barney looking for me, so she gave me the cordless phone and I took the call outside to the porch.

"Are you and Sandy OK, Joe?" "Yeah, Barney, why do you ask?" I retorted. Barney told me that there was a drive-by shooting at our house and the place was riddled with machine gun bullets. The locals were there investigating and looking for bodies. Seems it had come over the police radio a few minutes ago and there was an APB for a cream colored Buick with two or more guys in it. They were considered armed and dangerous, but so far it looked like a clean getaway. I told Barney that we would go there right away. He said that he would meet us there with Bob Goodman. Sandy, Sue, and Steve were royally upset and I felt the same way. Actually, I felt violated. I thought to myself that after thirty years of playing with the dregs of society, making enemies and friends alike, nothing like this had ever happened to me. I thought that here I was, lucky enough to find a great woman to love and live with, finally catching a break and working hard and diligently to make a better life for her and me, and this has to happen. Yeah, I was upset and I wanted to know who did this and why. Barney told me that Lucy had been shot! She was alive and taken to the veterinary hospital for emergency care, but they thought she would live. Now I was really upset. Shoot me, OK, maybe I deserved it, but not some innocent little family pet. I didn't tell Sandy, but I wanted my pound of flesh for this. We drove to the house, taking both cars. The cop standing at the police barricade stopped us and asked for ID. After identifying ourselves, we were permitted to go in and see the damage.

The captain in charge of the crime scene wanted to know who we thought could have done this. I told him about the Fauxmaster case and about my little excursion to Rikers Island today. He took that information, and just about then, Barney and Bob entered. The two FBI agents who handled the federal part of the Fauxmaster case were with them. They told the Yonkers police captain that this was just a professional courtesy visit and that the case so far was completely his. The guy was a pro, he handled the entire "quickie" meeting with tact and diplomacy, and he kept his investigation team hopping at the same time. As the investigators were digging out slugs from our wall, the feds, Barney, Bob, and I talked quietly on the couch. Sandy was busy checking her office upstairs to be sure that her computer was OK and that whoever did this did not come in to steal stuff. We saw Lucy's blood on the floor. Poor Lucy didn't know what hit her and I was sure that as the good and obedient watchdog that she was, she must have been hiding behind the big armchair in the corner. It was riddled with bullet holes. The cops found lots of casings out on the street and dug out about thirty rounds from the house. The picture window in the living room was blown out as well as the glass slider on the front porch. The vet called and told us that Lucy was being operated on, but she would eventually be all right. She took two bullets to the belly but only one did any real internal damage. They told us that we needn't rush over there; Lucy would not wake up until tomorrow anyway. We thanked them and let them know that money was no problem. We told them to do whatever they had to do for our much loved dog, the princess of road kill.

Captain Israel Burns wanted all of us to come to the police station for a fact-finding conference; Israel Burns? Ya gotta be kidding, I thought. I didn't say a word about his name as I figured he had been hearing that crap all of his life and it would do nothing more than bore him. Further, he would write me off as an idiot. Barney and I exchanged smiling glances anyway. We took off in a little convoy; Sandy and I rode with Barney and Bob. The fine city of Yonkers must have been having fiscal difficulties. This place looked like a dungeon carved out of some early nineteenth century granite and painted puke green. The inner sanctum detective den was adorned with furniture that looked like it should have become firewood a long time ago. We took seats around the war-worn conference table and Captain Burns welcomed everybody with a smiling and all-knowing flair. The captain left his second-in-command, Lieutenant Dobson, to gather and trade information with the rest of them while asking me to join him in his office for a quick and private talk. I sat down in his little glass cage with the blinds drawn and he asked me to listen to what he had to say without interruption for now:

"Mr. Donahue, we have done some checking on you and wanted to find out for ourselves anything that you might be hesitant in telling us. To that end, we have found that you enlisted in the Marines in '61 as a private. You had to get away from your alcoholic father who constantly used you for a punching bag. You slapped him silly on your last day home and you have not seen him since. You were sent to Vietnam in '62 as a Lance Corporal E-3 and earned a field commission to lieutenant after your company was almost wiped out by overwhelming enemy fire in an ambush. It is reported that you have earned the DSC and a Purple Heart amongst other awards for valor and bravery under fire. You are an expert shot with the .45 the M/14 and the M/16. You were sent back stateside in '64 but voluntarily returned later that year to do another nine months of combat duty. Eventually you were shot in the leg and sent home. In the VA hospital you punched out your old CO when he came to visit you, but you would never give testimony as to why you did that. You were allowed to leave the service with an honorable discharge but you had the option to remain and face a court martial. Since leaving the service in 1965, you were divorced from your wife. She said you were an alcoholic. You had three boys who seemingly do not want to know you. Since then, you have lived alone in some slum dump in the Bronx. You took a day-to-day position with Mrs. Grandly, now your wife, who is now seated right outside. You have had many one-day jobs from her office as a 'daily work, daily pay guy,' and in at least three of those jobs, you may have made enemies that would just love to see you pushing up daisies. In effect, we had the idea that there are many avenues to pursue in trying to find out who may have tried to kill you and your wife.

In the Fauxmaster debacle, you jammed up some powerful and influential people. A judge could have many friends that maybe would not be seen as fitting associates in his profession. A drop of a dime could get your testimony squashed forever if you met an untimely demise. It could be some resident alien Vietnamese ex-soldier who got a line on you. Further, it could be that you might have rubbed some of your Marine Corps compatriots the wrong way and they found out where you lived only recently. Your face has been plastered all over the papers lately. Finally it could be the mob guy that you just took care of this morning. The other jobs, the one with the old rock and roll dude and that drunken singer, didn't make the cut for us to look too deeply into them. Now, what do you have to say to all of this: is there any other person or persons that you might know of who would want you or your wife dead?" I stood up and congratulated him for his quick and thorough investigation but said that I could add nothing more to what he had already discovered.

We went back outside to join the others. After about an hour or so everyone was convinced that we were all on the same page and that the information was equally distributed on a "need to know" basis. Barney and Bob drove us home so we could start putting our little house back in order. It was ten PM already and a workday for Sandy tomorrow. We were both tired. We called Steve and assured him that we would be OK and that we would deal with all of this tomorrow. He offered whatever we needed, but he could not call me "Dad." That was fine with me. I told Sandy to go to bed and I would do a quick board-up on the window and be up as soon as I was done. I poured a double and went to get my hammer and nails.

I slept on the couch in the living room. Every now and then, I would take a peek to see if the cop outside was still awake and each time I looked, he was reading the newspaper or drinking coffee. A couple of times during the night, I heard another sector car come by, but all in all, it was an uneventful night with little sleep. I thought of poor Lucy in the hospital and knew that I would be going to see her in the morning. Gee, it was morning, but too early to even make coffee. When I heard Sandy stirring upstairs, I got up and plugged in the pot, washed my face and greeted the day. The cop was still out there but I noticed that it was a different guy. Housesitting was a boring detail and wisely they spotted each other off every two hours.

At 6 a.m., I brought Sandy a cup of coffee, for which she gave me her best and bravest thanks in an upbeat manner, but it didn't work. She was scared and I knew it. I told her that all of this would work out, the bad guys would get caught, and none of us would be harmed. Sandy went to work and I looked at the monumental mess in our house and decided that cleaning it was a task for professionals. I called the insurance company guy at 9 a.m. and he was there before ten for a look-see. Making provisions for a contractor to come over for an inspection and set up a repair schedule was easy. The contractor said he would meet me at the house at 4 p.m.

I went to the doggie hospital to see my little girl. It was pitiful to see her strapped to a gurney all bandaged up but she was awake and saw me. Her little non-tail wagged a few times after her eyes focused on me. I whispered to her that in my view, she was the ultimate top dog. I petted her and rubbed her behind the ears to assure her that all would be OK and that she was lucky to be alive. The doctor told me that we could take her home in three days after the wounds healed a bit and that the operation had been a success. A bullet had nicked her spleen and there was a lot of internal bleeding. We were fortunate that the police department got her there in time to save her life.

The doctor went on to ask me about Lucy's medical records: "Who is your regular vet?" and stuff like that. I was embarrassed but I told him the truth: "Lucy had never seen a vet in her life so do what you gotta do, Doc." I was sure that she needed every shot that a dog was supposed to have. The good doctor was not too pleased with that information and told me that after discharge she would need further care with a local veterinarian; I said OK, I would do that, and he seemed happy. The doctor tried to be gentle with me but said that he was surprised that Lucy had no fleas, ticks or illnesses. I thought to myself that those critters shied away from alcoholic dogs. I didn't say anything, especially since Lucy was on the wagon ever since Sandy and I got married.

I called Sandy; it was a slow day at the office so I went there and took her to lunch. "Who do you really think did this, Joe?" Sandy asked over her bowl of wonton soup. I said it was probably one of her dissatisfied wino workers upset with her about lousy pay. She didn't crack a smile and I knew that this was no time for my weird humor. I had to honestly tell her that I didn't know and maybe even that it was a case of mistaken identity.

She went back to the office and I headed back to Yonkers to meet the contractor. Lieutenant Dobson was waiting for me so I invited him in. He told me that the weapon used was a 7.62mm NATO cartridge used by countless weapons manufacturers all over the world for military use. The shooting was not directed fire, more like just sprayed haphazardly all over the house. He said that whoever did this didn't want to leave anyone alive inside but they didn't follow through by going inside the house to check. He told me that they also recovered an unexploded hand grenade: "Only sheer luck that the thing didn't go off, Joe; the spring on the release lever was rusted. They pulled the pin but the grenade could not arm itself. I think they are telling you that they do not want you around, Joe, if you get my drift."

There were no fingerprints on the grenade or anything else so apparently they did not even get out of their car. Forensics on the tire marks in the street were inconclusive, but there was still an alarm out for the cream colored Buick. A neighbor got a glancing view of the car and recognized it because he owns the same model but could not see the plates or occupants. He didn't know how many people were in the car. Lieutenant Dobson was not all that optimistic about finding the perpetrators but said they would keep at it and if anything turned up, he would let me and my buddies at the NYPD know. I thanked him and he took off back to his little warren up on snake hill.

Pouring my first of the day, the contractor pulled up in a nice shiny pickup truck neatly painted with his company logo on the door. I met him at the door and I saw the look on his face; he was amazed at the extent of the damage. As we walked the house, he made notes and it seemed that no room was spared damage. Four new windows would have to be installed. Some brickwork outside would need to be done to remove the chinks in the mortar and the downspouts would have to be replaced as well. The front door looked like Swiss cheese so it had to go as well. He said a new sliding glass door on the porch was needed and tons of holes had to be fixed on the walls inside. I was doing some mental calculations on cost to the insurance company, but made no comment. All of this would be followed by a complete paint job, interior and exterior. The insurance guy told me that we were covered from top to bottom, including furniture, so we should just get it done, and this contractor was the one they always used.

The contractor's interior decorator associate pulled up. She was a pretty lady that probably weighed more than I did but she was pleasant and thorough. I asked her to come back later when Sandy was home. I was a lousy color coordinator who did not want to be spanked by his wife unless we were into that, which we weren't. Chuckles all around, I was told that work would start the next morning. The decorator gal would come back at six PM and so far, our lives were getting rebuilt right on schedule.

I called Barney and "made a meet." I called Sandy and told her that I would be back later as I had to talk to the cops: "Don't worry, all would be OK and the decorator lady will meet you at six. Steve, Sue, and the kids are fine; I will see you later, I love you, have dinner without me." Whew! That went off OK, so I locked the broken front door and took off toward the Bronx.

White Plains Road was a north/south four-lane thoroughfare beneath a grimy elevated rail line that ended up two blocks south of Mt. Vernon. I used to love that area. North of Gun Hill Road was like no-man's land, but south of it, the area lightened up a little.

The Arbor Bar and Grill was a couple of blocks south of Tremont Avenue and, except for the names and faces filling themselves with beer and booze, little had changed in fifty years. Walking inside was like visiting the ghosts of Christmases gone by. I remembered oh so well all the family drinking bouts, the funny things, the fights, the cops, the blood, the tears, and the puke. It was a love/hate feeling.

With a smile on my face I envisioned the "great fish fight" of so many years ago. It seems that my Uncle Ed, who is long departed from us, had gone flounder fishing. It was a good day for him and he brought home over a hundred and fifty flounders. He brought some of them to the bar to give to his friends and family. Most of them were drunk, thanked Uncle Ed and then commenced to throw flounder at each other. It was havoc inside the Arbor that night and Uncle Ed never went there again. That was a long time ago and I am probably the only one left alive to remember that scene of humor and sadness. The rest of them have all gone to their final reward. I only hope that they each seized the brass ring of eternal life with God in Heaven.

I didn't know a soul inside so I took a table near the wall and sipped a beer waiting for Barney to show. A couple of local dudes were playing pool and I watched with a sly eye. I knew that I could beat either one of them. I did not make eye contact with them or anyone else. I didn't pose a threat and just sat there like a bump on a log, minding my own space.

Barney arrived looking like an aging Mike Hammer complete with the trench coat. Most of the patrons knew who he was and he acknowledged one or two with a nod, he walked by the rest of them. He sat down at my little oasis in the shadows. Luis brought him a Jack straight up and Barney told him to bring me one as well. Barney told me that some strange things were going on down at the precinct but nothing he could put his finger on yet.

For starters, Mario Lorenzo washed up on the shore at City Island with a neat little bullet hole in the head. "Since he was a mob kid, these things were almost expected, and on the face of it, it would have nothing to do with you, Joe." I felt bad for the kid and knew that this was just another waste of life. That was why the bad guys always said, "Waste him." It was getting rid of possible harm or testimony. It was revenge or just "comeuppance," but whatever the reason might be, a life was snuffed out with no regard for pain, fear, or anyone's family. Barney went on to tell me that Tommy McGuinnes, my cop partner from times gone by, had been asking too many questions. Barney said that he never asked anything directly and most times uses an intermediary, but all of it centered on my recent activities, my family, and me personally. "Tommy has nothing to do with any of the cases you are involved with, Joe, so why is he asking? Have you had any contact with him other than a week ago when you and I ran into him?" I told him no, that I had not, but that our dislike for each other went back a long way. Actually, it all started right here in this bar. We were just stupid kids trying to be Mr. Big Guy; we grated on each other's nerves even back then. We sipped some Jacks and tried to be light with each other but neither of us could come up with any clue as to what was happening in the periphery of my life.

A guy walked into the bar and both of our radar screens picked up on him immediately. I didn't know him and neither did Barney. It seemed that he had this aura-like thing around him, a dark foreboding aura. Nobody sat near him and he just watched us through the mirror. Barney said in his best English, "Whose dat?" I shrugged and our eyes locked. We sipped Mr. Jack and paid him no mind. To me he looked like Dracula; Barney laughed when I told him that. As we sat, we talked about the Fauxmaster case and the Lorenzo thing but we could not come up with any possible connections. Nobody was shooting pool. Dracula came over and plopped in his seventy-five cents and racked the balls. He was going to play by himself — how fitting. The pool table was near our booth. We got a close-up view of this assassin wannabe with the steely dead eyes. He broke the rack of balls with the force of a cannon and the eight ball skipped off the table and took off in our direction. It was under our table. I scooted it across the floor with my foot so Drac could pick it up but apparently he wanted me to pick it up for him and deliver it unto his throne of sport. I declined the honor and commenced my conversation with Barney. We paid no attention to him. Barney told me that Roscoe was at the ready and he said it loud. Actually we figured that Drac would not even know this fifty-year-old term for a handgun. We chuckled; we always chuckled in the face of potential danger. I think it was like some kind of mental flip-flop one used to hide fear but whatever it was, we were alert and of one mind. Preservation and victory through strength was the only way to honor peace and continued life, or so they said.

Drac left the eight ball where it was and continued to shoot the other balls into the pockets with a vengeance. I noticed that he did have some skill at the game, but if we were to play any kind of game this evening it would not be pool. I took the empty glasses to the bar and Luis filled them, pay first please. A glass in each hand, I started back to the table only to find that Drac was blocking the aisle with his cue stick in his hand. He was chalking it up, but staring directly into my heart with his best "I'm your worst enemy" glare.

Barney had enough of this guy and so had I. I said, "excuse me," but he didn't move. I placed the glasses on the little wall shelf and put my foot on top of his. I could stare better than he could but he put up a good front. He was about my size but a lot younger and a lot leaner. He was probably a lot faster too. I guessed he figured that I should walk around the other way, but then he realized that he was probably suffering from a case of poor judgment. I could see it and sense it. I could almost smell his fear. The anger was boiling in his heart and I knew that this guy was not a professional anything. Barney came up behind him and touched him on the shoulder. He looked at Barney's beautiful twinkling blue eyes and Barney said, "Why not just move aside young man; let the old man through." He did as he was told, then put away the cue stick and took his seat at the bar — good!

It was still early so we had a couple of burgers brought over to keep us sober or as close to it as possible. The more we talked, the more we kept coming back to the idea that Tommy McGuinnes was involved with the Lorenzos and they thought that maybe I knew something that I shouldn't. Drac had at least three drinks to our one. Yes, I was watching him. Judging by the way people in the bar acted, they knew him and Barney but not me.

Nobody would come near Drac; they gave him wide berth. It seemed that the more Drac drank, the sloppier he got. I saw the pistol grip sticking out of his pocket. Barney saw it too; he got up and went to the men's room and I took another sip of Jack. Five minutes later, as Barney and I watched, two plainclothes cops came in and walked over to Drac. They took his gun away easily, cuffed him, and took him away just as neat as could be. His name was Sean McGuinnes, Tommy's nephew, and we knew that the stuff would hit the fan pretty soon. Tommy would be yakking about police courtesy, cutting him some slack, making it go away and all that, but it was not up to Barney; he didn't make the arrest. Of course this family connection did pique our interest in the overall scheme of things. As for me, I grew weary of cops and robbers and those who tried to play both parts at once.

I knew in my heart now that McGuinnes was involved in all of this right up to his eyeballs. I called Sandy but she told me to have a good time; she was enjoying redecorating the house with the lady beauty queen. "A good time, huh? Yeah, right Sandy, I will do that and thank you." We parked our cars in the Parkchester Garage two blocks away and cabbed it across town to visit Barney's favorite watering hole. Tommy was sitting at the bar seething but said nothing to us. A patrol sergeant friend of Barney's came over and we were introduced. He told us of McGuinnes' nephew getting busted for a gun rap but made no mention of us even being there. The call came from a "concerned and unnamed citizen." His eyes were probing but we would not bite. The kindly cop said that it was a dangerous world out there. The message was loud and clear. Barney retorted, "So they say Sarge, so they say."

It was time for me to go. I didn't like this silly chess game in which I was holding only the rank of pawn: "Take care Barney, call me when you get a chance. I have to be at court in the morning for testimony." "Yeah Joe, you too, keep your powder dry," he said with a smile. McGuinnes didn't even look at me. I skipped out of there like Julie Andrews playing Maria Von Trapp on the mountainside in The

Sound of Music. I left the car at the garage and took a cab home.

Sandy was asleep so I tiptoed upstairs and crawled into bed beside her. She murmured and I hugged her close; our house was at peace at last. After morning coffee, Sandy took off for work, dropping me off at the garage to pick up my car. She said that we could have picked a neighborhood with a little more class to indulge ourselves, but she knew that I was born around here somewhere and let it go with a shrug.

I got the car and drove to The Grand Concourse, then south to 161st Street and the dirty marble courthouse. I took my seat and saw that Fauxmaster was at the defense table with his attorney. Barney and Bob Goodman were in the room as well. The judge came in, we all rose, he banged his gavel, and the game was on. I gave an honest, unembellished answer to every question put to me, with no anger and no emotion. The DA asked the questions, I gave the details and that was that for that. The defense attorney tried to get me to say that we had in some way entrapped his client, but there was no way he could make it stick. My time on the stand over, they released me for the day.

Goodman stopped me outside in the hallway. "McGuinnes' nephew drives a cream colored Buick," he told me. They had it down at the pound, and so far, it seemed that he was driving the car at the shooting. They found spent shell casings and other prints in the vehicle. They would be checking them today for a match. "Maybe we can corral these banditos before the day is out," he said. "The noose is tightening and the kid is squirming, ready to sing for a lighter sentence. Uncle Tommy is not too happy with all this, and has taken an emergency ten-day leave of absence." That was as far as Bob would go with me but told me to be careful about where I went and what I did. I nodded my thanks for the warning and while I was in the Municipal Building, I updated my pistol license.

As I drove north to go home, I was pulled over by a highway cop on a motorcycle for speeding in his precious domain, the Bronx River Parkway. I was nice and he was professional; he checked me out, gave me a ticket for seat belts, and let me go with a slap on the wrist. Kissing my insurance card for remaining unchanged, I went home, wrote the check for the ticket, and dropped it into the mail.

I was starting to hate my telephone lately; I never knew what kind of craziness I was going to hear after I muttered my cherubic, "Hello?" This time it was an unidentified person asking in a nice way to meet him at Nathan's on Central Avenue in forty-five minutes. I asked this voice why I should do that, and he said the one word that made me say yes: "Lorenzo." I clicked off, made another call and was there for the meeting. Captain Israel Burns was on the hill across the street with a parabolic microphone video camera and binoculars; all was well. I sat where I was instructed and let the guy clean off the mess that the last diners had left. I knew that there was no way that I could be seen or heard from anywhere outside the building.

The guy dropped into the seat across from me with his two dogs and a coke. "How ya doin', Donahue?" I said, "Ok I guess, you doin' OK?" Nods exchanged, we both knew that this was not an unfriendly or friendly meeting, something more like an infomercial. That was, however, the extent of the small talk. My new friend had a mouth full of hot dog with sauerkraut and way too much mustard. I sipped my coke and waited for him to open the dialogue; I was curious as a cat on a roof. The guy put down his feast and looked me directly in the eyes. He said that Lorenzo had nothing to do with the shooting at my house. Mr. Lorenzo was in mourning over the untimely and highly unfair demise of his only son, Mario. He wanted nothing to do with me and had only a slight idea how this might have happened. He went on to totally blow the whistle on my unsavory friend, Tommy McGuinnes.

I had to be honest here. I didn't care how Tommy McGuinnes, Mario "the dead kid" Lorenzo, or anyone else was breaking the law. I didn't care about Mario's parents, Tommy's nephew Dracula, or what kind of deal all of them had together. I cared about my family, my wife, our grandkids, my dog, our turf and myself. All the rest of it was for the cops to figure out. I got lucky; I figured I had a new shot at making a life and I was happy with all of it. I wanted a simple life and I wanted nothing to do with crime and/or punishment. I did admit that I wanted to deal with the would-be home shooter and attempted dog slayer but that was personal and man-to-man. I listened to the whole story and was hoping that Burns could hear because none of what I heard was legally binding or even provable. With all the twists and turns relating to Mario, Drac, Tommy, and the Lorenzos, all I was interested in on a personal level was that he told me that Tommy had ordered the shooting. His simple-minded nephew pulled it off, and in my own way, I would be sure to make them pay for that.

I told the guy that what he said was very interesting and I asked him why he was telling me all this stuff. He said that it didn't matter why, but he was a friend of the Lorenzo family; they asked him for the help and he was here to do as they asked. "Simple as that," he said and he got up and walked away. I took my coke and walked outside to the little porch and sat down to light up a Lucky and watch the world go by. I also watched through the plate glass window as the table cleaner removed the bug from under that tabletop; I thought, Isn't technology wonderful? I saw my unnamed friend drive out of the parking lot and I saw Lorenzo drive away in his own car. We made eye contact; he nodded, I nodded, and he drove away.

Burns sat down across from me; Barney and Bob Goodman were with him. I heard all they had to tell me, but Barney's eyes were conveying to me that there was a lot more that they were not telling me. To skip over all the little ins and outs of the clandestine stupidity of the McGuinnes vs. Lorenzo cloak and dagger routine, my family, including Steve, Sue, and the kids would now have police protection night and day until McGuinnes was brought in. The tape that they got from this spur-of-the-moment chat would be played for the DA and the FBI to see if there was yet a legal basis to make more and further-reaching arrests.

It all had to do with interstate drug traffic, turf wars, and murder. McGuinnes and crew thought that Mario had confided in me information that would hurt them. They told me that Mario had been tortured before his killing and must have made up some story about me to save his own skin. I guess it didn't save his life, but the bad guys believed the story.

Phil Fauxmaster was given thirty to life; Steve and Sue legally adopted the kids, and their names were unofficially changed. A little inter-governmental communication and requests got Steve a new location in Pennsylvania. For all intents and purposes, they fell off the face of the earth. Judge Carey was disbarred and, in a plea bargain, given a five year suspended sentence with one year of community service.

Under the RICO law, all of what Phil owned was seized for government auction to defray courts costs. What goes around comes around, so they say. "Damn," I said with a chuckle, "I wanted that BMW." The rest of Phil's partygoers were meted all kinds of punishment in varying degrees. Some got fines, others minor jail terms, and yet others were allowed to skate with a slap on the wrist. I wondered how the "upscale" house painter made out and thought that it would be poetic to have him paint my house just for laughs. Before I could make my escape from my cop pals, Barney slipped me a note. I wondered if he used crayon or his usual Etch a Sketch scribbles. He did it sneakily enough and so I stuffed it into my pocket just as sneakily. I drove to Sandy's office to tell her of all this and, sure enough, an unmarked was sitting in front of her office.

Sandy sent me out to the deli for some pastrami on rye and two beers; I wanted more but I let it go till later. I read Barney's note while waiting for the sandwiches; he wanted me to call him on his cell phone as soon as possible, which I did. Sandy and I probed each and every avenue of these new things that had come into our lives. I told her about the gun that I owned and that I was now carrying, complete with a license for a concealed weapon. I also told her that I bought another gun that was in the house inside the drawer of the table by her side of the bed: "Just aim and shoot honey, it's easy." My woman could be a cold-hearted babe sometimes; she said that if anyone ever broke into our home and I wasn't there, the intruder would be dead or at least needing a new set of family jewels. She said this with no hesitation, and I was glad to hear it. I bid her goodbye for now: "See ya at the house for dinner," and all of that. On the way out, I nodded to the spooks outside but they hardly acknowledged me.

I called Barney from my car and we met in the north Bronx near Van Cortlandt Park. I guessed that my "tag-along" hasn't yet been assigned because no one followed me, and I watched closely that no other cars parked anywhere near the meet. Barney came up on me from the wooded side of the park huffing and puffing as if he had done the U.S. Marine Corps three-mile forced march. I guess that you have to understand that Barney and I went back a very long time. Friendships were deeper than jobs and friends looked out for one another. He got right to it. Tommy McGuinnes was a dirty cop and they all had known it for years, but they could never make any kind of a case against him. He was too slick and, as a narcotics cop, he knew how to cover his trail and get things done for him without his direct involvement.

The story went down like this: "McGuinnes had Mario snatched off the street because they owed him a lesson in etiquette. Mario tried a shakedown on one of their suppliers. Not only did that occurrence land Mario in jail; it blew away one of their major suppliers. The Fauxmaster case also caused one of their best customers to evaporate. Old man Lorenzo let Mario run his own game since he had other, more important criminal dealings that required tending. McGuinnes and company didn't care to go against the old man, but they had to protect their turf and knew that to show weakness was to invite future inroads against them. They tortured Mario before they ventilated his brain-housing group and it seemed that Mario did indeed tell them a tale involving you. McGuinnes thinks you will be making moves on him and his business. He wants to snuff you out because of that, but more than that, he hates you from years gone by anyway." I thought of that cute little blue-eyed babe I stole from him back at the Arbor Bar a million years ago. I remembered his all-too-vocal threat against me at that time. It was almost forty-five years ago. Old hatreds died hard, I guessed.

Barney told me that McGuinnes had a little group of other cops that work with him. They knew who most of them were and IAD was doing an ongoing investigation on them, one at a time. "So far nothing worked, Joe, just a pile of names and hints, but nothing concrete. Just know this pal, one of them pulled you over on the Bronx River Parkway the other day: the bike-cop, remember? That was just a little show of force for them, a teaser actually, because that particular cop is supposedly their enforcer. He stopped you because he wanted you to remember his face. He wanted you to see him because when he kills you someday soon, you will remember him and die angry. Tommy's nephew, the kid that you call Dracula well his real name is Sean, and he is just a loose cannon and Tommy never could control him. When he shot up your house, he hoped to kill you and make himself look good to his uncle. He is an idiot and even McGuinnes knows that, but idiots pay the price too, so he will be off the streets for a long time. McGuinnes is still on leave and nobody knows where he is. His phone is tapped and so are yours and Sandy's." I said that was OK with me. Barney, Bob Goodman, and the FBI also knew that I now packed heat and to them that was OK as well.

I told Barney that this had been a long day and he agreed. I said I'd be right back and asked him to please hang out for a few minutes. I went across the street to the Bodega and bought two tallboy six-packs, all nicely frosty and clean looking. We walked into the park by a copse of trees and boulders. We had us a picnic of laughter and hatred, suds and tears, reminiscences and pontifications. In short, these two old, sixty-plus friends got bleary-eyed stupid drunk and sloppy. It was fun to escape.

Barney said, "Joe, if you head for your car, I will arrest you for attempted DWI with intent to leave me alone in the park."

"Barney, you are indeed a lovable idiot. I'll call Sandy and she can take both of us home to Yonkers for a good meal. Who knows, she may even get to like you someday."

Barney told me that he couldn't do that because Sandy had a tag-along, and he did not want to be seen with me. I said, "Oh yeah Barn, not bad for a broken-down, drunk cop; I guess you are on your own. Take care."

Barney's car was on the other side of the park, he walked over hill and dale just to meet me and be assured that we were alone. As Sandy pulled to the curb, Barney waved to her and then headed back across the great unkempt lawn to his car. Sandy's spooks pulled in right behind her but they missed seeing Barney. I'm sure that they thought I was one weird guy sitting alone in the park getting blitzed, but I really didn't care what they thought; just protect my wife and I am happy. I told Sandy that this meeting was Barney's idea and then I told her what he told me. I was inwardly hoping that she wouldn't be too mad at me for being in a semi-wasted condition. She laughed and said that she knew from the get-go that Barney and I were tight and she didn't mind all that much, as long as I called her and didn't drive a car when that happened.

McGuinnes' crew shot up my house and almost killed my dog; I could not get this out of my head. I promised myself that before he got busted, he and I would have a face to face about that, cop or no cop. No, I did not tell Sandy what I was thinking.

We went home for coffee and a proper dinner. I was beat but feeling my oats too, so I chased Sandy around the house until she let me catch her. I whispered into her ear that I was feeling randy about Grandly. She giggled and asked, "Are you sure you're up for this, old man?" Life was good, busted sheet-rock and glass on the floor and all. That night was probably the first uneventful night in weeks and we slept like two newborn babies. We awoke wonderfully late in the morning and my passion princess had her way with me again. "All this before breakfast?" I asked. She told me to get dressed; she was taking me out for a breakfast of steak and eggs. Thankfully, the week-end went off without a hitch: no phone calls, no visits, and no problems.

On Sunday, we took a ride with Steve, Sue, and the kids to

see the new house that they bought. It was in New Hope, Pennsylvania, about an hour and a half south of Yonkers, but far enough away from the past to make all of us happy. Steve would be working in the Philadelphia central recruiting office and that was about a forty-minute ride each way.

Life could be good in the suburbs and New Hope looked like Norman Rockwell created it. While we were there, Sue insisted that we have brunch in a restaurant that she discovered on her last trip here. We walked into The Raven on Route 179 and I was impressed. I was told that this place was noted far and wide for a fantastic Sunday brunch menu. First thing I noticed was the construction going on for a building extension, so I figured that life was good for The Raven too.

Steve and Sandy's new neighbor Aaron played host, and we all had a fine time dining with the upper and lower echelon of New Hope while we sipped on Bloody Marys. For me, Aaron was a trip to behold. All of my life I was satisfied to pay no interest in befriending a man or woman who had a different sexual identity. Aaron was so totally open with who he was that I couldn't help myself; I found that I liked him right off. He was a good man and a definite asset to our family.

The Raven had an interesting and varied clientele made up of both gay and straight patrons. Soon, this man Joe Donahue, the blue-collar, ex-Catholic, God-loving, ex-cop, ex-Marine, ex-construction guy, stuffed shirt, Bronx Irish, straight-laced man of knuckles and beer found a new way of looking at other people. Yes, I thought, we all gotta live on this planet, so let's do it with respect, peace, and love for each other. Barney would kill me if he heard that, but Barney would be wrong and he wasn't here. I made a mental note to bring him here someday to broaden his cultural enlightenment.

Right after this little mental flip-flop of mine, Aaron introduced us to the new owners of the restaurant, Terrence and Rand. They proved to be two of the nicest guys I had ever met. Openly gay, their smiles and quick wit were effervescent. I knew that they appreciated the fact that we were just as open to them. On some kind of metaphysical level we knew that there were no invisible walls separating us. For me, this was a new thing. I found that it wasn't all that hard for me to "get over myself" and realize that these two young men were just like everybody else in this world. They worked their tails off to make a living and they did it well and with class.

I smiled broadly, shook hands, and enjoyed a few minutes of conversation with them. I found that this restaurant and bar had been here for years and was running a bit stagnant. When Rand and Terrence took over, they poured more than money into this business; they invested their sweat, their hearts, and their minds as well. Building a great menu with world class chefs, servers, and additional staff, the business took off like lightning. Terrence laughed and said that sometimes it was more than they could handle on an emotional level. Thinking about the crooks and killers in the periphery of my life I said, "Yeah, I know all about overtaxed emotions."

Our server brought over the appetizers so the owners left us with a cheerful "bon appetit." As I dug into the paté, an old adage came to mind that related to the human condition. It went like this: "United we stand, divided we fall." Yes, I realized that there was room in the heart of my life for gay people and those of other ethnic or religious persuasions as well. Shamefully I admitted to myself that I had not always felt like that.

What I also didn't know was that Barney had been shot and was now in the Bronx North University Hospital Intensive care unit in a coma. My cell phone rang. Bob Goodman told me that Barney was found face down in some mud in Van Cortlandt Park Saturday morning. A gunfight, but whoever else was involved so far was still a mystery. Bob asked me where we were and I told him. He told me to stay in Pennsylvania with the family; I said, "Sure Bob, OK. I will do that." Steve, Sue, the kids, and Sandy had a safe place here in New Hope, and Aaron the neighbor was an excellent bodyguard. He could kill an attacking elephant with the forty pounds of gold that he had hanging around his neck and wrist. There was no way that I was going to sit there with them. Sandy knew that I could not stay, was worried sick, and told me so. Steve wanted to come with me but I said, "No way, Gyrene, this is my job, and the less involved it is, the better off it is." I told Steve that this was little more than settling a childhood problem and I was more than up to the job. In my mind, I told myself that little kids found adult toys and the rules of the game had changed.

I called the New Hope Taxi Company and some local yokel drove me all the way into the bowels of Sin City. Eighty-seven fifty the meter read, so I gave him a hundred and fifty dollars and wished him a safe trip back home. He had his own map and he couldn't wait to head for the George Washington Bridge happy to get out of there alive. His parting words were, "Ta-ta Prince Charming." I shrugged and said, "Yeah buddy, I'm a Prince Charming individual alright." I knew in my heart that McGuinnes did this to Barney and I walked right into the bar.

I could not believe my eyes. Tommy McGuinnes was sitting at a table with the bike cop and his nephew, Dracula. There were two other drinkers and one (of all people to be seen in a dive like this and much to my happy surprise) was Bob Goodman. I took a seat at the bar and Bob nodded to me. I saw the alarm and I felt the tension. I knew that my appearance was a total shock to everyone here, but I could not care less. I was here to play this hand, and to play it well. I cared nothing for the law of the land at this point. These guys did a nasty to my buddy and I knew it. Nothing was going to dissuade me from getting moral and rightful revenge. They shot my dog. They shot up my house. They shot my friend. No way would they walk away from "Prince Charming" this night.

Bob watched me through the mirror, but I was masked cool and unaffected. I was watching them in that same mirror and they knew it. Uncle Tommy was the big man of the night, and the rest of them were like toadies, listening and intent on grasping his every word, every inflection, and every nuance. Inside, I wanted to puke. Sean, who must have somehow made bail, was like the court jester: he smirked and groveled as he reacted to whatever Tommy was telling them. The bike cop was a cool cucumber and he made no effort to avoid my stare; he stared right back with ice blue eyes. He reminded me of a tombstone. I was getting up to approach the little table of devious hierarchy in this den of iniquity when Bob intercepted me. Very coldly and forcefully, he grabbed my shoulder and said, "Sit down, Joe."

Ya know, I love my wife! She knew me better than I did. She called Goodman at home and he knew where I was going. He told me that we were outnumbered, out gunned and off of our turf. Bob said that still there was no legal way to arrest Tommy McGuinnes for anything. Nothing could be proved. Barney was in a coma and had not been able to give any kind of clue as to what had happened to him. I felt guilty for leaving him alone in the park and I told Bob (off the record) of the meeting. I felt especially bad because I was out with my family for an entire weekend digging on good stuff and Barney had been lying in a mud puddle waiting to die. I told Bob that these guys did it and he said he knew it as well, but we had to prove it and do it right so they all would go down for a long time smashing rocks. I wanted my own justice and I wanted it now, but I did not say that to Bob. I just nodded in capitulation. Bob ordered two more drinks for us and I watched the bartender. He poured a Jack Daniels and water for me and a ginger ale for Bob.

Much to my surprise, Bob also said to Jake, the dude behind the bar with a million tattoos, "I want to buy all those guys at that table a round of drinks too." Jake's jaw dropped and his eyebrows raised, but he said, "Sure man, you got it." I put my hand on Roscoe and moved the safety to fire, but there was no round chambered and I knew it. I think Bob did the same because I noticed a lot of fumbling around as he took out his wallet to pay the tab. I thought of Barney lying on a bed unable to talk and unable to move. I wondered what he was thinking, did he feel pain, was he upset because he must have walked into a trap, and was he upset with himself for being a dummy? Was he mad at me? I loved that old sot and I would not let go of this in an easy way. Hey, what are friends for, huh?

Jake placed the drinks in front of each man with a false flair;

he even brought new napkins. "Drinks on those guys," he said, and they all looked at us. The bike cop stood up and walked over to Bob and me. "Ain't you the guy that I stopped for speeding on the Bronx River Parkway the other day?" I answered in my most charming voice possible that I was the self-same individual to which he was referring. I went on to inquire how was it that he would remember me, when his job surely caused him to stop many motorists. He said that I had a remarkable face, ugly and stupid looking.

I watched Dracula, but Uncle Tommy had his foot on top of his and he would not move. The bike cop was goading me into a dumb barroom brawl, but I was having none of that for now. Bob was like a coiled spring; I could feel it, but for now there was no need to unleash the fires of hell. Bob Goodman had a black belt in karate. Very quietly, I told the bike cop that soon he would be a dead man. I told him that I thought he or Tommy or both of them shot Barney and I was the equalizer. He laughed; I knew he would. He said, "Go for it, scumbag." I smiled and turned away from him. I knew that Bob had my back and I chuckled at the poetry of it all.

Bike Boy walked back to the table and Bob said to me that we should leave and leave now. Three strangers came into the bar. None of us knew any of them, two guys and some half-drunk gal. They took seats at the bar and one of them ordered whiskey for the entire bar. If you knew anything about Bronx etiquette, you did not refuse an offer like that. Even if you didn't feel like drinking anymore, you toughed it out and you smiled; those were the rules of the game. Our drinks were in front of us and we looked to our new found hosts, raised our glasses, and said, "Thanks buddy." Over the lips, through the gums, look out tummy, here it comes. I went to the men's room; I needed to pee, ya know?

I was at the urinal when McGuinnes stuck his gun into my back: "Tell me why I shouldn't just kill you right here, Joey baby?" I told him that it was not proper Irish etiquette to kill a man while he was so indisposed, but that if he had a beef with me, I was sure we could work it out in some other way. He growled. Shake, zip — I smacked him with all I had. I think I broke his nose but it didn't matter, he was up and ready in a New York minute, blood and all. In a way, it was fun; I was taking all my pent-up frustration out on him and he was the man on whom I wanted to release it. He was Barney's shooter, he shot Lucy and my house, and he probably tortured Mario before killing him. He was every enemy soldier I had ever come up against in times gone by. He was for me, right then and there, the total personification of everything in this world that I hated and everything in this world that was evil. I granted no quarter, would not let him get up, and I kicked him, punched him, and kicked him some more.

Sean was at the door, but Uncle Tommy's inert form was blocking his entrance. I heard Bob outside talking to Sean and they backed away as I opened the door. I was dragging Tommy McGuinnes by the collar and I looked at the bike cop directly: "Here's your boss buddy; take him and this idiot kid and beat it." He drew his pistol to shoot me but the FBI lady agent at the bar shot him dead on the first shot. Sean the idiot went diving for Tommy's gun that was on the floor. I will tell you the truth here, we let him have the time to get it and aim it but that was all. Another of the agents dropped him immediately with one shot to the head.

"Gee Bob, do you think they will ever serve us here again?" He said, "Joe, what goes around comes around, that's what they say." "Yeah Bob, and now all we have left is Tommy." Bob said to me, "That's good enough Joe, it is over." I looked around; Mr. Lorenzo nodded to me, wiped his lips with a napkin, paid his tab and left the bar with his friend, the guy I met at Nathan's.

"I'm such an idiot," thought Barney while still comatose. "Why did I even talk to Tommy? I knew he was a bad guy, and I knew he wanted Joe D. dead. He caught me unawares, walking back to my car in the park. He pulled his gun and I said 'Hey Tom, we are cops, man; what are you doing?' He shot me anyway, and I knew he would. I shot back, but I know I missed him. He shot me again and then again. He thought I was dead and so did I. I laid there in the mud and watched my life serum drain into the ground. Time stood still for me; no noise no pain and no people to help me. I was just lying there and slowly bleeding to death; I felt cold and clammy. I told myself that I refused to die. I asked myself if I was ready to die. I asked God if I was ready to die. I prayed to the God that I figured had long ago given up on me, but I heard his voice. I knew that I would not die. I knew that he would carry me through and I knew that he would make all things in my life right once again if I let him. I said, "Yes Lord, Yes Lord, Yes Lord."

A part of me died alright, but not my physical body; the old man who lived in me died, and I knew that I would emerge from this horror as a new creature. I knew that Joe and I had to prosecute the bad guys, but more importantly, Joe had to know that God is real."

I held his hand and whispered silent prayers for which I had no words. I even made the sign of the cross knowing that I was not even a Catholic anymore. "Barney, don't leave me pal, I need you in my life. I love you like a brother and I know all about your weaknesses and your strengths. I will get Sandy to cook us up some steaks and potatoes, man; just come out of this and do it now. I can't stand to see you like this."

I felt it, just the smallest little grip on my hand, but I felt it and I knew that Barney would come back. The monitor over his bed wailed an alarm and the little graph thing went nuts. Nurses and doctors came at the quick and Barney was rushed back into the operating room. I waited outside with Bob Goodman and we paced the floor. I heard a loud growl from inside the operating room and it was Barney's voice. I smiled and so did Bob; we knew our bud would be OK. The door opened and the doctor asked us inside to try to make Barney quiet and we did so with happy hearts. Barney told us that he thought he was dead but they just hit him with a shock thing that he didn't like and he had to rise to tell them to cut it out. Bob and I roared in happiness and kissed that damnable unshaven Irish face. The first thing Barney said was "Where's my gun that friggin' McGuinnes shot me."

CHAPTER FIVE

Court of Last Resort

D id I ever tell you that I disliked courtrooms? More than that, I couldn't stand lawyers, judges, District Attorneys, legal sec- retaries, depositions, copping a plea, testimony, and back room deal making. In short, I think if you captured the bad guy, then let's get it over with. I agreed to the premise that all persons had a right to a fair trial and if they couldn't afford a lawyer, we gave them one. To a degree, I guess the other "feel-good" line about being inno- cent until proven guilty had a place in some trials where an eyewit- ness was not involved. But if the overwhelming preponderance of evi- dence pointed a finger of guilt at someone, that's that, skip the appeals, and let's get on with the next case. Bad guys in my view had forfeited their right to coexist in my society. If you did bad things and the good guys caught you, then you paid the price and that's that, plain and simple. McGuinnes was a bad guy, as were Phil Fauxmaster, Judge H. Carey, Mr. Lorenzo and the rest of his crew that he so lov- ingly called associates. Lorenzo just hadn't been snagged yet, but that wasn't my job. That's Barney, Bob Goodman, Burns or the FBI's thing to do. For me, I was just not interested unless they crossed the line into my home turf. I was a simple man. I loved my wife, I loved my kids, grandkids, my country, my neighbors, my friends, and I loved my God. If I was left alone with only those good things in my life circle, then I was a happy, content and well-rounded man, at peace with my surroundings and myself. I did not go out looking for criminals, idiots, transgressors, con artists, druggies, peeping toms, or pickpockets. I went out each day clear-eyed, happy, and engaged in the conduct of living my life as a benefit and, yes, a blessing to others.

Fauxmaster crossed the line. By sheer happenstance, he and his little gig were brought into my life. I recognized the total evil in which he was involved. The worst part of it was his sick misuse of his own children. I couldn't give a hoot in hell about his drug use; I would only wish deep down that someone along the line had given him a "hot load" (overdose). He got caught, his cohorts got caught with him, and Sandy and I helped doing that, so I felt good. The best part of what I felt has nothing to do with how Fauxmaster would pay for his crimes; the best part was that we saved the lives of two innocent children. We gave these kids a chance at life that they would never have had with their father.

McGuinnes was always a bully, always trying to live up to his own image and always walking over other people to achieve his goals. When his nephew "Sean the Idiot" shot up my house, it was like a row of dominoes. Push the first one and the whole row fell. McGuinnes was shoveling coal with the demons of hell along with his nephew. Tommy was stabbed in prison by one of the other unfortunate dumb-bells of this world. The guy who killed him was a lifer anyway and Tommy sent him up for murder and drugs. He must have been overjoyed to see McGuinnes come in there in his prison greens, something like food for the ravenous tiger of hate that lived in every evil man's heart. The tiger was fed but would never be satisfied. When Barney told me that McGuinnes was no longer to be counted among the living, I ran the emotional gamut of "Good" all the way back to "what a wasted life." McGuinnes' life was one of constant escalation. He went from juvenile delinquent and bully to petty thug with brains. He carried his sick mental attitude all of his life but was smart enough to hide it from his superiors.

How he passed the shrink test to become a New York cop baffled me. Well, I guess it was all justified retribution that he paid for his crimes even without the benefit of a courtroom and judge. His slayer did society a favor and saved us some money. He too would pay the price for what he did. Crime, like sin, could never be appeased; it was always hungry for deeper and further-reaching thrills until the brick wall at the end of the road was met headfirst.

I totally believed that if a criminal was smart enough to elude man's punishment for his crimes, he still didn't get away with it. I believed in Heaven and Hell and I knew that, for all of us, the Ultimate Judge awaited to greet us, one by one.

In my alone time at home, I sat by the window watching some kid on a tricycle happily peddling his way alongside his mother. The kid was happy and his mom was vigilant and loving. To my eye, this scene painted a happy future for this kid, assuming that the rest of his home life was equally as healthy as what I was looking at. I thought my own personal final thoughts for McGuinnes and they went like this:

There is no atmosphere per se, just the void of empty space in matted grayscale. A wind, which may just be a thought, seems to blow down from a craggy cliff. No way to rationalize any of this. There's no moon, no sun, no clouds and no light; there is just the dank nothingness of possible existence. If Tommy could hear, he would know that the peers of his old reality are singing in the wind. He cannot hear. If he could see, he would see multitudes of angels rejoicing over others but there were none to rejoice over him. If he could feel, he would sense that he was in mightier hands than the ones that he let guide him all of his past life! He is, and always was, morally bankrupt. He views the vast expanse before him; he knows that he must enter and never return. He tries to look back, but he cannot turn from his fate. He wants to explain, but there is no one to hear what he has to say. He wants so much to hear the words that will prevent this atrocious act but the silence is deafening. He is alone with his thoughts and alone in his misery.

He wills his body to backtrack, to move from the lapping waves of churning white phosphorous on the sand, but he cannot do it. No longer will his body act in accordance with his will, and no longer is he able to undo anything that he has done. He is here in this place precisely because of his own doings and misdeeds. He is here because he refused to be set free. He is here because he himself predetermined this to be so and he cannot deny it. He spent his life in the pursuit of worldly gains and it did not bother him at all to hurt other people while doing so. He cheated, he lied, he stole, he murdered, and he manipulated in order for him to reap the rewards of greed, envy, ego and lust. Tommy denied the truth of the ages and now the price is to be paid.

The living spirit of Tommy McGuinnes feels drawn into the burning sea before him and he cannot fight the power that propels him forward. It is like a gigantic locked door at his back, a wall of steel pushing him slowly into this ocean of physical destruction. This, he knows, is the sea of everlasting damnation, the ocean of forgetfulness, the lake of fire, and the river of no return. He has passed the place of the Court of Last Resort; this is the entranceway to hell itself. He stands in total realization of all these things and he is terrified. The pressure to move into this abyss cannot be fought and he slides against his will ever so closely to the stench of rotting flesh and tortured spirits. His thoughts, memories, emotions, and capacity to feel pain are the only remaining attributes of a life lived separated from goodness, and he wishes this were not so. He is now alive in a new form; he is total spirit now, a wisp of wind, a thought or an idea, but he is in effect the same as he always was; he is evil. He has now come full cycle. Tommy's spirit is painted the color of gray forbidden and shunned reality from there to here. He is the surreal, macabre reality of somber truth, the evidence of living in discord with all that God created in peace and love. All he feels is terror and shame.

McGuinnes falls to his knees. His plea for mercy is unheard, so he curses God. The pain is overwhelming, the stench overpowering, and the noise of everlasting anguish deafens his thoughts. He cannot understand. He wishes for the silence and peace of death but it is not forthcoming. With unbelieving eyes he sees a horrible spirit entity rise from the polluted and smoking cauldronlike mire before him. Its red and flaming eyes pierce this unredeemed wretch with flaming arrows of pain. Somehow Tommy sees his flesh torn from his bones. There is no longer any human reasoning to be applied to this place. He is spirit, but yet he feels agony in the flesh. He has lost his ability to reason. He knows that he is now insane, insane and in terrible pain. He cries tears of acid and it sears his bare chest; his sputum is bile mixed with the blood of his teeth and gums. He is gnashing his teeth in pain and fear. He is shaking and burning; he notices that he is knee deep in this flaming sea of despair. The demon of everlasting damnation approaches him with festering boils of disease and rotting piglike flesh. The embrace cannot be repelled and all he can do now is moan in the certainty of an everlasting existence in this place of the unredeemed and lost souls. He remembers that it did not have to be this way!

The sea of misery has no end. There is no surface and no bottom in this quagmire of never-ending torment. Scenes of his sins, crimes and inhumanity toward other people are played for him over and over. He sees his father and his nephew suffering the same fate. His tormentors will not relent; sleep, rest, and running away are not possible. Who could endure such a place in all of creation? Throughout eternity, none could find any solace in this just punishment meted out to the unjust. This is the place of total darkness and anguish. This is hell and hell is everlasting. This is the rightful judgment of God on those who have no part in His mighty kingdom.

Goodbye Tommy.

I walked away from the vision of life outside my home and outside my sphere of influence. I turned to walk into the living room and I chalked Tommy McGuinnes up as a bad memory. I was headed to the wet bar for a communal sip and a congratulatory salute to the idea of punishment that fit the crime. I saw the piles of legal papers on the table but closed the folder and put them in the office. I would file them away later and with a little luck, I would be able to put the whole thing out of my mind and out of my life forever.

Sandy and I had planned a dinner party tonight. Some of her business associates, a few friends, and one or two neighbors were coming. The house was back in order and the cleaning ladies were just about finished doing their thing. Soon the caterers would be here with all the goodies and as much as I could not stand the hoopla of these things, I would be happy to see Steve, Sue, and the kids, Barney, Bob Goodman, Israel Burns, and Lieutenant Dobson again. This time there would be no intrigue; this time the talk would be of good things and positive mental attitudes. This time, we would not be thinking of guns, fear, or retribution. Sandy called with some final commands and I went through my "Yes, dear" routine. I assured her that the place looked great and all would be fine for a wonderful and happy time with our friends. Inwardly I was hoping that Barney would get a ride with one of the other guys but that was his call, not mine.

I cranked up the Explorer and drove to the liquor store to stock up for the night. Peter the clerk greeted me with a smile and I handed him a slip of paper with our order neatly typed out by Sandy. I scribbled in two more bottles of my personal "one on one" confessional libation and gave him my credit card. Peter said he would deliver the order in about an hour and that was fine; I had other places to go. I liked Peter; he was a purveyor of craziness, but he hid it well and downplayed the idea that I saw him all too often. Off to the supermarket I went, clutching the other list that Sandy had prepared. I just couldn't wait to hobnob with all those crazy women with coupons, mini-calculators, and crying babies strapped into carts. I especially got a charge out of the older or infirm shoppers driving around on those motorized carts like banshees on the hunt. They run over your toes and bump you in the rear end, and then they halfheartedly apologize.

It was all a goof; we guys just didn't stand a chance in those places. I found the paté, the dip, the tonic, the shrimp, the crackers, cheese, the soda and the beer; I even bought milk. I doubled the beer order for future use and added in my particular item of Planters Peanuts, lightly salted. I breezed through the checkout line, paid cash, no little discount card, thank you, and off I went.

Last stop before home was the pet store; we just had to cater to our heroine fat dog Lucy, the princess of road kill. Let's see here, a big bag of pig's ears, some dog bones, a few other yummy-looking treats, a case of IAMS dog food, and a big bag of dry Kibble that she hated. I loaded my booty into the gaping maw of the Explorer, slammed the lid, and then leaned on the car to light up a Lucky. It was a beautiful day. I watched some guy getting dragged down the street by this hulk of a dog and I remembered all too well my encounter with that same poorly-fed beast of burden. He leashed Trixie to a parking meter and went inside the pet store with a list that I imagined the drunken diva's house girl had given him. I walked over and petted the animal and for some reason I thought that this beast of human torture remembered me; she wagged her formidable tail. I stood back and chuckled as Sandy's employee unhooked the dog and set to the task of being dragged back home. Bye Trixie, I thought to myself and then said good luck to the hapless dude who was now learning how to surfboard on concrete.

I drove home a content man who had filled his every want, need and desire, the most important of which was making his wife happy. Lucy ran to greet me at the door; I guess she recognized the pet store logo on the bags I was carrying. Before I could even unpack all the veggies and supplies, I had to feed the dog. I had to feed the dog all the time; day or night, it did not matter to my sybarite ex-slum dog Lucy. She ripped a pig's ear out of my hand and darted off to her private dining area to make a mess on the carpet. Thanks Lucy, some-day I will teach you how to operate the vacuum cleaner, I thought. Lucy had healed well from her gunshot wounds, but she had lost her vigor to chase squirrels, skunks, and chipmunks. That suited us just fine. No, we were not contemplating taking her to a dog shrink. She adapted to her life experiences, and as far as we could tell, was doing just fine. We surely didn't mind her not bringing in her road kill trophies either.

The booze got delivered right on schedule and I set up the bar after putting away the other stuff, all in their proper places, thank you. Sandy came home looking harried, so I poured her a glass of wine to calm her down and to bring on a little relaxation. We talked, we laughed, and we were serious, but the crowning moment was when she told me that she had sent someone else to walk Trixie. I cracked up because I had seen the guy and he looked pretty much the same as I did when I had that job. She asked me if I minded giving my dog gig to someone else and I begged her to keep that guy with the diva and the canine tractor-trailer. I learned my lesson and all I ever wanted to know about poop scooping. She chuckled and said, "Wait until you see the next job I have planned for you, Mr. Big Guy." "Oh, I can hardly wait," I said.

I got lucky with Sandy upstairs and she said that she was a lucky woman to have finally found me. I snorted, "Yeah, just call me Prince Charming."

The hour arrived and all was ready. Steve, Sue, and the kids were early and it gave us a chance for some family talk and it was all good stuff. The kids looked great and I didn't notice anything in either one of them to set off any alarms. Sandy looked radiant in her hostess dress and I was pretty much at ease in my khakis, open collar shirt, and smoking jacket. Barney looked at me and cracked up. Bob shook my hand and I was introduced to his wife Phyllis. The rest of the guests trickled in two by two and introductions were made all around. One of my uppity neighbors kept staring at Barney, but I couldn't care less. To know him was to love him I thought, so get over it already. I was intrigued to see Captain Burns speaking Hebrew with my dentist neighbor and the guy was impressed to the max. Dinner was a semiformal sit-down deal and our hired butler served it with class, finesse, charm, and professionalism. Sandy whispered to me

that Theodore was one of her employees and that she had known him
for years. I looked around the table at our guests and realized that
there was enough firepower here tonight to ward off a full-scale attack
by the Taliban. I kept my thoughts to myself, engaged in small talk
with everyone, and the evening progressed better than I had imagined.

Barney did not touch a drop of booze and I wondered about
that. It turned out that Bob Goodman was a deacon in his church and
had brought Barney to a service when he got out of the hospital.
Barney saw the light of God and was bubbling to tell me all about it.
"Yes Barney, no Barney, sure Barney, I will do that," and on and on
he went. Bob came by and snagged dear old reconstituted Barney
from bending my ear and he winked at me in a knowing way. Bob
said to me that he knew who I was and was happy with where I was
in life. That made me happy and appeased Barney to a degree so he
left me alone about the God talk. I asked him if his new life prevented him from meeting me in Van Cortlandt Park next week and he
laughed, saying that he would pray about it. I knew then that it would
never be, but that too was OK with me. I was happy for Barney to
have finally found a reason to be and a reason to keep on being. I
loved the way Ralph and little Sue called him Uncle Barney; it made
me think of him like some character in the Muppet movie, maybe like
Barney the grouch? Yeah, that was him, or wasn't that Oscar? I didn't
know and I didn't really care; I liked that moniker for old Barn anyway.

Sandy was watching her husband interact with all the people
at the party and noticed that she did not see any of his rough edges.
She thought to herself that she was a lucky woman to have found this
man when she had actually given up the hunt. In a split second of
time, she measured Joe against her first husband, the abusive and
egomaniacal Bill Grandly. He was Bill the elder, Bill the first, and Bill
the one and only and forevermore gone. The whole thing passed in
her mind quickly, the whole sick story. Joe picked up on the momentary fugue-state that Sandy was experiencing and he scurried to her

side and put his arm around her waist. Bob called for quiet and announced a toast to their hosts, Joe and Sandy. With glasses raised and an aura of warmth and camaraderie, Bob told them all of the power of truth that lived in Sandy's heart; he touched on her bravery and resourcefulness against things out of her control. He told the others of Joe, the man who ran away from life only to have real life find him and bring him back to a better life than he ever had in the past. He said it was God's way of dealing with all of his people, be they Jew or Gentile lost or found. We are created in His image and so we are all His children. He got a little preachy when he went on about being wayward sometimes and making error judgments, but he capped it off nicely with thoughts of forgiveness and repentance. Everyone said, "Hear, hear."

Sips were taken and the applause ebbed. Sandy took the floor and in a very eloquent manner thanked each and every person in the room for just being who they were. She noted how important their friendships were to both Joe and her. Joe beamed at his wife with pride and said to all that he could add nothing to what his wife had just told them. The grandfather clock in the hall tolled twelve times and the pendulum of time marched on. Handshakes and hugs all around, the party drew to a close. Theodore was well ahead with the cleanup process. Sandy thanked him for his thoroughness and let him go home to his own family an hour early. Steve and Sue were in the guest bedroom and the kids were asleep hours ago.

The house was quiet. Even Lucy was snoring with a full belly of hors d'oeuvres. Joe brought Sandy a glass of white wine and they sat together for a quiet chat. Joe also had a glass of wine. It may seem quaint, cute or even old-fashioned, but they were holding hands as they sat on the couch. "What happened before Sandy? I noticed that for a few minutes back there you seemed to have slipped away to a place unknown." After almost six months of marriage they had never had a disagreeable word; they had found acceptance and understanding from each other.

It was time, she thought, time for Joe to learn of my past. I love this man with all my heart. More importantly, I know that Joe loves me with all of his heart as well. Sandy went on to tell Joe how she came to this fantastic place of being and she told it with no embellishments, no false truths and no lies, just the facts, as good or as bad as they were. "It goes like this Joe …

"Mom and Dad were second generation Irish immigrants and life was not all that easy for us back there in upper Manhattan. Dad worked as an automobile mechanic and did his best to support Mom and me. Like all parents, they wanted a better life for their child, and they encouraged me all the way through school and on to college. I majored in business administration, eventually taking a job downtown in human resources for a large electronics corporation. I liked the job and found that I had excellent people skills. This went a long way with the company and in a few years I was promoted to division manager. The extra money came in handy and I was able to help my parents. I often visited them, but generally I led a quiet and reserved life. I met Bill Grandly, and he was the most handsome guy I had ever dated. He was a mounted cop working Central Park South. With all of my resourcefulness and skills in people management, I failed to see that Bill was a flawed individual. He was unhappy with himself and whatever it was he thought he needed to achieve. He always wanted more, but was not willing to put forth the effort to earn it. He swept me off my feet in a whirlwind romance and within a year we were married. Bill married his meal ticket. Bill was not the shining star that he always thought himself to be. He was brutal on the job and received many departmental disciplinary reports. He cheated on his taxes all the time and we were audited more than once.

"I earned more money than he did but it didn't bother me. After all, we were in love, ya know? In about a year, I was pregnant with our daughter Sue, and in the last trimester, I took a leave of absence from work. I had enough vacation time and sick leave saved up so we didn't notice the loss of finances too much. After Susan was born, I noticed a drastic change in Bill. He was often late coming home, he drank more and more, and sometimes he stayed out all night. I thought that he might be cheating on me as well, but after a while I just didn't care any longer.

"One night in a drunken rage, he slapped me around the apartment with no provocation. For the next two years, Bill wandered into and out of NYPD treatment programs for alcohol abuse. The beatings started again and with greater intensity. I started to hate my husband, but I soon became pregnant again. This second child was not Bill's and he knew it. The next beating put me in the hospital with a broken nose and a miscarriage. I filed divorce papers from my hospital bed with my mother's assistance. Bill was a cop and cops stuck together, so Bill was never prosecuted and to this day, he is still on the job and still abusing people. I had a visit from the NYPD psychiatric physician who told me that Bill was suffering from a phenomena in which some men have the weird impression that their wife's womb was a sanctuary after birth. This causes them to stray and find sexual gratification in other places. I laughed him out of the room and told him that nothing he could say in Bill's defense would make me consider him to be a member of the human race ever again.

"I quit my job in an effort to hide from Bill and opened up my little business: Grandly's Extra Hands, Inc. Life went on; Bill never looked for me, and apparently wanted little to do with our daughter Sue as well. And then Joe, you walked into my life and I am thrilled to be blessed by you and all that we have achieved together. I love you."

Throughout this entire story I said nothing. I let it all come out and I felt anger and sympathy, which was quickly replaced by admiration for the courage and tenacity of the love of my life. She wanted to know about my past but it was getting late and I begged off for now: "Another time Sandy, OK? I promise." She said that it wasn't important. What was important to her was that this was now and we were the people that we were. I kissed her and we went upstairs to sleep in peace. I guess the drinks were working overtime on my poor kidneys, so I had to get up in the wee hours of the morning. I was wide awake.

My mind seemed to grow tentacles, if that was possible, and I seemed to feel every nook and cranny of the house. I sat on the couch with a glass of water and closed my eyes to enjoy this mental venture that was happening in my inner being. I felt peace and warmth, sort of like baby's breath. I felt security and I felt the power of good people living lives that were credits to society. I looked at the dog curled up in her bed and knew that if there were a reason for her to be awake and pacing the floor, she would be doing that. The doors and windows of our sanctuary were locked and the world was outside. Peace and love lived here and that was the way we liked it. Just like Scarlett O'Hara said: "Tomorrow is another day."

CHAPTER SIX

What Goes Around Comes Around

S andy called me around 11 a.m. while I was doing my domestic duties: "Joe, can you be a bartender for a private party? Theodore is not available and I'm in a pinch. This is a new client for us and I surmised from the conversation that there could be future business for us there. I really want to impress this lady so we can build a good relationship." I told Sandy that I would handle the job and wrote down the particulars. I had about three hours to get ready so I showered and shaved and found a clean white shirt, black tie, and appropriate slacks. All nice and spiffy–looking, I growled at the dog and she growled back. Obviously, she had no idea that I was only kidding with her. I grabbed some pastrami and rye bread just to show myself how far I have come in my culinary enlightenment. I made the sandwich all by myself, complete with mustard and pickle. Although I absolutely craved a cold beer to go with it I had to resist the temptation in order to make a good impression for our new client. I overcame the urge to leave the dish in the sink and dutifully washed it, dried it, and put it away. I thought with a laugh, Gosh Joe, you amaze even me.

Sandy was pulling into the driveway while I was backing out, so I blew her a kiss and told her that I would go off to this job and land her a contract that would make us rich. She laughed and said, "Yeah Joe, you really are Prince Charming, but you might consider wiping the mustard off your chin." I laughed, "See you later then." I drove down to Riverdale in the north Bronx.

Riverdale was an enigma; the street layout was designed to confuse the uninitiated and ill informed. Most of New York City, the Bronx included, followed a sensible pattern of numbered streets intersected by mainline avenues, but not Riverdale. One might follow Broadway or Riverdale Avenue south from Yonkers only to be forced onto a service road with no exits. If you were not vigilant, this would put you onto the Major Deegan Expressway and whisk you into Manhattan, bypassing the street that you wished to find. I had little experience with this place, but I knew enough to stick to the right, drive slowly, and watch the signs. Traditionally, Riverdale was the enclave of the moneyed elite of the city, their little hideout from the daily grind of consuming each other downtown on Wall Street. Designed to keep out those who did not belong, the streets were deceptive. Some were one-way and would not allow a quick loop back, while others were dead ends without the benefit of proper signage. I thought that Robert Moses could not have had a hand in the planning of this place. He was New York City's greatest planner and road builder, and everything he did was well thought-out and logically designed. This area of the Bronx was created in the warped mind of Alice's Mad Hatter. I pulled over under a tree and studied my little map. I had been telling Sandy that I wanted to install a GPS system in the Explorer but mirthfully she said that bad pennies always had a knack of turning up and that I always managed to find my way home.

I saw the street on the map and realized that it was right around the corner from where I was parked. Judging from my prior experience with the one-way streets, either I left the car here and walked around the block, or I drove to the corner, made a left, and hoped for the best. From there, I would have to go two blocks down, cross the park, go three blocks north, make another left over the parkway, then come back down. I was sure that if I missed the street, then I would forget this nuttiness and head for a gin mill. Discretion was the better part of valor; I locked the car and walked around the corner.

Any home here more than two stories high constructed of chrome and glass had to be the wannabes and the ivy stone edifices were the old money snot-nosed elite's. I wondered what and who awaited me. Ah, there it was: a refurbished but authentic English Tudor all tucked away well off the street, complete with new growth ivy and well-pointed leaded opaque glass windows. Subdued lighting along the slate path led to the ornate door where I slammed the twenty-pound knocker ring thing to announce my arrival. Ms. Debutante of the Year greeted me kindly, all the while projecting the feeling that I was the hired help, she was the mistress of the evening, I was to shut up, do my job, get paid and that was that. Suits me to a tee, ma'am, I thought, and I walked to the bar to clean and set up. I put on the little black vest that I found on the bar shelf and I thought that I was now transformed to be the quintessential "Jeeves." And I was!

Lots of high-end hooch here, I thought, and so I reminded myself to keep a quiet, low profile approach to all these people unless the expected demeanor of this party changed my mind. I would be Mr. Adaptable and fit my personality to meet each situation and person as presented. For now though, I just set up the bar and made sure that there was no dust on any of the glasses or bottles. I noticed that only two had been opened all the rest of the jugs were new. I took note of Mr. Jack up there on the glass shelf and I winked at him; I think he winked back. Good, I had a friend already to share this adventure with me. The party started to populate and after semi-formal greetings at the door, most of the guests gravitated directly to my little oasis amidst the subdued glitter and phony glamour. Ms. Penelope Gravis was the hostess and celebrant of the evening and the party was just a few friends to gather, sharing the trappings of the good life and all that. The queen of the evening icily asked me not to put out a glass for tips. I said, "Alright, Ms. Gravis, that's fine with me." Inwardly I cussed this broad, but gave her my best and most winning smile anyway. I detected the storm clouds beneath her façade of self-assuredness and knew that she was in over her head.

I paid little attention to those in the living room and merely concentrated on being the best and most professional bartender that these good folks have ever had the pleasure of being served by. I poured the Chablis, Merlot, and Chardonnay with class and style, offering a clean napkin with each drink. There were a couple of beer drinkers, and in some way their eyes conveyed a kinship to me. I chose not to allow my personality to get in the way of equal service to all. I just poured each drink or opened each bottle for each person silently and in a friendly way. Guests were still arriving, the night was early, and wine was seemingly the drink of choice for at least the time being.

"Got a Heineken buddy?" I turned to look into eyes that I had seen before. He said, "Long way from Nathan's, huh Donahue?" I nodded in agreement, gave him his beer and said, "Here ya go Mister. Uh, sorry but I never did get your name back then." He told me with a glint in his eye that I wasn't about to get it tonight either. We shared a laugh and I wondered why he was here. Sure enough, amid much fanfare and accolades of graciousness, in pranced Mr. Lorenzo with his Barbie Doll wife in tow. Although it wasn't reality, it seemed that the music stopped, the people were paralyzed, and the air had become quiet and still.

Ms. Gravis curtsied in respect and I expected her to kneel and kiss his ring. A toady ran over to me and asked for a glass of Asti Spumante for this unannounced guest of honor. I poured, he ran off, and my mind went into overdrive. Why was it, I wondered, that I felt a power over this man who represented all things in life that I abhorred? Surely, with a snap of his little diamond-studded pinky, he could have had me dragged outside, shot, and tossed into a Dumpster to be ground up for dog food. I knew that he wouldn't dare. I poured,

I served, I mixed and I smiled; the evening wore on.

Mr. Lorenzo was holding court in the corner to some of the suits that were there and the conversation was muted, respectful, and attentive. Earlier I had noticed that the Nathan's button man pointed me out to Lorenzo and our eyes locked for a fleeting moment. A waiter came by and slipped me a plate of shrimp to hide beneath the bar. I was grateful for the munchies and thanked him. "No problem," he said, and then went on to tell me quickly that he would "give my regards to Barney and Bob Goodman in the morning." Message received, I nodded; he smiled, and then walked away with tray in hand.

I guess it was around ten-thirty PM or so when I noticed that the guests were getting louder and looser. I had tons of empties in the trashcan and the conversations grew more animated, the jokes more risqué, and the music louder and faster. The cop-waiter was busy as a bee picking up, straightening out, and serving more. He was now relegated to picking up trays of drinks from me for them. I thought that they were now too lazy or blitzed to come and get their libations by themselves. Maybe they didn't want to trip and fall, whatever!

Every now and then, Ms. Gravis would stop by to check if everything was all right; she replenished the bar when needed. I guess she had a pantry in the other room because we ran out of nothing. Penelope came over a minute or so after talking to Lorenzo and she had "Thomas" the waiter with her. She told me that Mr. Lorenzo would like a moment of my time and Tom here would take my place until I got back. I told her, "Of course," but I wished I were wearing a wire. Thomas did too. I followed the hostess with the mostest to the throne d'affairs but I refused to genuflect.

Penelope said to the king, "Mr. Lorenzo, here is Mr. Joseph Donahue, the bartender, as you requested." He stood, he reached, I reached, we shook, and I retched inside. The guy from Nathan's was there with two other suited dudes who took their leave without instructions or introductions. Lorenzo asked me how I was doing and wanted to thank me for telling his son to straighten up and fly right.

(I guessed that Mario had told him). Sadly it was too late for him, and his past caught up with him too quickly and unexpectedly. I agreed and shared my condolences with him wearing my finest, most heartfelt I really mean it look. Lorenzo went on to tell me that he liked me from the first minute he saw me. He said that I "exuded trust, was a stand up guy," and all that good stuff. He said that he was proud of me back there in that sleazy bar dealing with McGuinnes. He went on to say that he wondered what a guy like me was doing working as an underpaid day-to-day odd-job worker. I told him that it was my choice, that I didn't need to make piles of money, and that I led a simple life with no entanglements. He asked me if I would be interested in working for him doing similar "odd, no entanglement jobs." I answered him straight:

"Mr. Lorenzo, I know that you are an attorney and I know that most of your clientele are people that I personally choose not to know or deal with. Although I find the opportunity that you offer tantalizing and maybe even challenging, I really don't think I could accept. Further, if you have been reading the papers lately about the McGuinnes case, you know that I have a loose association with the cops and the FBI. I don't know, nor do I care to know, what it is that you do in your professional life, but I could project a time when I would know maybe too much about you. This could be a source of trouble for me and by extension, for you as well. I certainly do not wish to insult you or rub you the wrong way, but in all honesty, I felt really badly for Mario because he never had a chance in life and just when he maybe was changing his mind, he got snuffed out. As I am sure you know, McGuinnes and Mario were in competition and that is how I got tangled up in that mess."

He was ready for that answer and he put on his serious face. Mr. Nathan's boy puffed up his chest. "Ok, Donahue you had your say, now listen to this and listen with both ears. McGuinnes grabbed my kid and they beat him badly before killing him. Rumor has it that Mario told you something on the ride back from Rikers and McGuinnes wanted to know what it is and now, so do I." I stood there with my big dumb Irish face hanging out wondering just what in the hell this guy was talking about. Mario told me nothing about anything, so both Lorenzo and McGuinnes were making something out of nothing at all. I told Lorenzo exactly that. Lorenzo looked at me and asked if I had been properly introduced to the Nathan's button man and I said no. With a devious smile he said, "Joe Donahue, I would like you to meet Mr. Bill Grandly."

No wonder he wore a smug attitude when we met back at Nathan's. No wonder he wouldn't tell me his name when we met here at the bar. They wanted to surprise or shock me or goad me into anger. I looked at him and said, "Sorry, but for reasons we both know, I cannot and will not shake your hand." I looked at Lorenzo and said that I had to get back to the bar job; I thanked him for the little chat, I enjoyed it — not! I turned and walked away knowing that I had just made an enemy, but I couldn't care less.

I relieved "Thomas" from the bar and he took off to grab his tray. Lorenzo and his lackey Billy left the party after bidding a thank you to their hostess. The party ended about a half-hour later and I cleaned up the bar rapidly. Tom and I worked hard, shuffling dishes and glasses into the kitchen for the overworked staff there. Soon we were done, Penelope paid us, and like a rocket, I was out of there with Tom running right behind me. "Where ya parked, Joe?" "Right around the corner," I told him, "and with a little luck, I may even find my way out of this nutty little corner of the Bronx." He said that I indeed would be lucky to find my way out since maybe some of the banditos were waiting for me. Maybe another less formal chat was on their mind. I felt good having Tom with me; I hadn't brought my cannon with me. Rounding the corner, Tom told me that his car was right behind mine and that we should wait just a few moments so he could call in to Bob Goodman for instructions.

A truck rounded the corner and double-parked next to my Explorer. Plainly marked on the side was New York City Bomb Squad. Bob told Tom that they had my vehicle watched during the party, and they had had a shootout with Lorenzo's little bomb maker making a hasty get-away. He unfortunately passed away to bomb maker nirvana, so no information could be gotten from him. He had no identification, so Forensics was burning the midnight oil fooling around with DNA and prints. My SUV was supposed to be my death trap. The bomb squad treated my beauty with the greatest of care and found this nice little package taped to the firewall alongside the steering wheel column. If it had worked, I would have worn a steering wheel in my mouth instead of teeth. Yeah, I shuddered.

Finally assured that the Explorer was safe, one of them started the engine; he was wearing a helmet, flak jacket, and a wire mesh groin protector. Bob asked me to come to the station for a chat but I asked him if the morning was alright with him. It had been a long and interesting night, and I wanted to go home and make sure Sandy was OK. Bob told me that he had talked to Captain Burns up in Yonkers a few minutes ago and there was a detail in front of my house right now. They checked with Sandy without alarm, and she was OK. I said, "Thanks, Bob, but I will still see you in the morning."

CHAPTER SEVEN

Wrapping Up With Things to Do

I t was a glorious Saturday morning; the sun was bright, no clouds, squirrels were frolicking, and the birds were chirping outside (making a friggin' racket which made me growl, but I smiled because I know that I was supposed to). All was well at the home front, but Sandy wanted an update on last night. She told me that Israel Burns called last night about ten-thirty PM to say hello and then all of a sudden, there was a police car parked out front all night. We took our coffee outside onto the back deck, sat at the glass table, and talked. I told her about the party, then Lorenzo, and finally the icing on the cake: I told her that I had met her ex-husband, Bill Grandly. She was livid with rage and I had all to do just to calm her down. "I'm sorry Joe, but that man is a snake who has gotten away with more bad stuff than most people would even think about." I told her that I knew that, and that Billy-Boy seemed to be keeping company with those of his kind. Maybe this would just go away. They thought that maybe I knew something, but really I didn't. I hoped I had put that little rumor to rest last night. I skipped the part about the bomb. She wanted to know why all of a sudden we had police protection again and I told her it was because Lorenzo was at the party. "They had an inside cop working the tables, but they didn't know that I was supposed to tend bar," I said. "What happened to Theodore anyway?"

She said that he originally took the job but had to cancel at the last minute as he had an intestinal virus. I thought that was pretty convenient and that the truth had something to do with Lorenzo wanting me to be there instead of Teddy. I made a mental note to check that out soon, but for now I just let it lay there. "Sandy I have to go down to the north Bronx and chat a bit with the good guys so let me go for now and I will be back as quick as I can, OK?" She said she was going shopping and would be out for a while anyway so she added, "Go on Joe, go play super hero. I know you love that." I waved to the cop, backed out of the drive, and made another mental note to sell the Explorer; it felt violated and tainted to me. Although I hid it from Sandy, I was in a somber mood. Something told me that this whole Lorenzo craziness was far from over and I was still just a pawn. I was a pawn whose life and family were in danger and I did not know why. I drove to the Bronx north precinct; it was 9 a.m.

Webster Avenue was filthy in the morning. In the brightness of the sunshine you could see the gray water in the gutter, dirt on the sidewalks, and newspaper pages blowing in the wind. Mix that with tons of beer cans, discarded smelly, flea-ridden clothes, and lots of garbage piled in front of the tenements with feral cats warring with the rats over the day's bounty and, for sure, "it's a long way to Kansas, Dorothy." The only good thing I noted about this armpit of the earth was that there were few people to be seen. Those that I did see seemed to be on their way to do the battle, seize the victory and maybe get themselves and their families out of this living hell. I felt good seeing working people trying to make a life and somehow, deep down I applauded, saluted, and encouraged them to success.

A lesser man would be very depressed to see all this wasted space provided for our more unfortunate brothers and sisters, but every city had places like this, every city in every state and in every country of the world. I wasn't depressed; I once lived in a place just like this. At one time I was one of these people, albeit by choice. Fate forced my escape, thank you, fate. I bought coffee at the corner deli (cop-provided coffee was radioactive, I thought), went inside, met the desk sergeant who made a phone call, and soon Bob Goodman was escorting me in to greet the day. The conversation was factual, quick, and businesslike. I listened but had little to add.

"Joe, we cannot ID the bomber guy, no prints on file; but he was not an amateur so we figured that he was a guy that had never been caught. The bomb was fairly sophisticated and would have killed you. It was not a warning; it was a real and direct attempt on your life. We knew that Lorenzo was coming to that dinner party, as Penelope Gravis is involved in his organization. That's why we had Detective Tommy Moore in there as a waiter. More on that we cannot tell you, but I can tell you that we knew all along that the guy you met at Nathan's was Bill Grandly; he retired from the force about six months ago with a full pension. A 'need to know basis' remember Joe? We didn't want you smacking him while he ate his hot dog; we needed information. We didn't want to play you like a pawn but we didn't want you to blow your cool either. That could make you dead and, gosh Joe, we like you," he said with a smile. "Lorenzo did not say or do anything to you that we know of that could be considered an assault or a threat, so we can't hassle him about it but we don't know exactly what he did talk to you about. Grandly is a creep and got off the job with a cloud of suspicion over his head. We think he has been working for Lorenzo for a long time. Now though, he is a full time and in your face employee.

Stay away from him Joe; we know the real reasons for Sandy's divorce from him, and if he met an accident, you would be first in line as the possible perp. Oh yes, Sandy's employee, Theodore, he got a visit from an unidentified messenger who handed him an envelope with three hundred dollars in it and a note. We spoke to him last night and he was helpful and forthcoming. We assume that Lorenzo manipulated Sandy into a corner where she had no other replacement at such short notice than you. Theodore is OK and not involved; he is just a guy who needed a few extra bucks for his family. He is scared but innocent, and as far as we can tell, he is clean and out of the picture for Lorenzo as well. Now Joe, what did Lorenzo want with you?"

I told Bob about the job offer and that Lorenzo pampered me until I insulted him after he told me Grandly's name. I told him that he thought that his dead son Mario had confided in me about his dealings with McGuinnes and company: "I told Lorenzo what I am telling you now, Bob. The kid said nothing to me about anything deep and personal. I drove the car, he slept halfway through the ride, and I don't even think the kid liked me all that much anyway. I do know that Mario told his dad that I whispered to him to straighten up and fly right and maybe that made him hate me, I just do not know. Come to think about it, last night I told Lorenzo to his face that his son never had a chance in life to live it decently so that too probably got him hot under the collar. I guess no father wants to hear that he raised his kid to be a cretin, but birds of a feather flock together, the apple doesn't fall far from the tree, and if you lie down with dogs you will wake up with fleas.

Mario never had a chance and I don't really care; he was a bum and his father is a bum. What goes around comes around, Bob, and King Lorenzo will one day meet up with his just desserts. I just hope that I can be there to see it happen. Sure, I am pretty damn mad at what he tried to do to Sandy and me, but I am a private citizen who can have little effect in bringing him to justice. That, my friend, is your job, so go out there and protect the public; that's me, OK? By the way, thanks for calling Burns and getting that detail to my house last night; that was good thinking and I appreciate it." Barney had the day off, so Bob and I concluded our chat. He gave me some fatherly advice to stay low, avoid Bill Grandly as well as Lorenzo and associates, and I said I would. "Take care of yourself Bob, good seeing you again." "See ya Joe, be well, and say hi to Sandy for me." I went outside and found my car that I felt shaky about, but quickly overcame the feeling. I put my cell phone on the seat, turned it on and it rang; it was Sandy.

"Hi Joe, how did the talk go with Bob and Barney?" I told her it went well, all was in order, and Barney had the day off. She wanted to know about Theodore and if there was any reason for her to distrust him. I allayed her feelings with the assurances that Bob gave me: "Bob checked out his story and it was true, he got a virus alright, a three hundred dollar virus, but he is clean Sandy. He is clean and OK, he just needed the money and had no idea what was going on." As an employer Sandy didn't like it, but as a human being, she understood it.

"Joe, I have a mission for you, if you choose to accept it." She said this in her best Mission Impossible voice, to which I chuckled, "Very good, Mrs. Phelps." I wrote it all down and started the forty-five minute drive north toward Briarcliffe Manor, just south of Ossining where the Sing Sing correctional facility was located. I was to be, of all things, a hired clown, straight man, and stooge for a standup clown/comic at a kid's birthday party. It sounded like a fun way to pick up a cool buck and a half. I was to meet the funnyman leader of the day's festivities at the Elmsford Diner for a little depiction of what he wanted me to do for his gig.

His name was Pete and he was on time and so was I. We had coffee and he told me that I would just stand there and he would make me out to be something verging upon the village idiot. He would be dressing me in balloons at times and pulling rabbits out of my pocket from time to time. He asked me not to smile at anything, just to play along, and everything would be fine. His regular partner was out of town and this job just came up yesterday. He called Sandy this morning and luckily for him, she filled the bill. We were to be there at three and it was already two, so he said, "we had better get a move on, OK Joe?"

I followed Pete and when he parked his car, I parked right behind him. He asked me to join him by the trunk of his car where he produced a box of miscellaneous party props and little boxes. I had no idea what they contained. He opened one right there on the street and did a fast "makeup" job on my face; I looked like a sad sack. He transformed himself into a clown in about two minutes and together with all the stuff, we knocked on the back door as instructed. The lady of the house, who was a fairly young mom of three and a very nice person, ushered us inside. She said that it was a birthday party for her six-year-old twins. The house was full of neighborhood kids and they were busy inside munching on candy and cake. We could hear the giggles from the other side of the door. She offered us coffee or anything else that we might want, but both of us declined. She told us that in a few minutes she would make an announcement to the kids that she had a special fun surprise for them and would then bring us inside. We nodded, and Pete asked me if I could handle this. I told him as I had told him before that this was new to me but I would play along like the trooper that I always wanted to be. He slapped my back, took a shot of Mr. Jack and said, "There's the bell Joe, let's go."

I was six foot tall and weighed about one-ninety; Pete was only five-six or so and a lightweight. We looked like Baby Huey and Wally Cox. I guess that made us look even funnier because the kids clapped merrily as soon as we stepped inside. I stood in the middle of the floor looking like an idiot, no expression and no talk. Pete was electric; he rapidly took control of the party and the kids were rapt in attention to his every word and every movement. He did as he warned me; he seemingly pulled rabbits from my pockets, slapped me upside the head with balloons, and generally made a jerk out of me. I acted along like some hapless buffoon and the kids either loved me or felt sorry for me, I couldn't tell. Pete slapped pie in my face, twisted skinny balloons to make animal shapes, and stuffed them into my pockets where he stuck them with pins. He had some crazy red and blue powder in the balloons so it looked like I blew up at times. He also had a small tape player that played hurdy-gurdy music, and Pete made me move as if dancing to his tune. I obliged his every move and started to anticipate his next assault on my body. I was laughing inside all the while. Really, I never knew how much fun this could be.

Pete called the twins up to the center of the room and they dutifully came up to him filled with giggles of laughter. They were good kids, smart and bright-eyed; I liked them right off. Pete put a top hat on me and handed me a telescopic cane. I had no clue as to what I would do next. I felt movement under the hat, like a crawling sensation on my head but I just stood there like the dummy I was supposed to be. With the kids sitting on chairs before us, Pete bent me over with one hand on my waist and the other keeping the hat in place. So I bent and stayed that way holding the cane. I didn't know that Pete had checked out this part of the act with the twin's mom and she said it was OK. Pete announced that Mr. Greenbeak and Mr. Hardshell were coming to live with Mary and John (the twins). He slowly allowed my hat to drop into his hand where he produced two live baby turtles. Pete amazed me in that he was also a ventriloquist. It seemed that the turtles were talking to the kids. As much as I tried to look, I did not see his mouth move. This guy was a funnyman alright. Each kid took a turtle; their mom was quick to produce a bowl for each. Pete then took the cane out of my hand and collapsed it. Left on my head from the top hat was a small skullcap plastic thing and he placed the cane onto it straight up. He then put my hat back on my head and stood me upright. I rose, holding back my own smiles, when Pete poked me in the stomach. The hat rose four feet into the air and the kids went wild. He poked me again and the hat sank back to my head. I rolled my eyes and the kids loved it. Pete sat me down on one of the chairs and I figured that he would leave me alone for a while. He ran all around the room pulling stuffed animals from kid's backs, pulling out puffy clouds of cotton from others and skipping merrily along, making all of them happy. The little girl Mary came over to me as I sat there and she said, "Are you OK, Mr. Huey?" What a great kid she was; I just winked at her and she smiled and skipped away in glee. Pete was busy painting little cat-faces on some of the kids, so I just relaxed and took a break from my straightman repertoire.

Finally it was over; I had to use the bathroom anyway. Back in the kitchen, Pete ran to his briefcase and took another hit from Mr.

Jack: "How did it go for you, Joe?" I told him that I loved the deal and would do it again any time that his buddy was away. Pete told me to wash my hair in the sink as the turtles relieved themselves while there. "Oh great, Pete! Thanks for the opportunity to play private privy to Mr. Greenbeak and Mr. Hardshell." He laughed and with my head in the sink, Mrs. Mom came in to thank us and pay us off for a job well done. She handed Pete five hundred bucks right in front of me and that was fine with me. Outside he gave me my share of the money. He then asked me for my phone number should he need me in the future. I told him that I was Mrs. Grandly's husband and that he could get me through her. He shook my hand and said that it was an honor and a pleasure.

I told him that he wasn't getting away so fast: "Open that briefcase, please." I took a shot of Mr. Jack and so did he. We hit it off and I liked Pete; he was a good guy and he was the kind of guy I wanted and needed in my life. Doing this bit with him was a catharsis for me. I was allowed to visit the land of clean fun and wholesome games. I was allowed to forget, even if just for the moment, Lorenzo and bad things. I called Sandy and I drove home. I knew that the fun was over for now and that I had things to do in order to wrap up the loose and dangerous ends in our lives. The clown was gone, the villains would arrive, and the white hat wearers would win the day.

The Hideout

Sandy was glad to see me when I got home and I told her all about the kids' party with Pete the comic. She told me that she would have paid a million dollars to see me getting slapped in the face with pie and so we both felt good about the quickly done contract. She told me that Sue had called and asked if we would like to come down to New Hope that evening for dinner. "Sounds like a good idea Sandy, let's do it." We didn't even mention the darkness surrounding our lives. That was not in our control, but we would take no chances either. We hurried through the preparations for a quick exit and we were on the road by four PM heading west on the thruway to pick up route 287 in north Jersey. We decided to take Lucy with us and give her some new air to breathe. The kids would have fun with her as well if we could keep her sober.

We took Sandy's Volvo and she agreed to sell the Explorer. She said that we deserved a Jag now: "Right, Joe?" I leapt for joy just like the little boy that I was. Heading south, we got off 287 and onto Route 202 South through Flemington, New Jersey. My mouth was watering seeing all those nice new spiffy cars lined up at the never-ending line of automobile dealerships: "Look honey, a HumVee dealer!" "Keep driving sonny-boy, you don't need an armored personnel carrier now, do you?" It was a good, light and happy feeling to be with Sandy; she was always an "up freak" and I enjoyed just being with her.

We drove over the Pennsylvania State line, crossed the viaduct over the Delaware River, paid the seventy-five cent toll and turned down Sugan Road into Steve and Sue's development. They lived just outside the village of New Hope and it was a world away from the grimy streets that I had walked this morning. We called ahead from the road so they knew that we were near and Steve met us at the door with the kids in tow. He was proudly standing next to a little ceramic elf dude that was holding a sign that read Welcome to the Manleys. Ralph and little Sue were all over Sandy and me. They were calling us Grandpa and Grandma, which made me feel hopelessly old. Lucy was in heaven with the kids as well because nobody played with her at home.

Sandy and I hugged the kids and kissed them profusely. Inwardly we were amazed at the transformation that Sue and Steve had worked in the lives of these two pure hearts. Seemingly they were able to chalk up the eighteen months with Phil Fauxmaster as nothing but a bad dream. Later on while sitting on the porch, Steve told us that little Sue did have bad dreams at night sometimes but the doctor told them that they would dissipate with time. The thing to do was keep her active and involved with projects, homework, school activities, and a fair amount of housework like keeping her room neat. The whole key to success, the doctor said, was love and he saw it in Steve and Sue. Sue told us that both kids were doing better than expected and she knew that to build character did not necessarily mean pampering. Ralph, it seemed, has turned out to be a football nut and had made the school team. The worst part of all that they had gone through was, of course, accepting the fact that their mother had passed away and they would never see her again. Steve assured them that he missed his sister as well and that soon they would be traveling to Chicago to visit the place where she was buried. I remembered that her name was Carol Manley and I felt sorry to have never met her.

We watched the kids trying to get Lucy to fetch sticks and balls but she wasn't into that. All Lucy wanted out of life was to be fed and walked, given water, and then left to her sleep. Of course a few beers would be great too, but as I said, she was on the wagon. The kids were happy outside rubbing Lucy's belly, so we were able to update Steve and Sue on the craziness that was happening in the periphery of our lives. We even had thought that selling the house and moving someplace like this would be a good thing for us. Sandy had an associate who had been pestering her to sell him the business, but thus far she wasn't interested. Actually, neither was I. Working as an oddball for other oddballs was a lot of fun for me sometimes. We had a wonderful barbecue outside on the deck and I pigged out on burgers, spare ribs, and hot dogs.

I gave Steve the benefit of one of my Uncle Ed's favorite Polish adages: "We get too soon old and too late smart." I told him that right this minute, he and Sue were in the most fantastic place and time of their lives. Steve said that combat taught him to put away childish things and enjoy the value of family. He knew that he had a great wife and two wonderful, if not mysterious, kids to raise. They hoped to have one of their own soon. Sandy and I could not have been happier. Later, Steve came out of the house with the afternoon mail in hand. He excitedly opened a selected envelope in front of all of us. He read the final decree from the court; Ralph and Susan, formerly known as Fauxmaster were now legally adopted and would forever be known as Ralph and Susan Manley. Applause and tears of happiness, we were now a real family with real and connected identities. The kids were as happy as can be and the joy was overwhelming. Sandy and I felt that finally we were away from the disturbing things in New York and we were relaxed for the first time in a long time. Life was good!

The ride home in the dark was quiet for us but we talked of the kids and how great it was to see them all once again. Lucy of course was happily snoring on the back seat, dreaming of dog yummies and road kill. Arriving back home at the Grandly/Donahue Estate, both of us noticed the absence of police protection but neither of us mentioned it. "A long day, honey." "You got that right, Joe." With that, we were off to sleep. Lucy beat us to it and was already in her little bed beneath the spiral staircase. Its funny how ten hours of sleep can go by like it was twenty minutes, but that was how it felt. We both awoke at 10 a.m. that Sunday morning and had ravenous appetites. The sun was gleaming through the new doors; it looked like it would be another beautiful day. Sandy rustled up some bacon and eggs, juice, toast, and a big percolator pot full of coffee. When we were finished, I helped her with the dishes and clean up in the kitchen.

I figured that I would step outside to get the paper and share it with Sandy so both of us could sip that last cup of coffee of the morning and just chill out for a while. I opened the door, bent down to get the paper and I heard the crack of a rifle. That was all she wrote; I went down like a ton of bricks; it was a headshot. The lights went out. If I could have guessed anything, I would have guessed that I was dead. Not in the cards this time though, and I awoke hours later in the hospital with the mother of all headaches.

They were all there, and Sandy was distraught with worry. Barney, Bob Goodman, and Captain Burns told me that I was one lucky guy. I got me a nice little crack in the skull but no internal damage. Fortunately it was a glancing shot. Another eighth of an inch and the life and times of Joe Donahue would have come to an immediate end. I couldn't hear all that well and couldn't smile either; thinking was just about impossible. Barney gave me a mirror and I saw a mummy laying in bed with my face on it. Geesh, when would this stop, I wondered. The doctor came in and he told me all of the technical information, but none of it made any sense to me. Sandy was paying rapt attention though so I knew that I was in good hands and would eventually be OK.

He told me that he was giving me painkillers and a sedative to let me sleep away my pain. "No questions and answers with the cops at this time for you Mr. Donahue," the doctor said so I guessed Sandy had told them everything that she knew, which wasn't very much. All I could say was that I had nothing more to add. I didn't see anyone, just boom, splat, that was that, and here I was. Everyone except Sandy left the room and I fell into glorious dreamland. I guessed that I finally came out of the fog late Monday afternoon because I felt overpowering hunger. I rang the bell for the nurse and an angel of mercy appeared at my bedside. Although I had poor balance, I made it into the john dragging the IV tree along with me. They say that Pepsi was the pause that refreshed: "Yeah, right!" I was able to eat, but chewing was slow and a little painful. I ate all of that bland hospital food and loved every bite of it. I asked for more and got it. I felt good and the headache was more like just a throb now. I could at least see and think without pain.

The doctor came in and looked me over, tickled my feet, and did some other neurological tests, and then they whisked me away to the X-ray room. Sandy came in around 9:30 a.m. and Doctor Steven Eric Enriquez was right behind her. The doc explained that the bullet had cut through the skin, and actually glanced off the bone in my skull causing a slight hairline crack. There seemed to be no internal damage and the X-ray showed that the healing process had already begun. The swelling was subsiding and the headaches should be gone in a day or three. He added that I should suffer no long lasting difficulties except a scar just above my right ear. Sandy was overjoyed, as was I, but a smile was a bit hard to conjure up at the moment.

The doctor told me I could sit up and get dressed, but to stay off my feet for the rest of the day. Tomorrow I could try walking around, getting my balance and strength back. All done in the right way while taking the medication that he was prescribing, and I should have little discomfort and be released from the hospital in two days. Barney (now Lieutenant Barney), Captain Israel Burns, and Detective

Sergeant Bob Goodman had other ideas. They were standing in the doorway and waited for the doctor to leave.

They laid their plan before Sandy and me. They wanted me to be dead. Not like really dead, but play-act dead. They were going to release to the papers that the shot was fatal and there was no more Joe Donahue. Burns and Barney outlined this three-act play for us: "Day after tomorrow, there will be a family only, one-day funeral service followed by a cremation. Sandy will go into isolation and whomever did this will hopefully fall for the ruse. You two will have to find some place to dig in so Joe can get better. This will give us more time to try to find out just what is going on and why." Sandy knew that her secretary Martha was capable of handling the business for a few weeks, as long as she was available by phone if needed.

Standing at my bedside, and fearing for my life, she made the decision to contact Mr. B. Arbitrary, the associate that wanted to buy her out; she would sell him the business. Her long-range plan was to sell the house as well, move us to a safer place, and life would once again become simple, safe, and happy. Maybe open a bed and break-fast, a place somewhere in Pennsylvania near Steve, Sue, and the kids, she thought. All of it sounded good to Sandy and after a few argumentative questions from me, the plan was agreed to by all. Sandy called Sue in New Hope and told her to do a rush locate on a place that she thought would be suitable for us to hide out in for a while. Sue was excited and said she would get on it right away.

The next day I was secreted out of the hospital in a panel truck and driven all the way to New Hope and into the loving arms of my relatively newfound but loving family. That same day, an empty casket was loaded into a hearse and driven to an unpublished funeral home for cremation. There was a police escort and they were sure that this procession was not followed. Sandy played her part well as she walked by the empty box weeping like a trooper. That evening, assisted by friends and neighbors, Sandy packed up basic necessities and drove the Explorer to New Hope. Again, she was escorted all the way and in contact with Barney via cell phone. They were not followed. One of the neighbors agreed to sell Sandy's Volvo while she was gone. Sandy signed the papers in advance for her.

Everything looked like it was falling into place and very well executed. Sue found an empty bed-and-breakfast place for sale in a town called Solebury, which was not far from where she, Steve, and the kids lived. Sandy and I would live there and pay all expenses, which made the absentee owner very happy. The owner wanted a "rent with the option to buy" deal, but we weren't ready for that yet. With assumed names we moved in, and I did a lot of porch sitting while Sandy was on the phone most of the day just about every day.

The Volvo was sold.

Money was transferred to Barney for forwarding.

Sandy took a loss with a wry smile.

Sandy and I traded in the Explorer for that Jaguar that we loved. We found a burgundy beauty up in Automobile Land in Flemington, New Jersey. The car was registered to Sue Manley in New Hope keeping our names and address off any records for now. Mr. B. Arbitrary bought Sandy's business and she made a small fortune.

Months went by and much to my surprise, I loved my new surroundings. So did Lucy who had "just made the cut" and was allowed to relocate with us. I healed well but sported a nice clean scar across the right sideburn; I looked very much in vogue.

Antonio Vittorio Lorenzo loved being a hoodlum. He often jokingly told his guys that he was born for this life. He said he was Al Capone reincarnated. He was quite proud of himself and hated with a passion anyone who would insult him or slander his family's good name. He told Bill Grandly that Donahue crossed the line and he paid with his life: "He had no right telling my kid to get away from his mother and me to 'get a life, fly right,' and all that stuff. When he told us that Mario 'never had a chance,' what did that mean, huh? It meant that the missus and me didn't do good for our own kid, right? I gave Donahue one chance to work for me; if he had agreed, we could have taken down the bomb in his car in a New York minute. Ok, so that deal didn't work out, but we got that 'sonamabitch' anyway. We worked too hard to build our business here and I wasn't ready for some broken-down booze hound ex-jarhead to get away with anything that causes me even a scintilla of concern. I'm a lawyer; I know how to kill and slip away almost legal-like."

Bill Grandly laughed at his mentor's snide tongue-in-cheek remarks: Just like the gofer that I have come to be, he thought. Since quitting the police department, he had made more money than he thought was out there for him. Most of the stuff he did was simple enough, doing drug meets and bringing in the bacon. He knew enough not to cheat Lorenzo as that would bring on a certain untimely demise. Sometimes he was the strong-arm guy who did some leg busting with that muscled idiot that also worked for "Fat Tony."

Every now and then Bill Grandly would think back to his childhood. Every now and then he would think back to his first meeting and subsequent marriage to Sandy. Every time he had those thoughts, he got angry and went out to pick a fight with someone in a bar. He did this often enough to know that he had a violent nature, but he really did try to keep it under control. He knew that he inherited this trait from his "dear old dad," Bill Grandly the first.

Bill couldn't pick and choose his jobs working for Lorenzo, but it gave him an outlet for his pent-up anger and he was happy. He remembered watching his father die on the street with a knife in his gut and he remembered that when he was about eighteen years old, he found the guy who did it and beat the hell out of him. He tied him up and tossed him off the Crossbay Bridge in Howard Beach Queens; the guy was still alive when he was tossed into the bay. Bill assumed that this was the end of that little piece of history but he did not know that the guy had lived, and was now a cripple living in a wheelchair over in Co-Op City. When he took the cop test, passed and was hired, he was amazed. Now he could play his game and had a legal gun with which to play it.

It didn't take long for Bill to learn the ropes and soon he had built up a little cadre of nondescript thugs covering all the illegal disciplines. Not really organized like a working crew or team, they met often and pulled off a lot of nasty little rip-offs. They were pretty successful, but Bill soon learned that he was encroaching on some protected turf so he respectfully asked for a "meet" with the local don, Tony Lorenzo. Tony handled Bill almost as a lark because his real activities were spread far and wide. He did however realize that he could not allow Grandly and his crew to ride unchecked. He demanded a cut of their take and allowed them to do what they did as long as they got permission before each caper.

Bill's marriage was suffering during this time because his mind was elsewhere. Sandy was a pain in the butt sometimes, living her naïve life, but he put up with it. His late night drinking bouts were fun for him and if she nagged him about it, a little slap went a long way to shut her up. After the kid was born, he had little interest in Sandy and the kid proved to be a nuisance as well. The last straw was when some guy who worked with Sandy knocked her up. What did she expect, me to raise that kid or what? I dealt with her in the correct way, but never did find out who the guy was. She lost the kid and divorced me, big freaking deal; she was outta my hair and that was good for me. Bill had a few close calls with the police department but nothing could ever be proven against him. After twenty years of play-acting as Bill the cop, he retired from the department under a cloud of suspicion. He threw in with Fat Tony full-time and life was good.

About a week after Donahue was "snuffed out," Tony gave Bill a little job over in Co-Op City. A couple of old men were running a numbers gig, a loan-shark operation and a little betting parlor playing the ponies. Bill took Harry, the muscleman enforcer, along and drove to the park on Co-Op City Boulevard two blocks east of Gun Hill Road. Just as Tony described, he found two elderly gents playing checkers on one of those little concrete tables that were scattered around the park. He saw the guy in the wheelchair and knew that he was the leader of the band. Bill and Harry sauntered over to the men and got right to business. With a smirk on his face, he told them that Mr. Lorenzo was not too thrilled to have them disobey him. They were told to deliver a ten-percent cut every week. Bill said to them, "It's been a month now and we ain't heard anything from you, so here we are to set the tables straight." That being said, Bill found himself looking down the barrel of a Colt .45 automatic held steadily in the hand of the man in the wheelchair: "Bill Grandly, how sweet it is to have you where I want you. It's been a long time since we last met, Billy-boy. I guess you thought I died out there in Howard Beach, huh?" The man had no fingers on his left hand. "Crap floats, Billy, and maybe I had to give up some of my fingers to the crabs out there but I made it back alive, busted kneecaps and all."

Bill's face was white with fear and his hands trembled. "Before you die kiddo, you are going to learn all about your rotten old man and why I killed him. I was nothing but the milkman delivering in your neighborhood. Your old man thought I was messing around with your mother but he was way off base. Your mother was an ugly old broad with a big mouth. No way would I go near her. Anyway, your old man killed my son John and got away with it. He wanted to punish me in his own way, but I turned the tables on him, Bill, just like this scene we are playing out right now. I stabbed your old man and he deserved it, and now you are getting what you deserve."

With that, the cannon went off, neatly turning Bill Grandly's face into hamburger. He fell like a ton of bricks and Harry just stood there. The wheelchair-bound killer looked at Harry, handed him the envelope with a smile, and said, "Tell Tony that I thank him for sending Grandly to me." Harry took the envelope and said, "No problem, see ya later." He walked away and the white phosphorus shores of hell had another customer.

Lorenzo laughed and told Harry that Bill was privately expanding and said, "We can't have that now, can we, Harry?" Harry shook his head and said, "No sir, we can't." Lorenzo told Harry that the only good thing that Grandly ever did for him was knock off that big-mouthed donkey Donahue. Harry laughed; Tony gloated, lit a cigar, and told Harry to get lost for now.

For Sandy and me, life eased up immeasurably. Even Lucy

was now a countrified dog of leisure. The vet said she was fat and lazy but other than that, she seemed to be in good health. We sat out on the rear deck of the "out of business" bed-and-breakfast and viewed the panorama of our surroundings. We were talking money and how we wished to live our lives from here on out. Both of us were satisfied to leave the past as it was. I vowed not to seek revenge because I wasn't sure who shot me or why. I was fairly certain that Lorenzo had a hand in it, but I told Sandy that I was grateful to be alive and wanted to stay that way. I wanted to be with her for a long time to come. "Let sleeping dogs lie," I said.

I had a good pension from construction, a social security check, and a disability benefit from the government. I owed thanks to The Veterans Administration for going to bat for me on that. I alone was bringing in about five large a month into the family coffers. My ex-wife had remarried so the alimony payments had stopped a few years ago. Sandy had invested the profits from the sale of the business into a healthy stock portfolio and took about three thousand dollars a month for spending money. She too had a social security check and the proceeds from her Simplified Employee Pension Fund (SEP-IRA) as living expense money. We were living comfortably, but had not yet replaced Sandy's Volvo that we had sold in New York. We saw Steve, Sue, and the kids often and I even joined a local golf club. I never played the game before but was willing to learn. My impetus to join this club was of course the well-stocked bar and the other retired lions that hung out there. Funny thing about me was that at that time, I had totally given up my long-standing relationship with Mr. Jack. I didn't miss it and Sandy sighed in relief. Every couple of weeks Barney or Bob would call on the phone but the investigation was now in the cold case file. Barney told me, "Joe, you made it home safely so enjoy your life, man."

When the news of Bill Grandly's death reached us, it was an unexpected windfall. Grandly never changed his last will and testament since the divorce from Sandy, and she inherited a cool million dollar insurance settlement. Further, she also would get the monthly retirement check from his pension and the two-year-old Mercedes Benz sports car that Bill the Snake loved so much. It was to be transferred to her name. She also was the owner of any and all other material possessions Bill had acquired in life. Sandy and I agreed to send in The Salvation Army to take anything that they wanted, free and clear. I took a bus to New York, met Barney at Pennsylvania Station, and he drove me to pick up the Mercedes. I had brought the plates and insurance papers with me.

Barney did a lot of backslapping and wanted to keep me up there in New York hoping to sit on a rock in Van Cortlandt Park with me. He wanted to once again chug a few frosty tallboys "just one more time." Barney, it seemed, was a little more relaxed since his religious conversion. "It can't be that way Barn, I would probably get busted on the way home, and for sure I can't spend the night. Why not take a week or two off and come down and stay with us for a while?" Barney said he would do that and would call us as soon as he could arrange it. I believed him because Barney always told me the truth.

It gave me some kind of "King Rat" feeling to be driving Bill Grandly's car. I liked it and decided to keep it, giving Sandy the Jaguar. The next day Sandy and I took it to an auto body shop for detailing and a new paint job. Those guys went over the car with a fine-tooth comb. They removed the seats and carpet, sterilizing everything that they could. Sandy hired the local Feng Shui expert who lit a smudge stick and did a "cleansing" job on the car. We had it painted burgundy to match the Jag and we felt that any "spiritual presence" of the last owner was totally removed. I didn't buy into that smudging stuff too much, but if it made Sandy happy, I shut my mouth and was respectful of her feelings.

I thought, Sure, go chase the boogieman out of the car, right. Sandy called her lawyer up in New York and all the necessary papers were drawn up to legally change her name. She was now Mrs. Sandra (Sandy) Donahue, and good riddance to the Grandly dynasty. A blissful year of peace passed for us and we were now the Donahues of

Solebury, with family in New Hope. We bought the defunct horse farm and bed-and-breakfast inn, naming it Donahue Downs. We were mysterious to some, friends to all, and an enigma to most. We fit right in with our other "mind your own business" neighbors.

Sandy, forever the businesswoman contracted with a local builder to convert the old horse barn and make it into a state-of-the-art conference center. The main house was enlarged and upgraded as well. We embarked on an aggressive marketing program to attract major corporations and local events as well. Every room in the guesthouse was wired for dual DSL computer hookups and private direct dial-out telephone service. Cable TV, VCR, and DVD access were available as well. No expense was spared to make Donahue Downs a showplace and a compelling "away from the office" business site for national meetings.

Tony Lorenzo kept his own countenance and business prospered. Harry was handling all the tough-guy stuff so there was little for Tony to be bothered with. He thought of letting one of his nephews take over so he could go out west and spend his fortune just for fun. He dismissed the idea. He just loved what he did too much to let it go that easily so he decided to expand his horizons. He sought a conference with the upper echelon of organized crime and he made his pitch. Fat Tony wanted to make a move on the other crime family businesses. He knew that some of the families had various politicians at all levels of government in their pocket. He knew that many opportunities were missed at the airports and docks and he went on to say that disorganized control of the municipal and trade unions was a mistake. He wanted to bring it all together under one umbrella, using all the leaders who were now in place. He said he would be fair; he said he would run those other business families leaner, greener, and more profitable for all of them. He was looking to become the Capo di Tuti (Boss of Bosses); Tony wanted to control all of it. They listened quietly and the meeting ended. After a well-appointed and sumptuous dinner for all at his expense, Tony went home to his palace in Yorktown to await the call that would catapult him to heights heretofore unknown or get him killed. He would not have to wait long.

Two nights later, Tony had a guest. Vito Scaglionne was conveying good news to him. The other families were not all that upset with his plan since they knew that there were other avenues right under their noses that they hadn't tapped into yet. They knew that Tony had the expertise and the nerve to pull this off and that it would benefit all of them. The only stipulation was that he would have to absorb a lot of the firepower and men. They didn't want to overload him with too many guys so a meeting was going to be scheduled to divvy up the staff and job assignments. Tony was blown away; he thought that he could have been rubbed out because of his suggestion, but it apparently went the way he wanted it to. He only wished that his son Mario were alive to take a part of this. He blamed his death on Donahue since he and McGuinnes were both "Micks." Vito told him that the meeting would take a month or so to set up but so far, it looked like a go. Lorenzo felt good.

CHAPTER NINE

The Reunion

I t was opening day at Donahue Downs and every local dignitary we could think of was invited. There were three mayors, two judges, one police chief, and a councilman from Philadelphia. The local media outlets were well represented, but the big guns in Philly stayed home. Radio WNHP-AM was doing on-site interviews, playing great music, and describing the accoutrements and festivities of our grand opening. Barney, Bob Goodman, Israel Burns, and Jim Dobson were all there, as were Steve, Sue, and the kids. Many of our new friends, including Aaron, Sue and Steve's neighbor, were there as well. Happy and moving music was playing from the outdoors stereo system, and the atmosphere was one of joviality and camaraderie. A hundred or more people were assembled and conversations were all upbeat and congratulatory in nature. We were having a blast.

A young man of about forty came over and said, "Congratulations, Mr. Donahue." I shook his hand and looked at him. I said, "Thank you for your kind words Mr. ... I'm sorry, I don't know your name." Sandy was watching me closely. A media guy had his camera trained directly on my guest and me. The man said to me, "Mr. Donahue, my name is Joe Donahue also, and I'm your first born son." We hadn't seen each other in over twenty-five years. I didn't know what to do. I didn't know what to say. I cried. I looked at this fine young man before me, and yes, he did look like I did when I was that age. I hugged him and would not let him go. He hugged me back with just as much gusto as I was holding him. He too had tears running down his cheeks. Flashbulbs were popping, people were clapping, and someone put on some loud music; it was the Marine Corps Hymn. My son Joe was also a Marine. He was a gunnery sergeant, stationed in Quantico, Virginia, at Officer Candidate School and he was attending college at night.

It was crazy how all other things that were going on had become secondary to me. The media ate it up. They were popping questions to Joe and me left and right until Sandy came over and announced that she was the guilty culprit. She did the trace on the family and when she found that Joe was a Marine, she had asked Steve to look him up. Steve visited Joe in Quantico and at first it was a bit touchy. After some talk about "the real Joe Donahue, Sr.," he agreed to come and see for himself. Joe Jr. said that he was damn happy that he did and always wanted to know me; he said that he missed me and felt cheated. I hugged Steve. I hugged Sandy. I hugged my son. The kids came over and hugged all of us, but I am not sure that they knew why. Barney, Bob Goodman, Burns, and Dobson were so overjoyed that Barney bubbled out loud, "Praise God!" I couldn't have agreed more.

If there were a sad heart anywhere at Donahue Downs that day, we would never have known it. Every person in attendance was caught up in the hoopla and general gaiety of the atmosphere. Pete, my favorite clown friend, was entertaining the kids of all ages and I admitted that he and I grabbed a shot of Jack behind the little curtain that he had set up. I was introduced to his "straight man" and I wished her good luck with a smile.

Pete was a funnyman all right, but now I knew that he was a

happy man too; his partner Marcy was a knockout. His gig enraptured Ralph and Sue, and Pete kept trying to lure me onto the scene. Ralph kept saying, "C'mon Grandpa, you can do it." Joe Jr. looked on with a quizzical grimace on his face upon hearing two kids call me Grandpa. I stepped into the act and Pete got me square in the face with a lemon meringue pie. The kids were filled with glee, Sandy rolled on the floor, and my son could not contain his laughter. He yelled at me, "Hey Dad, Mom said you had that coming for a long time." He said it in a joking and friendly manner, and everyone took it that way. The whole place busted up in laughter and so did I. I was back to my sad-sack routine, but this time Pete messed up a nice shirt. "No biggie," I said to him. The moment was worth all the shirts that a million little sweatshops in every underprivileged country in the world could produce.

I watched as Steve and Joe Jr. talked near the outer circle of people. I was glad to see that, as I genuinely loved Steve. He was a brave man, a great father, and a Marine's Marine. Finally, the act with Pete closed and we all gravitated to the banquet table that was set up outside in front of the newly converted horse barn. You name it, we had it, and if we didn't have it, we would get it for you in a New York minute. If that didn't float your boat, well, that was the way the mop flopped, so drink beer and choke on a burger.

It was a long but overwhelmingly joyous day for all and Sandy said that it couldn't have gone better. I couldn't have agreed more. After the party wound down, the locals slowly departed to their proper suburban retreats. Many of them were business people who worked in New York City or Philadelphia during the week but called this area home. It was what you would call an "eclectic" group, but I always hated that word because it seemed so snobbish, if not boorish. They were good people and I enjoyed their company, and that was that for me. We left all the outside floodlights on all night and our little haven looked like a diamond shining in the midnight terrain. All of the guests who traveled here spent the night in the guesthouse rooms or in our "not so little" remodeled and expanded home. It was all for free, from A to Z! In the morning, over a communal breakfast, everyone bubbled with a million different topics.

Bob and Barney had skipped out early to attend service at one of the local churches. Everything that was spoken about was interesting and intriguing, but the only thing I wanted to do was get to know my son, Joe Jr. Steve and Sue had gone back to New Hope with the kids and I missed their energy. We all laughed when Joe Jr. said to Barney upon his return from church, "If you think I will call you Uncle Barney too, you got another think coming, man." Everyone saw the comic energy in that and smiled graciously.

I knew that the cop guys wanted to fill me in on what was going on with the banditos, but I didn't want to hear it. Bob lightened up the talk by telling us that he and Barney went to the New Hope Pentecostal Assembly Church and thought the young pastor there was a great man of God. Both he and Barney said that I should go there next time I had the chance and I said that I would. Steve returned to Donahue Downs after breakfast as Sue had taken the kids to Sunday school. All of us guys went outside to sit under the tent to sip Bloody Marys. Sandy insisted that she was "one of the guys" as well, so she too was there. I was glad she was.

Initially we focused on Joe Jr.

First off, Joe apologized to me for not looking for me for so many years. He said that he had a right to learn the truth about me, but he had been listening to his mother's one-sided version about whom and what I was. He did not slam his mom and neither did I, but in a way, he apologized for her as well. As far as I was concerned, I understood her feelings and many of them were based on truth. I told Joe, "I cannot undo the past. I can only hope for a better future, and perhaps soon I could get to meet your brothers as well." Joe said that he would work toward that goal. He told me that I was a grandfather six times over now. He named names, showed me pictures, and my heart was breaking with joy. I sensed a void, a void that needed to be filled. Was that ennui? Yeah, I think it was. It saddened me in one way, but I saw the gleam of light under the doorway to the future and it was a happy vision for me.

I learned that Joe would be graduating from college in two months. The Marine Corps would then grant him a commission as first lieutenant. Joe was a career Marine and I was proud of him. It was funny to listen to Steve telling us that Joe had more time in the Corps than he did and in our company, he refused to allow Joe to call him sir. They traveled many the same paths in their careers, including combat roles, but they had never met before Sandy arranged it. Bob Goodman and Israel Burns were Army guys, so they respectfully kept their distance during this "jarhead" shakedown cruise. Eventually, Steve drove Joe back home to Virginia and many promises were made. Both of us vowed to keep them. A part of my emptiness disappeared forever.

It was time for the New York update and a more somber mood overtook all of us. Bob Goodman opened the talk and I noticed that Barney had produced a briefcase and a tape recorder. Bob said that before he got into details, he wanted us to listen to a tape produced by the FBI and shared with the New York City Police Department. Burns said that he had already heard it, so he excused himself to take a hike to the bathroom. Needless to say, Bob told us that this was confidential material and could never be discussed with anyone who was not involved or anyone who was not on a "need to know" basis. They were sharing this with us because unfortunately we were once again netted into the arena of Fat Tony and associates. Sandy groaned; I growled and said, "Hit the play button Bob and let's get this over with." He did and the scratchy tape rolled:

"Tony, we are making the gig. Chicago and Detroit are coming as well as reps from the five New York City families. Two guys are coming from upstate and one from Philly. Most of 'em know the haps but all of 'em got questions. Two or three don't trust you all that much and one openly said that you should have been put down years ago. That was Alphonse from Brooklyn, and I guess you know why he feels that way. You gotta patch up that little problem to win his OK on this deal but he said he was open to listen."

Bob told us that the voice we were listening to was that of Vito Scaglionne, the self-appointed liaison among all of the families in organized crime in the Midwest and East Coast. He also had inroads with the Los Angeles, Las Vegas, and Florida guys. Vito himself did little else besides run messages delivered in face-to-face meetings. He was trusted by all of them and did quite a juggling act at times. We knew that he knew everything we didn't, but there was no way that he would ever be broken. He was sworn to Omerta, the blood oath of silence in the face of death. Sandy almost fell off her seat. She knew why we were apprised of this information. She had accepted the weekend rental of the conference center only last week. The man that made the reservation was none other than Vito Scaglionne himself. He was articulate during the call and had presented himself as the CEO of a multinational banking consortium. She thought him a bit smarmy on the phone but since she checked and found that his business was a real and vibrant Fortune 500 company, she dismissed her feelings and happily took the contract. He made an electronic payment up front and the contract was faxed to him for signature. He signed it and returned it via FedEx overnight. There was no way to back out without being sued.

Goodman said that they knew this and that was why they had come up with another plan of attack. Bob said that the FBI was overjoyed at the potential of this gathering. They wanted permission to replace our working staff with agents and cops from all the involved jurisdictions. If we were agreeable to this, then a team would be here a week before the meeting to learn the ropes of our establishment. They wanted Sandy and me out of the area because Fat Tony would recognize us. They had two "countrified" looking agents to take our places. I didn't respond to that right away because I was more than a little angry to be hearing this on the first day after our grand opening. "Play more of the tape, Bob," I said.

He hit the button again: "Ya gotta be kidding me Vito, Donahue Downs?" Vito laughed and said, "Hey Tony, there gotta be a million Donahues in this world. You wanna whack em all?" "I can't stand donkeys, Vito, I had enough with McGuinnes, Grandly and the other Donahue, ya know? I snuffed him and I want to forget him, ya know?" "Yeah, yeah Tony, relax, this place is buried in the middle of nowhere and the guy is probably some old coot that don't know nuttin' about nuttin'. You can even drive there in two hours or less and it isn't too hard to find either. The sit-down is set for August 13th and I'm taking a ride down there next week to make all the arrangements for our associates."

I immediately realized that August 13th was a Friday, how fitting for them. Sandy chimed in that she expected Mr. Scaglionne to arrive this Thursday morning for a "walk around" inspection of the facilities. He would then give us his guest list. Some had special requests like front view, ground floor, or a smoking room. One needed a wheelchair-accessible accommodation. Bob told us that we would do the trading places routine before then to assure continuity and keep them unaware that we were on to them. The New York City District Attorney said that on the strength of that tape alone, we could bust Tony any time we wanted. The listening device that was planted in Tony's home was a Federal Court-sanctioned bug. Anything of evidentiary value was admissible in court. The FBI wanted us to hold off busting any of these guys for now. They wanted the meeting to take place. They saw much heavier charges and arrests coming from this little powwow. Lorenzo and gun charges would be the least of it. These guys were into some heavy stuff and their tentacles reached from coast to coast and abroad as well.

Burns said that none of them knew him and he would be a waiter in the dining room during dinner and a butler during the day for whatever these bums could want. Barney already had reserved a room in the Best Western for that weekend so he could be close by and maybe even play some cards with Sandy and me to kill time. The wheels of justice would start churning out this plan come Monday morning. Although Sandy and I realized that we were trapped into this situation, we wanted the Lorenzo problem behind us and it looked like it would be done in a grand way. Bob said that the rest of the tape would not be played for us. What we heard was all we would hear because the rest of the stuff was super sensitive. Barney whispered to me, "Politics," and I understood.

Sandy and I would have only four days to enjoy our little piece of heaven and then we would be handing over the keys to the boys in blue. Bob told us that tomorrow afternoon the first of the group would be arriving to get up to speed on the workings of the establishment. Sandy's replacement would have to know exactly what was said to whom and how to use the computer and everything else that was here. There would also be an electronic surveillance group wiring every room, every bathroom, the porch, and the outside gazebo as well. All the phones would be tapped and, where possible, video equipment would be hidden as well. Bob said that all this stuff should be up and running before Wednesday morning. Thursday, the first step of the trap would be set in motion.

Barney and Lieutenant Dobson had to go back to New York, but Bob and Israel Burns were staying with us for the rest of the week to help coordinate with the FBI. We were glad to have the company. Later on, I walked with Barney to the car. We stood there like we were embarking on the greatest adventure of our lives. We had traveled far together, and Barney said, "We will travel this road together as well, brother." We hugged each other in gratitude for a friendship that spanned more than forty years; then he drove into the sunset with Lieutenant Dobson.

It gave me a funny feeling to look at what Sandy and I had created here because I knew that our pristine homeland would soon host the scum of the earth. I told myself that this was my final fortress against evil. This was the hill worth dying for and this was the point of no return. We would win against this onslaught of evil because we had the King of Glory on our side. The FBI and the cops of course would help too (chuckle).

I went inside, grabbed a beer, and joined Sandy in the living room. The team of Goodman and Burns were already busy at the phones and things were moving along rapidly. Sandy looked at me and said, "Joe, I love you." It was a moving moment and with a glint in my eye, I told her that she was the reason for my life itself and that I loved her with all of my heart. We called it a night, leaving the two angels of righteous intervention alone in the room. They were busy with whomever they were talking with on the phones anyway.

"G'night Joe, G'night Sandy." "Goodnight Bob, goodnight Israel." We went upstairs to bed, to rest, to think, to pray, and to hope for the best for every person that we loved so dearly.

CHAPTER TEN

Changing Places

The meeting was hastily thrown together. They met at Chris'
house in Albany, New York. This was a quick two-hour hop
on the red-eye for Joe and a three-hour drive for Rick, who
came in from New Hampshire. Joe Jr. brought his brothers up to speed
about finally seeing Dad again. He showed them pictures of their dad
and Sandy, with Sandy's grandchildren and Steve and Sue as well. He
described the entire family as one of stability and love, built on a set
of high moral values. Rick was open to a degree and was at least willing to listen but the youngest of the three, Chris, wasn't buying into
it at all. They each had their vague recollections of who and what
their father was; most of it wasn't good. Now in their late thirties,
except for Joe, who had already turned forty, the memories were fad-
ing, but the pain remained. Their emotional stability had always been
tenuous at best and volatile at worst. Each had to deal with their
demons personally in the best way that they could. Joe, as the oldest,
remembered more of the good times than the other two, but the ugly
scenes were just as vibrant for him as they were for his brothers. Of

the three brothers, Chris had become the most financially successful. He was also the unhappiest of the three.

Rick had in some way found peace and was living his life as best he could see fit. He did not visit much of the family too often; he needed no remembrances of times gone by. To him the past was dead; long live the future. He knew that he buried his demons with a shallow shovel and that they were always there, always ready, often challenging him. He focused his life on his wife, his daughter, his home, and his job. Rick was also a hobbyist body-builder, and he knew that this gave relief to his anger at life and his frustration of living with a predetermined set of genes that would never be silenced. He was his father's son who could never admit it.

Chris was forever chasing rainbows and with determination, luck, and guts, he was amassing a small fortune doing real-estate ventures. Self-educated, he presented a fine physique and a surface charm to those he met. Long gone was his addiction to crack-cocaine. The psychiatrists told him that he had an addictive personality. "He believed it and when that final hurdle in life was overcome, he did not drink alcohol and totally avoided situations where illegal drugs or booze might tempt him. Chris trusted no one and was, for all intents and purposes, an isolationist. Women in his life were for fun; so many of them drifted into and out of his life. They were always much younger than he. Chris could never capture the valued things in life. The gifts of love, peace, trust, happiness, and self-respect were not, unfortunately, in his lexicon of living. Inwardly, Chris would have rather learned that he was adopted than admit that Joe Donahue was his biological father. He had believed everything that his mom told him about his father. More than that, he built a preconceived set of untruths and confabulations to embellish his thoughts in a derogatory manner. The already slanted image that he had of his father worsened each time Chris thought of him. He told himself that he hated his father and that suited him to a tee.

Of the three brothers, Joe Jr. was almost a clone of Joe Sr. The values of the white-hat-wearer were not learned behavior; it was more like instinct. Joe was always the champion of the underdog and took upon himself many a bar room brawl to prove it. Suffering more than his share of bloody noses, bumps, and bruises, he eventually learned that he could not save the entire world. Joe improved his mind and body and sought a proper avenue of life that would fit his character. He found it in the Marine Corps. He was happy to respond wherever they sent him to pick up the cause of the sword of honor and the shield of righteousness. He believed, and rightfully so, that he was the ultimate soldier, standing tall for the greatest nation on earth. He was a proud man who worked hard to earn the title of United States Marine.

Initially Joe told them all he had learned from Steve and Sue and it was a good report. He told them about Donahue Downs and about Sandy, their dad's new wife. He told them that their dad was now a fine-looking man, clear-eyed, intelligent, loving, and fully repentant about the past. He said that their meeting was healing for him and that Dad sincerely wanted to get to know them and their families. He had said that he always loved them, each one in their own way, but he could never show it. Joe's final pitch went like this: "Later in life, when Dad was living alone, he was afraid to even try to find us. He said that rejection would have been the final insult and wanted to avoid it for as long as possible. He was dying living alone in the Bronx, but as the angels would have it, he had met Sandy there and life took off in an upswing for him. Dad was as much a victim as we were, guys, and for me, forgiveness is more than just a word: it is a way of life. I think that Dad experienced more evil than any man should have had to back there in Vietnam. I think that ruined any chance that he might have had to live in a normal manner when he returned to civilian life. Unfortunately, we were affected as well."

Chris accused his older brother of being morally philosophical and an apologist for their dad. He said that the present could in no way change the past. Rick said to Chris, "We cannot live in the past because it will destroy any kind of vision toward a happy future for any of us." He told Chris that he was going to meet their father with

Joe and hoped that he would come along. Chris was noncommittal and presented a blockade to his brothers on every point. Joe and Rick always knew that their younger brother had a different set of values in life. They shrugged at each other and tried again and again to change his mind. They knew that their mother had filled Chris with all the things that she told them, but he was swallowing it all, hook, line, and sinker. The discussion verged on anger so they let it go for now. Going back to their respective places in life, they exchanged phone numbers and vowed to meet again with the wives and all the kids. They jokingly told Chris that they would eat him out of house and home. Chris laughed and said, "Bring 'em on, bro." His brothers left and Chris was alone with his steel-trapped mind once more.

Donahue Downs had not hosted an affair as yet and the place was booming with activity. Electronic crews were scrambling all over the place, installing wireless communication devices in the most unlikely places and installing bugged telephone jacks in every room. In the cupola atop the converted horse barn, a high frequency transmitter plus a cell phone decoder and recording device had been installed. Video cameras were set up wherever possible, with the easiest place proving to be the driveway gates that already had some electronics. When a guest was given a reservation, a pre-coded room number was issued before arrival. Each guest was emailed or faxed a confirmed reservation with his or her individual coded room number. This number was to be entered into the keypad by the gated entrance to Donahue Downs. Their reservation numbers were pre-entered into the gate's electronic system. When a guest arrived, all he or she needed do was punch in the room number and the gate would open. This made the vehicle stop and it was a perfect place to take a picture. After much testing and improved lighting, the system operated perfectly. When a vehicle entered the driveway, an electronic eye picked up the movement of the car and automatically turned on floodlights to illuminate the area for the ease and comfort of the guest. The keypad post was moved slightly to force the driver to slightly lean out of the window so he could punch in the numbers. This of course gave a perfect angle for the video and still camera to take pictures. None of the added paraphernalia could be detected by the naked eye. When the gate opened, the front desk was electronically notified that a guest had arrived. Bellhops met the vehicle at the front door and porters were on hand to help with luggage. It was a class operation, designed to ease the check-in procedure and minimize paperwork.

Sandy was teaching Agent Margaret Graham the nuts and bolts of all the internal operations. Agent "Marge," as Sandy came to know her, was a fast learner and eager to learn each step. Bellhops, chefs, busboys, bartenders, housekeeping staff, and waiters alike were teaching their replacements every nuance of Donahue Downs. The concierge, general manager, maître d', and the desk staff were all replaced as well. The entire staff was looking forward to an unexpected weekend off with pay even before they had the chance to prove their worth to Sandy and me. Each had had a background check and each was sworn to silence under threat of federal criminal prosecution.

My replacement was a guy that looked just like me; he even had a potbelly. I liked him right off and asked if he would be rooming with Agent Marge. I said it with a lilt in my voice, a smile on my lips and a twinkle in my eye that spoke the truth of my question. The guy laughed and said that he hoped so, but he was only kidding. He was a happily married grandfather himself and this was just another job to do before he retired in six months. His name was Michael McCormick; I was happy with that. I later learned that his nickname was "The Pugilist." The crew remained there until Wednesday night. Vito Scaglionne was due the next day and this was the first trial run for the bugging and surveillance equipment. Sandy and I packed up and handed the keys of the property to Marge Graham and Mike McCormick. We checked in at the Best Western Hotel in New Hope and then ran out to visit Steve, Sue, and the kids. I noted that the hotel was within walking distance to Giovanni's, a little Italian restaurant that sold packaged goods: "Pizza and beer anytime I want, I'm in suburban heaven!" Sandy laughed and reminded me to use a napkin instead of my sleeve.

Vito arrived promptly at 9:30 a.m. on Thursday morning and punched in his entrance code at the automatic gate. The gate opened silently and smoothly; Vito was impressed. His smiling and alert image was captured and marked as Exhibit One. "We are off to the races," McCormick said to Marge; all was ready. Vito stopped the Lincoln under the overhead canopy and a valet opened his door for him. The neatly uniformed attendant said, "Welcome to Donahue Downs, Mr. Scaglionne, it is a pleasure to have you visit us. Mr. and Mrs. Donahue are expecting you and await you just inside. I will park your car for you in the visitors' slot directly across the blacktop." Vito got out with briefcase in hand and, as the valet parked his car, he entered the grand reception area. Mike McCormick and Margaret Graham had assumed their roles perfectly. A warm handshake from Mike and a smile from Margaret put Vito at ease. He cordially congratulated them on this fine inn and its apparent attention to detail. He warmly noted that their establishment was constructed neatly and tucked into very beautiful surroundings. He said that he loved the ornate molding, It was indeed a class operation, he said. Mike, who was now Joe Donahue, invited him for a tour of the rooms, the convention center, and the dining room. He was proud of his inn and hoped that all would meet Mr. Scaglionne's demands for a successful business association meeting on August 13th. Margaret offered the use of a vacant room for his comfort while he was here for the final acceptance of the contract. They showed Vito to Room 112 on the first floor, just off the corner from the front desk. Vito went there to clean up, use the john, and make a quick phone call.

He met them again in about fifteen minutes, all set to see Donahue Downs in all its finery. He noted with interest that more than one room was wheelchair accessible and mentioned that only one guest coming would require that accommodation. "No problem at all, Mr. Scaglionne," said Mike, and they continued down the hallway and out the side doors toward the convention center. It was a large room with crystal chandeliers, subdued lighting, and a beautiful Berber carpet wall to wall. Although it was now set up as a dancing accommodation for tomorrow's reservation (a wedding), it would be outfitted with as many tables and chairs as Mr. Scaglionne needed for his business affair and dinner. Vito loved it and produced brochures from a standup comic and a cabaret singer whose partner was a piano player. They were bringing them in from New York for the evening of Saturday, August 14th. The pianist would need a piano for the evening and Mike promised to have one on the site by that time. Vito looked at the grounds, the gazebo, and the wooded lands surrounding the estate and was elated to have found the perfect place for his mobster gathering.

After looking at a few rooms, all was approved, and Vito handed them a guest list along with a list of special requests from some of the attendees. They went into the office to discuss price. "Thirty-two guests, double occupancy plus food for their privately contracted entertainers, right Mr. Scaglionne?" "Yes, Mr. Donahue, and I am prepared to offer a respectable retainer to close the deal." Margaret was deftly punching up numbers into the computer, then handed Mike a slip of paper. Mike said that the final bill including unlimited food and drink would come to a neat one hundred thousand dollars. This would cover three days and two nights, checking in on Friday, August 13th, and departing Sunday the 15th, at 1 p.m., which was their normal checkout time. Vito didn't bat an eye, signed the contract, and wrote a check for thirty-five thousand dollars payable to Donahue Downs. Handshakes all around, Vito thanked them and made for the door. Margaret pushed an intercom key and had Vito's car brought to the front door. His Lincoln now had a hidden GPS system and the functional cigarette lighter on the dash was a microphone. Vito did not smoke. Vito drove back to New York happy as a lark and used his cell phone often. After a fair amount of following to be sure that Vito had indeed left the area, they let him go on his merry way.

Margaret called us at the hotel and asked us to remain there overnight just to be sure that all was secure. "No problem," I said and Sandy and I took a ride to the little town of Lahaska for a nice dinner at Jenny's restaurant, our favorite. The following day, I called in and asked if we could come home now. I said that in a jovial way but I wanted to be in my own home and fumigate the place if I felt the presence of the creep that was walking on our land yesterday. Captain Burns said, "C'mon in Joe, all is well."

All was well indeed, as we were soon to find out. All of our regular personnel were back at their posts and none of the police activity could be noticed. Israel Burns met us and told Sandy and me that the meet with Vito Scaglionne went off without a hitch and that Donahue Downs even made a handsome profit. Burns went on to tell them that most of the law enforcement personnel would be leaving soon, but two agents would be left here just for assurance. "Treat them like guests Joe; the feds are paying the bill." "Thanks, Izzy," I said, regretting that moniker as soon as I said it. He laughed and said, "Call me what you want, man, but Izzy just don't make the cut." He gave me a friendly jab, thanked Sandy, and headed for his car. Bob Goodman was a bit more formal. He told me that three days before the mobsters would get to choke on their lobsters, the entire crew would be here and all set up once again.

Sandy and I had no problem with any of it and Bob took off back to New York as well. The two federal agents that were remaining with us introduced themselves and we gave them a room at the inn. No, it wasn't a freebie. We did, however, feel a lot more comfortable having them around. "Well, honey, it's work time and we have a wedding gig to take care of, right?" Sandy said that we did and we went to check with Milt, our man in charge of these things. He assured us that all was under control and the banquet room was already prepared. He said that guests would be arriving shortly and he would take proper care of everything. Milt told us that there was no need for us to be hanging out; he would let us know if anything difficult came up. He had our cell phone numbers so we took off again to go visit with Steve, Sue, and the kids. As I said before, life is good!

"Hiya Vito, c'mon in and bring me up to speed on the deal in Pennsylvania." Vito took a seat in Fat Tony's living room and took a sip of the Straga that was offered. "Tony, the place is great. The owners are quiet and semi-refined. I don't think they will be nosy or get in our way at all. I signed the deal and gave them thirty-five large as a retainer. I will handle all of the reservations for the crew and mail out the room assignments well before we go. I gave the owners a list and they said they would be making all the correct decisions as to who goes where and all that stuff." Vito didn't want to use the Donahue name to Tony any more than was necessary.

Tony said it sounded good to him and that he was busy writing up his proposal; he wanted to deliver his plan with professionalism, making sure not to miss a thing. He said that he spoke to Alphonse in Brooklyn in a face-to-face last week and that they had declared a truce by divvying up some territory and smacking down one or two of the gunslingers. Vito always thought it ironic that the little guys took the heat for the boss's decisions, but he said nothing. Tony grumbled, "Donahue Downs, huh?" he over-emphasized the name of his old nemesis. Vito laughingly told him to lighten up. They hung out for a while longer but Vito had to leave as soon as possible. He had a lot of phone calls to make in order to pull this off without any snags. "You take care Tony, I'll be in touch." "Yeah Vito, you too," and Vito took off to take care of business.

"Hi Chris, this is your brother Joe. How ya hittin' 'em man?" Chris answered, "Fine," and Joe told him that he would be in New York for a few days and would be seeing their mother. He asked him to meet him there for a little family gathering. Joe was once again trying to bond with his wayward younger brother. Although he never thought that Chris would agree to this spur-of-the-moment invite, life's flip-flops are made of crazier happenings. Chris said he would meet him this Saturday at their mom's house. Joe was floored and later called Rick, who was just as amazed: "Maybe our little brother is coming around, huh, Joe?" Rick said he would also be there, as he was on vacation now anyway. The pretense was a visit to Mom's, but they all knew that they would have some private time for each other. "Time to talk about the 'Dad' issue," said Rick; Joe replied, "Yup." Rick and Joe agreed that their mother need not know anything about their dad but if the subject arose, they would not run from it or lie to her. "Chris will tell her, Joe. You can bet on that," said Rick. Joe said it made no difference; they were adults now and could make their own decisions about their father. Rick just hoped for no fireworks, but said he would see him in a few days. Joe was the only one of the three brothers that knew that their mom had cheated their dad out of the money from the sale of the house. He knew that his dad would never have done that to her but he kept his own counsel and shut his mouth. Joe thought that this fact alone helped him to agree to meet his dad; he knew there was more to the story than what his mother had told him.

Carole; their mother, had remarried and took her new husband's name; she was now Carole Hewlett. Gene Hewlett was a successful businessman about two years from retirement and he enjoyed life with his new wife. The house was neat clean and at peace, just the way that both of them wanted it. Gene had heard the sad saga of Joe Donahue and felt pity for him. He didn't hate him because in his own way, he understood him. Carole was not in the habit of reliving the old pain and had adapted to this new life in grand style. Her kids were coming for a visit and she was thrilled, as was Gene; he liked all three of Carole's sons. Rick was the first to arrive and had just about gotten comfortable with a cup of tea when Joe knocked on the door. "It is good to be here," he said, as he shook Gene's hand and told him that he missed him as well. Chris arrived shortly thereafter and inwardly Joe and Rick were amazed, yet happy, that he decided to come for this visit.

They had a nice dinner all arranged and the conversation flowed easily. Nobody, including Chris brought up the infamous and mysterious father. Joe had a room at the Holiday Inn and Rick had called in earlier as well for a reservation. Around 10 p.m. they made their move to leave, and they received little resistance from Carole or Gene. A little convoy of Donahues merrily tooled across town to the Holiday Inn.

They sat down in the lounge for a chat. Chris (of all people) opened the conversation to tell his brothers that he had a great new girlfriend. He told them, "This is finally the girl I want to marry." His brothers were genuinely happy for him and they wanted to hear all about her. Both Rick and Joe saw a dynamic change in their younger brother, a change for the better. Chris said that before he would tell them about how and where they met; he wanted to tell them that this girl had an effect on him that he never suspected. Right off the cuff, he told them that he wanted to meet his father. Joe lifted his gin and tonic in a salute to Chris' new girlfriend and Rick said, "Hear, hear." The date was Sunday, August 8th, and they decided that an impromptu visit to Donahue Downs next weekend was the thing to do. They had a great and long overdue time with each other and Chris decided that he would spend the night at the motel as well. He had to!

Tony Lorenzo spent the week plotting his business plan of attack. His wife had her hair done.

Vito Scaglionne spent the week going crazy with details for the meeting. He also cleaned and oiled his guns.

The Donahues spent the week teaching, showing, and listening. The Manleys were snug as a bug in a rug.

The Hewletts went out to eat and talked of retirement.

Burns, Goodman and Barney were coordinating with the FBI all week. They were overjoyed with the guest list.

The new staff moved in and the regular employees hopped, skipped, and jumped their little butts off on a free vacation weekend. Phil Fauxmaster paced his six-by-eight cell in killer boredom.

Tommy McGuinnes, his nephew Sean, and Bill Grandly shoveled burning coals onto the fire that was consuming their flesh. They could not welcome death.

Judge Carey's wife filed for divorce.

Joe and Sandy moved to The Best Western and prayed for a

just conclusion to all of this craziness.

The three Donahue boys packed clothes for a trip.

The empty stool in the Arbor Bar was quickly taken by another wiseguy wannabe. And life went on.

CHAPTER ELEVEN

The Grand Affair

I t was Friday morning in Bucks County, Pennsylvania, and the sun was in its glory. Deer were feeding at the roadside and commuters made their way over to I-95 for the trip south to Philly or north to New York. It was 6 a.m. and Donahue Downs was bustling with activity. Breakfast for the staff was a hurried necessity. Even Mike "The Pugilist" McCormick and Margaret Graham had more important things that required tending. Lieutenant Jim Dobson and Captain Israel Burns looked stunning in their neat little bellboy uniforms. Their weapons could not be seen. None of the staff's weapons could be seen. Each male or female agent was armed and many of them were masters of martial arts. All of them were masters of illusion.

Check in time was 3 p.m. and they wanted the guests who were leaving to get hustled out as quickly as possible. Only one guest who had checked in yesterday would remain until Sunday afternoon and he was monitored all day. The electronics guys were putting the final touches on their wares and the newly appointed concierge was practicing his lines. The commander of the FBI group and his staff were given a prime location to monitor everything that happened; they were in a locked utility shed far away from the main buildings. In the shed were computer monitors, listening-device receivers, recording equipment, and live feed video screens attached to DVD recorders from all the video cameras on the property. Every room was bugged, as was every bathroom. Bugs were in every location, including the kitchen. The concealed antenna on the cupola sent a strong signal and all systems were good to go. They ran tests, made adjustments, and moved things around to cover every possible contingency.

The agent in charge, Major Richardson, called Mike in his office and told him to relax. All was completed and all systems were performing perfectly. The GPS blip from Vito Scaglionne's car showed him to be stationary at his Bergen County address. Outside reports came in by phone that some of the out-of-state guests were on their way to Pennsylvania, some by car, others are in airports or on the way to them. "We have hours, fellas, but keep on your toes and stay alert." The morning dew gave way to mist and the deer sipped and supped in tranquility.

"Tony, Vito Scaglionne is on the phone." Theresa's voice would never be called anything close to melodic; she screeched. Tony took the call on the kitchen phone, still chewing on a chicken leg, cooked but cold and slimy. Vito wanted to know if Tony was bringing Theresa with him because they had talked about bringing Harry, his lieutenant, instead. "Nah, I'm bringing Terry, she can lay out by the pool and sun her royal behind off all day, far as I care. Harry I don't need, ya know? A good guy to have around, but I couldn't take driving with him for hours, and he would never know what the hell was going on during the meet anyway." Vito thought differently but said nothing: "Ok then, see you this afternoon, everyone wants to hear your spiel." They clicked off. Tony left chicken grease all over the phone. He didn't care, figuring, so what, maybe it will give her something to do when she finds it. Tony smiled, and then he yelled upstairs to make his wife hurry up with her primping. He was anxious to get there and get this done. Tony felt the hand of fame calling him by name. "I really am the new Capone," he said to himself. His grin was chilling.

"Joe, Lucy smells like a horse." I nodded and said that the odor from the dog reminded me of life back in the city. "She always smelled that way," I said laughingly. Sandy would have none of it and asked me to take her out for her walk before we took off for the Manley home. Lucy had been out of sorts lately and her stool was a mess. Lucy had developed a new affinity for suburban life. She assumed that those jellybeans the deer left each morning were for her and she found them tasty and plentiful. Lucy had intestinal problems and as much as I hated the job, I noticed worms in her stool when I did my little scooping routine. We took Lucy to the Manleys with us, and Sue promised to get her to the vet come Monday morning. Sandy could not take to the idea of sharing a hotel room with a stinky dog. She told me laughingly, "Two stinky animals I cannot handle." I did my usual, responding with, "Yes, dear."

I scribbled a note for Barney and we took off with the dog on the back seat. I reminded myself to get the car cleaned next week and to keep Lucy out of it until she was cured. We took the Jag; the Benz was already parked in Steve's garage. As she drove, Sandy was going through her mental checklist. All traces of the two of them had been removed or hidden at Donahue Downs. Marge Graham and Mike McCormick had a good grasp on the business and the staff took to their jobs with little difficulty. Sandy wondered if Mike would consider a job with them after he retired and made a note to ask him when all of this nonsense was over.

Neither she nor I knew who was visiting our inn this weekend, so we just hoped that there would be no damage and that the Lorenzo debacle would come to a close. We pulled into the driveway and into a new frame of mind. All was at peace here at our extended family's home and we were glad to put evil thoughts out of our mind for at least the time being. I played football with Ralph and Sue asked Sandy to teach her how to sew. Sandy thought, "Sew? Hmm, OK let's see here. First, you thread the needle," — promptly sticking her finger with it — "then you make a knot." Sandy had forgotten but she ad-libbed it through. Sue wanted to fix the hem on one of her doll's dresses and this kept them busy for a long time during the day. Sue mastered the art quickly and soon she was bugging her mom for anything else that needed mending. Sue was enthralled with her daughter's newfound hobby and started digging out all kinds of things for little Sue to fix.

Lucy was outside on a leash sniffing the ground looking for jellybeans but there were none to be had. Steve read the morning paper and the whole scene was bucolic, filled with restful peace in the valley. Lunch was served as a buffet on the deck and Lucy begged for her share but was rebuffed and offered a snack of Kibble. I hate Kibble, thought Lucy, so she stalked off to find a tree on which she could pee. Properly relieved, she lay down in the shade and marveled at the silly humans doing whatever it was that they did. Inwardly she wished for the old days with yummy bones stolen from the goody-locker in the alley and a cold beer from Joe. She rightly guessed that those days were over. She resigned herself to play this "countrified dog" routine until they (or she) got bored with it all. Lucy fell asleep, malcontented as usual. I took a nap on the couch. Steve took the kids to the park. Sue and Sandy went shopping. It was noon and peace prevailed in the Manley home.

Rick was the first to land at Philadelphia International Airport. He had only a carry-on with him so he was free and clear to check on his brothers. He found that Chris was due in next and his oldest brother Joe would be in about twenty minutes after him. He waited in the lounge for Chris' plane to come in: "Amazing," he said to himself, "his plane is ten minutes early." Sure enough, Flight 1107 from Albany touched down at 9:05 and the passengers deplaned. Chris always traveled first class, so he was the third person to come out of the door.

A warm hug and the brothers Donahue went to American

Airline Terminal B to await their older brother. Checking with the Avis desk on the way, they were assured that their rental car was waiting for them. Joe's plane was delayed twenty minutes so they had a sumptuous breakfast in the terminal lounge. Coffee and a bagel for each, price $8.00. Chris moaned but Rick paid. With a growl in his belly, a smile on his face, and a scowl for the cashier, Rick forked over a ten-spot, took his change, and sat with Chris to wait for Joe. Finally Flight 860 from Washington D.C. landed at Gate 23-B and a stream of passengers alit. Joe had to be maybe the last person off that plane; the trail of blank faces seemed endless. Hugs and handshakes all around, these three young men, filled with anxious thoughts of slaying their demons, went to find the Avis desk.

Chris was thinking that he would not know what to say to his dad. Rick was curious as hell about him and Joe looked forward to the whole scene: "This is going to be a great surprise for Dad, fellas, so just let it happen; you'll see, it will be great." Chris had reserved the car, so he handed over all his papers to be photocopied by the clerk, who then handed him the keys. They found the car right outside and all gassed up. It was a bright shiny Lincoln Town Car with all the bells and whistles. Joe whistled and said, "Beautiful." Rick said nothing. He was thinking that Chris would never get over trying to prove something to somebody. Chris drove, Rick sat in the passenger seat, and Joe sat in the back trying to make sense of a map that he printed off his computer. "Just follow the signs for I-95," he told Chris. These latter-day Three Musketeers were off on a long-overdue adventure to heal hearts and put their ghosts to rest. Nobody other than their wives and Chris' girlfriend knew where they were.

Carmine and James Falcone arrived at O'Hare with time to spare; their plane was on schedule and they had no difficulty departing Chicago. Their flight was uneventful and right on time and they had planned ahead to be early for their little meeting before the big meeting. They had to be early because they had arranged for a sit-down with two of the Philly guys. They were picked up at the arrival gate and whisked away into the bowels of South Philadelphia. Their driver had little to say and that suited them just fine. The hoods from the Windy City were right at home here in the City of Brotherly Love. The trash looked the same and the dank aroma of broken lives permeated the air. Yeah, they felt at home.

Major Richardson called the FBI central office in Chicago; he had his counterpart on the line: "We got a make on the Falcones arriving in Philly Al, what's up with that?" Al told him that the electronic bracelet that Jimmy Falcone was supposed to be wearing was still active and showed his location right where he was supposed to be, at home. Richardson snidely replied that Falcone's St. Bernard was probably looking at the bracelet on his leg with a quizzical eye. "Ok Major, he's all yours I guess." They hung up and Richardson thought, yeah right, just what I need; two assassins to make my day. They had been going over the guest list that Vito had given to Agent McCormick and all of the names proved to be bogus. They had no idea exactly who was coming to this meeting of the upper echelon in organized crime. The deposit check was good and Vito was supposed to pay off the rest of the tab upon his arrival. To the supposed owners of Donahue Downs, Vito was the organizer and main man running this meeting. The FBI knew better; they knew that Tony Lorenzo was the star attraction. They wanted him and they wanted him bad.

It was 3:30 p.m. and the guests had been arriving every ten or fifteen minutes. Already, Major Richardson had collected a veritable "Who's Who" in organized crime. Every face was identified and each one was matched to the bogus name that was on the reservation slip. Marge and Joe would only greet Vito Scaglionne and so they remained in their office. The general manager was in the lobby and the check-in procedure was running just like any other mainline hotel. Each car was met and all the proper fuss and bother was extended to each guest. The valets had a field day driving the cars to the parking lot while quickly planting listening devices into each one for future use. Richardson was watching the video screen from the electronic gate when another black Lincoln rolled up to a stop. These guys sure do love those Lincoln's, he thought. A quick look at the distance shot pickup screen displayed two other cars directly behind this new arrival. The driver looked quizzically at the keypad but did not attempt to touch it.

Richardson was concerned but then the driver pushed on the intercom button to say something. He opened the speaker to catch what was said. "Donahue Downs, how may I help you sir?" said the voice from the front desk. The driver of the car said, "I am Mr. Donahue's son. Could you please open the gate for me?" All hell broke loose at the desk but the agent on duty responded quickly, "One moment, sir." Goodman and Burns studied the face on the screen and told the agent that they had met Donahue's son Joe, and this guy wasn't him. The immediate fear was that this was a car with some of McGuinnes' crew looking to even up the score. Chris sat patiently waiting for the gate to open but as of yet, it hadn't budged.

The driver of the car behind him honked his horn. Chris looked into the rear view mirror and Rick and Joe looked over their shoulders. "This guy is impatient, isn't he?" said Rick, but all of them paid no mind to the guy back there. "Let him wait just like we are," Joe said. Richardson ordered the gate to open but told his men to stop the car on the driveway, allowing the other vehicles to punch in their codes. The guy in the black Chevy wagon blew his horn again, and this time Chris stuck his head out of the window and angrily told the guy, "Hold your horses, man! Can't you see that we can't move yet?" The guy in the third car got out of the car and walked up to the Chevy. Carmine told Jimmy to calm down and wait. The gate started to open, but Jimmy Falcone couldn't resist being the idiot that he was. He yelled to Chris, "Move the car, prep boy."

Chris had had enough and his Irish temper got the best of him. He yelled back at Falcone, "Up yours, buddy! We're moving, awright?" Jimmy Falcone was not used to talk like that aimed at him. He was the big guy here and he was not going to allow this lily-white kid to insult him, especially in front of his brother Carmine. Jimmy ran over to the Lincoln and punched Chris right in the face. Joe and Rick jumped out of the car like water dropped in hot oil. Joe grabbed

Jimmy in a headlock and Rick smacked him with a fist that looked like a Virginia baked ham. Carmine drew his pistol and told them to stand down and to do it now.

Richardson yelled into the wireless transmitter to the agents that were playing security: "Get down to the front gate immediately; there is an incident taking place!" They were halfway there already to stop the Lincoln from getting to the front doors. Pulling to a smoke-screeching stop in their little two-door Chevy, they hopped out and read the scene. Both of them drew pistols and ordered all of these men to stand away from each other, and that the one with the gun needed to put it on the ground. Carmine saw that he was outgunned and put his 9mm automatic into his belt, refusing to obey the "rent-a-cops" command. Chris had a fat lip. Jimmy had a broken nose and was bleeding. Carmine snarled and the agents weren't sure what to do. Richardson spoke to the agents through their earpiece microphones: "Get the cars out of the way so other guests can come in. Identify these guys and if they are guests, let them come in without any further comment." Goodman got a make on the big guy from the first car; it was Donahue's son, Joe Jr.: "Hold those three right there and tell them that we will deal with them in a few minutes. Talk to them kindly; they are good guys and they didn't do anything wrong."

Jimmy Falcone said his name was George Smythe from International Banking Consortium and produced his reservation. Jimmy had a hard time talking and Rick grinned at him. Carmine did pretty much the same, saying that his name was Bernstein. The Falcones were allowed to drive into Donahue Downs without further ado. Inside Jimmy's room, Carmine shoved a piece of torn pillowcase into his nose and told him that it was probably broken. Jimmy said that he didn't even care about Lorenzo now; he wanted that big dummy that sucker-punched him. Carmine told him that it would all work out in its proper order: "Those guys are here at the hotel and we got all weekend to take care of them so relax and go fix your face. Lorenzo comes first."

Vito Scaglionne pulled up to the gate, punched in his code,

and drove right up to the front door. The valet greeted him, helped him with his bags and took the car to the lot. He had the same room that the Donahues assigned him last time and he appreciated such nice-looking digs. Room 112 was well decorated and had a nice view. Vito did not miss the Godiva chocolate on the pillow next to the little box of Torrone Amaretto nougat; he smiled.

The phone rang. Mike McCormick said to him, "Welcome back to Donahue Downs, Mr. Scaglionne. It is indeed our pleasure to host this affair for you. Please let me know directly if there is anything you need that has not been addressed since our last meeting." Vito said that he was sure that all was in order and he would be coming to the office in twenty minutes to complete the financial transaction. McCormick said, "That will be fine, Mr. Scaglionne." They clicked off, and McCormick breathed a sigh of relief that so far no red flags were alarming this thug with money.

Burns and Goodman had picked up the Donahue boys at the gate after the Falcones were allowed in. They drove them inside the property unseen by anyone. Goodman drove the Lincoln and followed Burns to the maintenance building near the fence line at the rear of the property. Richardson was livid, but controlled his rage because these guys had no idea of what they had walked into. Bob Goodman introduced Gunnery Sergeant Joe Donahue Jr. to Major Richardson of the FBI and neither was overly impressed. Joe introduced his brothers and demanded to know where his dad was. Richardson had no other alternative than to tell them what was going on. Rick thought it comical that he smacked an organized crime hood but said, "Well, he started it, right?" Richardson looked at Chris's lip and told him that if it was any consolation, Jimmy Falcone looked like Donald Duck. Chris got a chuckle out of that, but the brothers three wanted to know what happened from here. Richardson was thinking it through and told them that he would weigh his options and make a decision soon. He couldn't let the Donahue boys meet up with the Falcone brothers or anyone else for that matter. He knew that word would spread quickly about a little to-do at the gate with somebody that nobody knew. That would bring Vito running to McCormick for some answers to questions that they were not ready to answer yet.

At the very moment, Vito was in the office with Mike McCormick and Marge Graham, playing a double-sided game of charades. Both sides were cool and businesslike, even gracious to one another. Mike offered Vito a snifter filled with Napoleon Brandy; Vito accepted and toasted his hosts. Vito then handed Marge a cashier's check for sixty-five thousand dollars and Mike stamped the invoice PAID IN FULL. They shook hands and Vito made his exit with great fanfare, complete with the overdone and false moves of the European uppercrust. Both sides sighed in private relief. Vito hated brandy. Mike knew it.

Vito walked into the lion's den filled with the overblown egos of men with violent natures. Vito was an organizer and a sometime killer, but to his detriment, he knew too much about too many. He was a constant threat to some of them and for others, he had to earn respect daily. On the other side of that coin, just as many in the family trusted and protected him. He was a needed and sought after asset, too valuable to be silenced, yet too dangerous to be given a free hand. He was always watched and he knew it.

The lounge was full of men in suits and he knew all the leaders. Backslaps were many and he was engaged in many a light conversation with biting words. Vito parried well and danced away from the heat of each foray, threat, and inquisition. Tony Lorenzo entered the room. His three hundred-pound, over-indulged body nearly touched the doorjamb on both sides. Relaxed muscle he called it. He walked across the reception room floor with Barbie in tow. Vito thought of a ballerina following an elephant in the circus; he smiled and thought; "No disrespect of course." He smiled broader at that thought but he hid it well.

Mr. Herb Philbrick was the only guest in the place that had no part in these mobster shenanigans. He was there for some rest and relaxation, on orders from his doctor. He sat in the lounge reading the newspaper and paid no mind to the other guests. Herb was a Wall

Street stockbroker who lived in Briarcliffe Manor about forty miles from his daily grind in New York City. He suffered a severe heart attack at his desk, forcing him into this convalescent leave of absence. No family anywhere near, he chose not to tell anybody about his illness. He just did his time in the hospital and now he was here. He figured to remain until Sunday and return home for another week of rest and then back to work for him. Herb had a lot of work to do. During the day, Herb would drive all around the countryside, visiting antique shops and little villages that he found scattered around this beautiful area. He loved New Hope and fit right in with the rest of the tourists walking up and down the street. Herb was a nondescript person; he looked like a million other faceless people that we all see every day. Nobody here at Donahue Downs bothered with him and he found that he liked the peace, quiet, and solitude.

The staff treated him well and he had no complaints. Herb went into the dining room and sat at the same table that he had been sitting at for the past two days. His health wasn't all that good but he thought that as he grew stronger, he was getting there. He knew that eventually he would be OK. He had no idea that half the people at Donahue Downs kept an eye on his activities. Even if Philbrick did know, he wouldn't have cared at all; his visit here was for the purest of reasons. All he wanted to do was get well, go home and get back to his job. His own private, immediate, and illegal retirement plan was still just a germ of thought in his mind. Yes, he thought, the Canary Islands really were beautiful.

Friday evening at the inn was a light, fun-filled evening of business acquaintances meeting and greeting one another. Only the slightest of whispers about business occurred and nothing of real value was learned by law enforcement personnel. The eavesdropping equipment picked up snippets of meaningless jargon and some whispered hints that went nowhere. Things like who made out well, which guy got whacked recently and so forth were heard, but few names were mentioned and most of the information was old news. The dining room opened at five on the dot and all of them drifted inside to pick and choose where and with whom they would sit. Lorenzo sat with his wife and he knew that this made him look good to the others. A few others had brought their wives, some had brought their latest squeezes, but many were alone so more than a few tables consisted of just eight men.

Donahue Downs was decked out in a manner befitting a presidential visit. Crystal glasses and goblets, porcelain place settings, lace-frilled napkins, new linen tablecloths, tapered candles, and real sterling silverware surrounded centerpieces of magnificently constructed arrays of fresh flowers. An ample staff of waiters expertly took pre-dinner drink orders and handed out ashtrays as requested. It was obvious that some of the guests were out of their element but all stumbling was overlooked. Some were rude, but that was overlooked as well. All the tables were bugged.

Vito Scaglionne, Jimmy and Carmine Falcone sat with Jack "The Lip" Sullivan. Sullivan was one of the few ethnic outsiders to become a "made man." He earned this position as an attorney who knew every trick in the book to turn a jury. Sometimes when things looked their worst, jury panel members simply disappeared. Sullivan's reputation grew far and wide. The Falcones were his assassin tools of the trade and Scaglionne was the one who always planned in advance the winning outcome of trials that seemed to be open and shut against his clients. Sullivan was untouchable; Elliot Ness would die of old age before he could pin anything on Sullivan. Sullivan had his hand in every group of these cretins nationwide. His personal banking and savings accounts had nothing to do with the economy of the United States. With his retirement package well in place, none of his associates knew that he would soon be history, leaving them to fend for themselves. "Sully" hated these people but they were his meal ticket for now. His best friend and confidante within this organization was Ishmael Baum, the other ethnic outsider who was their mastermind of finance. An expert in international banking, he was considered to be the latter-day Meyer Lansky. Baum was not at this meeting but his liaison was and would contact him daily. Sully was only fifty-three years old and would be out of the country before his fifty-fourth birthday; at least that was his plan. He thought Omerta; yeah, right!

Major Richardson planned to have the Donahue boys transported by van to the hotel where Sandy and I were temporarily housed. We were not at the hotel and Richardson did not want to cause any disturbance at the Manleys'. He slated the call for later. Joe Jr. was watching the monitors all around the room; he thought of the war rooms that were simulated at War College. This was the first time he had seen an operation in real time and he was intrigued. Rick sensed danger and knew their position here so he was agreeable to let Richardson transport them under cover. Chris was still upset with Jimmy Falcone and wanted to do more battle with him. He thought to himself that he would shove big brother Carmine's gun where the sun didn't shine, then teach little brother Jimmy a lesson in etiquette. Chris had a vision of grandeur and a superiority complex over these hoodlums and he always hated cheap thugs. He had been warring with an inadequate self-image all of his life. That misunderstood view of his life was the motivating factor to succeed far beyond what he perceived others had expected of him. His new gal-pal had opened up new horizons for Chris and he had come to realize that some hills were just not worth the effort to climb. This, however, was like a personal insult to him because just when he was ready to re-associate his life with real people, these idiots had to get in his way. He would not have it and was now filled with hatred and revenge.

There were no windows in the utility shed, just a locked door. Without realizing it, the Donahue boys were prisoners of Major Richardson. Chris looked around and saw no ashtrays so he lit up a Camel. Richardson looked up and said, "Chris, there are no windows here so we don't smoke, OK?" Chris said, "I'll just step outside then, I'm hooked on these damn things." Richardson said, "Yeah, Smitty go outside with him, OK?" Agent Smith opened the door and Chris and he stepped out into the fresh air. Agent Smith lit up as well and said that Chris had a good idea. He smiled and so did Chris. They were standing at the backside of the block-style building; they could not be seen from the main house or from the convention center. Chris tried to pump Smitty for information about the guy that hit him but Smitty was a seasoned agent and told him that he would not and could not divulge anything to him. "It ain't fair," said Chris as he rubbed his fat lip. Agent Smith told him, "Life ain't fair, so get over it and get on with your life. You don't need to get involved with these dirtbags."

They went back inside to hear Richardson's plan. Chris dismissed the idea of smacking the agent and going on the hunt for Falcone; he knew that he would lose on that score. He told himself that he would think of something somehow. Richardson told the Donahue boys that they would be detained until well after dark. He wanted to be sure that their exit was not seen. "Yes, the Falcones will wonder where you are, but that's tough crap for them," he said.

Thirty tape recorders were eating up tapes like ravenous wolves. The agents could not monitor every conversation at all times so they selected the ones that they felt would be more enlightening for them. One agent laughed to hear that Herb Philbrick was talking to himself. He shut down the listening device at Philbrick's table; it was an illegal intrusion on his civil rights. All the rest of the devices were legally sanctioned. The writs named names and places.

Lorenzo was bored to death listening to his wife and gravitated from table to table, just like the diplomat that he thought himself to be. Finally greeting Scaglionne with a handshake, he stared into the dead eyes of Jimmy Falcone. Jimmy and Carmine were well schooled; they played the game and hid their hatred well. Sullivan shook his hand graciously and said that he was on pins and needles waiting to hear Tony's new proposal. Tony got a bit mouthy here because he was proud of what he was proposing. Tony was, in the final analysis, a pompous yet dangerous windbag. He sometimes talked too much for comfort; this was one of those times. He named a few senators who were being forced into corners with blackmail and said, "These guys are spread too far and too thin. We need to get them together as a unit, even sweeten the pot for them if we need to, but we gotta get some of these turds to exercise more clout on our behalf." Richardson paid rapt attention. Carmine excused himself from the table, opting not to enjoy the Biscotti Toscano desert. Lorenzo watched him leave, his mind working overtime with concern. His concern was well founded. Scaglionne knew Carmine would leave and said nothing. Scaglionne never said anything, but his mind was a steel trap of disjointed data that he was quick to associate and re-associate.

Lorenzo ran to his table so he would not miss the Biscotti desert. Scaglionne picked at it and listened to Sullivan talk about sports. Jimmy was quiet but thinking with a smile, broken nose and all. He now had two jobs to complete this weekend and that prep-boy would not get out of his sight. He wondered where those guys were!

Philbrick dabbed his mouth with the napkin and walked away from dessert. He went outside for a walk in the slowly diminishing sunlight. He sat on a boulder and lit up one of his cigarettes, forbidden by doctor's orders. When one of the guests came out of a side door, he had nothing else to do but watch his moves. The guy (Carmine) got into the Chevy wagon and backed it out of its parking spot. He then deftly parked it, nose out in front of the door that he had just exited. Weird, thought Herb; he took another drag, changed his view, and watched a squirrel play with some nuts.

Carmine went back inside to his room to await Jimmy; they had to talk now. Fat Tony belched, got up, took Barbie, and went to their room. Sully and Vito went to the bar and chatted with some of the other guys. Vito and Sully knew them all and they were a team: inseparable, unchallenged, and respected by all.

Jimmy came into the room and Carmine pointed to his ear while saying, "Hiya Jim." Carmine found the listening device and pointed it out to his brother. They talked of stupid stuff, Mom and Dad, their friends, sports, and baloney like that. Making a hand movement, he signaled for them to leave the room. He said, "C'mon Jim, let's get a drink at the bar." They left and went outside for a walk instead. If they saw Philbrick under the tree, they did not make note of it. Philbrick, however, made note of them. Although Richardson had long distance night vision telescopes fixed on all possible doors, this particular door opened to the parking lot and a wide field; there was no place secure to set one up so all that was there was an eaves-dropping device.

Some of the goon guests decided to leave the property in their rental cars to travel to New Hope or Doylestown and see the sights. They had heard how nice these towns were and supposedly there were plenty of pretty girls walking around. It was only seven in the evening. The gate cameras saw everything but none of it was impor-tant. Richardson wanted to listen in on the meeting set for tomorrow night. He figured that some of them would come and go as they pleased and he didn't even have them followed. Jimmy walked back into the dining room and found that Tony was not there. He looked all around and made sure that Barbie Doll wasn't there either. Correctly assuming that they had gone to their room to freshen up, Jimmy joined Carmine again by the Chevy.

Together they walked around the building and through the front door. They wanted to avoid the electronic door key at the rear door. They walked without hesitation to Tony's room and knocked. Tony answered the door, looking directly into a note that Carmine held up in front of his face. The note read, don't say a word; your room is bugged. Tony nodded and stepped into the hall with them. Jimmy opened the door with his knee and walked into Tony's room and silently urged Tony's wife outside as well. The four of them walked down the hall toward the side door. Both Tony and his wife received an injection in their necks. It was fast-acting poison and they were dead before getting to the door. Jimmy stepped outside and looked around, all clear. No words were spoken and they dragged the Lorenzos over to the car and crammed them into the empty rear of the Chevy with the tinted windows. Philbrick saw the whole deal; he crouched lower behind the boulder. As an added touch, Carmine used Tony's room card to activate the door, knowing that an electronic record was made.

As far as the Falcones were concerned, this part of the plan had worked perfectly. They drove out the gate smiling and laughing for the benefit of the camera that they now assumed was there. They took the bodies and dumped them in a cornfield somewhere in Pennsylvania. Even they didn't know where they were. "Damn shame I couldn't tell him that Bill Grandly was our cousin, right Carmine?" "Serves him right, Jimmy, he shudda done his homework before whacking Billy; most of the guys want him gone anyway. Besides, he said that he missed his kid Mario; now they can be together forever."

The deed done, they drove around for a bit and then returned to the hotel. They had a drink at the bar, and then went to their rooms and to bed for the night. They both slept soundly. The Falcones did what they did and they did it perfectly.

CHAPTER TWELVE

Payday

The king is dead, long live the king. Thus was the whisper at breakfast when it was discovered that Fat Tony and his wife were missing, yet their car was still in the parking lot. The feds didn't realize it yet. Everybody (including Herb Philbrick) knew what had happened; they just didn't know how or by whom but they would find out sooner or later. "Whatever," most of them thought, pass the cream, would ya Vinnie? Alphonse from Brooklyn was tickled pink and could now expand his horizons and yes, with company blessings granted beforehand. Jimmy took a shower, dabbed on some Old Spice, and sauntered out to enjoy the morning repast with his kinfolk. Carmine was more introspective; he wondered if now wasn't the right time to go back home to New York. He could leave Jimmy to handle Chicago and he would bump Alphonse. Yeah, he thought, this could work for an even bigger score than I thought. He, too, went to breakfast and wanted to toast a glass of orange juice to Vito, "the manipulator par excellence."

Herb was at the front desk checking out, in a rush. Penelope

Gravis was at the front desk checking in. Penelope was in a rush too. Herb was overly nervous. Penelope was on solid ground. Richardson was baffled. At least the Donahue brothers are out of my hair, he thought. They were trucked out last night and taken to the Best Western. Joe Donahue Sr. wasn't advised beforehand. The boys wanted to surprise him as best they could and if it had to be at this hotel on Route 202, then so it will be. "Who's the babe?" he asked Burns. "Damn, that's Penelope Gravis, she works for Lorenzo. Tony's got some guts bringing her down while his wife is here." Penelope was given a room and she went upstairs to dump her stuff on the bed. She returned right away and sat down with Carmine Falcone, her lover.

Vito took the floor. Herb stopped in his tracks to listen. Penelope checked out her face in the compact mirror. Carmine was attentive. Jimmy had his hand on his gun. Sullivan ate eggs and hardly paid attention. And twenty-six other upper echelon "dons" of organized crime listened with rapt attention. Every bellhop, table server, desk person, janitor, and listening device paid attention as well. Richardson was jamming the earpiece into his ear so hard it hurt.

Vito looked at every face. He smiled at some and had hard eyes for others. "Ladies and gentlemen, this is just a little announcement to let you all know that Tony Lorenzo has taken ill and had to leave last night." There were murmurs all around the room, mixed with some muffled chuckles. Vito went on, "Although Tony had a great presentation to make to us this evening, I want you to know that I have a copy of what he wanted to do and I will present it to you instead of him, assuming that this meets with your overall approval. I will cut this short to let you all enjoy breakfast." Most nodded in agreement, some just dug into the eggs, but Jimmy winked at Carmine, who smiled at Vito. Penelope had her hand on Carmine's leg and she said, "Let's go to my room honey, OK?" They took off to do their long overdue exercises.

Richardson was aghast; he called McCormick: "Mike, did you hear that crap about Lorenzo?" Mike said that he had and wanted to know what the good major would like to do about it. "Get two of our people into Tony's room. Use the housekeeping ruse but get it done. If there is a Do Not Disturb sign on the door, go in anyway but knock loud first. I want to know right away what is going down. Lorenzo ain't sick; he was excited about this meet and I know that this whole deal was his idea." Very quickly it was determined that all of the Lorenzos' clothes and personal effects were still in the room. The bed had not been slept in and their car was still outside. Richardson said to himself, "Damn, he got whacked; I can feel it!" How right he was.

Joe Donahue Jr. knocked on the door to Room 111 at the Best Western. It was nine in the morning and the Donahue brothers had an interesting first day in Solebury. Sandy opened the door and was overjoyed to see Joe Jr. standing there. Behind him were two other strapping guys that just had to be the other Donahue boys. I was shaving in the bathroom and stepped out wearing my shorts and skinny-strapped undershirt; my hair looked like I combed it with a mix-master. Shaving cream and rumpled underdrawers notwithstanding, I hugged my older son and stared into other eyes that I had not seen in over twenty-five years. I collapsed into a sitting position on the side of the bed. Sandy had unstoppable tears of joy freely flowing down her cheeks. Barney rushed into the room with his gun in his hand. He heard the commotion and thought that Lorenzo had found us. A joyous and overpowering reunion was had. Everybody sobbed in heavy emotion that could not be stopped. I tried to put on my pants and they all laughed. Chris said, "This is the dad I remember: a guy who couldn't put his pants on straight." I asked, "What happened to your lip, Chris?" The boys told me all that happened at the inn and I said that we weren't going to allow those dirtbags to get in our way: "This is our time and we will make the best of it, right?" They all agreed, but Barney ran to his room to call Burns to find out what was going on over at the inn.

I dressed quickly. No one had eaten so all six of us went to a chrome and glass diner about a half-mile up the road. I turned my cell phone off. Barney didn't. Conversation was excited and convoluted, pictures were shown; names were given, and I was happy to hear that Joe Jr. had named his son Joseph Donahue the Third. "A chip off the old block," I said. Joe the Younger said, "Maybe so Dad, but he's going to college and with a little luck he will never see the Bronx." I couldn't agree more. Then Rick started in about his family in New Hampshire. More pictures, more names, and a picture of a beautiful, smiling wife. "My grandkids and my daughters-in-law! I'm blown away," I said happily. Chris was a little more reserved, but chimed in about his real estate stuff and his new girlfriend. They all promised a real and complete family get-together at Donahue Downs as soon as it was possible. Barney didn't want to put a damper on the festivities but he did say, "Yeah, as soon as we can sweep the banditos out of there." They all laughed and I said, "This problem will be done with by tomorrow and from then on, I want nothing to do with any bad guys wherever they are and whoever they may be."

Sandy was silently listening to the inner spirit of Chris. She felt the unsettled questions and knew that he had a lot to deal with if he would ever find the truth. He didn't know whether all the things he was told about his dad were true or just made up stories that he was told by his mom. She felt that Chris was guarded even with his brothers. She knew that someday soon she and Chris would sit down for a deep powwow.

Barney got a call on his cell and excused himself to walk outside the restaurant. When he came back, he told me that Lorenzo was most likely dead but the mobsters were still there. They had a meeting and floorshow scheduled for later this afternoon stretching into the night. I told them all that Tony Lorenzo and his wife were the only ones at the inn who knew the real Donahues by face. I wanted my family to enjoy this day on our own property. "Too dangerous," said Barney. "The three gladiators here smacked one of these dudes and they don't take kindly to that." I told Barney that the goons would all be in the convention center so we could come in to the hotel and go upstairs where we would stay for the day. There were plenty of bedrooms up there and room service could tend to our every need. Barney said that he would have to call ahead to ensure safe passage but I told him, "Yeah Barney, you do that but we are going home to the Donahue residence, the government and the mob be damned."

Richardson said, "NO WAY." Burns and Goodman did their best to stop this crazy move. They tried to get me to go to Steve's house with my entourage but there was no changing my mind: "Steve, Sue, and the kids are out of town; they went to Chicago to visit Steve's sister's grave site. We're not going there and we ain't staying here either." I was lying but he didn't know it. "The Donahue family is coming home and don't even think about trying to stop us." Richardson asked me to give him an hour to make a plan and put in some reason to get the goon squad over to the convention center right away en masse. Watches synchronized, they agreed to be at the main gate at 10:45 a.m.. Chris drove the Lincoln, I drove the Mercedes, and Sandy took the Jag. Barney came with me, leaving the unmarked New York City police car at the Best Western. I was the lead car. I punched in my private code and the gate opened silently. We were coming home.

Captain Burns was waiting at the gate with a local cop from Solebury. Both were resplendent in Donahue Downs security staff uniforms. He drove the company Chevrolet and we, in our three vehicles, followed him to the private parking lot behind the residence building. Entering through the kitchen, we used the rear staircase up to the second floor family quarters. "Joe, this is Major Richardson with the Federal Bureau of Investigation. He is the lead agent in charge of this operation." Bob's intro was formal, but Richardson and I knew each other. The major smiled and extended his hand. He said, "Bad pennies have a way of surfacing." I nodded my agreement and told him that we could deal with the "chump change" later. Richardson was my commanding officer back in 'Nam.

I shook his hand (regrettably), and we agreed that the past was dead. My mind was like a cement mixer though and I remembered the whole scene. When this was over, I fully intended to air the laundry with this guy, but for now we needed each other. Bob Goodman entered the room with some stranger in tow. He greeted us warmly and said that for such a big place, we were running out of room to hide people. He said to Richardson, "This guy was checking out when Jimmy Falcone stopped him in the lobby." Jimmy was intimidating to Herb Philbrick and he had told him not to leave the hotel. Bob said, "Mr. Philbrick is scared, but has an interesting story to tell us. Let's let him have his say and see what we can do with this new information. We also have to protect him somehow, but we will get to that." All the Donahues took seats, as did Bob Barney, Captain Burns, and the major.

Philbrick told us that he saw two men drag two bodies into the rear of a Chevy station wagon and drive out of the complex. He said that he had seen these men from time to time and that they were guests here at the hotel. He went on to describe Jimmy and Carmine Falcone. He also described Tony Lorenzo and his wife with definitive clarity. Knowing that he had seen something that could endanger his life, he was checking out of the hotel when one of them (Jimmy) stopped him and had told him that he wanted to talk to him privately. He guessed that he was seen hiding behind those boulders and the guy talking to him scared him badly. That conversation had been seen by countless agents and cops in the lobby and was clearly displayed on the monitor in Richardson's office. Richardson ordered an intervention. He had the concierge interrupt the conversation on the ruse that there was a difficulty with Mr. Philbrick's credit card. He was asked to come to the office to straighten it out and here he was blabbing his little heart out. Herb would testify, sign a statement, do anything, but he wanted out and he wanted out now. He told us that he had a bad heart and could not take all this craziness; he was a sick man. Richardson saw that the easiest way to deal with and protect Mr. Philbrick was to get him out of here under police escort all the way home and arrange for protection while at home as well. It was arranged for in less than half an hour.

Jimmy and Carmine were having coffee together at a table in

the corner. Jimmy told his brother that he wasn't sure but when they left the parking lot with Lorenzo in the back, he saw something red by a rock. This morning at the front desk he had seen that red patterned shape again and recognized it. It was a shirt and this guy was checking out in a hurry and seemed nervous. Jimmy told his brother that he stopped the guy for a quick "feeler out" talk and the guy had eyes like a cornered rat; he was scared. Jimmy said that he knew that he had seen them: "I was just about to get his name and stuff when he was busted for a bad credit card by hotel security and taken away. Where he is now, I don't know, but this is a loose end that we gotta take care of." Carmine told his brother that he would run this by Vito: "Vito can get the hotel records and we will deal with this as quickly as we can." Jimmy also wanted to know why Carmine hadn't told the others that he found the listening device in his room. Carmine told him that the best way for them was to keep quiet and let the others get cooked: "The more of them to take a dive, the better it is for us." Jimmy thought that his brother was really a smart guy. It was high noon, lunchtime, and time for Vito to make his spiel. They went into the main dining room at the convention center. Carmine walked with Vito Scaglionne and whispered all the way. Jimmy tailed along behind them, scanning the lobby for Herb but he was a no show. Lunch was a feast to behold.

When everyone was seated, Vito Scaglionne went to the podium that was set up and centered at the rear wall. He gently rapped the gavel and the room fell to silence: "Ladies and gentlemen, friends and esteemed colleagues, in a special arrangement with our hosts here at Donahue Downs, we have prepared a lunch befitting of who we are and why we are here. Please enjoy it and join me in thanks to our hosts who have gone overboard to provide for every detail of our convention." Vito clapped and in a friendly gesture, saluted Mike McCormick, the supposed Mr. Donahue. Everyone else clapped too, even the Falcones. Vito extended the podium to Mike who told them that it was indeed an honor to offer his humble inn for their enjoyment and he was proud to have them here. A drink for a toast, everyone sipped, and Mike took off to join Richardson. "Everything set, Mike?" Mike said that he wanted them to get their money's worth and the major said that we would all have a nice little payday today.

The gigantic salvers of antipasto were brought to each table followed by bowls of minestrone soup. Goblets of imported water were freely filled and refilled over and over. Lunch entrees were more fitting for a complete sit-down dinner and included choices of egg-plant parmigian, sausage and pepper scaloppini, Italian marinated grilled chicken, and any kind of steak that one could wish for. The refreshments flowed and special orders were well tended to. The wine was decanted at the tables. There was Gaja Lenghe Nebbiolo Costa Russi from Piedmont Italy for some of the diners, yet others selected the white wine, Schiopetto Sauvignon from Friuli-Venezia (vintage 1932); it was the best in the house. Most, however, opted for cheap Chianti or beer. Vito was in his glory. After an hour and a half of feed-ing these creeps, the waiters served the espresso and silently closed or manned every door.

Unannounced, Mike McCormick and Margaret Graham entered the room. Mike was resplendent in his formal tuxedo, and Marge was decked out like the Queen of the May Day Parade. They walked to the podium arm in arm. Gently rapping the gavel, the first to come to attention was Vito Scaglionne, who was wondering what Mr. and Mrs. Donahue wanted to say and why they did not run it by him first. Nobody else cared; they were having a good time talking manipulation, crime, death, and destruction, all of which had been lovingly recorded and marked as evidence. Mike took a deep breath and commenced his announcement referring to notes that he had placed by his side. The room was filled with servants of every descrip-tion. At least two waiters or bus persons were at each table. The room fell to silence; a few sipped their drinks, yet others were tuned out from what was going on. The Falcones were attentive.

Mike opened his speech: "Ladies and gentlemen of organized crime," and with that, Mike flipped his leather-bound FBI badge out from his waistcoat pocket. The staff stopped the immediate noises of shuffling chairs and movement. "As you know, the guest of honor, Mr. Lorenzo, is no longer with us. Matter of fact, he is no longer to be counted among the living, thanks to Carmine and Jimmy Falcone who are under arrest right now for murder in the first degree." Guns were aimed at each table and the Falcones were disarmed and cuffed. One of the agents at their table read the Falcones their rights and they were shuffled out of the room. "Mr. Scaglionne, you are under arrest on a federal warrant of conspiracy to commit federal crimes of interstate distribution of illegal narcotics and murder. Further, we have an extradition order from Italy for your arrest as well. It seems that you deserted the Italian army back in 1963 and they too would like the pleasure of your company. We will honor that warrant after you serve your sentence here in the United States." Two pistols were removed from Vito, and after a minor struggle, he was cuffed and ankle-chained.

"Ms. Gravis, you, too, are under arrest as a criminal facilitator engaged in engineering the murder of Tony Lorenzo and his wife Theresa." Penelope screamed in despair; she was quickly searched then cuffed by a female agent, and ordered to shut up and sit down. "Mr. Sullivan, the United States Attorney General has revoked your license to practice law 'for cause.' You, sir, are to be detained under house arrest until we transport you to Washington DC. The charges are jury tampering kidnapping and murder." Jack "The Lip" Sullivan was silent and submitted to handcuffs with no complaint. "We would like you all to know that Mr. Isaac Baum, your national CFO, has been arrested in the Florida hospital where he is recuperating from a heart attack. Two U.S. Senators have also been arrested, but for now we will not name names as there are others implicated."

Mike droned on and on naming names and citing charges against each one. He finally finished his litany of names and charges with his closing comment. "By the way, dinner and the show have been canceled." Every guest in the room was arrested and taken by bus to the Philadelphia Federal House of Detention. Their possessions were all confiscated. The Donahues and Herb Philbrick watched the entire thing via closed circuit television in the inner office. Philbrick was driven to his home in Briarcliffe Manor, New York. He was told that they would be in contact with him very shortly. He was assured that nobody knew his name except the good guys so he could go about his life normally for now.

My family and I went downstairs to watch the grand finale of the proceedings. Penelope Gravis stared directly into my eyes and I remembered her telling me not to put a glass on the bar for tips. I chuckled and said silently, "Honey, this is my payday, and what goes around comes around; you can keep the tips." Chris, forever unruly, yelled to Jimmy and Carmine, "See ya around, big boy." They snarled at him. Barney laughed and slapped Chris on the back saying, "Yer da bomb, man."

As they say, "Life goes on," and the big, the bad, the ugly, and the good guys alike do what they do in order to survive this thing we call "life in the good old U. S. of A."

The Donahues of Solebury

CHAPTER ONE

Home Sweet Home

We were sitting on the back porch playing chess, Barney and me, just two old friends passing the day. We were evenly matched at the game, both being sorta like novices. "Check," I smugly chortled. "Not so fast, fat man. Lemme analyze this here situation," said my linguistic opponent. I loved Barney; we went back to our teens in the Bronx getting dragged through the growing-up process together. In those "macho" Bronx teenage gang situations, we gravitated to each other more often than not. Fat lip or black eye, we usually walked away together. Both Barney and I had a long-standing, albeit deleterious, relationship with "Mr. Jack" as we so lovingly referred to our personal choice of escapist booze.

Jack had no part in our lives today, but both of us missed the "good old times" that we shared, with him being the focal point. During those days, we drank too much, fought too often, loved too little, and matured too slow. Whatever the case, Barney and I thought that in every situation, we were the good guys. We were the self-appointed avengers for the downtrodden and the protectors of the weak and ill informed. Win, lose, or run away to fight another day, whichever way we did it, we did it together with a laugh. It was drama, but fun drama for us. Barney and I eventually became New York City cops. Barney stayed for the long haul, but I went my own way after only two years. Others from our little "Rock Around the Clock" gang went on to be cops also: some good and some not so good.

It was a great day, not hot, not cold nor windy, just a great day. Sandy came out; she was my wife, my lover, my savior, my friend, and my comrade-in-arms. She once introduced me to others as her business associate; it wasn't true then, but it was now. With three glasses of inexpensive white wine on the tray, she sat down to bust our chops a bit. I guessed that business was slow at the hotel and she wanted some entertainment to round out her day. I was glad that she did. I always enjoyed her spontaneous visits, especially when she brought the libations with her. "Joe?" I looked up. "Yeah, Barney?" I asked. "Umm, check mate, brother," and he busted up laughing. So did Sandy. I scowled; it was my usual response to losing another game to this loveable nincompoop in the rumpled suit. I studied the board and he was right; I had lost another game to this over-the-hill graduate of the school of hard knocks. I tried to distract him so I could cheat but he was on to me and said that he would shoot my kneecaps out if I tried. Sandy lifted her glass and saluted the reigning champion of the Donahue Downs Chess Club, Barney. This was the self-same Barney who had no last name (but in actuality, it was Tunney). Yes, his great uncle was Gene. We just didn't use his full name because we liked to call him Barney Rubble or Barney the Grouch or, as the kids liked to call him, "Uncle Barney." Only Barney called himself, "Captain Bernard Tunney, Chief of Detectives, Bronx County, New York Division, retired." I think he wanted me to stand at attention and click my heels when he recited that, but I didn't; I told him, "Sit down, your majesty." When our old friend Bob Goodman called, he always asked, "How's the chief?" Yes, we answered respectfully. We told him that Barney was as well as could be and put him on the phone if he was around. They used to work together back in New York and Bob was also a near and dear friend to all of us.

In my alone time, I often wondered how Bob Goodman was able to isolate himself from the job; his family life was excellent. Cops dealt with the dregs of society and often they fell prey to their own weaknesses. This destroyed them and those that they loved. So often we heard of cops getting divorced over and over or falling to alcohol or even drug addiction. Some went all the way and deep throated the Glock. Bob, and now Barney, marched to a different drummer. In a boom-box society, they heard psalms. In a grimy alleyway, they would look at a weed growing in a crack in the concrete and consider the wonder of its greenery. I have seen lesser men back away from situations that Bob and Barney would walk right into and come out victorious. Yeah, I liked these guys; they were men's men. Barney never got married; that was a good thing, I thought mirthfully, because the world was not ready for another generation of little Barneys walking around. Although Barney and I had been friends for years, I only met Bob because of the craziness of the McGuinnes and Lorenzo deal. It was fate's way of creating new, lasting, and deep friendships. I had been vegetating in the Bronx living alone with my dog and working daily work, daily pay jobs. I worked for Sandy, who was now my wife and the queen of our new digs here in Solebury, Pennsylvania. She was second in command after Lucy our dog who, of course, ran the whole show. The net of criminal deceit spread far and wide, but powers beyond our comprehension used each seemingly impossible situation to bring all the white-hat wearers together. The story involved kidnapping, drugs, police corruption, murder, illicit sexual activities, and organized crime. People died, but as we all looked back on it, not one of the good guys was called to the court of last resort during that time.

Barney kept telling me about a bible scripture that he had learned. He recited it into my ear ad infinitum. It went like this: "All things work for the good for those that love God and are called to His purpose" (Romans 8, Verse 28). He always concluded those words by saying "Amen" as if it were a question. I knew my lines by then so I looked at him with trepidation and awe. I shakily said, "Amen Barney, OK?" Yes friend, I had to admit it: when he cornered me like that, I chuckled in my heart but I didn't let him know it. However, when I was alone musing, I sometimes thought of what Barney was telling me, and as I analyzed it or parsed it down, it rang true to my heart. He said, "All things, not some things, work together." Surely what Sandy and I had gone through in our separate lives ended up as working together. "For those that love God." As I thought on that, I ended up really thinking about God and if I knew him at all, no less "loved" Him. Conversely, did He know me? Hmm. And the last part always threw me for a loop: "And are called to His purpose." Thinking on the whole scene of the last few years, my alienated children, the kidnapping of the Manley kids, and exposing them to horrors that children should never experience, caused me to think deeper into that whole sick and crazy scene. The deaths of some unsavory people like McGuinnes and his idiot nephew Sean, the entire Lorenzo family being wiped out, even a New York City motorcycle cop getting whacked in a bar, all had me chagrined. I guess that the topper on the cake was the taking out of Bill Grandly, who had been my wife Sandy's first husband. "For those that are called to His purpose," huh? Yeah, as I looked back at it all, I guessed that Sandy, Bob Goodman, Barney, and I were called to a higher purpose that even we could not see. We just did what good people did and were electrified at that time to take action.

In the past this man would have merely shrugged his shoulders, had another beer, and chalked it all up to "that's the way the mop flops." To realize that the power of eternal goodness decided to bring together a bunch of mobsters right here in my home only to have the FBI orchestrate a massive sting operation and bust twenty-six of them from all over the place seemed to me like poetic justice. So, in my private time, I thanked Barney for telling me that the God he knew so personally has passed this message down to me. It quieted the demons that taunted me from the past and quelled any concern I might have had for the future. As I looked further into the branches of each family involved, I saw that the good seeds had yielded good fruit. Even Chris, my problem son, had seen the logic of living a peaceful life. He was now married and happy for the first time. Yes, I was a grandpa again. I sometimes lost count and had to think about names and do a count, but that was OK; when I saw them all here playing and swimming in the pool, I was overcome with love and thanksgiving. Love for me was a word with little meaning for far too many years. I guessed that Barney's recitation of St. Paul's Bible gem had helped me more than I knew. It was all good stuff!

Mike McCormick came out to join us. He had a cordless phone with him and told me that I had a call from New York. It was Israel Burns, Chief of Detectives up in Yonkers. He was another good friend of ours. He was wondering if he and his wife Phyllis and Jim Dobson and his wife Betty could come down for a week of restful vacation time. Jim was another good guy that we found during the crazy time and Sandy and I both said that we would be overjoyed to host their vacation; I told him, "Come on down, buddy."

Mike took the reservation and Sandy and I agreed that this would be a comp for them. Those guys deserved a freebie sometimes and this was one of them. Phone call over, we asked Mike to take a seat and have a sip of the grape with us. No glass, so I gave him mine, I was just at home slugging from the bottle. Sandy just loved it when I did that — NOT! Mike and his wife Helen bought a little piece of heaven over in New Hope not far from Steve and Sue. He had retired from the FBI just after the mass gang arrest here at our house. He was a big burly Irish-American with twinkling blue eyes and our grandkids loved him. He was a gentle giant whose favorite pastime was boxing and weight training. In his spare time he refereed at the Doylestown Amateur Boxing Arena, which actually was just a club of like-minded guys playing around in their old age, teaching younger guys how to stay out of trouble while building up their minds and bodies. Mike was a civic-minded guy and a definite asset to our little establishment nestled in the woods.

Thinking back on the time when we first met him, it seemed like it happened to someone other than us. It was just a foggy remembrance to us now. After the mass arrests here, the government confiscated the mob guys' privately owned vehicles. The cars were stored here in our lot for months but they eventually filtered down to our ownership as payment for the usage of our hotel to facilitate the arrests. On Sandy's orders, all of the mobster cars were traded in for other more suitable vehicles. Actually, Sandy couldn't look at them and would never ride in one. They had to go. I never gave it another thought; to me they were just machines and I didn't care who owned them before us, I personally didn't give a hoot. I guess Sandy's Feng Shui gal struck out on that deal; the boogieman was too deeply entrenched. We traded in seven Lincolns and two Chryslers, none over two years old. We walked away from the GM dealership owning five new Buicks. Yup, we thought we got a good deal, yeah right. We had the double-D logo of Donahue Downs painted stately on the car doors, creating an instant fleet of hotel courtesy vehicles and another asset to our growing company. When Sandy and I first came here, we never envisioned this fine independent hotel that we had created. We were hidden here in this out-of-business bed-and-breakfast inn/converted horse farm under assumed names. At that time people wanted us dead and that was not a good thing. We owed much to Bob Goodman, Lieutenant Dobson, Barney, Israel Burns, Mike, and his ex-boss Major Richardson, who I disliked and forever would. All of them acting in concert saved our lives and the lives of our family as well. As Barney loved to say, "It all worked out for the good." All of the bad guys from that time were either deceased or in the slammer now.

Only one of the bad guys slipped through the net and he wasn't even mob-connected. Herb Philbrick had become for us a mystery man with brains and guts. He was to us what D.B. Cooper was to the airline industry, a magic man who just disappeared with the goodies. At that time Philbrick had gone back to his job on Wall Street and stood tall at the trial as a witness for the federal prosecution. He never failed to show up court when needed and he seemed to be a fine upstanding citizen. Nobody realized that he was doing his own deal all along. Soon after the trial, Philbrick fell off the face of the earth with millions of dollars stolen from his company and their investors. He abandoned his wife and child who lived in Idaho then disappeared without a trace. We thought of him from time to time and Barney would often say, "Ya just never know what is going on in a person's mind."

Barney was right about not knowing what was going on in someone's mind and I would usually reply with my old standby adage taken from an ancient television show: "Eight million people in this town and eight million stories; this is just one of them." It might be true that Barney and I spent a lot of time remembering the things of old, but we also had a vibrant vision for the future as well. We agreed that we would not allow the craziness of the past to affect our future and that included the elusive Herb Philbrick. We saw what we did in the now of our lives as contributing good things to good people and assisting those who tried to walk the fence or were too weak to stand for what they believed. We coddled and urged, probed and pondered, were forceful when needed yet encouraged positive thinking with a smile and a laugh.

So far we had been lucky with our employees; we had never had a theft or incident of any kind. The guests arrived in anticipation and departed fulfilled, knowing that they received the service and care for which they paid. We were one of the few independently owned hotels with a five star rating by the Hotel Association of America. We were proud of that distinction and worked hard to protect it.

The other night we had a "men's night out." Mike, Barney, Steve, and I went to Doylestown to a boxing match. One of Mike's protégés, an "up-and-coming" boxer named Luis Ortega, was to be the second bout of the evening. He was a welterweight and according to Mike, a fine young man with some rage issues. Boxing was his vent, his answer to the crummy things that prevailed in his life and he was good at it. He had had some minor trouble with the law but so far with luck, nothing too serious. We met him during the first event of the evening and I looked into the eyes of a youth that seemed unstoppable. He had a well-built body, strong face, serious as a heart attack, yet filled with humor as well. I liked him right off. Mike laced up his gloves, clasped hands with him and told him, "Go get 'em, tiger." We went outside to cheer him on. Luis's opponent was a little bigger but a lot slower and by the third round the end was near. Just before the bell in the fourth round, Luis sent home a strong right uppercut and the fight was over. We cheered loudly and Luis raised his gloves in victory. We felt good for him; it was a well-fought, clean fight and Luis helped his luckless opponent off the floor and hugged him. It was good to see. We stuck around for a few more bouts, grabbed a couple of cold ones at a local inn, and headed back to the Downs. It was good to get out for some entertainment and it was good to share it with Mike, Barney, and Steve.

There were many more cars in the lot now, so I assumed that business was good. Sandy was in her office talking with our front desk manager. "What's all the hoopla outside?" I asked of whoever would choose to answer. Sandy told me that there was an affair scheduled at one of the American Legion Posts nearby, but far too many people had signed up. They exceeded the fire department rating for safety with relationship to the floor load capacity, as a matter of fact; their building was ancient and should have been demolished years ago. "The Post Commander called us just after you left to see if we could take the entire party and we said yes. Business isn't that great this time of year anyway and so, here they are, just a bunch of guys with their wives wanting to have a good time. I gave them a discounted rate and they came in as a convoy. They had arrangements with a local caterer and I allowed it to be diverted here instead. We will only pick up the slack if they run out of food, but the drinks will be tallied and paid for by the Post. It is only an overnight stay and the commander promised to try his best to keep the legionnaires in line as well he could."

I told her that it was a fine thing to do for the guys and since

I knew many of them, I would go out and mingle a bit. It had been a long time since Barney and I got tipsy together so he came with me to hobnob with the veterans. Our bar was filled to capacity and most of the booths and corner tables were taken as well. Walking into the bar area, I saw that these were my kind of people. Some came over to say hello and one guy wearing a moose hat said he always wanted to be Ralph Kramden so this was his time to be his fantasy. I told him, "Go for it and have a good time." I bought the entire place a round of drinks on the house and saluted them all with a nifty little speech of thanks for their service and all that stuff. I saw more than a few Marine Corps insignias and I knew that my kin were here as well. Marines shared an uncommon bond, kind of like a brotherhood association of unity written in honor and paid for with blood. The Marine Corps bond transcended all else, race, age, and time itself. You could see it in their eyes and most of them knew that I also was a Marine. Steve was beaming to see this and wondered if we couldn't have a November 10th celebration for the next Marine Corps birthday party. I told him that I would run it by Sandy and maybe contact the USMC auxiliary to see who ran that affair. I had been to a few of them and had a wonderful time reminiscing with old comrades in arms. As the evening wore on a few got a bit rowdy but nothing serious. The members took care of each other without us getting in their faces. Barney and I downed a few; Steve went home early to his family, but Mike hung in there with us for a while. He said that he wanted to make sure I would find my way home.

I slurred my words a bit but laughingly informed him, "I live here, remember?" Barney said pretty much the same thing in his forever joking, Irish brogue. Mike was fairly satisfied that we would not get into trouble so he finished his Guinness Stout and he also went home. Sandy dropped by and told me that she was going to bed and I could stay as long as I wanted. I was easing into this affair and felt pretty good. I kissed her goodnight and thanked her for her ability to let me be myself from time to time. Barney didn't want a kiss goodnight and he headed out to his room for some sleep. "G'night,

Barney." "G'night, Joe," as we did our forever poor imitation of Chet Huntley and David Brinkley.

Barney stopped half way through the lounge and was drawn into a conversation. I paid him no mind but was glad to see that he had developed his own set of friends. He was talking to a lady about his age and she was smiling with an unmistakable twinkle in her eye. I sat back at the bar and watched slyly through the mirror. Sure enough, they danced and my heart was overjoyed to see Barney finally shedding his macho cop image to join the human race. Barney was smiling too. I did not want to cramp his style so I left the bar with my drink in hand and went out to the reception area to see who was still around. It was almost midnight. I couldn't help thinking about that crazy time almost three years ago when all the mobsters were enjoying my hospitality. Gladly, after all the trials and testimonies, I had never seen any of them again. We never got any threatening phone calls or mail. I guess that the bad guy associates let it go and so did we. A lot happened after that major mob bust but it was none of my business. I just read the papers and hummed a gentle "Ho-hum."

I watched a tired late-night traveler check in at the desk, a single bespectacled guy in a well-worn trench coat and floppy little rain hat. I couldn't see his face but something about him reminded me of someone somewhere way back in my memory banks. Mr. Walter J. Lewis signed the guest book and was given a room. He was part of a convention that would start tomorrow morning.

I was pretty tipsy by then and so I just chalked it up as a silly Irish half-baked non-ability to conjure up ghosts. I chuckled and talked to the Post Commander, Richie Robben. He had a little jug of Mr. Jack with him and offered me a drink to toast our graciousness to host his affair on such short notice. Well now, no self-respecting man could refuse such a kind offer, and we clicked glasses and swore a never-ending friendship. What baloney, huh? I gobbled up that sip of remembrances and savored every drop. With each sip, other times came to mind. Other places, faces, and situations manifested themselves into my thoughts in milliseconds, but all of it worked out well in the final analysis.

"Another, Joe?" "Pour away, Sir Richard, the evening is still but young." His wife came by and snatched poor Rich away from me. He went willingly enough but put up a phony "poor little boy" face, complete with the pout. Rich, his wife, and I laughed. They went upstairs for the night; he left Mr. Jack with me for safekeeping. The new guest had taken off to wherever our clerk assigned him and I forgot all about him.

I took the almost empty bottle of Jack Daniels and went back to the bar to see who else was left around to play silly mind games with me. Barney and his new lady-friend were sitting in a candle-lit corner booth totally engrossed with each other. I did not interrupt, but in my mind I was clicking my heels and jumping up and down in joy for them.

Our bartender came over to me and asked, "Anything I can get you, Mr. Donahue?" I said, "Yes Johnny, bring over two empty glasses please." I emptied the jug of Jack, filling each glass about half way. I asked him to take a drink with me but he said that if he did, he would be fired from his job. I told him that this little secret would be safe with me and I would not tell his boss. He laughed and hoisted the glass with a clink to mine and said, "Here's to Donahue Downs, the finest family-run hotel on the East Coast, run by the finest people that I have ever had the pleasure of working for." Wow! I drank with him but told him that his little toast would not grant him the opportunity to have another drink at this time, nor would it get him a raise in pay. Johnny laughed and told me that he had been waiting a long time to tell me how he felt about us. I thanked him and I meant it.

This was a privately owned business and Sandy and I called the shots. I told Johnny to keep the bar open as long as there were customers, unless someone became so intoxicated that he had to be cut off. I told him not to break the law, just to use his discretion, and stay flexible: "These are good people John, so let them have their fling if they want to." "You got it Mr. D. I will let you know how it went tomorrow when I come back on shift." I thought this to be a fair arrangement and I went upstairs to bed.

CHAPTER TWO

Oh, How Easily We Get Bored

The man who once was Herb Philbrick had been living in the lap of luxury for more than three years now. He could not have wished for a better place to call home. He was free of the job that he hated back in New York but more than that, he was free of that woman who made his life a living hell. The first and most beneficial thing that he was able to do for himself was to get his company to transfer him to the home office in New York City and away from Idaho. The next good thing that he manipulated was the arrangement to leave his wife back home. He told her that he hated New York and didn't want her and their son to have to suffer in such a terrible place. The truth of course was that he loved it and cherished the freedom that living alone offered him. He willingly sent money back home and never missed or was late sending her a check. He wanted her quiet and content, because down deep he suspected that she didn't care one way or another if he were with her or not. She just wanted the money and that was OK with him for then.

He was correct in his summation: Mrs. Philbrick was happier

with the gardener. He was biding his time to spring his trap, and when the time came, he did not hesitate for a minute. His plan had to be put on hold while he was recovering from the heart attack and then even more so when he had to testify in court about some mob activities that he witnessed in the hotel where he was staying. The FBI had guarded him night and day so he was afraid to make a move while the trial was going on. It took six months but he could handle it and he did. He knew that the brass ring of freedom was just around the corner so he played Mr. Nice Guy, concerned citizen, and dutiful employee.

Making the financial arrangements at the bank in the Canary Islands was a snap and he only transferred his limited savings into the account. That was seed money to get him established. He then contracted with a real estate outfit via the Internet and put a down payment on a house there. All was done legally, if not a bit slower than a face-to-face arrangement, and trust was a big factor. He expected to get the shaft a bit and he did, but it didn't bother him. He knew that he would be there soon to make things right and all he actually needed was a real address under the phony name that he created. He was now Mr. Walter J. Lewis, a retired gentleman from Crystal Springs, New Mexico. A social security card from an unfortunate deceased person paved the way to his freedom, even if he had to spend a lot of money to acquire this new but clean identity. His fortune was well invested, as that was his forte in life. The principal generated more than he could spend in any given month.

Herb was home free. Herb made no phone calls stateside and his created identity was so perfect that he had new credit cards issued to him right there in the islands. Herb was in good health except for that one-time heart attack, but he never had been an Adonis. He tried to live quietly and was at peace with his neighbors. The first year or so, he lived on the edge, going to bars and buying women for entertainment. A few close calls with some of the local lowlifes corrected this little fling mindset and he focused himself on higher things and better people. Herb did not make friends quickly; trust did not come easily to him. Thus, for the first year he kept an extremely low profile; he busied himself setting up his house at 62 Avian Street, Sardinia, Gran Canaria Island, which was known as "The Little Continent." In this idyllic setting Herb, who was now Walter Lewis, acquired a working knowledge of the Spanish language; he started to blend in. He established relationships with the local merchants, visited the beautiful beaches often, and grew bored rapidly. He expanded his horizons and traveled often to the other islands in this paradise lost. When he met American tourists, Walter was a bit standoffish and always let them do most of the talking. He never divulged his past or his profession; fabrication was his new game in life and mystique was his persona. He would laugh with them, entertain them, point out places of interest, and sometimes score a one-night fling with a lonely secretary from somewhere in small-town USA. His finances were secure, his weekly income was better than he expected, and the food was plentiful. Even the house servants were inexpensive, yet trustworthy and efficient. Walter had fulfilled his dream of freedom in luxury and as he looked into the mirror, he would command himself to be happy.

Walter Lewis stood in line waiting for his turn to talk to the clerk at the passport office. He knew that he had all the facts of his fabricated life committed to memory. He filled out the forms, handed them over, had his picture taken, and as easily as he had expected, he was now a bona fide world traveler. He went on to apply at the Spanish consulate for citizenship in Spain. For a while he was a resident alien but eventually, after a sloppy and inexact background investigation, all was in order and his wish was granted. For all intents and purposes, Herb Philbrick was a memory that only he knew; he was now, and indeed IS Walter J. Lewis, a one-time American, now a citizen of Spain living in the Canary Islands. Perfect!

Philbrick had done an excellent job with the identity transfer and every contact with his future home in the Islands was initiated through the Lewis name. Just before he disappeared, he cashed in his insurance policies, maxed-out all of his credit cards (mostly as cash advances), and even had a yard sale to get rid of his furniture up there in Briarcliffe Manor. He removed and destroyed the hard drive from his laptop and tossed the computer into a lake. He burned all of his personal records, up to and including his banking files, social security card, and birth certificate. Herb did not leave any kind of trail for the investigators to follow. He took his time and did it right; he never missed dotting each I and crossing each T. A week prior to departure date, he sold his car and took the train to work. He knew that after the last day of employment he would take a cab to the airport and Philbrick would be no more. He converted every asset possible into ready cash and became nothing more than a bad dream to many. That was a Friday and he knew that come Monday morning, his ex-employer would be awash with complaints from their clients. They would try to sort out what he had done, but this would not be an easy task. Every investment portfolio that Mr. Philbrick was in charge of had been tapped and converted to negotiable bonds. They were converted to liquid assets, electronically transferred into Philbrick's personal account then withdrawn as cash to disappear forever. Apparently he was able to do this all in one day. That was as much information his employer could find out at that time. They called the FBI immediately.

The already overburdened New York City division of the FBI was handed this case and all available assets were assigned to investigate and apprehend the perpetrator, one Herbert Philbrick. The Bureau has seen this type of crime many times before and they had perfected precise criteria to follow. They took fingerprints from Briarcliffe Manor and matched them with employment records. They interviewed other employees at the firm, likewise his neighbors and business associates. They dispatched a team to Philbrick's home in Idaho, but his wife was devastated and ashamed of her husband. His picture was shown at all the airports, bus depots, and train stations. They even tried the taxi stands near the office where he worked. Nobody could recall this innocuous little man with the boring face. A working profile was created for Philbrick and matched to others who had committed like crimes, but he was so unremarkable that he became unique to them.

This was not Major Richardson's area of expertise so he never even heard of this investigation. If he had, he may have been able to connect Herb Philbrick to Donahue Downs and the now-closed mob investigation, but it never happened. Richardson would find Philbrick's name a year later and only then, by happenstance. Some of the investigators would chide one another by saying that Philbrick was the mouse that roared. They were right. His file was stamped "Ongoing," neatly packaged, then shoved into the cold-case files. The thought was that soon there would be a rookie arriving at the office and the Philbrick file would be dumped into his lap to waste his time and get him some experience as a white-collar-crime investigator. It never happened and Walter J. Lewis, also known as Herb Philbrick, was home free.

At Beaufort, Scotch and Byrnes Investments, where Philbrick worked his dastardly, albeit felonious, investor schemes, they thanked God for Lloyds of London. The clients were compensated and given some perks to keep them with the firm. Most of the other employees were given lie detector and alcohol/drug tests. In the grand scope of things, Philbrick was only a blip on the insurance ratings nationwide and was soon chalked up as a bad dream and forgotten.

Nobody was looking for Herb Philbrick. Nobody had ever heard of Walter J. Lewis of Crystal Springs, New Mexico. The good people on Avian Street of Sardinia, Gran Canaria were happy with their gringo neighbor. And life went on in Happyville for our bland-faced, non-gregarious felon with an exciting history.

Walter needed an outlet for his creative devious and over-worked imagination. He took a meaningless job on the islands. He became, of all things, a bartender at one of the hotels. He thought, and rightly so, that this position would allow him to overcome his inability to communicate with others. Slowly with the passage of time, he was able to interact with both the locals and tourists as well. When speaking to an American tourist, he used perfect English but sprinkled with a Spanish accent. He did this to succinctly put forth the idea that

English for him was a second language; the ruse worked every time. Walt was fast becoming a master of illusion but it was just fun to him. He considered all people groups and governmental establishments to be stupid, slow moving, and inept. Walter had to keep himself in check many times; he knew that a bad move on his part would bring his little house of cards tumbling down around his ears. He never really let on how much he knew about any given topic. He often purposely made errors just to see if whomever he were talking to would catch the error and try to correct him. Walt loved the game. He became a valued employee and his daily receipts were always correct. Walter J. Lewis was in a way, recreating his old life working a steady job and he knew it.

He was not one to sit on the beach looking at the girls while sipping rum either. Cultural entertainment was all of the Spanish flair and Walt was not all that interested. If he wanted the latest movie, he had to order it from the Internet, which he did often. The theatre was almost nonexistent on the islands, so that part of his life had to be put on hold unless he wanted to travel to Madrid two hours by air. He did that sometimes, but not often enough to suit him. He was starting to miss the hustle and bustle of the fast life and Madrid was fast becoming a magnet for him; he was making friends and contacts there as well.

He was about ready to quit his bartending job at the hotel, thinking that it was fun while it lasted, but it was getting to be a bit too confining. It had become routine, matter-of-fact, organized, and demanding; Walt was bored. Mr. Alejandro Pignataro, his boss at the hotel, recognized the symptoms and asked Walter into the office for a chat. He told him that he was a much-valued employee and wanted to make greater use of his multi language skills. "Piggy," as the other employees called him, offered Walter a better position inside the hotel. The job offered daytime hours at better pay and a private office. He offered him the position of concierge, a newly created position for this hotel. Expansion and increased tourism demanded a higher level of ambiance and professionalism. The ability for management to relate to the guests more easily and in their own language had become a necessity. Mr. Pignataro told Walter that he would be perfect for the job with his skills in English and Spanish. He said that he had been watching him at the bar and his manners were impeccable, he had developed a winning smile laced with good humor, and his physical appearance was neat and clean. He would fit the position perfectly. Walt wasn't so sure if he even wanted to keep this job or any job for that matter. He only signed on because he was bored at the time. He never intended it to be anything more than a lark, a way for him to test his talents and perfect his skills as a Spanish-speaking islander with a working knowledge of English. He admitted to Mr. Pignataro that when he first started the bartender job he had loved it, but now with the passage of time, he was getting bored.

Alejandro said that he wanted to send Walt to Pennsylvania in the U.S. to an international meeting of hotel management personnel. Immediate flags went up for Walter but he listened on with feigned interest: "It would be a four-day learning experience, all expense-paid mini-vacation for you, Walt, and I think you are the best man here for the job. They will have a series of half-day, in-depth symposiums on many hotel-related subjects including the role of the concierge, more efficient computer programs used for reservations and the speedy check-in/check-out for guests. Security, housekeeping, and employee ergonomics would also be addressed. Walt, do you know anything about computer programming?" Alejandro posed this sincere, yet quizzical, question to Walt, hoping for the best.

Walt did indeed know more about computer programming than most people here on this island and he responded, "Yes Mr. Pignataro, I have a pretty good working knowledge of computer operating systems and could probably pick up a new program fairly easily."

Piggy was overjoyed and asked Walt to call him Alejandro. He told Walt that the system they now used was hopelessly outdated, poorly maintained, very slow, and crashed often. This too was an issue that had to be addressed if he wanted his hotel to enter the twenty-first century of proper and efficient hotel management. He had wanted to replace the entire system here but had no idea what he needed. Walt did not want to show Alejandro just how much he did know about computers but he knew that the computer problems at the hotel were child's play to him. Walt did not talk technical terms; he spoke only on a generic level, but Alejandro was impressed all the way. Walt promised his associate-wannabe Alejandro that he would sincerely consider this offer and get back to him as soon as he made his decision.

"Let me know as soon as you can, Walt, as I need to contact the hotel in Pennsylvania and reserve your spot. We have only two weeks to enroll, so time is of the essence." Walt nodded and started to make a respectful exit but Alejandro told him to take the rest of the night off: "Go home. Walt, relax and think on this; we really need you here." "Thanks Alejandro, I will do that and once again, thank you for this kind offer." Walt did go home; he had a lot to think about.

Walt considered the shipment that he had buried. His mind was playing dangerous games with him. He was contemplating teasing the FBI. He knew he could pull off the ruse of the century and get away with it. For Walt, it was all in fun; his life was fast falling to boredom. He no longer cared about quiet security; he missed the drama of living a covert, dangerous, yet fun-filled scam. Herb was like a chameleon and loved being an unremarkable-looking person who blended in and was never noticed. He concocted a plan that would not harm people in a physical way, but would line his pockets with more riches. Riches that he did not need or necessarily care to have, but it was just a game to be played for the fun of it. Herb also wanted to help his best friend, a guy that he had grown up with in Boise. He called Piggy and told him that he would take the job. He also made definite provisions in his mind to protect and reward his long-time friend, John Shaft.

Looking back on the first four months of his life here in the Canary Islands brought great joy to him. He remembered the excitement of the heist and the fear he had caused in other people as he unfolded his plan. Those that he ripped off in that scam did not know that if they bluffed him out, he did not have, nor did he want to have, the wherewithal to do the terrible things he had threatened to do. The story went like this:

Commercial Charter Flight # 107 out of Kennedy International was headed to Morocco with a cargo of brand new U.S. currency. The highest denomination in the shipment was the hundred-dollar bill. The plane was a retrofitted military GU-11 complete with a rear-loading cargo bay. Reclassified as a civilian commercial airplane, it now had the acronym B-1-RD; it was a powerful, responsive, and versatile aircraft. The precious cargo was strapped to the floor and as Morocco was the first of three destinations, the pallet of money was the last of the cargo to be loaded into the bay. The money would be the first of the cargo to be off-loaded; thus it was the first item facing the cargo bay ramp. Everything was properly documented and perfectly legal.

This money was the physical financial balance used to stabilize international banking institutions. The originator and owner of this shipment was a regular client of the transport company, known as the Global Asset Management Corporation of the United States, located in New York City. Their business was the transfer of cash from one country to another, a dangerous but exacting business, heavily regulated, inspected, and documented. Security was, needless to say, very tight. American dollars would be shipped to many different nations and that nation's currency would be sent back to the United States in the proper rate according to value. It was a neat and clean business; extremely rewarding to Global Asset Management Co. and they had been doing it for many years without a problem. This company and others like them were a needed service to the U.S. Treasury and to the world banking organizations. For without them, the governments of each nation would have new responsibilities. Internal strife, wars, and destabilization made it difficult for various nations to agree on anything; thus a sort of middle-man service industry was created and required. Global Asset Management Co. answered this poser and even the exacting Swiss banks were happy with them. All the bills were new, in numerical sequence, strongly packaged, and palletized. Armed personnel from the carrier guarded this valuable and highly sought-after shipment; it was door-to-door service. These security men were all ex-military or law enforcement people who took their jobs seriously. Each man was well paid, well armed, and extremely professional. Walt knew though that the human condition would dictate to them that no job and no amount of somebody else's money were worth dying for.

The pilot of the aircraft was Walt's co-conspirator John Shaft, a man that he has known all of his life. They had grown up together, and way back in their crazy teenage years in Boise, they were the best of friends. They confided in each other, they had many an adventure together, and they shared their fantasies, which were all "visions of grandeur." John joined the Air Force and became a pilot. Walt was a 4-F deferment and entered the stocks and bonds industry. They kept in contact often and saw each other from time to time when John came home on furlough.

After leaving the military, John bounced around flying for a few different airlines, finally settling on the commercial carriers. He has been with his company for ten years and had become a valued and trusted employee. Global Asset Management Co. may well have been just another shipper for the company, but it was one that was highly valued. The carrier assigned only their best flight personnel and most trusted security people to protect these money transfers.

Walt stayed in Idaho, married, and hated his life. He didn't even care for his own son very much. The plan had been two years in the making and finally they pulled it off without a hitch. John lived a higher lifestyle than his salary could support. Walt, who was Herb Philbrick at the time, had his own reasons to depart the life in which he was stuck. They got together in Boise one night and hatched this scheme which would grant them their fondest wish, freedom with no financial worries.

As the plane followed the normal flight path to Morocco International Airport, all was normal and the crew under John's authority was relaxed. There were no passengers on this plane other than company personnel. There was, however, an alien device happily ticking away under the sink of the small lavatory. It appeared to be a bomb. Displaying a digital LED countdown clock and a little blinking red indicator light, it looked authentic as hell. In truth however, all that was in the box was a Global Positioning System (GPS) transmitter and some inert material that was totally harmless.

Walt was tracking the plane from lift-off; he bided his time waiting for the exact moment. Everything was in place. Months ago Walt had bought a one-man submersible submarine from a black market contact. Totally under cover, Walt learned all there was to know about his little ship and he piloted it to the most northern island in the group. Lanzarote was his first destination and then on to the smallest of the island group, to the deserted and wild beach of Punta Delgada. There he constructed a safe deposit location underneath four feet of easily dug sand. He lined this hole with heavy plastic and camouflaged it with some broken ferns small trees and stones collected from the terrain. He had transported a small International Harvester Cub Cadet lawn tractor to the site and it too was well hidden.

The moment had arrived and Walt turned on the shortwave radio already preset to the proper airway frequency: "Attention pilot of Flight 107 from Kennedy. Turn on the speaker system to the entire plane as every person on that ship must hear what I have to say. You have five seconds to comply." He counted down and he knew that John had done as he commanded. He also knew that John had to open up the transmission lines so that the tower in Morocco heard what he had to say. Also, via skip-jump transmission format, New York at Kennedy was able to hear as well. "5-4-3-2-1," he said, and then Walt told his new and vast audience, "There is a bomb located beneath the sink in the lavatory and it will explode by remote control from my location. You have five seconds to check it out but I warn you not to touch it because if you move it from its pedestal, it will explode immediately. 5-4-3-2-1.

"Listen carefully and do not make any mistakes. Start to

decrease your altitude and come to five hundred feet. In exactly two minutes you will drop your cargo of U.S. cash out of the bay door and into the sea. Open the ramp now; I have a visual on your aircraft." That was the truth; Walt was leisurely riding on smooth seas and watching with powerful binoculars. The men in the ship scampered all over, John called New York for instructions, and Morocco scrambled a military jet to the location but they were at least an hour away. New York said, "Do as instructed." Walt watched as the ramp slowly opened from the bottom of the plane. The sea was so calm that he was able to keep his little boat ninety-percent submerged; he knew that he was not visible from the air. He jokingly told himself that the mother bird was gonna drop her nest eggs right into his lap. The plan went off without a hitch; the plane dropped the pallet and it splashed down about a quarter-mile to his starboard side. The ocean floor was only between forty and sixty feet in this area and the little boat was certified safe for two hundred feet of depth.

Walt had a bit of difficulty locating his prize but with a little luck, he soon found it and had a grappling hook snagged to the bottom of the pallet. Towing the load was not so easy but he made shore in forty-five minutes. As he broke the surface he looked around searching for any kind of air traffic. None was visible to him so Walt beached the boat, walked to his hideout location and returned with the little lawn tractor. He thought to himself, "This is indeed, a beautiful day." He placed a plastic skid on the shore and dragged the pallet to it. He then dragged the money on the skid and right into the hole. He removed five hundred dollars just for kicks, telling himself that he had worked for a day's pay. He promptly buried his loot. He then drove the tractor back to the boat, hooked up the towline, and went back underwater dragging the tractor with him. He knew where some submerged rock formations were and he dropped the tractor into them and broke the surface once again. Walt flooded and sank his boat then swam to shore to finish off his camouflage. He raked the sand to hide the tractor tire marks and he was satisfied that he had left no trace of his presence. A rather tiresome hike to town and all was well. John and he agreed that the money would stay hidden until John was able to cut loose from his job and without suspicion, move to the Canary Islands. From then on out what they did with the money was their own business. Mission accomplished; they had done it!

That was then and this was now and Walt was bored. It has been over eighteen months since that heist and Walt checked his cache only once during that time. All was safe, the investigation never turned up any clue as to how the robbery was completed, and John was cleared of any wrongdoing. Walt never touched the money; he didn't have to. He buried the five hundred dollars he took merely as a lark. He also knew that John was "retiring" from his job six months from now and he could not wait to see his old friend again. He figured that he would kill time living the sham of a hotel employee and deeply involved in Alejandro's hotel in paradise.

To Alejandro, Walt was a committed and valuable person; he had come to like him even if sometimes he seemed a bit distracted. "Big world," Alejandro would say, "lots of different kinds of people in it." Finally the day came for Mr. Pignataro and Walt to discuss the trip to the United States. Walt had already promised to complete this learning experience for Alejandro so he updated his passport. Alejandro greeted him the next morning with a smile: "Good morning Walt, let's go into my office and review the travel arrangements and conference agenda." Alejandro handed him his flight itinerary; he was to fly to Madrid where he would board a direct flight to Philadelphia International Airport. There a private car would take him to a hotel known as Donahue Downs in a little town called Solebury.

Walt had an immediate case of diarrhea. His mind went into warp-drive; he ran the scenario rapidly, could he pull this off? Could he so disguise himself as to be totally unrecognizable to the staff of Donahue Downs? It was almost three years since he was there and he had grown a beard. He was heavier now and a pair of eyeglasses might help as well. He thought of all of this in a split-second and never once changed his facial expression in front of Alejandro. He nodded in agreement that he would be overjoyed to learn more about the hotel business.

All said and done, Walt took the next two days off from work and prepared for his trip to his private adventure-land. He dug up his hidden five hundred dollars and smiled. The game was on!

CHAPTER THREE

Let the Games Begin

Monday morning at the Downs brought in a new, previously scheduled convention of hotel employees from all over the world. It was a teaching conference of new computer programs and different techniques for various positions of executive level employees in the hotel business. We asked Mike to attend the conference as well to pick up some new ideas as we had been playing this business pretty much by ear so far. The inn was packed but we did have a few open rooms to let. Sandy was in her glory as she looked out upon hotel management professionals; even the large chains were represented. We had a nice looking marquee standing on an easel center place in the main reception room that read International Association of Hotel Management 2004 Information Technology Conference. The four-day agenda was neatly printed below it and brochures were stacked in a holder for the taking. Needless to say, Donahue Downs was decked out with the best of everything. We were proud to host the conference as it gave our inn a stamp of approval as an established five-star, independently owned hotel.

Sandy and I were honored to meet many well-known leaders in the industry. Surprisingly to me, they were not the stuffed shirts that I always imagined them to be. They were like us, just plain folks making their way in life doing what they loved to do. I couldn't help but think that I had come a long way from that flophouse that I lived in back in the Bronx with Lucy, the alcoholic dog. I gave Sandy a lot of credit; she had cleaned me up pretty good. Even Lucy got regular grooming and now looked like a normal family pet. We had asked Mike to find out about computers linking us with other independent hotels and getting into their reference guides. Mike was happy about this new challenge as it coincided with his technical skills. Sandy and I wanted to know all there was to know about the hotel industry. We were pretty successful for now but we were more interested in creating a legacy for our children and those that came after them.

Although we offered our employees a fair benefit plan, as members of a network of other hotels, we would be able to do even more for them. Mike would look into that as well. "Sure Mike, you always wanted to be a double dipper," I said, and he jokingly scowled and told me that the FBI retirement package was not all that it was cracked up to be. The first event of the convention was a scheduled "after breakfast" networking social gathering in our lounge called the Winner's Circle. We had our waiters walking around the group, serving champagne. Others had trays of canapés, hors d'oeuvres and some weird-looking fish things. Sandy told me that it was sushi, I said, "Yeah, OK Sandy, whatever you say, sue-she." Sandy lovingly punched me in the ribs and I told her, "I love it when you hit me." Sandy had work to do in the office, so she left me there in the reception room. Barney had the day off to take his latest squeeze out for -- whatever they were gonna do, I don't pry remember? Mike was off hobnobbing with the hotel executive elite and I had nothing to do. I crept upstairs to catch up on some reading.

Mr. Walter J. Lewis of the Royal Gran Canaria Hotel was doing very well at this affair. He found a few Spanish-speaking guests so he was able to minimize his English language usage. He was well tanned and looked like an authentic Spaniard. Sporting a well-trimmed goatee, eyeglasses, and a sharp-looking suit, he knew that he would never be recognized as Herb Philbrick. He noticed Mike McCormick at the Faculty Development seminar. He was sporting a Donahue Downs blazer but he remembered him as a federal agent. His presence concerned Walt at first but then it became more of a challenge and thus, more of a thrill for him. Walt had a gift for rapid deductive reasoning and figured that McCormick retired from the feds and signed on here in the same role that was a ruse during the sting operation. Now he really was the manager of Donahue Downs. With his mind forever gleaning over snippets of data from three years ago, all fell into place and he knew that he was right. Walt had remembered overhearing the conversation between Agent McCormick and Major Richardson relating to his retirement that was only six months away. He remembered that McCormick said that he liked this part of the country and he seemed to be perfect in his disguise as hotel manager.

He snapped his fingers and said to himself: "Yes, this all fits what I see in the here and now. Agent Mike McCormick is now a private citizen and real-time manager of this hotel." Walt knew that this gift for clear, concise thinking was why he was on top of his game, and soon he would be able to broadcast just how smart he was. He was formulating a "tease-trap" for no other reason than to show the authorities just how inept they really were. He would sit in his room after dinner at night and extrapolate his plan down to its finite detail. Almost in a fugue state with his television on, he would stare into nothing and make facial expressions as he went over each step of his devious, yet admittedly dangerous, plan. His villa in Madrid was paid for and debt free. John was due in the Canary Islands next month. He had the time, he had the money, he had the plan, he had the humor, and he had the nerve to pull this off just one more time for the sake of the "legacy of Herb Philbrick." He knew they would eventually find out what happened but he knew that once again, he would be untraceable and long gone. Mr. Pignataro would never see Walter J.

Lewis again. John Shaft would not even be suspected of anything so he too would be alright.

Walt took a shower and prepared to attend the Faculty Development seminar scheduled right after lunch. It was the second day of his plan. He sat next to the vice president of a competing hotel from Sardinia but he didn't know him. They shook hands and spoke in Spanish; Mike McCormick was directly in front of them. The speaker opened the seminar and everyone was excited to listen, learn, and take notes. Most of the attendees assured themselves that they would pick up the recorded tape of this seminar for future use. Everyone that was, except Walt; he looked interested but his mind was a million miles away. He couldn't wait for this boring talk to be over but he took notes as well. He put up a good front and played his role perfectly. After what seemed like an eternity to Walt, the speaker opened the floor for questions. The seminar was winding down and he knew that he could disappear from the hotel for a few hours: He had work to do.

Using a pay phone at the hotel, Walt called a taxi for a ride into the village of New Hope. Decked out in his phony suit that hid the real man, he walked the streets of this quaint village but he did not blend well with the hundreds of tourists that walked the streets with him. He went into one of the tourist trap men's stores and bought a complete set of jaunty tourist type clothes. He admired himself in the mirror: Bermuda shorts, slip-on sneakers, no socks, and a Jets football tee shirt. "Cool," he said. He bought a dumb-looking hat and sunglasses to round off his costume. The store boxed up his business outfit and Walt rejoined the crowd outside. He paid cash for his purchases and spent eighty-five dollars. Walt used one of the serialized hundred dollar bills that he had saved from the airline heist. His plan was now in motion; Walt chuckled.

Taking another cab, he went to Doylestown, a much larger town not far away. He treated himself to a fine meal in one of the upscale restaurants where he dropped another of the hot hundred dollar bills. He reckoned that tomorrow he would spend two more of these telltale clues around the area but would save the last bill for his coup d'etat. He wanted to spend the last bill at Donahue Downs and hopefully he would get Mike McCormick himself to receive the bill with some fanfare. He wanted Mike to remember him after the fact and he wanted the Philbrick connection understood just for the fun of it. Herb thought about something he had read in Shakespeare: There is the rub; Walt smiled.

Walt took another cab back to Donahue Downs and had the driver park by the rear entrance nearest his room. Using his electronic key, the door swung open like "Open, sesame" of Ali Baba and the Forty Thieves fame. This was the same doorway where he had witnessed the murder of Mr. and Mrs. Tony Lorenzo three years ago. It wasn't the first time or the last that he would see Jimmy and Carmine Falcone, the murderers. Both of them were sitting on death row in Attica State Prison in upstate New York. He couldn't care less; that whole debacle was for him a terrible waste of time. It set his master plan back almost an entire year but there was little else he could do. The night was calm, a nice breeze, about seventy-two degrees and the sky was without a cloud; it was 8 p.m., time for bed.

The hall was empty; no noise anywhere, so he entered his room to look over the papers for the convention. He saw that tomorrow morning there was a talk on computer systems and programs, right up his alley, and time to spend some of the "Mr. Piggy" money. Tomorrow, after all the business hoopla was over, he had planned another trip. This time, he would go down to Philadelphia and spend another two of the hot hundred-dollar bills. He also would contact Johnny Shaft in Idaho, per their plan. Walt felt good, really good — his plan was going flawlessly. All was quiet at Donahue Downs. Only two guests were at the Winner's Circle Bar on this Tuesday night and they too would soon be off to bed as well. Barney was one of them and his gal-pal was the other.

Captain John Shaft caught the red-eye special from Newark International, a direct flight to Boise. He would be home soon and he was tired after another international run to London, Dublin, and

Berlin. For John, the hardest part of this job was the never-ending waiting. He was not responsible for the manifest of cargo or the loading/unloading process. He did not accompany the deliveries from the airport through customs, and from there, to the final destinations. He sat in airline terminals and hotels all over the world waiting and waiting. Most times (like this time) he would have to sleep over. More than once, he had violated company rules by drinking just a little too much, but he always got away with it. He was never late, never looked disheveled and always went through the pre-flight checklists with the maintenance people at the airports. John had no negative reports in his personnel jacket with the company and he was up for a pay increase. The robbery off the coast of Morocco was seen as totally unavoidable. The heist was considered well orchestrated and not attributable to anything that John had done. They never found out how the phony bomb got onto the aircraft and they never found out how the loot was picked up by whoever did the deed. The money never turned up and the major banking institutions of the world were notified of the serial numbers. The insurance company hired countless teams of people to scour beaches all over the area but not one clue turned up.

He and Herb had gotten away with their caper and soon he would be free to do as he pleased with the rest of his life. He would file his papers soon. He was going to quit this job and in thirty days, he would move away from Idaho and the U.S. forever. He was so squeaky-clean that he did not even need false papers. He could remain as Mr. John Shaft, formerly of Boise, Idaho, and now a citizen of Spain, just like Walt. The two of them would be just two more rich Americans living abroad. Walt would call him tomorrow night and he couldn't wait to see how they were progressing with the master plan of life for them.

On a bright and sunny Tuesday morning at the Downs, the dew rose as mist, creating puffy little sections of fog on the ground. The flowers along the walks dripped with moisture and one could almost sense the vibrant life forces at work in this healthy area that Joe and Sandy had created. Lucy needed to go outside and Joe decided to take her for a walk around the estate. She was itching and hopping to make an exit to relieve the call of nature, so she hurried Joe along as he got dressed. Casually clad for the morning, Joe opened the door and Lucy ran like hell over to the back fence near the maintenance shed at the rear of the property, her favorite "dumping ground." Joe and Sandy finally trusted their dog not to violate the rules so Lucy never disturbed the manicured lawn areas. Joe chuckled as he thought; no poopie-bags needed here. He leisurely walked to where she was and sat on a rock to light up the first Lucky of the day. Sandy had been trying to get him to quit but she was having a hard time of it herself. They decided to check out some of the programs that were around to quit smoking but something always got in their way and it was put off for "just another day."

Lucy was stock-still; she had assumed her "I'm the great hunting dog" stance and Joe looked up and into the face of God's pure and wonderful creatures. A fawn was standing not ten feet away, looking at them in a big-eyed and quizzical way. Joe said to the deer, "Good morning kid. Where's Mom?" Sure enough, gently through the foliage came the doe with another fawn walking behind her. They knew that there was nothing to fear here; Lucy sat down and did not move. Joe rose and took the apples out of his pocket, keeping eye contact with the doe. Joe moved slowly closer and closer. He extended his hand with an apple and yes! She finally allowed him to feed her directly. Most times she would back away or bolt back into the woods but Joe has been working on building up trust with her. The doe took an apple and turned to one of the fawns and put the apple on the ground for the little one to take.

Joe had three apples and he felt almost Godlike, caring for these creatures of the forest. All three apples dispensed with peace, love, and trust to propagate the species, Joe turned, Lucy rose, and the two of them left the deer to feed. He whistled. It was 6 a.m. and the guests would soon be up, so he headed to the kitchen for his "morning repast," as he liked to say. Sandy was already there so they sat at one of the small tables for breakfast. Lucy of course was begging for food and wouldn't let the cooks alone. The cooks smiled and said, "It is a violation to let dogs in the kitchen, Joe." They all knew it and so Lucy was scooted out of there and into her little fenced-off compound. She was fed royally and did not miss the alleyway diner back in the Bronx.

Today would be a good day for the Donahues; Israel Burns and Jim Dobson were coming down with their wives for a six-day vacation. Joe and Sandy had planned a sightseeing trip to Philly as a group using the hotel limousines. It would be Barney and Ellen (his newfound girlfriend), Jim and Israel with their wives Betty and Phyllis plus Joe and Sandy. The eight of them were in the same age group and mostly the same cultural background, except Joe and Barney who were still learning. "That's for tomorrow, Sandy, so let's just reacquaint ourselves with our friends today."

Sandy nodded and said, "It will be a fun-filled few days and long overdue. Hopefully," she said, "I can get Steve, Sue, and the kids over for a grand dinner all together once again, with Mike and Helen too." She planned to call them and set it up for Friday evening. After breakfast the Donahues of Solebury went up to inspect the rooms set aside for their friends. Two luxury rooms right next to each other, both made fresh with flowers and little candies on the pillow. Joe remembered that the room for Israel was the same room that Vito Scaglionne had had, but it had long since been fumigated. Sandy muttered that it should have been exorcised.

"Where does the time go, Sandy? It is almost nine-thirty and they are supposed to arrive around eleven, we gotta get hopping." They were setting up a private luncheon out on the veranda, set for six. Everything was arranged down to the finest detail. After check-in and their luggage was put away, Mike would escort them to the veranda where champagne was set up along with some gifts for all four guests. Joe was dressed in his new Armani jacket and Sandy looked resplendent in her Ann Klein dress. The computer program seminar was already in progress so most of the other guests were gone for a while, attending the conference in the ballroom across the way. The lobby was relatively empty.

Right on schedule, the Burnses and Dobsons parked in one of the guest parking spots. They came down in one car: a brand new, sporty-looking black Buick Lacrosse. We had the staff make such a fuss over them; they were not allowed to touch their luggage. With appropriate class and attention to detail, our guys and gals handled everything for them. Checking in at the desk, they were told that no paperwork was needed and all was ready for them. Our desk clerk handed each of them a set of electronic keys and they were directed to the rooms. Mike was right there to walk with them and to make a formal greeting. We waited on the veranda in great anticipation. After dropping their stuff in the rooms, the four of them joined us outside. It really was a warm and fuzzy greeting with smiles and hugs all around.

Mike stood at the head of the table, playing maitre d'. He lifted the glass of champagne and toasted our guests with a royal flair that even I did not know he possessed. Israel Burns, who was half-Jewish and half-Irish-Catholic, responded to the toast with, "Spoken by a true Irishman with the gift of blarney." We all applauded and shared a good belly laugh.

Shortly, Barney came by, looking spiffier than I had ever seen him. I thought that it was just like Barney to schnor another free meal, but we were all glad to see him. "Where's Goodman?" he wanted to know. Looking into his eyes with a smile on my face, I told him that Bob wasn't able to get the time off, "because you, Barney, had left a manpower shortage up there in the Bronx when you called it quits, and crime takes no holidays." He jokingly said that maybe he should go back to lend a hand but on second thought, he was finding the Pennsylvania lassies quite appealing: "I ain't goin'," he said with a laugh. Sandy and I told him that we wouldn't have it any other way and we were glad that he was our maintenance manager. Barney responded back about the perks being pretty good: he had free lodgings, food, and a pretty good salary for an old broken-down cop. Everyone smiled. Sandy had gifts for the ladies, really nice gold bracelets with the double D logo of our inn engraved on the backside with the date of our get-together. The guys got box-seat tickets at Yankee Stadium for a game next month. Barney got a handshake. We ate in grand style out there on the veranda and afterwards we enjoyed some coffee and some "bring em up to date" chitchat.

Israel, Mike, Barney, Jim, and I took a walk around the grounds to let it all hang out a bit. I offered cigars all around and we spoke of the Falcone brothers, Vito Scaglionne, and Fat Tony Lorenzo. "Shame they had to snuff the guy's wife at the same time," said Jim. "Mrs. Lorenzo was just a dippy broad hanging on to the easy money; she didn't do anything and she didn't know anything." A few adages were tossed around, things like, "When you lay with dogs, you get fleas." Jim came back with, "Yeah, well it's a damn shame anyway, ya know? The Falcones should roast in hell for that." It was one of those few times in my life when total clarity busted into my brain and all the parts fit. I looked at my friends and told them about Barney's Bible quote, the one that says all things work together for the good. Both of these guys had heard it before and just looked at me for a further explanation. We went down the list of characters in that now three-year old scenario:

"Tommy McGuinnes was a bad cop who got whacked in prison. Sean, Tommy's nephew, was dead at the ripe old age of twenty-six. Mario Lorenzo, another young man with his whole life ahead of him, was now dead because he was living up to his father's image as a gangster. The motorcycle cop in the Bronx, one of McGuinnes' hit men, also was shot dead in a crummy bar with a dirty floor. Bill Grandly, Sandy's ex-husband and Lorenzo's ex-cop hired gun, also turned up dead when his private history caught up with him. Mrs. Lorenzo was in the thick of it; she was not an innocent party. She allowed her husband to ruin her son's chances for a decent life. Maybe it was unfair that she got whacked, but I am not the judge of that. Vito Scaglionne is out on bail but under house arrest. He is fighting a twenty-year sentence in a federal pen, and when he gets out, the Italian government has other charges against him. Jack Sullivan lost his attorney's license and is involved in the legal battle of his life to stay out of the slammer. His assets frozen, his vacation from 'the life' is now on hold. The Falcones killed the Lorenzos and only with luck or the grace of God, we had an eyewitness testify at their trial. Both of them are doing all kinds of legal maneuvers to avoid lethal injection. Penelope Gravis is still in the slammer but should be getting out soon with a shortened sentence due to turning state's evidence and good behavior. Phil Fauxmaster was the beginning of this whole deal. Because of him, Sandy and I saved the two kids who are now my grandchildren. His case brought all of the others into play. He is in jail now and will be there until he is almost seventy years old. I say good riddance to him and to all the others as well. The world is a safer place today without them.

"The only bad guy that was never caught really didn't have much to do with what the rest of them were involved in. Herb Philbrick had slipped through the net but then again; at least he wasn't a violent person. His time will come," I said. I then reminded them, "The Bible scripture says all things, not some. The good in all this is that the kids are safe with my daughter-in-law and Steve; they will be OK. Not one of the good guys suffered any real damage, although Barney did get shot full of holes. McGuinnes did that, and he was a 'brother-cop' at the time. Barney emerged from that hospital a changed man, a man with direction toward higher things in life. I say that God used this whole criminal happening to slap the bad guys and reward, or call, His children. They tried to kill me a few times, shot up my house, and injured my dog; then they shot me, but all in all, look around you fellas. I can't call it merely luck that I have evolved from that slum that I was living in back in the Bronx. I really see that the real beginning of this whole deal was when Sandy and I finally got together. There is no way that I could have engineered this plan. This whole thing, with you guys involved as well, is the classic war of good against evil and we won, guys. Correction, in this drama

in our small corner of the world, HE won if you get my drift." Israel
Burns said, "Amen, Joe." Jim said that he now knew that in a crazy
kind of way, we were all connected in a spiritual bond that we may
never understand.

We walked past the convention center. "Big meeting goin' on
in there, huh Joe?" "Yeah Jim, a convention of hotel executives and
Mike is supposed to be there, right Mike?" Mike said, "Not this particular talk, Joe. That talk is computer systems-related and we have a
state-of-the-art system now. I did however, talk to the guy giving the
talk yesterday and he was impressed with what we have, so I skipped
this little get-together. I'm glad I did because your round-up of the bad
guys and good guys puts my little Irish heart to rest about the grand
scope of things."

Walt watched as they walked past the large window to his
right and he had another case of instant diarrhea.

Mike then asked, "What ever happened to that Philbrick guy,
anyone know?" Israel Burns told us that he apparently fell of the face
of the earth and after over two years of investigation, there was still
no trace of him or the money that he stole from his job at Beaufort,
Scotch and Byrnes. The investors were protected but this little creepy
guy had pulled off his caper flawlessly. Burns said that he was probably living in the lap of luxury somewhere in the sun, pinching
bunny-butts and drinking mint juleps: "Ya gotta hand it to him
though, he's got some stones." Jim told us that Major Richardson had
been transferred to white collar crime and was in the process of looking at long-term relocated U.S. citizens. It was only a shot-in-the-dark
investigation, but it kept him busy. So far, according to their last talk
about Philbrick, there had been no good hits to investigate.

As this was said, they were only fifteen feet away from the
infamous Mr. Philbrick. Walt was sitting there seemingly engrossed in
the computer talk and taking notes like a maniac. He was telling himself to remain calm; there was no way that any of those guys would
recognize him. He already had sat right next to McCormick, who
made nothing of the meeting other than he was just another guy at

the convention. "Focus on the plan, all will be well," he told himself but he had to pinch his sphincter muscles to retain control. The posse walked down the path and away from the window to join their wives back on the veranda just as the speaker asked for questions. A short while later, Walt approached the table set up at the rear of the room and initiated a seven hundred thousand-dollar order for Mr. Pignataro. He used a company credit card to place a substantial down payment. He chuckled to himself, wondering if Piggy could handle this new debt load. The system would be an in-house server network with access to each room. A dish antenna would be set up on the roof to access the World Wide Web. With all kinds of firewalls, anti-virus programs, Internet server-based Spam scams, pop-up controls and surge-protected servers and routers installed, their system would be fool-proof. This new and unique system, with on-site setup and a three-year maintenance contract, was subject to credit approval and Walt gave the salesman a business card from Mr. Pignataro. The installation required a complete wiring job of the hotel to install DSL cables to each room and every office. He was told that this was the reason for the exorbitant cost. This shipment would be put together tomorrow and shipped out immediately upon credit approval.

The computer salesman told Walt, "With luck, Mr. Lewis, your equipment should arrive in ten days and our technician will be arriving with the shipment to help set it up and train your people. Thank you for your order." Walt said and did all the proper things that a customer did, and after signing the contract, moved away from the area. He made a mental note to call Piggy and tell him to expect this delivery. He knew that he wouldn't be there see the new computer installation but he was a nice enough guy to care that his boss would be helped by what he was doing here at the convention. Walt went to his room to use the john. The seminar came to a close. There would be a networking social gathering this evening, but Walt would not be there. He had things to do. He had to call John Shaft. It was time to put the next phase of the plan into motion. Herb loved John and would never hurt him. He trusted his friend to a fault.

He changed clothes and, in his tourist outfit, called a taxi from his room. He was going to Philadelphia for the evening. He always wanted to see the Betsy Ross house and the Liberty Bell anyway and this would be his last opportunity to do so. He would make all of his phone calls from Philly as well; he wanted to leave no trace of this part of his activities here at Donahue Downs.

He went outside to wait for his ride into Fantasyland. "Philly is a big town buddy, where exactly do you want to go?" asked the driver. In response, Walt told him that he wanted to see some of the historic sites. They were off to the old section of the city, the place where the birth of our nation was celebrated. Walt didn't know where he was in Philadelphia, but he told the driver to let him out in the general area and he would just walk around. Paying his fare, he walked along the cobble stone streets marveling at the sights that were parts of our national heritage. He picked up a brochure from a vendor on the street and figured out where he was and what he wanted to see. First though, were the phone calls that he had to make!

He placed his first call to the Canary Islands and got Mr. Pignataro on the line. He very excitedly told him of the computer system and made sure that all was OK with him on the purchase. Mr. Pignataro was excited as well and told Walt that he had done well. "I will see you in a couple of days then, Alejandro, and thank you for your trust and confidence." That done, it was time for the call to John and he checked his watch to be sure that this indeed was the agreed-upon time. It was, and he dialed John in Boise from this street corner phone booth.

John picked up the phone on the first ring; he had been standing in the booth on South 9th Street waiting for the call. They updated each other on their plan and the timeline was right on schedule. As far as they could see, the plan was perfect. John had resigned from his job and was even able to get a pension and reduced medical benefits for himself. Herb chuckled and so did John; they knew that it all had to look right. Herb did not tell John that he was in Philadelphia because that would have gotten him nervous for no reason. They agreed on a time and place in Madrid for their first meeting and only briefly mentioned their prize hidden in the jungle of Punta Delgada. "See ya on Thursday then John, OK?" John was as happy as a kid in a candy store and clicked off the line smiling. He was on his way home to pack; his reservation and passport were all taken care of weeks ago. His flight was without charge thanks to his old job as a pilot. He also made arrangements with his landlord to sell his furniture and send him a check sometime in the future. John knew he would never see a dime of that money but it didn't bother him at all.

Walt took a walk to see the sights and sprinkle some hints to baffle the FBI. He looked down Elfreth's Alley and let the ghosts of the past whisper in his ear. This was the first continuously occupied residential street in the United States. He could almost visualize the carriages and powdered wigs; with his imagination in warp speed, he thought that he could hear the clip-clop of horses long since dead. Not far away, he visited the Betsy Ross house on Arch Street and thought the rooms to be very small. He liked the displays though and looked at the graves outside. He was nothing more than just another tourist enjoying the flavor of Philadelphia. He went on to visit the Rockwell Museum, Independence Hall, and the Liberty Bell, but he saved his last stop for his coup d'etat. After two hours of walking the streets and taking pictures with a cheap camera, he found his way to the U.S. Mint at 5th and Arch Streets. In the Rittenhouse Room, Herb saw the precious gold coins displayed on the walls. He salivated at these beautiful baubles knowing his greed would never be satisfied. Finding that some of the semiprecious coins could be purchased, he did exactly that. He found a five-dollar gold coin minted in 1872 and bought it for ninety-seven dollars. Handing over number three of his stolen hundred dollar bills, he knew that within two or three days it would be found to be part of the heisted shipment heading toward Morocco. If anybody were to take notice of this three-year old, out-of-circulation bill, it would be the U.S. Treasury Department. He however, would be long gone by then.

Herb exited from a side door; he was hungry and would find

a nice little restaurant nearby. At that very moment, Joe Donahue, Jim Dobson, Barney, and Israel Burns entered the U.S. Mint with their wives, Sandy, Phyllis, and Betty, and Ellen, Barney's girlfriend. Luck was still on Herb's side and none of them saw their Spanish-speaking guest make his exit. Herb did not see them either and thought that this was another beautiful late afternoon. Herb enjoyed a sumptuous dinner at The Bistro St. Tropez in the Marketplace Design Center on Market Street; he was treated like royalty. He paid for his dinner with a hundred-dollar bill and, chuckling under his breath, told the waiter to keep the change. Well satisfied that all was in order for the day and that he had accomplished all that he set out to do, he grabbed a cab and made his way back to Donahue Downs. Tomorrow was Wednesday, his last full day in the United States.

As he walked through the lobby of the hotel, a desk clerk called after him: "Mr. Lewis, you have a telegram, sir." Herb didn't miss a beat; with nerves of steel, he approached the counter where Mike McCormick was talking to one of the front desk employees. He and Helen had not accompanied their friends to Philly, as someone had to stay behind at the hotel. He looked at the clerk who handed him the telegram. He did not look at Mike and Mike only barely noticed him. "Thank you," he said in his best Spanish accent as he took the cable without opening it. Curious, he thought, it was from Mr. Pignataro. He hurried to his room to see what he wanted. The message was short; all it said was call me.

Punching in the numbers for the Canary Islands, Walt felt his world coming apart. For some reason, he had a foreboding feeling in his heart. Alejandro picked up the phone on the first ring and was glad to hear his best employee on the line: "Walt, I received a phone call from the FBI in the States asking after you. I acknowledged that you worked here but said that you were off on a business trip for a few days. I did not tell them where you were but I did tell them that you would be back here Thursday evening and would be in your office Friday morning. The man, a Major Richardson, said he would call back then. Is everything OK, Walter?" Herb, always the "cool as a cucumber" criminal reassured his boss, "I have no idea what the FBI would want of me but I will tend to it on Friday, just as you told them." His next call was for a taxi. Mr. Lewis wanted a ride to Philadelphia International Airport. He knew that the noose was tightening and a change of plans had to be made immediately. He left via the rear exit, luggage, laptop and all. He did not check out of the hotel but left the room key on the night table next to a large gratuity for the housekeeping staff. He was not seen by anyone. At the airport he had to pay an additional hundred dollars to update his ticket to Madrid but again he saw some twisted humor in the fact that the bill he was going to try to pass to McCormick would now be traced to the airport. They would know just how close they were to catching him.

He waited an interminable two hours, but Flight 6271, nonstop to Madrid, was on time. He would be a day early in Madrid but he would use the time wisely. The plane took off with a contented Herb Philbrick aboard. In Madrid he would once again go through his pre-planned metamorphosis: he would meet John Shaft as Mr. José Lorenzo; he had always liked that name. His plan was put into effect months ago but would now be accelerated by one day, no big deal.

Mike couldn't shake the feeling that he had been had. He was a federal cop too long and had learned not to deny those gut feelings. He knew that something just happened that he should have understood but he missed it: "I know that I know that guy." Checking the computer registration file, Mike found that the guy was a Mr. Walter J. Lewis from the Gran Canaria Hotel in the Canary Islands. "He is here for the convention, perfectly normal, but there is something that I can't put my finger on. That man bothers me. I'll sleep on it; tomorrow it may come to the surface. Maybe I will try to meet the guy, who knows?" As the Donahue party re-entered the hotel grounds, Mike put his head down on the pillow next to Helen. Sleep would not come easy. The Donahue group went to their rooms and all slept soundly after a full and fun day. Barney had to drive Ellen back to New Hope but he wasn't gone long. Everyone was tired and all had a good time.

Walter J. Lewis breezed through customs in Madrid, waited

for them to finish checking his luggage and then caught a cab into the city. He located the small hotel that he had been told about last time he was here. He went inside to check in. Plenty of vacancies and he was given a room on the ground floor with a little porch overlooking a weedy garden. Walt paid the man cash up front for a two-day stay, the clerk smiled, bad teeth and all. Walt used an assumed name and was not asked for identification. He was tired and needed sleep but it would not come easily for him. He spread his stuff on the bed and sat at the cheap desk staring into the dirty mirror. He thought of his wife back there in Boise screwing the gardener and waiting for a check from Herb Philbrick, a check that would never come to her again. He thought of his son that he had abandoned the kid that always complained and was constantly mollycoddled by his mother. "She spoiled that kid rotten and he too looked at me as just the food and money provider. Little Herbie will have to grow up one of these days. Maybe he will learn how to be a gardener like his mother's boyfriend."

He thought of Beaufort, Scotch and Byrnes, where he used to work. His bosses there always considered him to be just a little bespectacled man who was a stickler for details. They kept him on because he generated business and his work was flawless. He was not the company superstar but he didn't want to be. Herb had been playing his role for years waiting for John and waiting for destiny. The bosses at Beaufort, Scotch and Byrnes did not know that Herb Philbrick really was a superstar; he was just not their superstar. Herb used his hidden talents only for personal enrichment. Tossing a few crumbs to the company from time to time ensured his employment and his access to the client list. It all worked so well, he thought. He was actually working two full-time jobs: the company job and his own demanding caper, which took more of his time than his paid position. Herb thought that the heart attack that sent him to the hospital almost ruined his plans. He would not allow that. He listened to the doctors; it was only a mild attack. "Consider it a warning," they had said. He was told to take a two-week rest, go to a hotel or something and just find a place to relax and to not think of work for a while. Herb did that at Donahue Downs, selecting the hotel at random. At the hotel he witnessed the type of crime that is seen only on television. He did not want to see any of this but once he had, he had to protect himself. He allowed the FBI to protect him because the video camera clearly showed his face hiding behind some rocks as two murders took place. The FBI had their witness, the Falcones suffered for their sloppiness, and the Lorenzos paid for their crimes with their lives. Philbrick saw it all and he lost six full months of his self-created retirement plan.

Returning to Donahue Downs as Walter Lewis was risky but he loved the game and his disguise was perfect. His thoughts ran like this: I know that McCormick thinks he knows me, I saw it in his eyes. When he awakens in a few hours, maybe I will call him on the phone to say hello —.NO! He warned himself again that this was not the time for foolish mistakes. His time was now and he knew it; strike when the iron was hot, he thought, but the second idea came crashing in immediately. This iron was getting too hot to handle so he had had to accelerate his plan by one day, right? "No big deal," he said. He admonished himself to take no more crazy chances. No phone calls to anyone and no contact with any other person except John and "Carlos," the man that he was to meet tonight. The man with a new set of papers for him, the man that would allow him to become Mr. José Lorenzo of Madrid, Spain. Herb started to consider his first alias as Walter J. Lewis working at the Gran Canaria. Mr. Pignataro was a pretty good guy and a small-time operator just trying to make a living. "The computer system I bought under his name will help him in that business but, alas, I will not be there with him to guide him along," he thought.

Considering his dangerous trip to Donahue Downs — seeing all those cop people again! — caused a raucous outburst of laughter, but he knew that it was nervous energy and could have been captured easily. "Piggy saved my life with that telegram. I owe him a favor and somehow, I will find a way to repay his act of kindness." As soon as Piggy mentioned Major Richardson he knew that if Richardson were to see his picture he would run it through their electronic imaging program and Philbrick's face would outshine Mr. Lewis'. The game would be up, as they said. He then thought of John, his best friend who right this minute was somewhere over the Atlantic Ocean on his way here. Of all the people Herb had ever known, even his parents, John Shaft was the only person he ever trusted. John was always there for him and conversely, Herb was always there for John. Never did they cross each other and every time a problem arose, they worked on it together. That was how and why this master plan to freedom was conceived. John lived high on the hog; his monthly bills exceeded his income. He was doing the losing dance of life called "one step forward, and two steps back." Herb was suffocating in his little house with two cats on the lawn and three sick people inside. He deserved better; he worked too hard in life to accept this emotionally draining relationship. Rather than hate his life, he planned the escape with John, a plan that would ensure a prosperous forevermore for both of them. And so far it was working.

CHAPTER FOUR

Nothing Left to Lose

Who knows to what heights Herb Philbrick could have risen had he been happy, but happiness just wasn't in the cards for him. Herb could never be content with any particular plateau in life; he would forever be driven to get more. He would, even on his deathbed, strive to cheat the devil of his due. If he had stayed the course and run the race to attain victory in any field or endeavor, he would have been a true master. His mind was a wonder; he never forgot even the smallest or most mundane item of data. When needed, everything he had learned about any given subject was right there on rapid recall. Herb could have been the Einstein of our century, but he chose to be nothing more than a cunning criminal. With all of his brilliance, he never stopped for the briefest moment to realize that he was going nowhere. His "need to win" was inbred into his spirit by his parents who told him that he was nothing and never would be anything. Herb rejected them early in life and walked to the tune of the discordant drummer from then on. He didn't have the need for money. It was the game of getting something for nothing that was his driving force. He needed to thwart the authorities just as he thwarted his parents. He felt no love for his wife and child because he received no love from his parents; he did not know the emotion of love at all. The only tangible thing in Herb Philbrick's life was his relationship with John Shaft. Throughout life, they suffered equally and rose together overcoming all situations, one for another. For Herb it was more than friendship; it was a blood-oath bond, it was true brotherhood. John made a similar vow to Herb for his own set of reasons. John considered Herb to be the love of his life and did not deny it to himself.

Herb suffered no fools in his life. If you showed the slightest weakness or fault, he would exploit it and use it to manipulate you all the way to personal disaster. Herb was callous and would not "feel another's pain;" indeed, he would walk away with someone else's gold under his arm and a chuckle in his heart. Herb had none of the personal flaws that other people had: he was not a drinker, never gambled nor felt drawn to illicit sex, and his smoking was down to only a casual cigarette from time to time. He told himself that his personal discipline enabled his intense focus on his projects. He never forgot a name, place, or date; once he saw a face, he would not forget it. Herb would always marvel that he himself was so nondescript to others that he could walk into and out of situations without so much as a nod of remembrance. What Herb did not know was right at that moment, Mike McCormick was sitting on the side of his bed thinking about him.

"I know I have seen that guy before; he is a bad guy, and I know it." Mike could not shake it; he had been trained too well to disavow his gut instincts. He knew that the more he churned this face and voice around in his mind, it would eventually come to the surface. It was already almost midnight but Mike decided to check on "Mr. Lewis" anyway. He called the hotel and told the desk manager to fax him whatever information they had on Mr. Lewis; Mike McCormick would not sleep this night. While Mike was waiting on faxes and doing a lot of thinking, Herb was walking down Coronado

Street in Madrid looking for number forty-seven and whistling. They were thousands of miles apart, but at this very moment their individual spirits were entwined in a game of show and tell.

Mike stared at the telephone on his desk but he wasn't focused on the phone itself. His mind was viewing mental newsreels of crime and punishment. Mike was focused on the mob bust at the hotel three years ago. He was, in a crazy way, seeing internal television before his very eyes. He saw the mobsters, their faces, smiles, and sneers. He heard snippets of talk; he remembered how hard they all worked to pull that bust off and how bad they felt not to have prevented the Lorenzo murder. As soon as he thought of the name Lorenzo, the image of a little man hiding in some rocks came into play and he saw the face of WALTER J. LEWIS. Mike could not contain himself; he literally shouted to his sleeping wife, "I knew it!" Parts of Herb's plan would become clear to Mike tonight, but not clear enough. Mike could not learn enough about what Mr. Walter J. Lewis really was up to. Mike couldn't prove anything at this point as it was all circumstantial data. Mike knew that what he understood was neither the beginning nor the end of Philbrick; his knowledge of this guy was midstream information. Both identities, Philbrick and Lewis, could be checked backward to the origin and forward to wherever this little man was hiding with his fortune. He called Major Richardson and left him a voicemail: "I know where Philbrick is, call me."

Walt opened the door and walked into the bookstore just like any other customer. It was here that he would meet Carlos, who worked for Mr. Baum. Baum was a master forger. He was a day early, but he did not want to sit in a drab hotel room waiting for fate to catch up with him. He needed Walter J. Lewis to disappear immediately and without a trace. He needed this done now, not tomorrow. Herb knew that by this time, Donahue Downs would know that Mr. Lewis had slipped away during the night. Herb entered the shop and started to browse among the dusty books. Carlos was on him like a moth to a light bulb: "Welcome sir, may I assist you with something?" Carlos said this while wearing his most subdued smile and probing stare. Herb told Carlos that he had a special need and asked to talk in private. Both Herb and Carlos knew the routine and all of the code words were executed flawlessly. They walked past Mr. Baum working on a table with an eye loupe and they walked past a customer as well. The girl at the register rang up the sale for another book and the last of the customers left the store.

Carlos shredded all the personal documentation of Mr. Walter J. Lewis: the passport was gone, the birth certificate gone as well, and all credit cards and picture IDs, including his driver's license, were tossed into the shredder. He also shredded the airline ticket for the flight to the Canary Islands and the social security card that bore the name of Walter J. Lewis. Mr. Baum came into the back room and greeted Herb with a smile and a handshake. He set to the task of recreating a new Herb Philbrick and he snapped a picture for the new passport and driver's license. Mr. Lewis disappeared without completing his trip home. His last known record was deplaning at Madrid and checking through customs. He did not make the second part of the trip to the islands and would forever be a mystery to his ex-employer Mr. Pignataro.

Herb Philbrick walked into 47 Coronado Street as Walter J. Lewis but emerged as José Lorenzo. He remembered something he had heard at Donahue Downs a few years ago. I think Vito Scaglionne had said this; yeah, he did and it went like this: "The king is dead, long live the king." Once again, Herb Philbrick was on top of his game. He took a cab back to his fleabag hotel where he picked up his luggage and laptop computer. He would meet John at the airport in a few hours, but for now he was going to introduce himself to his neighbors. Taking another cab across town, he moved into his own home. Herb, forever the stickler for details, had all this in place weeks ago. Even the car was delivered and left where Carlos was told to leave it. The keys and all the necessary papers were in the mail slot signed, sealed, and perfect. Carlos and Baum did an excellent job for which they were well paid. Herb was good to go and Walt fell off the face of the earth. Mr. José Lorenzo stepped over the threshold of his new home for the first time and tossed his gear onto an overstuffed armchair. "Three hours and John will land; I can't wait to see my friend again." Herb breathed what for him seemed to be new air.

John Shaft was a man consumed. John loved and trusted his friend Herb, but he had always been a straight-laced and law-abiding guy. John was not on sure footing in this new life. Herb had convinced him that the theft would work and he was right, it had. It was the first criminal act with which John had ever been involved. He was nervous during his testimony with the FBI, but he stood tall and toughed it out. He had mastered the art of fooling the polygraph test at Herb's request and he found that it wasn't all that hard to do. He and his friend would be home free in just a few short hours. He couldn't wait to find out how Herb hid the money and he couldn't wait to see it. He knew that it was now his passport to a free and happy life. John was on pins and needles when the plane captain announced that they would be landing in Madrid in fifteen minutes. He fastened his seat belt and looked at the lights of Madrid, his new city of residence and freedom forevermore.

It was 8:30 a.m. at Donahue Downs and the meeting was called to order. Joe and Sandy, Mike McCormick, Barney, Israel Burns, and Jim Dobson were all inside Mike's office at the hotel. Major Richardson was on the phone hooked up on a conference line with FBI bureau chiefs in Madrid, New York, Philadelphia, and The Canary Islands. Mike started because he was the one to finally recognize Philbrick as being Mr. Lewis. He told everyone how he had the room inspected early this morning but Philbrick had checked out, seemingly in a rush. Richardson told them that they were already checking the local cab companies and would find out soon enough when Philbrick had left the hotel and where he had gone. Mike said that he was at the desk when the clerk gave Lewis the telegram but nobody knew what it said. Richardson said he would check it out as soon as possible. Within an hour, an agent had interviewed Alejandro Pignataro at the Gran Canaria Hotel and gotten Walter Lewis' address on Avian Street but he had apparently not been there.

It was soon discovered that Walter Lewis did not take the second leg of his flight from Philadelphia. The search had to originate in Madrid. Richardson was not happy about this because traditionally, the police in Madrid were slow to move and somewhat uncooperative with the U.S. authorities. This investigation was in the hands of the FBI now and Richardson thanked Mike and Joe and the rest of them for all the help. What Major Richardson did not tell them was that he had a gut feeling about Philbrick. Richardson was connecting the dots and felt that the elusive Herb Philbrick engineered that international money transfer theft from New York to Morocco last year. In his own way, Richardson respected Herb Philbrick: he was smart, cunning, a master of disguise, and a non-violent criminal. Herb would prove to be a worthy adversary and when this case was solved, Richardson could retire to sit on the porch and count squirrels too. The very thought of it made him chuckle; he knew it would never happen. Richardson had his own personal demons to slay and they went back to Vietnam. There would be no way in hell that he would sit idly anywhere just to think; his memories would drive him insane and he knew it. Further, he could not live down the shame each time he saw Joe Donahue and knew that at some point he would have to face him with the truth. He needed to avoid that for as long as possible. The voices in his mind would never be silent until he talked to Joe; he owed his fallen comrades that much.

John Shaft deplaned in Madrid and breezed through customs. Waiting for his luggage, he found a private car driver carrying a sign with his name on it. "I'm John Shaft," he told the driver and the man responded in fair English that his name was José and that he would take him to his friend Herb. The man said that was all he knew but that was good enough for John. They found the luggage and John jumped into the black Mercedes for what would prove to be the second greatest adventure of his life. John sat in the back seat of the car looking at the city of Madrid as if for the first time. He had been here before but hardly ever went any further than an overnight stay at the Arturo Soria Hotel near the airport. His driver just passed it on the M-30 road and John felt a little better after seeing a familiar sight once again.

"Anything familiar to you, John?" the driver asked. With that, the car pulled to the curb and the driver shut down the engine. Turning around in the seat, Herb said, "Welcome home, John." Herb was not recognizable; John had no idea that his lifelong friend had met him at the airport. They got out of the car and in the streets of Madrid, these two old friends knew that their destiny was unfolding before their eyes. They hugged, they laughed, and they shook hands as if for the first time. For John, it was freedom with peace, security, and riches never before considered. For Herb, it was the happiness that he would be able to share his mind and the fruits of their labors with his friend John, the only friend he had ever had.

Their reunion was wonderful, but oh so short. "There is much to do," said Herb as they settled into the living room with glasses of Vega Sindoa Cabernet Sauvignon Tempranillo, Herb's new found wine of choice. Herb told John where the money was hidden and how he had done it. He knew that John would be excited to know this because he was not a rich man. In fact, he knew that John wanted to keep his old identity so he could draw on his pension plan and social security. Herb had to tell him firmly but gently that it could not be that way. Herb placed his hand on his friend's arm; he had to tell him the truth of his new reality. With all the love and friendship that he had for this man, the only person he had ever trusted, he told John that he would never draw on his pension, his investments, or his social security. He told him that he would realize far greater rewards in the long run: "John, the connections are too easily made from the pilot of the airplane who retired and moved to Spain so close to where the hijack took place. Add that to the fact that this pilot, you, John, grew up with me, Herb Philbrick, already an internationally wanted criminal; the connections are too easily made and the FBI is not stupid."

He told him that the FBI had already made the connection. He did not tell him that he had only recently been in Pennsylvania teasing the FBI and the Donahue clan because that was, to him, privileged information. Herb played his games alone.

Herb told John only what he needed to know but added that he would have a new identity tomorrow. For the first time in their lives, they relaxed and enjoyed the company of one another without constraint. They drank more than they should have, laughed as much as they wanted to, and all inhibitions were dropped. One thing led to another, one man touched, the other let it happen, and both fell to the embrace that they each needed to fulfill their overdue desires for one another. The kiss was deep, passionate, loving and filled with mutual respect. They were in love and they knew it all of their lives. It was just that now, with all of the restrictions finally lifted, they were allowed to be who they were. They remembered the first time, the time of their youth, and the tears and laughter finally burst forth and echoed from one to another. They were free, free at last, and free to be. They both said, "Life is good." Herb and John visited Mr. Baum in the morning and started the task of making John Shaft disappear forever.

ACTOS-2.5A CIA/NASA orbital reconnaissance satellite clicks along, snapping its daily allotment of digital images of an empty beach a barren coastline and a pristine ocean not five miles off the coast of Punta Delgada. All was as it was yesterday and as it had been for all of the yesterdays since they added this location to the reconnaissance list almost three years ago. Soon, this mile-high, highly technical and super expensive "eye in the sky" would earn its keep.

CHAPTER FIVE

The Chameleon

Major Richardson made some phone calls and assembled the lead agents that were assigned to the two different investigations concerning the elusive Mr. Philbrick. It was a great source of embarrassment for him and his old associate Mike McCormick to have let him slip by unnoticed. The good major was grateful that Mike finally made the connections but he chastised himself over and over: "He was right there, back at Donahue's hotel, what nerve the guy has." Very quickly it was ascertained that Philbrick and John Shaft were childhood friends back in Boise so the heist from the airplane was now a no-brainer. They knew that Philbrick had become Walter J. Lewis and was working for the hotel in the Canary Islands. From there, all trails stopped. Shaft quit his job and records showed that he had gotten a free one-way ticket to Madrid. Philbrick never returned to his job at the hotel and disappeared from his little paradise in the islands.

"OK guys, so what do we do about all this? Some of the stolen money turned up around Donahue Downs and of all places, one of the hundred dollar bills was cashed at the U.S. Mint in Philly. Philbrick is rubbing our noses in it and although it may be great fun for him, I will not allow this twerp of a church mouse to get away with his scams." The major went on to tell the other agents that as far as he could tell, Philbrick was sitting on at least forty million dollars from the airplane robbery and another eight million from the investment thefts. The airplane money was all marked and would have to be laundered to be of any value to them but the money from Philbrick's original theft was untraceable. Philbrick and Shaft were living in Fat City and by now they were probably so well covered, only a miracle would bring them to justice. Richardson asked the other agents for some input, any crazy idea that could be used to capture these two bandits, but nothing of real value came forth.

The agent in charge of the airline heist told the major that Interpol had been investigating that robbery for years and had come up with nothing. Only the "eye in the sky" held any hope for them, but they knew that there were hundreds of miles of beaches to cover on at least three different islands or atolls that could have been used to pull off the caper. Richardson then told the other officers that he was packaging up the entire portfolio and bringing it to the U.S. Attorney General with the hope that he would hand it over to the Central Intelligence Agency. If the CIA would undertake Philbrick as a covert operation there was still a possibility for closure. That and the reconnaissance satellite were their only hope. It would also remove these issues from the cold case files of the FBI.

The meeting closed and Richardson breathed a sigh of relief. At least now he had direction. He told himself that he has done his best on this case but now these two men were out of his jurisdiction. From here on out, it was no longer in his control nor was it his responsibility. He knew though that down deep, his professionalism was tarnished, if only in his own mind. He wanted to catch Philbrick so he could then face Donahue and put that unfinished Vietnam business to rest as well. Perhaps then he could finally hang up his guns, ride off into the sunset, and sit on the porch like the rest of them. Again he scoffed at the idea with a growling, "Yeah, right." He thought about going on vacation, a month, maybe six weeks if he could get it. He would vacation in Madrid. The more he thought of it, the more the idea appealed to him, so he called the personnel office to check out the schedules.

Herb and John walked into the shop and Carlos was surprised to see them. Code words quickly breezed through, Carlos knew right off what the menu of the day would be; this was the friend that he was told about months ago. "Good morning, Mr. Lorenzo, so good to see you again," he said. Carlos played the perfect shop clerk and, looking over his shoulder, Herb noticed that Baum was already studying John for the work at hand. Later that afternoon, José Lorenzo and the newly created Mr. Justin Bourne walked the streets of Madrid hand in hand looking for a sidewalk café. Carlos and Baum smiled about their newfound source of income. Mr. Lorenzo was proving to be a very valuable customer.

Joe Donahue gave up trying to teach Lucy to fetch.

Barney was in love.

Richardson was finagling schedules.

Mrs. Philbrick filed for divorce and let her lover move in.

The Manleys returned home from their time of grief.

Chris, Rick, and Joe Donahue Jr. ran their lives as credits to a society that could not appreciate their individual gifts of wisdom. Joe Sr. often referred to them as the Three Musketeers awaiting their call to stardom.

Mike assembled complete dossiers on Herb Philbrick and John Shaft and sent them to his ex-boss, the major. They had discussed plans off the record. Mike was even more frustrated by Philbrick than Richardson was; he was right under his nose and he did not recognize him. Mike wanted him so badly he could taste it. He would relish the day that Philbrick was brought home to face the music.

Steve and Sue tended the garden of love that they had been blessed with and told the world of the new Manley child on the way.

Alejandro Pignataro was a bit confused, but since hiring the technical representative to stay at the hotel on a long-term contract, he was satisfied that Walter really didn't hurt him too badly.

The crummy streets of Webster Avenue up in the Bronx had not changed and the Arbor Bar had a capacity crowd.

The silent satellite clicked away watching, forever watching.

CHAPTER SIX

Let's Take a Vacation

H elen hugged Mike and told him that she understood his need for closure. Richardson filed for and was granted an extended leave of absence from the department and Joe reluctantly agreed to come with them. Sandy loved Joe with all of her heart but knew that her man was a man of integrity that would not sleep knowing that the quintessential creep Mr. Philbrick had gotten the best of him. She reluctantly bid him, "Farewell my love, and good hunting." She followed that loving statement with a gentle reminder to keep out of harm's way and come back to her safely. There was firm resolve in her voice, so Joe assented in an almost sheeplike manner.

Three burnt-out warriors were going to Madrid without official sanction. They had no plan: just guts, intelligence, and motivation, and for them, that was enough. Joe and Mike were waiting for the major who was going to spend the night at the hotel prior to leaving out of Philadelphia International Airport in the morning. Joe wasn't all that happy about working with him but, like Mike, he wanted Philbrick brought to justice. He felt as though Philbrick had made him out to look like a monkey's uncle. Joe didn't like that feeling at all, especially from this little smart-aleck dude with steel nuts, a straight face, and an unremarkable appearance. To Joe, Philbrick was the untended "Irish Pennant" still hanging from the Phil Fauxmaster, Tommy McGuiness and Tony Lorenzo affair; it left a sour taste in his mouth. Richardson arrived with minimal baggage and a more reserved attitude toward Joe. He knew that this was the time to slay his demons and to finally tell the truth, the truth that had haunted him on a daily basis for over twenty-five years. The meeting commenced in Joe's inner office and after handshakes, Joe broke the ice:

"Ok fellas, we agreed to do this and all of us understand that we will get no help from our government. The best we can hope to do is find this guy and hold him for the Interpol cops or Spanish Police if they will even listen to us." Richardson said nothing; his mind was elsewhere and Joe recognized the symptoms. Mike tensed up; he felt a storm in the air. After the proverbial pregnant silence, Richardson gulped and looked Joe straight in the eyes. Mike opened three bottles of Guinness Stout and placed one before each of his comrades. Major Richardson was thankful for the interruption but knew that he would forge ahead with his explanation anyway. Joe knew what was coming so he sipped, sat, and waited. Mike didn't know what to do or say so he held his place in silence.

"Joe," said the major, "I don't know if you will believe what I am going to tell you, but you and I have to bury the ghosts of the past and be done with it. There is not a day in my life that I don't think of that time when I sent you and the platoon out there on that mission. I see the faces of our buddies, Joe, and I remember all of their names. I have written letters to every family and as for me, I wanted those letters to be closure or a cleansing, but for me, they were not. For the families, they were tributes of heroism to the fine young men that they sent to that crazy place in the craziest of times, but I was the man to lead them. I was responsible and I felt the pain of loss almost as much as those wives, children, mothers, and fathers did. Joe, only you were left alive to exact rightful retribution and vengeance from me and I can see God's mighty hand in the wisdom of it. When you punched me in the jaw back there in St. Albans Hospital in New York, I knew I had it coming. In a way, down deep, I wanted you to finish the job and be done with it, but I knew that you were a better man than that. You are many things, Joe Donahue, but a murderer you ain't, even if in the long run had you done so, it would probably have been better for me. I did not push a prosecution against you, the Corps did. I've led a miserable life, Joe, and every day I am reminded that I have a debt that I cannot repay. If you will let me, I want to tell you how that decision came about; but just know this, I am in no way trying to shift the blame to anybody other than myself."

I looked at him with pity and remorse, shook my head and told him, "Let's do this once and get it done with; I too hear the screams and agony far too often and I've harbored a hatred for you ever since. It almost ruined my life."

The major went on to tell them of the pressure exerted upon him to reconnoiter and take that God-forsaken hill back there in Khe Sanh. The pressure came from the division commander who expected miracles from men that were battle weary, ill fed, and undermanned. "I knew that ammunition was running low, I knew that there was no air support to call in for you and I knew that I had no other platoons or even a complete squad to come to your aid if you should need it. I was promised a promotion if we could pull this off and I was hoping against all hope that the mission would be a success. I didn't know until after you left that the hill was overridden with North Vietnamese soldiers; the initial reports had said 'light resistance.' The radio back at command was shattered and I got a note from the Colonel, but it came too late. Although I tried to call you on the walkie-talkie, I remembered that I put you on radio silence so all I could do was utter a silent prayer and hope for the best. I looked at who was left; two of my lieutenants were dead and Captain Johnson was shot in the leg. I could not leave them to run after you and I had nobody else to send in to help you. When reinforcements finally arrived, we found you and the bodies of the kids that I had sent into that meat grinder. When we got back, I notified command that I wanted you as my lieutenant and it was approved as a field commission. You had to spend some time getting your wounds fixed, but when you healed up and returned I had already gone back to Saigon and then stateside. I heard that you got shot up pretty badly a week later and were sent to St. Albans on the next available airlift. You got there ahead of me, Joe, as I had to report to command headquarters in DC and fill out tons of bogus reports and file papers. I sent a letter resigning my commission but they wouldn't hear of it. I ended up in the same hospital as you under psychiatric evaluation. Although they gave me a clean bill of health, they discharged me from the Corps to fight my demons alone. The only way I found that to be possible was by putting all I had into my job with the FBI. I never married, ain't gay, and I'm a closet alcoholic. Joe, I know that this may be too much to ask but I am asking you to understand what happened and please try to forgive me."

He was crying. So was I and so was Mike.

I stood up and faced the wall, hoping to find closure or some kind of peace, when all of a sudden I felt like, well, I can't explain it; it was like how I felt when looking at "The Wall" in DC. It was like the guys from my squad in 'Nam were hugging me and telling me that it was alright. Like they were telling me that Richardson wasn't the one to blame; it went much further than just him, he did what they had told him to do and really, none of them were suffering anymore. In a crazy way, I knew that the souls of my buddies were at peace and somehow or someway, all of this would work out in the long run. The words placed into my heart were resoundingly clear: "Remember Romans 8:28, Joe."

I turned, walked over to Richardson, and he stood. I guess he didn't know whether I was going to smack him or shake his hand, but he soon read my face and we hugged in tears of remembrance and forgiveness. Mike stood as well and shoved those beer bottles under our noses; we all clicked, saluted, and sipped. The deed was done.

Healing took place and peace reigned supreme. We had become a team of three with unimpeachable trust, honor, and integrity toward each other. Right off, Major Richardson told us that his name was Pete and suggested, "Why don't we just drop all this 'Major' stuff, OK?"

I always knew his name, but never wanted to use it. Calling him "Major" was my way of keeping him at arm's length, but he was right; the time for change was now. We all agreed and he went on to say that in this matter, we were equals and should decide as a group how we would proceed. Again, Mike and I nodded our agreement so we all took another swig from our liquid refreshments saying, "Hear, hear." Our cause was right and we wanted nothing more than justice in this matter. I knew that finally we would be able to function as a real team with singleness of purpose with no outside agendas or hidden dislikes.

We asked God to bless our mission and then sat down to formulate a plan. Pete said that through some of his associates, we now had a contact in Madrid who knew the turf and some of the bad guys as well. We may have to deal with some of the local underworld but what better way to find a mouse than to use some rats? We of course were the cats and pretty cool ones at that, even if we were more like the over-the-hill gang.

We all got a good night's sleep and left in the morning; Sandy and Helen drove us to the airport. They say that parting is sweet sorrow, but in my mind I almost chucked the whole idea and stayed home. I didn't want to leave Sandy, had doubts that Johnny the bartender could fill in for Mike, and I missed the kids already. Down deep though, I had one of my more famous gut instincts and knew that we would pull this off. The excitement of the chase won over my better judgment and businesslike thoughts, so I kissed Sandy, hugged Helen, and we entered that big-assed bird that would take us to Spain. We flew first class.

CHAPTER SEVEN

The Chase Is On

We depleaned in Madrid rumpled, hungry, grouchy, and tired but we smiled anyway, trying to look like seasoned travelers. In truth, we were three aging and angry men, each of whom hated airline food and did not fit all that well in the small seating spaces. Sleep was fleeting and Mike snored like an old Chevy with a bad carburetor. Well anyway, we were here and this was phase one and that was that for that. Grin and bear it, we told ourselves as we looked for an English-speaking cab driver that would most assuredly rip us off. Sandy always told me that I had too little faith in the goodness of humanity and she was right. Now that was a scary thought and inwardly I chuckled. We were booked at the Holiday Inn with reservations made beforehand by Mike and we were given a complimentary discounted rate. The driver said he was from Brooklyn but I didn't buy it because I said that downtown Flushing was pretty nice and he agreed. Flushing was a part of Queens County, New York and it isn't pretty, nor was it nice. Brooklyn is in Kings County. He tried the "nice guy" con as best he could but I gave him credit because we got to the hotel without the aimless circles to build up the fare. We paid him U.S. cash and for that he seemed to be grateful. We tipped him an extra five just because he smiled a lot and didn't talk our ears off. Maybe we wanted to get right into this affair but we were so tired that all we did was get something to eat and hit the sack. I didn't know about those other guys, but I slept like a bear with a tummy full of honey. Yes Ms. Scarlett, tomorrow really was another day.

We each overslept and around noon we met in the lobby to get some brunch and make our plan to catch the elusive Mr. Philbrick and company. Pete called this guy named Santos, who was a CIA mole. He was asked off the record to lend us some ground support on this mission and to pave the way where we would most assuredly fail without help. He sauntered into the lobby about an hour later, looking like a native Madrid businessman, which he probably was. Santos was really a Chicago-born Hispanic American but he fit in exceedingly well here in Spain. His English was impeccable and his command of the Spanish language was high class Castilian. He also said that he could speak the street language of a Bronx-born Puerto Rican as well. We all liked him right off. We went up to Pete's room to bring Santos up to speed on our quest. The talk took over two hours and Santos wasn't shy about asking questions. We created a sort of flowchart of the assumed activities of Philbrick, showing his original caper at the brokerage house after the mob bust in my hotel. From there, we pointed out the airline heist and his known occupation at Mr. Pignataro's hotel down in the Canary Islands. We presented the evidence collected that showed John Shaft to be the most likely co-conspirator as they were childhood friends and he too had left the U.S. for Madrid. Shaft was the pilot of the plane that was robbed using the bomb scare ploy. With some minor embarrassment, we told Santos how Philbrick toyed with us by returning to my hotel in disguise and that he got away with it. Spending some of the stolen and marked hundred dollar bills in the Philadelphia area had really stuck our noses in it, so to speak. His tactic had the desired effect; we were now super-motivated to extract a little payback. We wanted him bad and yes, now it was personal.

When we told Santos that Philbrick had over forty-eight million dollars of stolen money, he whistled. We told him that only eight million of it was liquid as the airline money was too hot to handle and had to be laundered. That was where we hoped that Santos could help us with our plan to trap Philbrick. We assumed that both Philbrick and Shaft now had new identities and most likely, they were created right here in Madrid. Shaft flew from the US under his real name and Philbrick got here under an alias, which was now untraceable. That name was Walter J. Lewis, but we were sure that by now, even that name had been obliterated. We now needed to know who did the forgery on all the needed documents, what were their new assumed names, where were they, and how could we bring them out under some sort of guise. Santos was hopping up and down; he knew of only two master forgery pros in Madrid and one of them only specialized in currency. He told us that he would bet his bottom dollar that the bookstore owner, Mr. Baum, was our man. He was a German-born Jew with a history, but like many of these guys, he hid his talents well and only sold his wares to an exclusive clientele. Santos said that Baum's hired clerk, a guy named Carlos, was his go-between and shooter when needed.

The three of us were private citizens from America; we had no right to own or carry guns in this country. The American consulate would only tell us to go home so we knew that we would have to walk easy but act tough. Santos could not get involved without permission from the Agency but told us that he would cover us in any way that he could. He also had an idea. We agreed to meet this evening after dinner and Santos would be bringing some help with him. We stayed close to the hotel because if we ran into Philbrick we probably wouldn't recognize him, but he would surely recognize us and run for the hills.

Kudos to the Holiday Inn in downtown Madrid, their dinner menu was superb. I opted for the seafood paella, while Mike and Pete ordered something called gazpacho (spicy tomato soup), then chorizo, which was spicy sausage and Mike felt that he almost caught on fire. After that, the waiters brought out a magnificent roast lamb; we ate like kings. Santos showed up while desert was on the table so he had a cup of coffee with us and nibbled on the munchies. I asked him where his promised support team was and he told us that we had just sampled some of his work. He went on to tell us that the cook here at the Holiday Inn was a guy named Raoul and it was his life's dream to immigrate to the United States. He was a young man: strong, honest, and brave. Santos told us that Raoul would most likely agree to this dangerous mission if we could pave the way for him to come to the U.S. on a work visa. We had no right though to put him in harm's way, so we all knew that this plan must be foolproof and go off without a hitch. We met Raoul later that night; we liked what we saw and we liked what we heard. I promised him a job at the Downs and Pete said he had contacts at the consulate that would pave the way and fill Raoul's dream. Raoul was excited about working for American justice and hoped that in the long run, this adventure would shed a good light on him when he applied for full U.S. citizenship. We got the ball rolling right away.

The next morning, I called Sandy back home in Solebury who faxed us a Donahue Downs employment application. We helped Raoul fill out the form and I signed it approved. Pete called his buddy at the consulate; he faxed us an application for a work visa for Raoul and the guy was so happy, he bubbled with excitement. Raoul took the day off from the Holiday Inn and ran over to the consulate for fingerprints and background information. He returned to our room around 3 p.m. and we sat down to business. Santos had one of his ne'er-do-well Spanish underground contacts call Baum and set up an appointment for Raoul to get a false identity for reasons better left unsaid. Baum liked it that way and trusted Santos' contact since they had done business a few times in the past. Raoul would be wired with the smallest transmitter I had ever seen; it was embedded into his scalp under the hair and could not be seen or detected. We would set up a camera with a telescopic lens in a vacant room across the street and the state-of-the-art parabolic microphone could penetrate six inches of concrete. Santos was able to borrow that from the Agency, but somehow I doubted that they even knew it was missing.

Our plan was to entrap Baum with the evidence of his real occupation and on the threat of turning him in to Interpol and the local authorities, we would strong-arm him into cooperation. We would tell him that all we wanted was Philbrick and if he cooperated, we would walk away from him and he would not be in any trouble. Philbrick and John Shaft would be sent back to the U.S. to stand trial for their crimes, and everything that started well would end well. Santos told us that he would be nearby in case any artillery was needed, but he too hoped that this seemingly simple plan would go off with no trouble. Raoul was as cool as a cucumber and I admired him for his ability to adapt so well to this scene. I suspected that he was no stranger to the underground, but I put that idea to rest; we needed him to do this and if he prepared meals at the Downs as well as he did here, he would have a new life.

It took a week to get all this lined up so to ease the boredom, Mike, Pete, and I flew down to the Canary Islands to snoop around. We spent the night at the Gran Canaria Royal Hotel in Sardinia knowing full well that this was the place that Philbrick had worked as a bartender and then almost-concierge. We made a point of meeting Mr. Pignataro, but just as a friendly bunch of tourists. We did not let on who we were or what we were about. We asked no questions, but casually strolled over to Avian Street where Philbrick once lived. I felt like a bloodhound picking up the scent; I could almost feel him here. The house was occupied so we walked by, seemingly paying it no mind. Seeing the topless babe on the front porch assured me that our church mouse Philbrick no longer lived here. We stopped at one of the tourist trap shops and bought a map of the island groups surrounding this area. Going back to the room, we made a list of all the most likely places that Philbrick could have stashed his loot. We plotted the spot where the money drop was made and calculated the time needed to move it to a safe spot. How he managed this was still a mystery to us, but either the money was still sitting on the bottom of the ocean floor or he had had a masterful plan. We knew the elusive Mr. Philbrick well enough to know that he had managed to secrete his pile of greenbacks somewhere, somehow. We would find it and we would find him. That was our oath, that was our promise to ourselves, and that was our mission fait accompli.

And the satellite clicked away. "Boring," thought the CIA operator back in Langley, so he had another cup of coffee and lit up with his feet up on the desk.

Herb and John were bounding over hill and dale in their rented four-wheel-drive Range Rover, headed for the beach at Punta Delgada. John had expressed a desire to at least see the money, even though he agreed that for now they could not use any of it. Herb told him that he was thinking of locating someone to help them on that score but he too wanted John to at least know where it was hidden in the event that something happened to him. They drove right on the beach in plain view and stopped the vehicle within walking distance to the buried vault.

Actos 2.5A orbital reconnaissance satellite saw both men plainly and obediently snapped pictures. The clerk in Langley caught it all and laughingly decided to take some close-ups of the occupants complete with the vehicle license plate number. He thought them to be nothing more than fishermen or tourists with a flair for wild adventure. The men disappeared into the jungle with shovels and the operator thought that to be strange. He knew that the satellite would be out of range in five minutes so he made note of all that he saw and printed out pictures of the men and the vehicle. He immediately faxed them to the Director's office for deciphering and action, if required.

John did most of the work because he was in better physical condition, but Herb tried mightily to keep pace with the digging. The sand had hardened up some since he was last here and the foliage had now grown a good root-base. Finally they lifted up the cover and saw the money still neatly wrapped in plastic. John noted that one corner was torn but made no mention of it, thinking that it was damage due to handling and the drop. They embraced on top of the money like two kids reveling over Christmas presents; in their own way, they took marriage vows right there: "Till death us do part," they each said. There was nobody there to celebrate with them, nobody to officiate, and nobody would have cared anyway.

"Nightfall will be soon," said Herb, so they set to the task of re-burying the stash and making everything look the same as it was. Smoothing their tracks behind them, they got back into the Rover for the long, bumpy ride back home. John was not satisfied living off of his friend's money and wanted to hurry the laundering process as quickly as it could be done. Herb understood John's need for independence and promised him that he would see if Mr. Baum knew anyone who could do that for them. Herb told him, "Ya know, John, we will take quite a whack on the money but there is enough of it to ensure each of us financial independence for the rest of our lives when it is over." He made a mental note to garner the best deal he could get and knew that Baum would have his greedy hands in the mix as well.

The ride home was a tough road to go, but they filled it with interesting deviations of clandestine financial plans of international intrigue. For John it was spooky, but for Herb it was merely another challenge that he knew he could win. John was fairly clueless on all this, so Herb took a lot of time to explain every detail as best he could. He genuinely loved John and would not hurt him, but his mental acuity was sometimes sorely lacking; this caused some concern for Herb. He decided that he would handle every aspect of this deal by himself and only use John for the minor details. Further, he decided that he would call Carlos in the morning to set up a meeting where he would explain his needs.

The magnificent trio was getting bored hobnobbing around this island paradise, for they soon discovered that there was little useful information to be gathered here. They stood out as men on a mission. Three aging, Caucasian guys all over six feet tall, all gray, and

Joe with his potbelly; well, they just did not blend in well and they knew it. They took the next plane back to Madrid. Santos met them at the airport and drove them back to the hotel. The ride back was interesting as Santos told them that he had gotten permission to put a surveillance team on Baum and his henchman Carlos. He told them that the office wasn't all that busy anyway and the boss saw the merits of the job. One of the investigators, a lady named Maria who was actually an American-born Hispanic with South-American roots was able to sit on a bench in a park not twenty feet from Carlos as he met with another man. She took pictures and Joe, Mike, and Pete looked into the eyes of the elusive scarlet pimpernel wannabe — Herb Philbrick. All agreed that Herb had once again done a masterful job in disguising himself; each said that they would have walked right by him on the street. Joe chortled that Herbie reminded him of an out-of-shape toreador. Santos gave them an update on the Philbrick file and it seemed that back in Boise, Mrs. Philbrick had been murdered. Herb Philbrick was now elevated in their eyes as being more than just an intelligent thief; he was now looked at as a dangerous man who would stop at nothing to win his game and severely punish those that came against him or rubbed him the wrong way. It could not be proven, but they knew that Herb had had that job done. They also felt that the only way that Herb could have accomplished this was by using Baum. Santos decided that after this was over, he would approach his boss for permission to move against him as well. They started to rethink how they would use Raoul; he must not be placed in harm's way and they did not want him to even meet with Philbrick. Upon completion of this mission, whisking him out of the country immediately would remove him from any future retribution from Baum also. All was agreed to and the final plan would be put into motion tonight.

Raoul walked into the bookstore to be greeted by a condescending Carlos who inquired after his needs. Raoul asked for a copy of "The Picture of Dorian Gray" by Oscar Wilde, and Carlos knew who he was and what he needed. Carlos said his lines and Raoul responded perfectly; price was no object. Santos heard every word. So did the tape recorder. Mr. Baum peered at Raoul and, after a limited, yet drastically incriminating conversation told him to return tomorrow for the documents. He took three pictures of Raoul and after a down payment of ten thousand dollars U.S. cash, the deal was struck. Raoul left the store and walked down the block, circling a few times to be sure that he was not followed. Actually though, he was being followed and he didn't even know it. Santos had a tail on him ever since he left his fleabag apartment back on Rio de Oro Street. Raoul disappeared into the woodwork and slowly made his way back to the Holiday Inn to meet with his American benefactors. He was on his way to America! Santos, Maria, and a beefy-looking associate walked into the bookstore as if they owned the place. Carlos approached them with his usual clerklike demeanor but they weren't having any charades. Santos put his hand on Carlos' shoulder and told him to sit down. The aide was also right behind Mr. Baum, who looked scared. Nobody else was in the store so Maria drew the blinds and posted the Closed sign on the door. Santos relieved Carlos of his pistol in order to remove any thought of using it. He opened his briefcase. Producing the tape recorder, Baum was aghast at what he heard and Carlos knew that he was looking at an awful lot of years behind bars. They were told that nothing would happen to them if they agreed to cooperate in snagging Herb Philbrick. Baum nodded and Carlos looked for a way out, but there was none. They spilled the beans like a broken piñata. They told him that Walter Lewis was now José Lorenzo and John Shaft had become Mr. Justin Bourne. They did not know where they lived — a small lie there — but did have a phone number for them. Santos told both men that they were to wear electronic bracelets around their ankles and every word they said would be recorded. They were instructed not to leave the shop unless they were going home, and then not to leave their homes unless they were going to the shop. Both would be followed and the shop would be wired with a listening device and hidden cameras. Both home telephone lines would be tapped.

They were trapped, they knew it, and they agreed to all of it. The phone rang and interrupted the conversation. Baum looked at Santos who nodded that he should answer the phone as if nothing was awry. As luck would have it, the tape recorder was already set up on the phone and it was Philbrick on the line. Baum was a master of his trade and there was no hesitation or variance in his voice. Philbrick wanted to chat about a new matter that he did not want to discuss on the telephone. He was told to come to the shop tomorrow at 3 p.m. sharp. Santos hid his glee in a professional manner but inwardly was jumping for joy. He couldn't wait to share this with Mike, Joe, and Pete, and of course his boss, from whom he would need lots of support to pull this off.

Carlos and Baum were told that the bugging team would be here in a few minutes and they were to let them do what they wanted to do without comment or interruption. There would be an agent watching both the front and rear doors to prevent an escape. It was found that there was no basement so Carlos and Baum really were like two trapped animals. They were told that after this was over, all the devices would be removed and they would be left alone from then on out. Santos was of course lying like a trooper; he wanted these perpetrators in the slammer post haste. The trap was set, the bait in plain view for the quarry to pounce upon, and all of the forces of legal entrapment were in place. With all systems a go, Santos headed back to the Holiday Inn for a sit-down with his semi-legal comrades. Raoul was already packing to make a 6 p.m. departure to Philadelphia. He would settle his affairs long distance but couldn't care less; he had few assets anyway. He carried a computer-generated picture of Joe's dog Lucy to assure Johnny the bartender of his identity. The cell phone broke Santos' feelings of certain victory and so he pulled to the curb to answer it. His boss, Charlie Daniels (no, not Jack's brother) told him that the satellite got a make on two men that fit the profile for Philbrick and Shaft. The assumed location of the money was identified and a team was on the way to look around. The license plate was traced back to the rental agency and the name José Lorenzo popped up. Charlie was hoping that this all made good sense to Santos who could not contain his glee. Charlie would meet them all at the Holiday Inn as well; he smelled a promotion in the air.

Raoul called the hotel to thank Santos but was told that he wasn't around right now. Mike told him to have a safe trip and to enjoy his new life. He and Joe would meet up with him back in Solebury soon and he told Raoul that he had better find a way to make that gazpacho for him once again because he loved it. A good laugh was shared and Raoul told him that it wouldn't be a problem. He had a few other hot little items he wanted to try out on them as well. He went on to say that maybe he could revamp the menu at the hotel, but Mike told him to slow down on that: "Those Pennsylvania home-bodies ain't used to Spanish cooking yet." Raoul put on his best clothes and took out the trash one final time.

Sandy told Johnny to head out to the airport and be there at 3 p.m. this afternoon, carrying a picture of Raoul, and to bring him back to the hotel. They had prepared a room for him and knew that the jetlag would be taking its toll on him. Lucy was depressed, Sandy was lonely, and Sue and Ralph missed their grandpa.

Shaft and Philbrick were motivated to make this new money deal that would ensure their everlasting happiness in financial free-dom. Six men in wetsuits alit onto the wild shores of Punta Delgada with metal detectors, a sat-phone, and shovels. They would have lit-tle trouble locating the loot and whistled a happy tune when they did. Faxes flew, calls made, congratulations all around; all that was left to do was shackle the bad guys. Daniels looked at the rubber stamp on his desk, the one that said Case closed and he couldn't wait to use it. Carlos and Baum had little to say to each other and filled their time in isolation cleaning the shop and thinking how weak they were. Baum made phony papers for both of them hoping that they would have the chance to use them. He also sent faxes to his bank with transfer orders to Switzerland but a sick little feeling was growing larger and larger with each silent move. He knew that the game was over for them but tried the best he could to cover each contingency for a possible escape. It was useless and he knew it; they closed up shop and went home to ponder their futures in dismay. Charlie's office intercepted all of Baum's faxes and they somehow never got delivered to the right place.

The meeting in Mike's room was standing room only and Joe decanted a bottle of good wine. The toast made by Mike was to Santos and his crew for the much-needed assistance, but of course Charlie took a bow as well. Santos had assembled a formidable team against Philbrick and every avenue of escape was covered. The arrest was to be made on the street even before they entered Baum's shop. Lookouts were to be posted at every possible avenue to the store and every agent would have a picture of the villains. They finished a magnum of wine and, in hopeful joviality, they called it a night. They all went back to their own rooms for some much-needed sleep so they would be ready for the task at hand tomorrow afternoon. Joe liked Charlie and told him to come to the Downs if he ever got the chance and to bring Santos with him.

Trapping the Fox

It was an overcast day with a hint of rain in the air. Herb told John that he was welcome to come along for this meeting but that he preferred to handle it alone: "Less distractions that way, ya know?" John, being the good submissive that he had become, capitulated and agreed to stay at home and await the outcome. Trust was not an issue here and both men knew it. Deciding to wear his worn-out trench coat and his stupid looking fisherman's hat, Herb set out to see Carlos and Baum to talk about his money problem. He took the car and drove into the city, only to find massive gridlock and frazzled nerves. Finally, he found a parking spot a block and a half from the shop and decided to brave the breaking rainstorm. Thunder and lightening opened up and heralded in a downpour that in no way could dampen Herb's spirits. He sloshed away down the street without even quickening his step. He told himself that rain was a good thing; it sort of cleansed the soul of mankind. He whistled a merry tune and the agents that saw him felt for sure that they had a nutcase on their hands. They did; Herb Philbrick was a certified psychotic. Right on cue, an agent departed the store to purposefully bump into poor, trapped Herb and he was in cuffs before he could say, "Excuse me." U.S. laws aside, nobody bothered with the Miranda rights; they just searched him and removed all of his personal effects. Baum and Carlos were sitting at the table in cuffs as well but were told that this was just for effect. They didn't want Herb to know that they had squealed on him to the law. They sat there looking grim and worried, but they did not know that they really had good cause to be concerned. Santos found the Baum-to-Boise connection, which resulted in Mrs. Philbrick's murder so now he really did have plans for their futures.

It was quickly determined that Herb came to the shop alone but they now had an address and John Shaft would be taken into custody soon. Agent Erik Bronkowski looked anything but Spanish but he was the agent nearest to where John and Herb lived. He volunteered over the radio to walk up to the door and play it by ear in order to make the arrest. "Who's there?" John said to the soft and gentle knock on the door. Bronkowski responded, "I am Erik, a friend of Mr. Baum's; he and Mr. Lorenzo would like you to come down to the shop." John was elated; he finally thought that Herb needed him for something more than just the physical stuff. Here was his chance to prove that he too could think and add some insight about what they wanted to do with the money. He shouted back to the locked door that he would be right out. He slipped on his loafers and stuck a .45 caliber Glock model 36 into his shoulder holster. He thought that it made him look manly. The gun gave him confidence as it filled his need to prove that he was brave, strong, and courageous. He wanted to be seen as a man not to be taken lightly. Actually John was a coward and he knew it but the gun felt nice anyway. Erik took it off him with no trouble and John was relieved.

Shackled hands to ankles, sitting in the back seat of the Fiat coupe, John demanded his rights. Erik wasn't listening and just turned up the radio; Elton John was singing "Funeral for a Friend." All in all, it was a fine meeting of the foxes and hounds in Baum's little bookstore. Carlos and Baum sat there looking all glum while Erik and Santos told Herb Philbrick and John Shaft who they were why they were here, and where they were going. Neither of them said a word. In walked Mike, Pete, and Joe, and this time Herb could not control his diarrhea. He stuttered and stammered but could hardly utter an intelligible word. The only thing anyone could understand from him was, "You guys?" and "How?" John sat there totally confused; he didn't know anybody in this room but knew that he was in deep trouble. So was Herb, he soiled his pants. In walked the U.S. attorney from the consulate and a local dude from Interpol tagging along with some dignitary representing the Madrid Police Department. The room was crowded and smelled of feces, garlic, humidity, body odor, and hot rice, but no one paid it any mind. Herb and John were doing the most sweat work and Joe, Pete, and Mike loved every minute of it.

When all was said and done, arrests were made (a multi-twisted affair). All the stolen money was recovered (whisked away by chopper). Lloyds of London was elated (and why not?). Baum and Carlos were tossed into the cooler ("But you told me, yadda-yadda"). Beaufort Scotch & Byrnes were redeemed (yeah, right!). Global Asset Management Co. was compensated for their losses (rightfully so). Herb and John were sent to the federal lockup for prosecution (What goes around comes around, ya know?). Pignataro never got the thanks that were supposed to come from Herb. Raoul was an immediate sensation at Donahue Downs. The grass was green over Carol Manleys final resting-place. Joe, Mike, Pete, Santos, Charlie, the U.S. attorney, and two Spanish cops got bombed.

It was a Wednesday morning and I cranked open a bloodshot eye, wondering if I would ever drink again. The night before was a task of joviality, happiness, and thanks for a mission well done. I felt terrible; I HATED RED WINE. The party never ended: Pete was lying on the floor, Mike was on the couch snoring, and the U.S. attorney was lying in puke, which I think ruined his suit. The Spanish dudes were making breakfast like nothing happened and dammit, they looked all refreshed and raring to take on the next Captain Courageous task. I thought that I would hate them by now, but the eggs and stuff smelled good to me at that point. The bell rang and it was room service delivering some champagne ordered by someone late in the night. They set it up in the middle of the floor, making special arrangements not to step on anyone and they split quick, holding their noses.

I painfully rolled off the bed and fell on my butt. I was fully determined to show those Spanish cops that we gringos could handle our booze. My nose was running and I suffered a severe case of Montezuma's revenge. I washed my face and gargled while trying to make my diminishing crop of hair look fairly presentable. When I made my UN-triumphant return, I found Mike and Pete sipping the bubbly and slobbering over some kind of weird-looking egg omelet mess. I almost ran back to the bathroom, but managing a quip about ironclad stomachs and intestinal fortitude, I instead joined them for breakfast. It was time to think about going home.

We got no special recognition.

Didn't want or need it.

Flying with a severe hangover was the pits.

Pete retired from the FBI.

I walked the grass of Donahue Downs and felt lucky to be alive. I had found a place on this earth to call home and a place worthy of family, friends, and long-lasting relationships. I was indeed a very blessed man, but for what purpose, surely till this day eludes me. Lucy was getting long in the tooth but then again, so was I. Sandy and I still clicked on all eight cylinders and Barney wanted me to be his best man at his wedding. I was wondering if I had to give him Pre-Cana instructions. My son Chris wanted to buy us out of our business so that he could build some condos, but I lovingly told him, "I don't think so." Steve made Captain and was transferred to Iraq and so was Joe Jr., who was now a lieutenant. Both got shot, both came home, and both wanted to go back. These two were made of the stuff that made America proud. Rick slaved away, protecting his little bit of heaven without any help asked for or needed from me; I loved that man. And so, I walked my little path here in the greenery of Solebury, far removed from the grime of the Bronx. My cell phone rang; it was Sandy. I had another call from Bob Goodman. I told her that I was not available and would call him back soon.

CHAPTER NINE

Epilogue

T he gray stone walls of Dannamorra Prison were not con-
ducive to friendly chitchat. The general ambiance of the place
left much to be desired. The main culinary ingredient of each
meal was a mixture of bland, colorless, and tasteless. All there was to
do was read or work out in the weight room. Herb did not fit in well
with the others and neither did Phil Fauxmaster. Herb had never met
Phil before, but they had a lot in common. While playing their third
game of checkers, they discovered that the Lorenzo family played a
big part of each man's incarceration.

Firstly, Tony because Herb had watched the Falcone brothers
kill him and his wife Theresa in that hotel hallway. Because of that,
he had to delay his life for a year under the watchful eye of the FBI.
Secondly Mario, because Tony's esteemed son was Phil Fauxmaster's
supplier of illegal drugs. Phil was a major buyer and supplier to the
white-collar crowd. When McGuinnes killed him, Phil had no other
source of supply. When Sandy Grandly and Joe Donahue came into
his life it was the beginning of the end for him.

Herb said that meeting Joe and his friends at the hotel in Pennsylvania was the beginning of the end for him as well. They shared stories and marveled at how they missed meeting each other by only a few months back in New York City and Westchester.

Phil asked Herb whatever happened to his lifelong buddy John Shaft and Herb could only hang his head down in mock shame:

"John is houseboy for big Nicky Byrnes down on cellblock C; he doesn't want to know me anymore," Herb answered with a wry grin. "Just as well Phil, because the guy had no nerve and I had to pull him along every step of the way." Shaft was sentenced to three to seven for conspiracy. With good behavior, he would be free in thirty-six months. Phil and Herb had a few other things in common, and over the course of the next few months they would discover hope for a bright light in their future.

Both men were smart.

Both men had contacts outside the prison walls.

Both men had secreted large sums of cash unknown to any other person. But most important, both were lifers and would stop at nothing to live again in freedom.

Family, Friends and Enemies Alike

CHAPTER ONE

Down and Dirty

My mind is a wall of gray granite; it is impervious to any and all assaults from forces beyond my control. I have made a personal decision to not allow anyone to tell me what to do. I am in that place between sleep with constant nightmares and consciousness with a different kind of constant nightmare. I do not know which is the better of the two options. I am the quintessential rock that gathers no moss because the good things that I gathered were taken from me. I am a man without a home, a ship without a berth, and a spirit emptied of everything worthwhile. Although I am not dead, I dream daily of the day when that sweet mother of eternal rest visits me. She will end this daily humdrum existence of living in a vacuum, living with nothing, and trying to live with who I once was. I do not want to hear from anybody about anything. I am OK with where I am and what I am doing.

I want no visitors, I want no friends, and I want nothing other than the tonic that deadens my thoughts. I crave oblivion. I have regressed to a point that I think is well past the point of no return. I have no chance for spiritual redemption. If God dismisses me, I would nod my head in capitulation and say, "Yes, this is my just deserts." Hell cannot be worse than the torture that I am inflicting upon myself, so bring on the devil. He would probably deal with me better than I am dealing with myself at this point.

I toss and turn in the sweaty sheets after ten hours of drugged sleep. I find that I slept with one shoe on and my pants down around my knees. I know that I must have passed out at some point last night – again!

It can't be morning already, but the dog is whimpering to go out. It can't be morning, but the sun is blazing unwelcome rays of laserlike heat on my face. It can't be morning because my head is pounding and my stomach is gurgling against the abuse of last night. I am going to be sick, as usual.

My heart is stampeding and my coughing almost brings me to unconsciousness; I spit up a wad of phlegm. No trash basket, so it fell on the dirty floor. Movement is difficult, shaky, and hurtful. My ice-cold bare feet are rebelling against the cold dirty linoleum. I stepped in the phlegm. My ankles feel thick and numb; I am wobbling. There are pins and needles in all my extremities. My eyes hurt and they are crusted; it is difficult and painful to open them for my eyesight is blurry. My mouth is dry and my tongue feels like sandpaper. It doesn't seem to fit in my mouth and I am gagging. There is an overwhelming pressure in my stomach but I don't know which way the release is going to happen. I can taste the burning rancid stomach gasses forcing their way up my throat. I am going to puke. At the same time I feel the horrible onslaught of gases and pressure in my bowels screaming for release.

It can't be morning because I wanted to die last night. I wanted to cash in my chips then, but now I want that everlasting rest even more. I deserve it; I have earned it. This has to be the worst hangover I've ever had in my life, I can hardly move and just the act of thinking causes me utter distress.

Holding onto the bedroom door, I seek stability on buckling

knees but it doesn't happen. I crash to the floor puking my guts up where I lay. I pee my pants and the diarrhea is uncontrolled. I can't make it to the bathroom. I make a total mess complete with snot on my lip, tears on my face, and saliva pouring out of my mouth. I can only moan in utter despair. I hate myself.

The dog hid behind the couch in fear, confusion, or maybe sympathy; don't know, don't care. I can't move so I just lay there in the filth of my own excretions, my own addiction, and my own stupidity. Prostrate on the floor, my head in the unprocessed swill of last night's booze, my eyes pop open and my ears scream at my brain; I hear a siren in the distance. I know it's a fire truck because nobody would call an emergency unit just for a broken-down drunken neighbor — especially for this drunken neighbor. I haven't made any friends in this run down tenement here on Taylor Avenue in the Bronx. This is the ramshackle hovel that I now call home. The door is locked; the dog couldn't hold it any longer and as usual, the place is a stinking mess. Even the roaches moved on to better, more affluent apartment dwellers.

I wonder how far down I have to fall until I can fall no lower. I wonder when I will stop the self-made punishment for letting myself sink into this ongoing state of depression. The admitted embarrassment that I am who I am and that I am guilty of crimes, both real and imagined, keeps me in a never-ending spiral of defeat. I think that this is who I always was and knowing this is the shame of being me.

As I lay there, I realize not for the first time that I have allowed the past to ruin my present and compromise my future. I have set the mold and I cannot escape the chains of my own bondage. I have given up on life; I have given up on friends, family, and career, and now I am alone with my worst enemy, me. My heart is still pounding in my chest so I guess that I am still alive. I hope for a heart attack, a quick demise, but it doesn't happen. I am doomed to continue my spiral to disaster and self-degradation.

Just the way I want it and just the way I like it. At least, that's what I tell myself. I start to sob and I am not sure why.

Lying still, my mind does an instant replay to further the cause of personal destruction. I have made my defeated return to my roots, the Bronx. I have surrendered to powers beyond my control and I want nobody to tell me otherwise. I always knew that life was unfair; this is just the proof of it. What I am living now is testament of that misguided, albeit all-knowing, negative attitude. I allowed this mindset to control my present — I gave up and now I want to die.

How is a person supposed to shut down the mind other than daily anesthetizing it? If there is an answer somewhere, I ain't never heard it. I cannot forget where I was and I cannot forget what Sandy and I had accomplished together. But now it's all gone. Just thinking of her name causes me to weep in despair. I will never forget Sandy, the love of my life. She was the only reason that I stopped my craziness and became a man. She was taken from me in the blink of an eye. In my mind, I no longer needed to be anything other than what I was made to be: a drunken broken man, a bum of little value to anyone.

The fire took it all away and under a cloud of suspicion, I left Pennsylvania as an alcoholic millionaire widower. They said it was arson; the hotel was completely destroyed and they never found Sandy's body. I was the prime suspect.

Bob Goodman didn't believe it; neither did Barney, Israel Burns or Pete Richardson. Mike McCormick and Jim Dobson did their best to stand by my side through thick and thin. I was like a zombie and I shut them all out of my life. Even with all of their attempts at caring, I slipped away in the dark of night. I merely packed what meager belongings I wanted to take with me and left my car in Steve's driveway. I took Lucy, hired a cab, and took off for New York City and the Bronx. I disappeared into oblivion just like a coward. I was a man in shame and I could not face my friends or family. Here I was, killing myself with no food, gallons of booze, nightly horrific dreams, and a mind that would not stop.

That was three months ago and I notified the Pennsylvania DA of my new address. I did not want to appear like a fleeing felon, but I told them in no uncertain terms not to divulge my address to anyone. I also told them not to bother me unless they had an arrest warrant. I never heard from them and that suited me fine. I did not have a telephone installed; I didn't need one and I still didn't want one. I don't even check the mail.

I knew that Barney had moved back here as well, but I would not call him even if I knew where he was. I would not, and did not, call anyone — not any of my sons, my friends, or Steve, my son-in-law. I gave Mike McCormick unlimited power of attorney but I was smart enough to secrete a ton of money to support myself during my sojourn into personal dizzy-land: my trip into attempted alcoholic suicide. I took it in cash, spending money to be used as I saw fit until I died of alcohol poisoning or malnutrition.

Every other day I had these thoughts of victory in the face of defeat, but this caused me to herald in the idea with another slug of wine or beer or whatever else happened to be around. I let the thoughts go; I drowned them and wasted another day. The only thing that made me happy was that the Bodega was only a half block down the street; I got my butts and beer there. Sometimes, I even bought a sandwich.

I looked at the dog and realized that I was being terribly unfair to her. I couldn't punish her just because I wanted to punish myself. After halfway winning the battle of the mother of all hangovers this morning, I went to the pet store and bought a dog-shipping container. Took it home, boxed up poor confused Lucy, and sent her by private car to Steve and Sue using Mike McCormick's return address. It cost me five hundred dollars to do that but it made no difference to me. I could not take care of myself; there was no longer any semblance of an idea that I could properly care for the dog that I loved so much.

I was now more alone than I had been in the last six years or so. I had suffered mental and emotional overload; I had to work this out and knew that so far, I had been doing a lousy job of it. I didn't seem to be dead yet.

I sat at the war-worn metal table and rethought that last day, the last day that I spent as a whole man. I tried to stop these recollections from invading my mind, but I could not. Just like instant replay, the movie in my mind unfolded and, as usual, I cried real tears and looked for another beer.

CHAPTER TWO

Resurrection Day

Sandy and I had a wonderful evening with our friends and business was good at the hotel. It was a Friday night and aside from the normal "business as usual" snags of operating a busy hotel, there was no drama in our lives. Mike and Helen went home around ten and Sandy went upstairs around eleven. Barney and I talked and laughed a bit, getting plastered and enjoying every minute of it. It had been years since that happened and it was good to remember the things of our youth. We took a staggering walk out to the maintenance barn because Barney wanted to show me some new equipment that had finally arrived. This was his domain and he was proud of it. We took a half bottle of bourbon with us.

He showed me the new riding mowers, weed-whackers, trimmers, and an updated gasoline storage tank outside. I was chiding him about extravagances but he laughed at me reminding me of the tax write-off that our CPA told us we should start to use. I asked him why we now had medical-use oxygen tanks and he told me that it was a new law for hotels. We were supposed to be equipped for any emergency that a guest might have. The tanks were secured in a locked metal container outside the building. In it were the tanks for guests and some oxyacetylene setups used in the shop. In another bin nearby were the used and unused gas cans.

Stacked neatly behind a locked wire-mesh cage were the propane tanks used for temporary heat in the shop or sometimes when a barbecue was planned. Barney proudly showed me the Bucks County Fire Department inspection tag and it was dated only two days ago. We drank more, gassed up two mowers, and in our silliness, cranked them up so we could play bumper cars out on the back lawn. We stayed away from the hotel so we wouldn't cause a disturbance to the guests.

Barney got sick and was throwing up behind some rocks and I was laughing at him. When he came back looking all ashen and wiped out, I told him to go to bed and that I would secure the mowers and lock up. He staggered away and I was alone in the dark with two gurgling lawn mowers and a wee bit of the much-welcomed libations. They found me sleeping it off in the maintenance shed the next morning.

I had a very difficult time making sense out of what they were telling me but soon it came to light. At some time during the early morning hours, the hotel had suffered some sort of major explosion and devastating fire. All of the guests and staff were accounted for except for Sandy and me, who they had now found. Sandy was still missing.

What little information they could come up with during the next few days went like this: The fire started in the kitchen but none of the staff had arrived for work yet. One acetylene tank and an oxygen tank were missing from the storage bins. They found their shattered remains in the kitchen. All the bins were found still locked and the electrically controlled key-box had no fingerprints. It had been wiped clean. I was the only person with access since Barney had gone to bed and that was where they had found him. It was supposed that Sandy had gone down to the kitchen for some reason or another, the explosion happened, and she was immediately incinerated. No remains were found but they were still looking.

The cops and fire investigators from Philadelphia interrogated Barney and I for days. But like the story goes: "The truth will set you free." We told the same story because that was what happened; we had gotten bombed, plain and simple. I had apparently passed out in the garage after moving one mower inside. It had a nice shiny dent on the fender where I guess I crashed into the doorframe. The dents matched and the other mower was found on the back lawn out of gas with the key in the run position. The bottle of bourbon was found near where I was sleeping on some old boxes and that was that for that. I had nothing more to add and neither did Barney.

We had no body to bury and we all held on to a glimmer of hope that somehow Sandy was still alive. The local pastor officiated at some sort of "closure" service, but it only served to deepen my depression and sense of loss.

The hotel needed drastic renovations, so in my despair I just closed up shop and walked away, leaving Mike McCormick and his wife Helen to handle all the details. The investigation was ongoing and I think I had been drunk ever since.

The dream came in the middle of the night to visit my fears and tell me the truth of the lies that I live. As I lay there in that sweaty bed, I felt that my body was in some sort of electrified aura-like thing that I didn't understand. The hair on the back of my neck was bristling and I had goose bumps on my arms. I opened my eyes in wonder and awe; something was happening here. It started with a whispered thought from a place outside of the physical realm. I knew that Sandy was alive! It was some kind of inner knowledge from who knows where. I bolted upright in bed as if she were in the room. I croaked out the words, "Sandy isn't dead and neither am I!"

I could sense her, smell her, and feel her but I saw nothing in the room other than the mess that I had created. It may have been my brain swimming in a sea of poison and I knew that I was drunk, but I thought that I heard her telling me to come to her rescue.

I tried to make sense out of the various shades of darkness in the room. I hoped to see her; I hoped that she really was there with me and that my life had been a nightmare up until now. My mind, or maybe it was my shattered emotions, whispered to me that she was trapped in a place of danger. Maybe it was the wind whisking the tattered curtains, but I could swear that I heard her voice.

I ventured to speak to this unseen entity in audible terms. I wailed her name and I cried in desperation. I told her that I loved her. I asked her for clues. I asked her for direction and I begged her to tell me where she was. All I heard in return was my sobbing and the labored sound of my own breathing. I suffered no hallucinations and heard no real-time voices; it was 3 a.m. and I was shaking, salivating, and sweating.

I cradled my face into my hands and let out a primal scream of total despair. I sobbed and wailed at the unjust turn of events that had come against my family and me. I knew that I had been doing this just about every day. I asked God for death but only heard my own voice telling me that she was alive. I knew it was not probable and not possible. This was wishful thinking, feeding myself further anguish to fuel the misery of my total emptiness. I told myself that I was drunk and I probably still was.

Sunlight interrupted my craziness once again and I cranked open my bloodshot baby-blue eyes. I thought about what had happened to me during the night and knew that Sandy and I totally loved each other and we had a karmic connection that transcended time and space. I felt that in some way, she had communicated with my spirit in the power of our shared love. I shook my head in dismay and wondered if any of this could be true. My metaphysical thoughts were interrupted because somebody was pounding on the door.

I was Joe Donahue, the proprietor of Donahue Downs in Solebury, Pennsylvania. I was a wealthy man and I was a man in ruins. Whoever it was would not stop pounding on the door. I said, "Go away, I ain't interested," but the pounding only got louder. I knew that I looked terrible, I would allow no person to see me in this condition. I shouted again to the door of my great fear: "Go away, I won't open the door and I don't care who you are."

It was Barney. He said, "Joe, open this friggin' door or I'll kick it down." He stopped me dead in my tracks; there was nothing I could think to say. I don't believe that there was any other person on earth that I would have allowed into my dungeon of personal despair but Barney and I had both been here before. I reluctantly unlocked the door. He walked in and smiled at me.

"Geesh Joe, do ya want me to shoot ya?" He was trying to be light but I wasn't buying. I was in my skivvies and dirty tee shirt, so I just sat on the bed looking like what I felt like, crap. Barney sat next to me. I threw up on the floor. He put his arm around my shoulder and told me that nothing was gonna happen in this life that could separate our friendship.

"Joe, we are going to make this right somehow; I loved Sandy too, ya know." He told me that I wasn't doing anybody any good living like this and that Sandy would want me to stand on my feet and face reality.

"Joe, you stink, get into the shower. From there we are getting some food and you are moving out of this dump today. I got a two-bedroom pad over on University Avenue and we are now embarking on what both of us have done a thousand times before for each other. This is the rebuilding process Joe, and like YOU told me a zillion times in the past, I will not accept no for an answer."

What could I say? What could I do? I took a shower!

When I came out, Barney had already put my junk into a box and packed up what clean clothes I had left. He said that we would come back tomorrow to finish cleaning and packing but for all intents and purposes, today was sayonara for this dump. He said that he had a lot to tell me and I needed to get straight fast. He took me to The Thruway diner over in New Rochelle and I couldn't shake the thought that we were so close to where Sandy and I had first met.

Barney ordered two plates of poached eggs on toast, tomato juice, and coffee. He wanted to talk to me and he said that he had important stuff to tell me. It was only 11 a.m., too early for me to think; I waved him off for now. Nothing made sense, my head was swimming, I was dizzy, and my guts felt like a cement mixer. I really tried to eat but I had the shakes and I was still in a mental fog; I couldn't understand what he was trying to tell me.

My stomach couldn't hold the food and I had to run to the john to puke again. I wanted to be angry with someone but there was no way it could be Barney. I wished that Tommy McGuinnes were still alive so I could hunt him down and pummel him again, but I was fresh out of enemies. The only one I could vent my anger on was myself and I had been doing that for the last four months. Somewhere down deep I was thinking that I really had caused that fire somehow. My hands were shaking uncontrollably and I spilled coffee on my shirt. We left the diner but Barney almost had to carry me to the car. Whatever it was that he wanted to tell me would have to wait until some other time. I couldn't eat, couldn't talk without crying, and all I felt was shame and emptiness.

Barney took me to his rented apartment on University Avenue near the corner of Kingsbridge Road. This was probably one of the last of the upscale old-style high-rise apartment buildings left in the north Bronx. It still had an elevator operator and night watchman in the lobby — amazing! He told me that the rent was ridiculous, but he wanted to be here and he needed to find me. Barney was driving Sandy's burgundy Jaguar still with the Pennsylvania plates.

Barney gave me some sort of pill and I nodded off on his couch. I could barely hear him using the phone. I didn't care who he was talking to so I just allowed the warmth of sleep to overcome me. I awoke around 5 p.m. because they were poking me. Barney had company: some guy older than dirt, which I thought, meant that he was two years younger than I was. His name was Dr. John Bagdonis and he was a retired New York City police surgeon; I called him Dr. Feelgood and tried to tell him to get lost.

He talked to me, asked a lot of questions, and did a lot of probing, jabbing, and neurological testing. Yeah, right there in

Barney's living room he did a colon examination and a ball squeeze. He took blood, a blood pressure test, and a urine sample too. I thought of the AIDS patient I had once tended to so I just shut my mouth and let it happen. Barney was chuckling.

Doctor Feelgood (or was his name Dr. No or Dr. Zhivago or Dr. Death, I couldn't remember; maybe he was Dr. Frankenstein) told me that I hadn't managed to totally burn out my health past the point of no return yet. He gave me a few injections of vitamins, a flu shot, and some other stuff that I couldn't remember. He told Barney to get me into a sauna every day for a week followed by a dip into a whirlpool and then a massage. The pills were to be taken every day and no booze — ever again!

He wrote out a diet for me and told Barney that it must be followed to the letter without fail. I hated diets, I hated medicine, and I hated doctors almost as much as I hated criminals and lawyers, which sometimes I thought were the same people. But most of all, I hated anyone telling me what I had to do. I wanted a drink but hid that idea from them. I just said that I would do what they thought I should do, but I was not sure why. I told Barney and the doc that without Sandy in my life, I was a man without purpose. I felt empty and alone and did not want to continue living like this. I opted to go out the way I wanted and didn't see any reason that anyone should try to stop me.

Then Barney hit me with a bombshell: "Joe, Sandy is alive."

I couldn't help it, emotion overcame me, and I sobbed like a baby. My dream was becoming reality and I could almost see Sandy standing in the room with us. She seemed to have tears in her eyes. I started blabbing nonsense interspersed with my questions, my hopes, and my fears: "How do you know this? Where is she? How did she escape the fire? Who did this to us? How did you find me? What can we do about it?" I said all these things mixed with spit, tears, and sweat, but I went on and on with a voice that was cracked and damaged by booze, nutritional neglect, and depression.

Barney dug out a small package from his pocket and handed it to me. I opened it and saw Sandy's wedding ring. It was not damaged by fire and I knew that she never took it off.

Barney shook the doctor's hand and thanked him. "No payment due Barn; I remember our past too buddy. You're a good man and so is Joe, so take care of Donahue and let me know if you need anything else." With that, he was gone with his little bag of torture devices under his arm. I was relieved.

Barney made coffee while I got dressed. I was still shaking but I knew that the food and medicine was going to work; I would be OK, I needed to be OK. I had a reason to live once again.

CHAPTER THREE

The Mission

I spent a week in Barney's care, and with each new day I grew stronger and more filled with resolve to find Sandy and bring her home. Barney fed me more rabbit food and dead steers than a man was supposed to eat, but he assured me that we were following the doctor's orders to the letter. The yogurt and cod-liver oil were especially disgusting to me. The medicines and vitamins made me urinate something like battery acid for a while, but I figured that it was just the booze purging from my body a little bit at a time. Dr. Feelgood called Barney and told him that all my blood tests came back OK but my cholesterol was through the roof. The urine test told the doc that my liver was in questionable condition. I played the obedient patient and Barney didn't have to bust on me too much. Eventually after a few days of recuperation, my brain started to function fairly normally.

Barney told me what he knew of the story: It seemed that two weeks ago, an unexpected package was delivered to Mike McCormick at the hotel. He and Helen were staying there while the clean up and investigation crews were digging around. Mike was the addressee on the package and it was delivered by a private messenger service. Mike checked back to the Messenger Company in Philly but it was a dead end. They were paid in cash and the receipt had a bogus return address. The only thing the dispatcher remembered about the guy was that he was a young European guy with a thick accent.

"There was a note, Joe, and it said that we had to find you and get you back to Pennsylvania in three weeks. They said that they would be in touch and that we shouldn't tell the cops about this; we were to just sit tight until then. That's what we did and so far there has been no further communications. Joe, you gotta come back to the Downs with me, the three weeks are up the day after tomorrow. Mike and I need you to help sort this out."

I knew that something was about to happen and Barney was right: I had to get back up to speed fast and I had to return to Donahue Downs right away.

All totaled, I was lost in the Bronx for three months and two weeks. Barney was searching for me for a couple of months until finally Mike got my address from the cops and handed it off to him. We settled up with the landlords, packed up the car, and headed south back to my real home in Pennsylvania. My head was swimming with all sorts of possibilities but I was so filled with medications and good food that I slept for most of the trip. I kept thinking how little we had to bring back home. I had accumulated nothing while there and had worn out what little I had brought with me. Barney's stuff was neat as a pin and I thought about how much we both had changed. It wasn't all that long ago that I dragged him out of a similar situation and we pulled a lot of strings to save his job. When I awoke, I was staring at the front gates of Donahue Downs.

Mike met us at the residence quarters and he didn't bat an eye about how I looked. I knew that my face was bloated and my skin had a sallow appearance. He gave me a gigantic bear hug and told me that he was happy to see me again. In my mind I thought that Mike was a man of class and a great guy to call a friend. He was also one tough cookie. Barney wanted to play mother hen and insisted that I take a seat on the porch with Mike as he unloaded the car. I wasn't buying into that; I wanted the accelerated course in this rebuilding process so the three of us did the job all in one trip. I gotta admit though, I did get tired quickly bringing the two boxes upstairs to my quarters, the quarters that Sandy and I had called our oasis. We met again back down on the porch and this time we sat for a couple of cups of coffee and some "bring me up to speed" talks.

Mike assumed his businesslike demeanor and gave me the bare unvarnished facts about all that transpired since I had split the scene. It went like this:

The cops and fire investigators did not find any human remains at the fire scene. They thought that Sandy took off, maybe with another man.

They also thought that Sandy might have started the fire as a ruse to cover her tracks.

They could not pin the arson on anybody yet, but I was still the prime suspect.

The insurance company would not pay on the policy until the police investigation was complete.

All of the staff had been interrogated and cleared of any suspicion. Everyone employed at the Downs was given two weeks salary and let go until further notice.

There was enough money in the accounts to cover rebuilding but right now there was a demolition company clearing out the debris. We still had assets, the courtesy limousine fleet was untouched, and the land was mortgage free.

The maintenance shed and all the goodies there were not damaged except for the stolen oxygen and acetylene tanks and one slightly dented mower.

The main residence quarters suffered no damage and its kitchen, with all the utilities, was still working.

The fire investigators thought that the oxygen and acetylene tanks were slowly opened inside a cabinet under one of the counters to trap the gasses. When the coffee urn automatically turned on, it created the ignition to cause the explosion. The wires were rigged. Those gases, combined into a small space and then ignited, caused a bomblike explosion setting fire to the cooking oil that was set up for the morning buffet. Traces of gasoline were also indicated in the residue. The smoke alarms and sprinkler system had been turned off and shut down.

The FBI seized the company books for over six weeks but found no discrepancy and no financial shenanigans. They were OK with the money that I had taken with me to the Bronx and didn't see it as a big deal. Apparently the feds had been watching me self-destruct up there in the Bronx but left me alone in my misery.

Mike said that the destruction of the hotel was as big a mystery to him as it was to everyone else but when Sandy's ring was delivered, the whole scene took on new meaning: "Joe, this is some sort of revenge, I can feel it."

I asked Mike and Barney if they knew where Johnny the bartender was and Barney said that he was working in some tourist trap down in New Hope. They told me that Raoul disappeared and they thought that he went back to Madrid. Everyone else was scattered around; most had found jobs, and others were unemployed.

After a walk around the fire scene and thoroughly depressing myself, I asked about our liquid assets. Mike assured me that I was still a very rich man and could walk away from all this with no problem. "That is not my nature, Mike," I responded and he said that he knew that.

I had a few requests and I rattled them off like a freight train gone amok: "Mike, use your connections and find out whatever happened to Vito Scaglionne. Barney, get Johnny outta that tourist-trap ginmill and tell him that he is back working here at the Downs; he is a stand-up guy. Tomorrow, we track down Raoul — something bothers me about that guy."

I was feeling better and better with each passing day and once again felt energized to become a man with purpose, a man on a mission, and a man with an overwhelming desire to live. I wanted my wife back home and I would allow nothing to get in my way.

A small gray car came into the driveway and parked in the semicircle right in front of us. Pastor Phil from the New Hope Pentecostal Assembly Church walked up to me and thanked me for deciding to fight against my personal demons. Barney and Bob Goodman told him about me leaving in a state of desperation and he started a daily prayer circle on behalf of Sandy and me. He said that although he had only met me twice, he knew that God's hand was on my shoulders and indeed on my destiny. Barney wanted to rattle off his favorite Bible quote from Paul's Epistle to the Romans but I told him that I knew it by heart now. I had been listening to him for years on that score and agreed that it worked just the way he said it would. Phil smiled at me, shook my hand, and told me that it was good to see prayers answered. He said, "Welcome back home, Mr. Donahue." Phil had a cup of coffee with us, shared some small talk, but had to hit the road on his daily ministry visiting some shut-ins. He left with a smile and a handshake.

At the same moment that Phil slammed his car door a cell phone rang. We all looked; it was over in the corner of the porch. I was closest and picked it up trying to hand it off to whoever owned it. Both Mike and Barney shrugged their shoulders so I pressed the button and said hello.

Sandy spoke the words that will forever live in my heart: "I love you, Joe. I'm OK. Vito Scaglionne wants to talk to you." The phone was snatched from her hand and I had the dubious honor of speaking to the devil incarnate.

"Good day to you, Mr. Donahue. I'm glad to find that you have decided to crawl out of the beer bottle. Sit tight, nothing will happen to your wife unless you screw up. I will be in touch with you in a few days via email. Do not tell anyone about what is going on except those two friends of yours sitting across the table from you." The phone went dead.

One of the construction workers put away his cell phone and

continued to work with the Demolition Company clearing out the fire scene. He was an associate of a shady man in Spain known as Pedro. I asked Barney and Mike who owned this cell phone but neither of them knew. Both of them thought it was mine and I thought it was one of theirs. It was just lying on a small table in the corner of the porch. I had the fleeting thought that Pastor Phil put it there but told myself that it could not be so.

Pedro's man got into his pickup truck and drove off the property before we could add two and two. The boss on the demo job later told us that a construction company associate — an unsavory character — asked him to take this guy on as a favor. He said that he owed the guy and hired the unknown worker on the spot with no background investigation at all. I fired him and told him to get his men and equipment off my property. We couldn't tell the cops any of this but we scared the crap out of the contractor.

CHAPTER FOUR

Devious Caper

Raoul was a man with a shady past and a bright future. He had made it to the U.S. and was overwhelmed with gratitude and respect toward his benefactors. He worked hard as the chef at Donahue Downs and increased his knowledge and talents. He was all that Joe, Sandy, Mike, and Barney had hoped that he would be. His menu preparations were par excellence and he always had a clean appearance. His work visa led to a green card and he was studying hard for the citizenship test. He was earning a great salary, had his own car, and a nice little apartment on Bridge Street in New Hope. He was taking courses in English at the local community college, had a growing bank account, and a cute little American girlfriend whom he called "Fluff." The American dream had become a reality for him and life couldn't be better. Raoul was a happy man until the knock on the door a few months ago.

Raoul didn't know who it could be and greeted the stranger with curiosity. He was forced to allow him inside because his visitor said; "Greetings from Madrid, Raoul, Pedro, Mr. Baum, and Carlos send you their best wishes." Raoul was stunned with disbelief. The past had caught up to him but he hadn't as yet learned just how devastating it was to be. The man pushed him onto the couch, pointed a gun at him, and told him to listen with both ears. They spoke Spanish but the gist of what was said went like this:

"Back in Madrid, you were a two-bit hood and drug mule. You worked for my compatriot, a man whose name is Pedro. The American CIA used you as a double agent in a few small-time capers and your contact to them was a Mr. Santos. We trusted you Raoul, but then again, so did Mr. Santos. The truth is Raoul, you were a rat, and nobody likes a rat. Pedro knew what you were doing but you never hurt him so he allowed you to live until someone else killed you. You were caught in a no-win situation when Santos offered you a way out and a chance for a new life. You took that opportunity and sent our friends Mr. Baum and Carlos to jail for a very long time. We do not think too kindly on that, Raoul, and now it is time for you to pay for your sins. If you do what we need you to do, you just may live and we will not kill your mother and sister in Madrid. By the way, they are still confused about your disappearance."

Raoul was trapped and he knew it. He thought about telling the FBI about this meeting but knew that his family would be killed before anything could be done to save them. He agreed to do as ordered and set up the fire at the hotel and the kidnapping of Sandy Donahue. He was told to wait for the right opportunity but only given two weeks to carry it out.

That fateful Friday evening when he saw that Mr. Donahue and his friend Barney were getting drunk, he knew that this was the time to strike. After closing down the kitchen that night, he hid on the premises until Joe and Barney went out to the maintenance shed. He then called Sandy on the phone, told her that Mr. Donahue was in the kitchen drunk and acting belligerent. He asked her if she would come down and help take him back to the apartment. Sandy walked across the back lawn toward the rear entrance to the kitchen but she never made it. Raoul grabbed her and put a chloroform rag over her face until she fell into unconsciousness. He had already rigged the wires needed to ignite his bomb and disabled the alarms and sprinklers.

He couldn't have been luckier; Donahue passed out in a drunken stupor in the garage and Barney went to bed. Raoul was in good condition; he had merely climbed over the fence and tossed the two tanks to the ground. He carried them over to the hotel rear entrance and nobody was the wiser. He was home free. He crammed Mrs. Donahue into the backseat of his car and made the call from his cell phone. He met Pedro's hired thug at the deserted rest area on I-95 where he transferred his benefactor's wife into the hands of the enemy. He went home and got some rest. All hell would break out soon and he had to be ready.

Raoul arrived for work at about four-thirty in the morning as he always did. The fire was roaring at that time and the local fire department was losing the battle to save the hotel. He helped care for the guests and worked along with the other employees trying to save what they could from fire damage. He played the game and he played it well. He was interviewed by the police with all of the other employees, gave his statement, and was allowed to go home. Three days later, he was called by Mike McCormick to come in for a meeting with everyone else. Even though he was told by the police and fire investigators to be available for further questions, he picked up his two weeks pay, withdrew his savings from the bank, and disappeared. It was assumed that he had gone back to Madrid. The police looked for him but found no trail. He was marked as a "person of interest" and was not forgotten.

Raoul got a phone call. He was told to go back to the rest area and wait for a man who would give him some cash and an airplane ticket back to Madrid: "Midnight tonight Raoul, and don't be late." Inwardly Raoul was happy; he knew that his talks with the police would soon grow a lot more in-depth than they had been and he really had no alibi to account for his time. Other hotel workers knew that his car was on the property well after quitting time.

Pedro called from Madrid and passed the message to his associate in Philadelphia that the best kind of rat was a dead rat.

Sandy was taken to a hideout where all of her needs were tended to and she was treated well, at least until the plan was set in motion. Four days after the fire and her kidnapping, she was injected with a drug that simulated death. With forged documentation and a phony grieving spouse, her coffin was loaded on an airplane at Philadelphia International Airport. Destination, Madrid! From there, and unbeknownst to any person except her captors, she was driven to a mountainside winery on the foreboding slopes of the Pyrenees Mountains. She was now the prisoner of Mr. Vito Scaglionne, international crime creep extraordinaire and the master of illusion. When she awoke, he greeted her with his usual display of phony European elitism and culture sprinkled with false egalitarianism:

"Ah, Mrs. Donahue, so good to see you awake and in good spirits. I intend you no harm. You will be well cared for while you are our guest and your slightest wish will be obeyed short of setting you free. I apologize for the manner in which you have been treated until now, but we both know that you would not come here of your own accord. As you know, I have an unpleasant matter to settle with your husband and Mr. McCormick resulting from my visit to your hotel in Pennsylvania. I am sorry but you are the bait, they are the prey, and I am the trapper. My associates and I are sorely upset about that sting operation and our business suffered greatly because of it. We intend to exact our pound of flesh, so to speak."

With that, he offered Sandy coffee, which she promptly refused. Sandy tried valiantly to tell Vito that they were helpless in that scheme and that they did not organize it. She tried to come up with all kinds of excuses and reasons but Vito would hear none of it. He waved her off to silence, breaking his false-friendly demeanor with a scowl. Sandy was terrified. She thought that she would be killed here; she thought she would never see her family again. Scaglionne took his leave and a chambermaid came into the room who told her that she would be her ongoing servant and guard. Her name was Gertrude and she was a Nordic bodybuilder, complete with tattoos and nose ring. Gertrude asked Sandy to call her Gert and said that she wanted to be friendly. All Sandy had to do was obey the rules and there would be no problems.

Gert attached a tracking device ankle bracelet to Sandy and told her that she was free to walk the grounds of this walled and guarded estate. She would be watched constantly and would be shot if she attempted to escape. The mere appearance of Gert scared Sandy but she was determined to find a way to triumph over this crazy and terrifying situation. Sandy asked Gert exactly where she was but Gert told her that she would not answer any questions for her: "We know that you are hungry, Mrs. Donahue; you haven't eaten in two days. Dinner is on the way up, but from now on you will dine with the rest of us living here."

Sandy took a shower, changed clothes, and cried where prying eyes could not see her. She ate, she had to; she was starving and she was sick with worry. She looked out of the window and saw nothing but snowy mountains. She was a long way from Solebury.

In bed that same night three months ago, Sandy closed her eyes with the prayer of those with no hope: "Joe, oh my precious Joe. I love you and need you more now than ever before. Find me Joe, save your life, save mine, and somehow let's rebuild our family." For Sandy, it was a prayer in the night, words said with eyes closed and goose bumps on flesh. For Joe, (he was in the Bronx at the time) it was a hell of a lot more real.

Mike, Joe, and Barney were aghast. They were deluged with overwhelming thoughts, ideas, and questions to each other. Right off the bat, they knew that Joe had been watched by more than just the FBI while he was in the Bronx. Scaglionne knew he was here at Donahue Downs and that he had arrived only a few hours ago. Mike called the regional headquarters of the FBI in Philadelphia knowing that he no longer had any viable contacts with them. He was trying to find out the disposition of Vito Scaglionne and would ask after Raoul if he got the chance. His queries were rebuffed and he could not divulge any of the new information to them so he had to keep it light.

He clicked off and after some discussion; it was decided to call Pete Richardson who was once in charge of that office. Pete had opened up a small local attorney at large office in Binghamton, New York and specialized in divorce and slip-and-fall cases. He hated what he was doing, but it paid the bills, kept him sober, and life was, well, I guess he would say that life was so-so. Yes, he was bored to tears and would welcome hearing from his old compatriots.

Joe picked up the phone and started to dial when Mike grabbed the base and shut down the call: "Joe, you are the primary suspect in the arson case; you can bet your life that this phone is tapped." Joe looked at Mike, shook his head, and Barney produced a brand new store-bought throwaway cell phone: "Yeah Joe, we gotta think of everything, ya know?" Mike made the call; he and Pete had long ago devised a code speak and since nobody wanted to take any chances whatsoever, the conversation would not be understood by any possible eavesdroppers. At 7:30 p.m., the three of them would meet Pete Richardson at the Ferris wheel ticket booth in Hershey Park in Hershey, Pennsylvania. They weren't followed. They used Mike's weather-beaten Saab and the three of them were now legally armed.

The state police found Raoul's car in the rest area on route 95 just south of Morristown, New Jersey. Two severed hands were found on the front seat. Cradled in this bloody mess of hamburger, they found a dead rat. The rest of the body was not found. The forensics guys found human hair and traces of saliva on the back seat but that was all. Eventual lab examination proved this trace evidence belonged to Sandy Donahue. The prints from the hands belonged to Raoul. This information was passed down to the FBI as well as the local police investigating the fire and missing person report on Mrs. Donahue. They all knew that this case was getting legs. Raoul had become a major suspect but they also knew that he would not be found alive. They were right! Raoul's remains were now part of the concrete infra-structure under the new bridge crossing Lahaska Creek. Pedro had accomplished what his associate Vito Scaglionne had asked him to do. Vito was happy with him and glibly commented, "Thank you for lend-ing a hand, Pedro." They both snickered at the irony and hung up two phones, Vito in the Pyrenees and Pedro in Madrid. They were a mere two hundred miles apart, but they had an associate right there in Donahue Downs, thousands of miles away. It was time to bring him back home; his part of the job was complete.

CHAPTER FIVE

Heroes, Villains and Walls

All the phones were removed except the one in Vito's office; only he and Gert were allowed in there. They had the only keys and the windows to this room were locked. Sandy had been an unwilling guest here for a couple of weeks now and she found that Gert and Scaglionne had told her the truth; she was treated well – for a prisoner that was.

Sandy walked the perimeter of the grounds often. She would follow the wall and search for a way out without getting shot. Any place she saw a weakness, a low part of the wall, or a doorway, she would find an armed guard with a radio and usually a dog by his side. She would just stroll by with a friendly greeting, noticing that the dog never wagged its tail; it just stared at her. Its glare would usually send shivers down her spine and she knew that she would not want to have one of those dogs chasing her. The guards would not talk to her; like the dogs, they just stared at her until she left their area.

As far as Sandy could tell, the large stone house was very old, but like the grounds, it had been well cared for. In her own way, she tried to look innocuous but she was forever probing, forever testing, and forever seeking a glitch in the security. She would use the library often and from time to time help out in the kitchen. She would do anything to kill the boredom and try to stop worrying about her husband and family back in Solebury. Sandy didn't know about the fire or any of the events that led to her kidnapping. She only assumed that Raoul had something to do with it because he made that call to her and here she was.

One day Sandy stole a knife from the kitchen, but Gert was on to her in less than half an hour. Gert was angry, as she pushed Sandy to the bed and tied her up. She demanded to know where the knife was and would not untie her until she had it.

Sandy gave up the knife easily because she knew that a knife would not be her weapon of choice anyway. Gert told her that kitchen utensils were counted after each meal and not to try it again. Untied once more, she was locked in her room for two days as punishment. Amongst Vito's latent talents and abilities, he knew how to run a jail; he had had a lot of experience.

Sandy had nothing to do but think, pace the floor, and stare out of the window to a place that she did not know. She gathered what she knew into her mind and made a mental checklist and inventory of facts. She had seen a Spanish newspaper downstairs so she assumed that she was not in the United States. Judging by the Snowcapped Mountains, she figured that she was not in South America. She was either in Portugal or Spain and that knowledge wasn't much of a comfort to her. Sandy did not know much of the geography of either nation for her to determine by the mountains where she was. She also thought that the armed guards near the wall and gates did not speak English but she wasn't sure about that.

She made a mental note to really try some communication with one of them on her next trip out for a walk. She thought of those dogs and she knew that it would be more difficult to deal with them; animals obey without question or emotion. They would do what they were trained to do. "The dog must die first!" was her first thought. If she were to escape this place, it would have to be done at night, unseen, and the dogs must be silenced.

Sandy looked deeply into her soul and found that she still possessed the abilities she would need to act independently and beat Scaglionne at his own game. As she paced the floor in her room of solitary confinement she would silently utter words. She formulated them on silent lips but engraved them into her heart. Wisdom, courage, bravery, intelligence, patience, manipulation, and perception were the first thoughts that she had. She sat on the bed to rethink each word in depth. After a few moments almost in a fugue state, Sandy knew that there was an ability that she lacked and that was the killer instinct. Scaglionne had it, as did her husband and Barney too. Most of those cretins that were at the mobster's ball at Donahue Downs had it also, but she knew that she could not pull the trigger to snuff out a human life. In self-defense maybe, but as an assassin lurking behind a rock, never.

Almost in tears, this truth of her character traits initially seemed like a fault.

"How will I ever get out of here if I can't fight my way out?" she wondered. There was a voice in her heart that told her that her love for truth, peace, and life itself was strength, it was not a weakness. She exuded trust and nobility of carriage to all that she met. In most situations people took to Sandy right off. She had an intangible aura that transmitted power. Her inner spirit conveyed to all: "I will never hurt you; you can trust me." Most persons were quick to accept Sandy, quick to loosen up, and if necessary, they would be quickly won over by her. This was an essential tool that she used in the business world and brought her much success in her endeavors. When Sandy walked into a business meeting or a room full of strangers, it had been said that she had a "presence."

Using her real personality to win in this imprisoned scenario would be one for the books, even for her. She formulated her plan and made up her mind; Sandy would beat them with no shots fired. Sandy discovered that she had the courage of Samson but prayed that she would have the wisdom of Solomon to use it wisely. She knew that she had the will to live and the brains to beat Scaglionne at his own game. Sandy knew that somehow she would prevail.

Gert finally opened the door and apologized for the needed punitive measures. Sandy told her that she understood and would not give them any more trouble. They smiled at each other and Sandy saw cold eyes in a false face trying to camouflage a blackened heart of stone. Gert looked away and Sandy knew that she was weak of spirit but strong in physique. This made her dangerous because Gert would kill before crying and stomp your face into the ground before she would kneel to pray. Sandy sensed that this person was capable of torture and had probably done it before. She resolved to stay on Gert's good side until it was no longer possible. Then, like the dogs, she too would have to be silenced.

Another uneventful week passed and Sandy was busy bringing the tools for her plan together. While working in and around the kitchen she found some rat poison in amongst the various cleaners and utensils. She thought that this could prove useful to her as part of her escape plans; she helped herself to a small portion of it and put it into a plastic bag. As time wore on, she eventually had about a half-pint of poison but dared not take any more as it may be noticeable. She hoped it would be enough to put down a full-grown German Shepherd. She kept this kernel-looking substance hidden between her mattress and box spring. The night of her planned departure, she would take a raw hamburger from the kitchen and mix up her delicacy for the watchdog. Sandy knew that the dog would suffer greatly before dying but there was little she could do about that; rat poison was all that she could get her hands on.

That part of the plan on hold for now, Sandy would next try to establish a rapport with the guard near the low spot on the wall. She had a particular guy in mind because one day he smiled at her and she smiled back. She had to admit to herself that her plan had not really been finalized in her mind. She figured that mostly she would be playing this by ear. All she had to do was get to a town she thought; from there she would find the local authorities and the rest would all fall into place. Well, at least that was what she thought. Gert was still a formidable blockade to her and Sandy knew that she would have to come up with some way of slipping away unnoticed.

Pete was the first to arrive at the ticket booth so he bought some popcorn from a vendor and leaned on a wall to wait. He hadn't allowed his physical condition to deteriorate since retirement and he felt good. Popcorn was one of the few treats that he allowed himself and he had cut down on the booze dramatically. His cell phone rang; it was Mike. They were just outside parking the car and would be there in a few minutes. Pete strolled over to the wall that overlooked the parking lot and wondered which of those moving specks down there were his friends. In a few minutes, he saw three men walking with purpose and he realized that it was Mike, Barney, and Joe.

Pete watched from this vantage point to be sure that his friends were not followed. He watched further as Mike fell away from the other two and hung back to watch the parking lot; they too wanted to be sure that they were not followed. Pete called Mike on the cell and told him that he was watching from the wall and as far as he could tell they had no tag-along. "C'mon in, Mike," and like an orchestrated maneuver out of a military textbook, the four of them met by the ticket booth, arriving from three different directions.

Greetings all around, Pete made no mention of any of the bad stuff that he had already heard. He noted Joe's apparent detoxifying appearance and he felt badly for him but said not a word. Pete wanted to listen without comment so they all walked over to this little tented catering place and sat with their backs to a man-made forest. Mike brought them all up to speed as far as he could. He ended the story with questions put to Pete, the ex-major of the FBI, his old boss.

"Pete, we need answers," said Mike and Pete felt like a man in a cement mixer. On the one hand, he knew and loved Joe's wife Sandy and felt badly for what happened to them, but also knew that he had no right to compromise an ongoing federal investigation. Pete had to take a moment for some inward reflection and to ponder all of the hypocrisy that he had witnessed in the past. He remembered all of the cases that were built on trumped-up charges just to put the real bad guy in the slammer. He knew that justice was really only what was true in the court of last resort. Pete had witnessed the "Rule of Law" casually dumped into the trashcan in order to bring the bad guys to justice. Witness and evidence tampering were the least of it, the thought being that if the perp got his due, then the ends justified the means. This time, Pete knew the truth but he had to prove it. He projected in his mind that whatever he did in assisting Joe Donahue would someday come to light and he wanted to be sure that his actions and those of his comrades would stand the scrutiny of legal investigation. This time, his license to practice law was at stake and this was the last time for him to take a stand for the truth if he had the guts to do so.

Failure to play by the rules could put them all in jail and Pete took it upon himself to build in every possible legal safeguard. Pete knew that this was his opportunity to stand for the truth for Joe Donahue and he needed to do that as payment. Not so much for Joe and his wife, but for his comrades-in-arms left on that stinking burying ground in Vietnam. Pete looked into Joe's eyes and he hid the tears; both of them did: "I'm with you all the way guys; I have never in my life been associated with a finer bunch of men than you three. I'll make some inquiries and I will get the information; I have strings yet to be pulled."

Pete called his associate in Binghamton, told him to keep a lid on his ongoing cases and only to call him in emergency. He gave him his private cell phone number and told him not to use it unless Jesus himself gave him orders to do so. Pete then called another friend and made some special arrangements. The brothers four were creating a base of operations on an old farm just outside Ringoes, New Jersey. Nobody else would know about it. A weather-beaten Saab driven by Mike followed a nondescript late-model yellow Ford driven by Pete across the state and into New Jersey. Somewhere on Route 179, they drove up a dusty road and stopped by a boarded-up farmhouse. It abutted an abandoned railroad trestle and looked like something out of a scary movie.

"Home sweet home, gentlemen," Pete said. "This is an old safe house that is no longer used but owned by a good friend of mine." Joe sat down, Barney took a peek out the back porch, and Mike wanted to know about the phones. Pete was too busy to answer any of them; he was checking to make sure that the old surveillance systems had been removed, and they had been. Pete sat down to make some calls, Barney made coffee, and Mike and Joe went on a tour of inspection.

They moved both cars into the barn, locked them, and brought the keys back with them. They locked the barn from the inside and jumped down from the hayloft. Joe almost broke his leg but came up OK with a minor limp, a wee bit of embarrassment, and a little self-reproach. Next they opened up the steel trapdoor leading to the basement and went down damp and dirty concrete steps. This unlocked door was ground level at the rear of the house. It was a terrible security flaw and Mike wanted to secure it to prevent the possibility of any unwelcome visitors in the night.

"Nice cobwebs, Mike; thanks for this little tour of yours," said Joe with a chuckle. Mike handed Joe a bolt and nut that he found on the workbench and told him to secure the door from the inside. They found that all the windows were locked and well; actually, they were sealed with grit and hadn't been opened for generations. The basement had nothing of interest to them but they did notice that the electrical hook-ups had been upgraded. Mike said that it was because this place needed some heavy-duty communications gear at one time. A quick check determined that the water and electricity were both on and the sewer drains and bathroom worked fine. They were good to go as far as the infrastructure and accoutrements went and everything was as secure as could be. They went upstairs, locking the basement door behind them, and found Barney and Pete waiting for them. It was time to share information and form a plan.

Pete told them that his cell phone should be ringing in about five minutes. His contact had to leave the office in order to make the call and this was most likely the only time they would be able to make this connection. The call came; Pete asked a few questions and did a lot of listening. The call lasted about twenty minutes and then finally Pete said, "Thanks Mel, I owe you man." That phone call provided a wellspring of needed information. Now, after all of the confusion with the hotel fire, running to the Bronx, and Sandy's kidnapping, the picture had become a lot clearer. Pete had the floor and the rest of them sat to listen.

"Jack 'The Lip' Sullivan was disbarred from his legal practice, but he had a lot of money and a lot of friends. One of his lawyer buddies represented him and Scaglionne and he managed to keep both of them out of the slammer citing various technicalities. Both were indicted and both made bail. Scaglionne had to put up millions in bail money but apparently it was no problem for him to walk away. Vito skipped out and it is assumed that he has left the country. They have an unproven paper trail that leads to Barcelona Spain but that is where it ends. Our contacts in Italy have come up with nothing further on him yet but interestingly enough, Jack Sullivan is no longer with us; he had a heart attack. A steel jacketed .45 caliber slug went right through his plasma-pumping machine. I guess that his friend Vito didn't want to leave any loose ends lying around. The Falcones are in Attica Prison and will be there forever playing chess, reliving the bad old days and legally fighting a lethal injection. Philbrick and Fauxmaster were both up in Dannamorra Prison but now they are the federal lockup in Allenwood PA. John Shaft is there also and has become house mouse to some prison warlord named Nicky Barnes.

All of these guys are safely locked away or dead. That probably includes your ex-chef Raoul. All signs point to the fact that he was involved in setting the fire in the hotel and kidnapping Sandy. He's gotta be dead fellas; they found his hands chopped off and left on the seat of his car holding a rat. Sandy's hair and traces of saliva were in the back seat of the car but so far that's where the trail ends."

Pete closed down his briefing by telling us that he would next try to contact Santos in Madrid to see if he could add something to this Raoul mystery: "There has to be some kind of connection between Scaglionne, Carlos, Baum, and Raoul. If there is, then we gotta assume that we have a starting place to look for Sandy. Scaglionne is too hot in Italy and cannot stay in the U.S.. If he has friends in Spain, well, we gotta do some heavy probing and thinking here. I hope Santos can help. Although it is still possible that Sandy is being held somewhere here in the States, I know Scaglionne well enough to know that he takes pride in direct contact with his capers. I think we should prepare for a trip to Europe."

Meanwhile in the Pyrenees, Sandy had been studying the guards but always kept a low profile. It seemed to her that Vito was away from this place more than he was here. Only Gert was the constant; she was always around and seemingly popped up in the weirdest of places and at the craziest of times. One time, she almost caught Sandy with some of the rat poison but she had just crammed it into her pocket in time. She casually dried some dishes and put them away as if Gert the Gestapo babe wasn't looking.

Sandy would always bust on Gert in her tongue-in-cheek manner; most times "loveable" Gert didn't even know that she was being made out to be a jerk. Sandy would often muse aloud about combat boots, leather jockstraps, and studded jackboots with whips and chains, but she always did it in a joking manner. Gert's response was a scowl and her inner thought was just how right this Mrs. Donahue was. Gert lived for the day when Vito gave her permission to whip this uppity bitch into submission. Sandy had her thoughts as well but they weren't as goofy as Gert's. She thought of cramming some rat poison down Gert's throat but she knew that this latter-day Amazon could break her in half like a matchstick. Hey, ya know? A prisoner gal can have some fun too; for Sandy it was entertaining just to think that she could win.

Anyway, Sandy was getting sick and tired of this day-to-day nothingness of being the captive pigeon. She was determined to at least try to fly this coop of boredom and veiled threats. She had to get back to her life and her family. She knew that the guards didn't live here at the estate as each of them drove their own cars to their appointed duty station each day. This caused Sandy some concern because it told her that the nearest town was probably not within walking distance. If she stole one of the guard's cars, she had better be assured of her direction and quick escape. She was getting desperate though and felt ready to take her chances, ankle detector bracelet be damned.

The next morning she had to suffer breakfast with Vito and Gert. Sandy was not one for small talk with these two so she helped the staff clean up in the kitchen.

Vito was acting strangely, like a man who needed something but wasn't sure what it was. He came into the kitchen and teased Sandy with rude comments; this was out of sorts for him. He asked Sandy if she wanted to watch as the dogs ripped her husband apart down on the patio while his two friends watched and waited their turns. Sandy was boiling inside but refused to show it; as much as she didn't want to admit it to herself, she was starting to genuinely hate Vito Scaglionne and Gert. She merely peered into his eyes and told him that he was in greater danger than he would ever know. "Mr. Scaglionne, your little house of cards will soon come tumbling down around your ears, and I will receive great joy watching the law enforcement people drag you away in chains." Vito sneered and, totally out of character, slapped Sandy hard across the face.

This act of cruelty startled Maria, who was the maid and cook. It also brought Gert into the kitchen on the run. Sandy was smarting but controlled the tears with a will of iron. She knew that she had struck home; Vito was not on sure ground and now she knew it. Gert was just about to lay into Sandy with a riding crop but Vito held her in check. He said, "Your time will come with Mrs. Donahue, Gertrude my love. I promise you that. She will be the last to die and that pleasure shall be yours." Sandy shivered.

That afternoon with Vito gone to wherever it was that he went, Sandy managed to steal some raw hamburger from the refrigerator. Her plan would now be on the fast track. She casually took her time, walking about the estate a bit, and then went back to her room. There she mixed up her dog slayer elixir with a silent prayer and a yet-to-be formulated plan of attack. Gert was nowhere to be found, but Sandy knew that she was always close by. Actually, Gert was in her office staring into the monitor with a live feed from the hidden camera in Sandy's room. Sandy surmised as such.

Gert smiled and knew that today she would get her first licks into the American bitch that she detested so much. She radioed the four guards on the perimeter wall and instructed them to unleash the dogs but to keep them calm and within eyesight. She further told them that if the American woman were to approach them, they should be on guard as she was probably trying some sort of escape trick. Her final instructions were, "If you have to shoot her, be careful not to kill her."

Ramon was sick to his stomach upon hearing this message. He was the guard posted where the wall had collapsed. He hated this job and only took it to feed his family. He was an imposing man but inwardly he hated violence. He was hired because he talked a good game, was an ex-con, had good connections, and was well muscled.

He was also the guard that Sandy had selected because he was the only one that smiled at her that one time. She saw in his eyes that he was not like the other guards and now she was betting her very life on that intuition. Hiding the poisoned hamburger in her jacket pocket, Sandy left her room and, using the side door leading to the kitchen, she found Maria. She was nervous, had many doubts about the dog, and was totally unsure about the rest of her haphazardly put-together plan. She also felt as though she was being watched.

She was being watched; Gert was happily observing the blips on the monitor being transmitted by Sandy's ankle bracelet. Gert left the office, fairly sure where Mrs. Donahue was headed, Gert used a different approach path toward Ramon's post. She wanted to give Sandy plenty of time to try her game. Gert was almost salivating as she thought about drawing blood from Sandy with her whip. Mental images of Sandy tied to the post in the basement, stripped naked and writhing in pain, gave her a near orgasmic experience; she couldn't wait to snare this stupid woman and beat the hell out of her. She thought, oh, how I need this; it has been much too long since the last one.

Maria strolled casually down the path toward the wall where Ramon was waiting in anguish. Sandy had asked her to bring a special treat to Ramon. She told her it was just a little hamburger for the dog and a little charm bracelet that she no longer wanted. The package, however, contained the electronic tracking ankle bracelet that Sandy had managed to dismantle and repack without causing an alarm. Sandy did this in the shower stall, fully aware of the hidden camera in her room. Maria liked Sandy and she liked Ramon as well. She welcomed this request with the wanton desires of a woman who had not been with a man for far too long. Sandy told her that Ramon had been asking about her and, in her naïveté, she fell for the ruse.

Sandy, however, was busy elsewhere. She only had minutes to complete her task and, putting the noise aside for the moment, she used a heavy candelabrum to smash the lock on Vito Scaglionne's office door. Breaking the glass of the gun cabinet, she grabbed two pistols and loaded them. The house was empty and nobody heard the noise; she was lucky. Running from the rear of the building, she made for the garage where the mechanic was busy drinking red wine while supposedly fixing a broken wheel on a cart. She ordered him at gunpoint to start the truck and lay down in the corner or she would shoot him; he complied, fearful of this crazy-looking American woman with a gun pointed at his groin. He understood not a word of English, but he got the message quickly enough.

"Thank God for Chevys," Sandy muttered, and she shoved the gearshift lever into four-wheel drive low range and roared through the weakly constructed garage doors. She put the pedal to the metal and tore down the driveway toward the front gates. She did not let up; she pushed that Chevy for all it was worth and crashed through the padlocked steel gates, ripping the hinges out of the concrete pillars.

There was only one road so that was where she headed. Checking the fuel gauge she found that she had only a quarter-tank of gas, but that seemed to be enough. She slipped the gearshift into two-wheel high gear and took off down the road. Bullets were crackling in the air but she did not stop and so far, none had hit her vehicle. Sandy had no idea where she was going, so she just pushed the truck up to ninety miles per hour and roared down the hill slowing only for the curves. She saw the two chase vehicles but they seemed far enough behind her for now so she silently prayed for guidance and protection. The road was narrow, there was just barely enough room for two cars to pass each other safely, and Sandy was speeding well above reasonable limits.

Vito was headed up the same road leisurely listening to some rock music and smoking a joint. They were headed directly towards one another, Sandy doing ninety coming downhill, only slowing when needed, and Vito lost in his own world just tooling up the road thinking of another romp in the sack with that crazy killer-Nazi chick, Gert. The distance closed quickly and Sandy almost lost control as her Chevy four-by-four slammed into Vito's Jag, but she kept going, almost smiling at the irony of it all. Her mighty Chevy pushed the Jag aside as though it was a mini-bumper car. She was one fender short of a six pack but that was OK with her; she saw in the rear view mirror that Vito was crunched into some rocks and she hoped that he was dead.

She came to a four-way intersection with no signs. In a split second, Sandy considered which way to go and what to do. She unhesitatingly turned left only because that road looked to be in better condition and had lane markers on the blacktop. Her decision made sense to her and the road was flat; she pushed the truck up to a hundred miles per hour heading towards who knew where. Sandy was trying to put the mountain range behind her, figuring that in the valleys or lowlands she would find a town or village, some help, or at least a telephone.

Gert came upon the wrecked Jag and extricated Vito from it

easily; he was relatively unharmed except for a bloody lip where the airbag had hit him. The Jag was on fire and Vito knew that he would soon lose about a half-million dollars of cocaine that was in the trunk. He also knew that they had to get the Donahue woman and she was more important. He jumped into Gert's car, wiped the blood off his chin, and chambered a round into his pistol. He was filled with rage.

Soon they came upon the intersection that Sandy had reached. They easily saw the tire marks on the pavement so they made the same left turn that Sandy did. Gert floored the Mercedes, rubbed Vito's groin, and laughed with glee. They knew that they would be trapping their quarry soon enough. She was headed into home turf! Vito picked up Gert's cell phone and dialed.

Sandy was filled with wild excitement mixed with fear of the unknown; she needed to find help and find it soon. As she sped down the road, she passed many small ramshackle farmhouses and vineyards, but she figured that she needed more help than what would be afforded from a farmer who may not even have a telephone. She also assumed that the language barrier would take too much time and that she would be caught. Soon she noticed that there were more buildings and even a few small business places, but no sign of anything that looked official. She was looking for a cop or a militia person, anyone with a uniform and a gun, but so far, nothing.

She drove like a banshee for a few more miles until she finally saw her salvation: a vehicle on the side of the road with a blinking blue light on its roof and was plainly marked Policía. Sandy maneuvered her three-fender Chevy to the side of the road and screeched to a halt directly behind the little Fiat police cruiser. The cop inside was waiting for her, gleefully anticipating his reward from Pedro's friend, Mr. Vito Scaglionne. Sandy noticed that the truck was overheating; she found this cop just in time as steam was pouring out from both sides of the hood and the front grill of the truck.

She hopped out of the truck and ran to meet the policeman who was walking toward her with a look of false consternation. He was nattily clad in a black uniform complete with epaulets, a Sam

Brown belt, and insignia badges. Sandy could tell by the stripes on his sleeve that he was a sergeant and she was elated to have found a cop with some rank. She also noticed that he sported a gigantic sidearm, just what was needed in this situation.

They were three miles from the nearest town on a stretch of highway that was flat, barren, and hot. There were no homes to be seen; they were quite alone. Just as Sandy was about to try communicating with the police officer, he roughly slammed her across the trunk of his car and wrenched her arms behind her back. He put handcuffs on her without a word and all Sandy could do was finally release her pent-up emotions with a scream of despair.

Vito and Gert parked alongside the policeman and both got out of their car. Vito smiled at Sandy and said, "Well done, Mrs. Donahue, but you lose." Gert showed an evil grin and slapped Sandy hard across the face. Gert hustled Sandy to the backseat of their car and roughly pushed her inside face first, making sure that she suffered some abrasions. As Sandy lay on the seat she held back the tears and vowed to be strong. Gert came to the other side of the car and opened the door. She leaned down face to face with Sandy and whispered into her ear, "Ah, Mrs. Donahue, my sweet; now you will see just how much I adore you." From someplace down deep inside, Sandy told Gert what she felt in her heart: "I have dealt with lots of different kinds of creeps in my day, Gert, and measured against some of them, you're chump-change. It will give me great pleasure to be a witness at your trial and if they find that you are the murderer you seem to be, I will take even more pleasure watching you hang. You won't break me, and since I am the bait for your scumbag buddy Vito, you won't kill me either. In the end, goodness will win, but since you have no idea what goodness is, I guess that it will take you by surprise."

Vito was busy paying off Sergeant Madera and thanking him for a job well done. He offered him a position as security officer in his organization if he should decide to quit being a cop. Madera thanked Vito, shook his hand, took the money and, without a second glance, drove merrily down the road. Vito took the driver's seat with Gert by his side and electronically disabled the door locks. Sandy said nothing but her hands were growing numb from the too tightly snapped handcuffs.

Gert was wild with sexual energy and Vito had a hard time controlling the car as he drove back to the estate. The car was bobbing up the road and so was Gert. As Sandy lay there, she was thinking that these scum-of-the-earth people mortified her. Vito called a mechanic friend and arranged to have the Jag and the truck towed to his garage for repairs, but he figured that the Jag was a total wreck. He would make Donahue and McCormick pay for that too, he told himself with an evil chuckle.

Upon arrival at the winery, Vito parked in the middle of the courtyard and dismounted from the car. He forgot to zip up his pants, so he clumsily did so with no shame or embarrassment. Gert used her sleeve to clean off her chin and got out of the car as well; she was definitely one high-class lady. Dragging Sandy out of the car, Gert roughly pushed her down onto the ground. Vito called his security head and told him to assemble the house staff and all of the guards into the courtyard. Gert parked the car by the garage then walked back with some rope. The half-drunk mechanic was with her.

Near the large and beautiful marble steps leading into the house were two cast iron black painted ornate poles that were only for decorative purposes. Supposedly they were used to tether horses for visiting guests in days gone by. Sandy was stood up and tied to one of them. Vito told the mechanic to tie Maria to the other pole making sure that Ramon was standing center place and had a good view of what was going on. Vito made his speech for all to hear:

"Mrs. Donahue asked Maria to bring a package to Ramon and she did so with no hesitation. This is totally against the rules of this house. Ramon is not guilty of anything because he did not allow Maria to even get close to him." He went on to say, "Ramon, you are to be congratulated for doing your job well and I thank you. Juan the mechanic was drinking on duty and allowed Mrs. Donahue to overpower him and steal the truck. For this, there is a price to be paid."

Vito blew Juan into hell with one shot from his Beretta and then, without hesitation, executed Maria as well.

Not a word was said by any of the staff or the guards but each one was shocked and scared beyond belief. Ramon was thanking his lucky stars for the dog because he wouldn't let Maria get close to them. He was snarling and ready to attack when Gert came upon them and realized what had happened. Ramon knew that he would have let Maria approach and was just about to leash up the dog. "What a lucky break," he said to himself.

Sandy could not handle what she had witnessed; she couldn't help it, she fainted. Vito instructed his employees to clean up the mess, bury the two traitors outside, and be sure that they had learned never to disobey any of the rules. He also told them that they were now in his employ forever and would not be allowed to leave the property. Those with wives or family outside would bring those families in and use some of the out buildings as living quarters. Any disagreements would result in death. Gert grabbed Ramon and told him to help her carry Mrs. Donahue back inside and down to the basement. Ramon put up a good front but inside he knew that he was not the man that these people thought he was. He complied with Gert's demands with a broken heart and great fear for this American lady. He also knew that he would be killed if he refused.

He looked at Gert as she struggled with Sandy's limp body and he realized that he hated her. Gert was not being gentle with the American lady and she didn't care that her head bumped the doorway or that her foot got caught in the banister. Sandy's ankle was mauled and the pain of the mishap abruptly brought her out of her temporary state of unconsciousness. Ramon gently untangled Sandy's foot from between the banister baluster and the lower rail, only to watch as Gert angrily dragged her with even more force and speed. Ramon said nothing but tried to protect Sandy from further harm as the trip to the basement proceeded. He was shocked with disbelief to see that the basement was a sort of medieval torture chamber, complete with shackles bolted to the granite wall. Gert dragged Sandy to the shackles and had Ramon lock her up against the wall.

Dismissing Ramon with a nod of her head, Gert looked at Sandy with an evil grin that was probably her best smile. She was wet with anticipation and toyed with a leather whip. It was Gert's favorite phallic symbol and one of the tools that she enjoyed using the most. Ramon was happy to get out of there and in his heart he prayed a silent prayer for the well being of this poor woman who was now in a place of great danger. He looked back one last time and saw that Sandy's face was bleeding and her ankle was red and swollen. He saw the plea in her eyes; she wanted him to help her.

Ramon turned his back, closed the door behind him and walked upstairs, hating himself for his cowardice. Vito Scaglionne met him just outside the basement door. "Where is your dog, Ramon?" Vito asked. "Bruno is still tied up back by the wall sir, back at my post," he answered. Vito told him that he had hired four more guards and he was now elevated to inside security. No longer would he have to sit in the sun or shield himself from the rain. He told him that this was his reward for being faithful and steadfast to his duties. Vito said, "From now on Ramon, you will get more money and added responsibility; bring your wife here to the winery, for I have assigned you one of the better living quarters. Your wife will be our new cook and I will pay her as well. Life can be good for you if you do as well as you have today."

Ramon thanked him profusely, but in his heart he wanted to escape this place of death and danger. He knew that he would not bring his lovely wife Theresa to this horrible place. He longed for the old way of life when he was just a lowly peon picking grapes in the vineyard but he knew he could not refuse this murderous man that stood before him. He nodded and said he would tell his wife right away.

Meanwhile back in Ringoes, New Jersey, Pete Richardson was talking to his ex-associate Santos, the CIA agent in Madrid. He had helped in locating, trapping, and arresting Herb Philbrick, John Shaft, Carlos, and Mr. Baum, the document forger. It was there in Madrid two years ago that Santos and Joe Donahue had first met, and they too now had an enviable friendship. Santos said that he had never heard of Vito Scaglionne but told Pete that Baum had been chirping like a canary trying to get a lighter sentence. He said, "One of the names he gave up was a local hood named Pedro who supposedly had ties to the American and Italian mobs. So far we haven't been able to pin anything on him, but we suspect him to be involved with narcotics traffic and the Asian slave trade market. Even though he is a very visible character in Madrid, he appears to be squeaky clean. He has a large winery up in the foothills of the Pyrenees, but seldom goes there. Pedro lives a high lifestyle even though his legitimate business is not overly profitable. The only connection we could come up with was that Raoul, Joe Donahue's ex-chef, once worked for this clown as a low-level numbers and drug runner. Raoul was playing both sides against the middle and we bailed him out with the Baum bust and gave him a new life in the States."

Pete updated Santos about Raoul and told him that now he was most likely pushing up daisies somewhere in a forgotten cornfield in Pennsylvania. Santos told him, "Hadda happen, Pete; they say that he was scheduled to get whacked here in Madrid anyway. It all makes some kind of sense now because Raoul's mother and sister died in a suspicious fire. We figured that it was retribution and now that I hear that Raoul's cover was blown, I guess it was. Pete, these people suck, man, so anything I can do, even without sanction, I will do it." Pete was overjoyed and told Santos that he would get back to him, as this thing seemed to be on the fast track. They clicked off for now.

Barney was out grocery shopping. Joe was sleeping and suffering more bad dreams. McCormick was updating passports using his cell phone and laptop. Pete did a quick inventory of weapons and ammunition. He cleaned and oiled all the guns just for kicks. Barney came back loaded with all kinds of microwave food, vitamins for Joe, and the local newspaper. Joe woke up and groggily came downstairs smelling Barney's lousy cooking. Mike printed out some passport update applications and signed his. Pete put away all the artillery and cleaned off the kitchen table. He even washed some dishes and glass-es. They sat to a royal evening repast, complete with bottled water and nasty-looking cutlery. Mike's cell phone rang and broke the mood of the feast; each man stared at another. Mike picked it up and said hello. It was Scaglionne.

CHAPTER SIX

The Scene Unfolds

el Hairston was an intimidating-looking black guy who had twenty-seven years with the Federal Bureau of Investigations. He loved his job. He stood six-feet-two and weighed in at around two-twenty. Mel was a computer analyst and cyber-cop, hunting down web perverts and scam artists. He had two great kids, a winning smile, and a black belt in jiu-jitsu. One of his more clandestine duties involved using his talents to monitor, listen to, and record satellite-generated cell phone calls from a special list that was given to him. One of the "hot" buttons lit up and Mel immediately pushed the record key. He was so totally committed to chatting with some online pedophile that he could not monitor the call, but knew that he would listen to the tape as soon as possible.

For the moment though, he was Martha, an eleven-year-old girl listening to some filthy language from some weirdo who called himself luvloaf69 on the Internet. He lived in Massachusetts and he wanted to come down to New York and meet sweet little Martha with the hot pants. This particular probable felon had a long history with

Mel and according to what had already been surmised he had raped a child in New Hampshire. Mel would not cut this conversation short; this bastard had to be stopped. Mel's associate was sitting next to him doing a reverse trace on Mr. Luvloaf's ISP and DNS numbers. After a quick telephone call to the web-server, he came up with a name and address in Cambridge, Massachusetts. While Mel was sweet-talking and typing a lot of "Oooh-Ahhs" and some other nutty talk like "Yes, oh baby," he would toss in a few moans and groans merely for kicks. His goal was to get a JPEG photo of Martha's overage amorous cyber-buddy and keep him online for as long as possible.

A quick phone call to the FBI office in Cambridge dispatched two agents over to Mr. Luvloaf's street within twenty minutes. Mel was being imaginative and very creative as he milked this perv to deeper levels until finally he talked him into uploading a picture of himself. This, according to the fictitious Martha, would be the only way that she could agree to meet him. The guy was using a dial-up server so the upload took three minutes. "Martha" told him that she too had a dial-up, so she needed a few minutes to download what he had sent.

The agents in Cambridge turned down Mockingbird Lane and parked two houses short of where Mr. Terrence Twyst, Ph.D., resided. They were connected through their laptop computer to Mel in Philadelphia, their boss here in Cambridge, and Mr. Twyst sitting at his computer just a few feet from them. They were waiting until the real felony was committed and soon it was. Mel looked at a photo of a naked balding man standing tall for all to see. Within seconds, the agents outside the house saw the picture as well. They hopped over the white picket fence very quietly. One agent went to the window where the drapes yielded a half-inch field of vision, just enough for a telephoto enhanced 35mm snapshot. The picture taken, complete with flash, clearly showed the computer monitor with the text of what was on screen. It also showed in a sequence of six more photos, Mr. Twyst going to answer the door. The other agent was knocking.

Mel sent the file over to the prosecutor's office for further action. He would later say that he felt good about nabbing this creep; all he wanted to do now was go home and take a shower. He felt soiled. The next day's newspaper in Cambridge displayed a glorious picture of Mr. Twyst with certain areas blocked out. The faculty saw it, the staff saw it, and so did Mr. Twyst's students. He was disgraced before his family, lost his job tenure, and would eventually face divorce and four years in jail. The rape investigation in New Hampshire could not be proven; the victim would not testify and was uncooperative in the investigation. If she had, Twyst would have been removed from society for a much longer time. Mel noticed that the "hot" button on the console was still blinking and he muttered to himself, "Oh yeah, that." He put on his headphones and keyed up the tape noticing that it was already a bit old:

"Good afternoon, McCormick; I'm sure you know who this is. This will be the last time you'll hear from me on your telephone. Just listen and listen well. I have taken the liberty of sending you an email, which you will find at the Donahue Downs web address. I urge you to see it right away. Although I do not know exactly where you are right now, I hope that you are close to that location because you and your friends are now operating under a time limit. Further instructions will be found in the email along with a very interesting MPEG movie that is attached. Goodbye for now." With that, the line went dead.

Mel would hear this call two hours later but by then, the brothers four had secured the safe house and were sitting in Sandy's office with the computer booted up. The email opened and there on the screen were the words from hell itself. Vito had written the following message to our stalwart white-hat-wearers:

"Gentlemen, I want you to know that I have the power to kill all of you right where you are in that burned out wasp's nest in Pennsylvania. However, I have far better plans for your demise. The plans I have in mind will be a lot more fun for my loving associate Gertrude and me. You will meet her in a few minutes; she is caring for Sandy in her usual professional manner right now, as a matter of fact. Once again I remind you to keep the authorities out of this because if you don't, sweet Mrs. Donahue will be killed and none of you will be able to find us. I have enough firepower in and around the Philadelphia area to mount a total and all-out armed assault against Donahue Downs and I could accomplish this with merely a phone call. If you recall the movie 'Scarface' with Al Pacino, that final scene where Pacino got whacked is reminiscent of how it would be at your broken-down hotel. It would be over in mere minutes, but that is not how I operate.

"That FBI sting operation of two years ago totally disrupted a large portion of our dealings in the States and many of our friends and associates were put out of business. Of course others have stepped in to take their places, but I do not control them as well as I once did. I attribute this to you Mr. Donahue, and to you, Mr. McCormick, because you acted in concert and were happy to do so. By the way, Mike, how's Helen lately? Still cleaning up and answering the phone at the hotel, is she?"

Mike shivered and grabbed his cell phone. He called Helen who was — thank God — at home. He told her to pack a bag, call a cab, and go visit their daughter in Cape May, New Jersey: "No questions Helen, just do it, and DO NOT start the car. I'll call you tonight."

The email continued:

"I am throwing down the gauntlet to you two; come and get Mrs. Donahue and we will see who wins in the end. On Rio Del Oro Street in the city of Girona, Spain, you will find an out-of-the-way hotel called El Diablo Rojo. Your reservations for two are already arranged under the name of Donahue. Only McCormick and Donahue are invited to this party; leave that broken-down sot Barney Tunney at home. I will be in touch with you at that location in three days. Now, so that you know that time and secrecy is of the utmost importance to you, take a look at the MPEG attached to this email. You tell the cops, she dies! A reverse trace on this ISP will prove fruitless. It is being relayed to you from a ghost laptop computer in Philadelphia, but Mrs. Donahue and I are thousands of miles from there."

Barney, Mike, Pete and Joe sat in silent shock. Barney said,

"This guy's one sick bastard." Joe wanted to open the download but all of them were afraid of what they were going to see. Finally it was decided that Joe alone should see what was on the file and if he felt it appropriate, then the rest of them could take a look. Barney and Mike knew that Joe's nerves were shot and it had been less than a week since his binge of booze. They were genuinely worried for him but their hands were tied; it had to be this way for now. They left the room.

Mel didn't know how to handle this without tipping his hand to his bosses and compromising his job. He had clued in his old friend Pete Richardson only this morning about Scaglionne and now the guy calls him on a tapped cell phone. "Screw this," he said, "I gotta do my job and these guys are in over their head." Mel took the tape into the inner office and sat in front of Major Wilhelm Schmidt, his boss, who was known to be a stickler for details, yet a straight shooter and street-smart guy.

Mel shivered at the recollection of a rumor about a Prussian horse soldier somewhere back in Schmidt's family history that collected the heads of his enemies. "Got a minute, boss?" he asked, and the major waved him to take a seat while still on the phone. After the call Schmidt asked him about the dirty-talking nut on the computer who hit on kids. Mel only gave him a brief overview and told him that he had something much more important but wanted to talk to him kind of off-the-record first. "No problem Mel, go for it," said the major.

"Will, this morning I extended a professional courtesy to an old friend, Pete Richardson, the guy you replaced when he retired. He and I are close friends, Will, and if he is anything, he is a good man and a fine professional cop. I would trust him with my life and once, I hadda do just that. He asked me about an ongoing investigation that actually was started by him when he was still here. He wanted to know about Vito Scaglionne, the mob guy who skipped bail and probably killed his ex-pal, the lawyer, Jack Sullivan. All I told him was that the guy had probably skipped bail and gone back to Europe, whereabouts unknown. I didn't think too much of it because he is friends with this guy Joe Donahue and Mike McCormick. McCormick is another agent who retired and works for Donahue at his hotel; he's a good guy too.

"They were all mixed up in that sting operation of three years ago. You read the file, right? Anyway, I guessed that they just wanted to be sure that they were safe from any further doings with the bad guys. I think that they thought that Scaglionne had a hand in the fire and now that I think deeply about it, they are probably right. Since the arson at the hotel and the kidnapping of Mrs. Donahue, we had a judge issue a warrant and we had all the phones tapped, including McCormick and Barney Tunney's, Donahue's right-hand man.

"I have been sitting on those hotlines for a couple of months and nothing of interest happened. That is, until now, while I was dealing with the cyber-sex nut, Terrence Twyst in Massachusetts. McCormick's cell phone hotline went off, but I could not disconnect with a case that we had been working on and was finally showing some results. Will, that thing goes off ten times a day and it is all usual run-of-the-mill baloney between him and his wife or the contractor cleaning out the debris. I didn't think it was too important but Will, I always listen in anyway; ya never know! I put the call on automatic record and continued what I was doing. Boss, this call came from Vito Scaglionne and it is a freaking bombshell. Ya gotta hear this, and if you can cut me some slack on the momentary indiscretion of blabbing to Pete, I would appreciate it and it will never happen again."

Major Wilhelm Schmidt, distant nephew of the infamous Prussian horse soldier and head chopper, looked at the formidable personage of his underling and had pity, while showing a face set in steel. Without the tiniest facial inflection or show of forgiveness, he told Mel to play the tape. Schmidt listened with deep interest and he noticed the matter-of-fact way in which Scaglionne selected his language. He spoke perfect English but with an undertone of hatred, mixed with a sick kind of false humor. The major knew now that

Scaglionne was a dyed-in-the-wool sociopath and psychotic killer: "Mel, we got other tapes of this Scaglionne guy so get someone hopping on doing voice identification on this thing. I want to be absolutely sure that this is really Scaglionne. Also, let's forget the first part of what you told me, OK? We go from here with what we've got. Call Charlie Beesworth; get him to check on the status of Donahue's, Richardson's, and McCormick's passports. I don't want a bunch of dead American hero wannabes on my hands. Get hold of Phyllis and have her crack the Donahue Downs email server; I want to see this freaking email this clown is talking about. Mel, this is already a couple of hours old and we got no idea what Richardson and his pals are up to; every minute is critical now. Do all this right away and get ready to take a ride into the woods; we are paying a visit to a burned-out hotel in Bucks County." By that time, Joe had already seen the video. He was crying his eyes out and his friends had lumps in their throats and rage in their hearts. They were going to Spain alright; this crumb Scaglionne had finally bitten off more than he could chew.

The video showed Sandy Donahue chained to a wall, nude except for her panties. Some bloodthirsty woman whom they guessed was Gertrude was whipping her. Sandy was screaming, crying, and bleeding. She had welt marks across every inch of what could be seen and her face showed swelling, black and blue marks, and some open cuts. The torturer was laughing and taunting her, calling her an American bitch and an upper crust whore. The final scene was a close-up of the sadistic broad, face to face with Sandy and spitting directly into the open wound under her eye.

Barney hugged Joe; he was crying too. Pete and Mike were in shock and hatred was in their hearts for Scaglionne. All four of them wanted to catch these creeps but it was deeper now. Now, they wanted to kill them, law or no law. Call it murder, assassination, or retribution; nobody cared. What was important now was getting out of this hotel and on to the first flight out of the country. Pete, the least directly involved with the Donahue family, was the only one with misgivings about breaking the law, but he was willing to go along as far as it went. He felt that when he came to the point of no return, he would make his decision. For now, these were his friends, and friends who were really friends stood in the gap; they took the heat and they didn't run from adverse situations. Pete made up his mind that he would not turn his back and go back to Binghamton to play lawyer until this horror tale was over with. He wanted to puke while watching the video.

Joe's mind was playing sad games of despair, mixed with a dichotomy of crazy emotions. He loved Sandy with all of his heart; in his mind she was the only reason that he was able to return to the land of normalcy. He thought of Steve, Sandy's son-in-law, and wondered what he and Joe Jr., both Marine Corps combat officers, would do after seeing this video. He could not hear Barney, Pete, or Mike; he was lost in a shell, a void where all things had become dull. He was burning with rage and fueled by the quest for ripping the throat from his adversary, Vito Scaglionne. Joe wanted to kill and he wondered if he still had the unattached emotional ability to do so. Other parts of his thought processes had him trapped in a merry-go-round of repetitive actions; he kept seeing himself in his mind's eye pushing that Play button on the computer: When the MPEG opened that first time revealing a close-up of Sandy's bruised face, Joe was immediately filled with rage.

He saw his wife in humiliation, pain, and tears. He saw her black and blue marks and the open bleeding wound on her cheek. Yet, beneath it for only Joe to see, there was the courage of a strong woman who had inner nobility under pressure. He saw her courage, wisdom and strength and only Joe could read in her eyes what she was thinking, This too shall pass and the evil of this world would be put down to the pits of hell. The camera panned back to expose more of the torture scene of his wife and already Joe wished the film to end; he had seen enough.

Unmercifully there was more, and Joe knew that Scaglionne wanted him to suffer through all of it. No sooner had he taken in the entire horror-scene, a whip snapped across Sandy's belly with uncontrolled force. Another welt formed and Joe heard laughter. Sandy's head sagged as she entered what Joe assumed was unconsciousness and he gave thanks to God for that small act of mercy.

This movie was taken with a late model digital camera; the scenes were in full color, crystal clear, and the audio captured every sick, evil, and hurtful sound. It seemed that the camera was placed on a stationary device, a table or tripod, because the next scene revealed the image of the devil's female child clad in black leather with silver studs. Gertrude turned to face the camera, full focus, and said with a sneer, "Up yours Mr. Donahue and McCormick; you will get even worse treatment when you come for your visit with us."

She turned and unsnapped the cuff on Sandy's left arm. Her body sagged and dangled from the other arm. This beast of a woman showed no gentleness or care. She finally and ever so slowly unsnapped the other cuff and allowed Sandy's limp body to fall to the floor. Scaglionne entered the scene and lifted Sandy to a gurney and the movie ended.

All Joe could think about was his own selfishness. He ran to the Bronx at the drop of a hat, wanting to forget the horrors of that which he assumed was his wife's death. He was guilt-laden and so morose that he wished he had died in the Bronx. He incorrectly thought that if he had, maybe things would be different. Barney shook him back to reality: "Joe, Mike and Pete put all the guns into the wall safe and we are packed up and just about ready to leave here. Pete is making some kind of arrangements to get us to Spain real quick and maybe even without anyone else's knowledge that we left."

Barney had assumed that the cell phones were tapped and none of them wanted to take any chances of getting trapped here. No sooner than he had that thought, Mike's cell-phone rang. It was the Philadelphia area commander of the FBI, a Major Schmidt. Mike answered in a business like manner and pushed the speakerphone button for all to hear: "Good afternoon Mr. McCormick, my name is Major Wilhelm Schmidt with the FBI in Philly. I hope all is as well as can be expected." Mike played his hand perfectly, divulged nothing, and answered the caller politely and almost honestly. The major went on, "I would like to take a ride up to see you about a few things so if you can be available in an hour or two I would appreciate it." Pete vigorously shook his head to Mike and intimated that he should say yes. He quickly scribbled a note and handed it to Mike, who read his lines without missing a beat. "Well major, it's 2 p.m. and I am away from the hotel doing some business with a new contractor, so why not make it around 4:30, OK?"

Barney was already packing the car with what little they were taking with them. Joe was coming back to reality but his head was swimming in dizziness. One side of him wanted a drink but the more logical side told him to take his medicine. He did that, popping a B-12 tab and two lithium pills. The call over, they grabbed their phones, Mike's laptop, locked the doors, and beat it the hell out of there in a New York minute.

Pete told Mike to head toward Binghamton New York and by the time they got there, his plan would be all nailed down. Pete spent the entire trip on the phone and the laptop. Barney and Joe sat in the back. They were all fairly sure that Pete's phone was the only one that wasn't tapped yet. Joe thankfully fell asleep in depression, the great escape mechanism. They were driving Pete's Ford. Sandy's Jag and Joe's car were left right in the driveway by the front porch of Joe and Sandy's residence quarters at the hotel. Mike's Saab was covered with a tarp and locked away in the deserted barn in Ringoes, New Jersey. Pete had a comical mental image of Schmidt banging on the doors at the hotel and wasting even more time: time that they needed oh so desperately. At four thirty-five they parked the Ford on a shady street in front of a converted house with a lawyer's shingle hanging outside. The sign read, Peter Richardson, Attorney at Law.

Mike's cell phone had been ringing for the last five minutes but they would not answer it. Finally, Pete figured that he could milk the major for another half-hour by telling just one more little white lie. He told Mike to answer the phone, apologize for missing the call, that the phone was in the car while he was outside talking, and to tell him that the contractor would drop him off at the hotel at 5 p.m. The call was a bit testy but it seemed that the major believed him. Mike turned the phone off and put it into the glove compartment along with Barney and Joe's. The guy waiting for them was Pete's friend, a retired Albany cop that Pete used for divorce investigations. He had Pete's Hyundai Santa Fe all gassed up and ready to go. They transferred cars and Pete's pal drove away in the Ford without even an introduction. Pete explained his plan as they headed East on I-88 toward Albany. "We have a meeting at 7 p.m. with another friend of mine. He has all of our passports with him. From there we head north and cross the Canadian border north of Plattsburgh, New York, and into Montreal. We have to catch a 12:30 flight on Swiss International Airline to Barcelona with a transfer at Paris.

"This is going to be a long night but Scaglionne won't be expecting us this soon and with a little luck, we will have outrun the good major who just probably broke down Joe's front door." Mike said, "Thank God for wireless laptops and cell phones, huh guys? Let's make all this work." That said, he used Pete's phone and called Helen.

Major Schmidt and Mel Hairston had Scaglionne's email forwarded directly to them as they sat in their car waiting for Mike McCormick. After they had read the message text and seen the MPEG, they knew that McCormick wasn't going to show up to meet them; they had been had. Mel said, "Geesh boss, I wouldn't be hanging around here either, but McCormick and Donahue didn't commit a crime; what can we do about this?" Schmidt knew that he had no time for mistakes; he knew that Donahue and McCormick were on their way to Spain one way or another. He wondered about their friend Barney and Pete Richardson as well.

He called the Binghamton police department and had them find out if Pete was at home. The call came back in fifteen minutes that the sector cop did a drive-by, saw Richardson's Ford in the driveway, the lights in the house were on, and he saw a male figure puttering about inside. A rapid records check revealed that the car was indeed Richardson's Ford. It was assumed that Richardson was at home and not involved with the other three.

Pete's associate played his hand well, making sure the blinds were open and he walked around every time he saw headlights of an approaching vehicle. He was prepared to do a face-to-face if needed. Once he saw that the last car to pass by was a cop and that he didn't knock, he shut down the lights and went to sleep on the couch. Schmidt wasn't convinced so he got Richardson's home phone number and called. He wanted to be sure it was really Pete walking around in that house up there.

"Hello?"

"Hello, this is Major Wilhelm Schmidt with the FBI in Philly. Is this Pete Richardson?"

"Yeah, what's up? But make it fast please."

"Pete, I just wanted to ask you a few questions if you don't mind."

"I don't mind at all major, but drop by in the morning. I'm busy with my lady friend for now though, so goodnight."

With that the phone was cradled and the call disconnected. Schmidt smelled a rat.

Mike drove but didn't want to risk getting stopped for speeding so he drove just like everyone else: eighty in a sixty-five zone. He always allowed those going a bit faster to pass him and he referred to them as his own private radar detectors. He pulled onto State Street in Albany with seven minutes to spare and right away, Pete recognized his old buddy walking down the street. One door opened, the guy got in, and they leisurely drove down the road. All the documents were legal but it looked like the ink hadn't even dried yet on the official stamps. The guy's name was Al and he had the airline tickets and a printed itinerary for them. He told them to drop him off at the next corner and to beat it; they didn't have any time to spare. Plattsburgh was almost three hours away. It was another two hours to Montreal International airport.

Mike stopped for coffee all around and then put the pedal to the metal as soon as he entered I-87, also known as the Northway. While passing Glens Falls and Saratoga Springs, Pete was in deep talks with Santos in Madrid. He didn't want to divulge the nuts and bolts of what was going down, but he sent an encrypted email with a copy and paste of Scaglionne's original email to Donahue Downs. The MPEG was attached and Pete knew that Santos would understand what was happening. He told him to find a safe place for Barney and himself not too far from El Diablo Rojo hotel in Girona. "A place within eyesight was best if possible," he said. Crossing the border was painfully easy from New York into Canada, homeland security or not. They each showed a driver's license and that was that. They told the border cop on the Canadian side that this was a pleasure trip and would be returning to the U.S. in about a week. "No problem sir, enjoy your stay with us," said the guy at the gate. They drove right through and into relative safety from Schmidt and company.

The Swiss International check-in attendant was amazed that three men from America were going to Spain and the only bit of luggage they had was a carry-on laptop. A few questions were asked, identification freely shown, and they breezed through customs and the metal detectors. They made their flight with a half-hour to gulp down some bland airline terminal food. Mike told Joe, "Food is a tool. Our bodies need it if we want to think clearly and act quickly; you gotta eat something, pal." Hearing Mike use the word "tool" jogged Pete's imagination and solved a small problem for him. He immediately booted up the laptop and zipped another encrypted message to Santos. We need tools, is what he wrote to him. He was tempted to sign the message using the word "snug," meaning guns, but he knew that Santos would get the idea.

CHAPTER SEVEN

Krazy Kops

The next morning in the bureau conference room in Philadelphia, a staff meeting was quickly assembled. Major Schmidt headed up the fact-finding and data-sharing gathering. In attendance were Mel Hairston, Charlie Beesworth, Phyllis Lilly, T.D. Brown, the major's immediate supervisor, and René Starker, the liaison officer between the FBI and the CIA. Also, Randy Gomes, representing the U.S. Consulate to Spain, was there to convey any important data forward to the Ambassador. George Wheelwright, who was sent as a representative of the U.S. Attorney General, wanted to be there only to get a heads-up on what may eventually prove to be a colossal problem for his boss.

It was a Tuesday morning and Mel had been up all night signing papers. Mel decided to sit in on this meeting and only drop his personal bombshell when the talks were over. He wanted to know all he could know and then his time would come.

Coffee all around and the meeting came to silent anticipation of what the major had to say. He brought them all up to speed and did not skip any details. He went into great length describing the mob-related sting operation of a few years ago and how Scaglionne was the only felon still at-large. He described the arson, the Raoul connection and his probable death. He told them of the kidnapping of Mrs. Donahue and about Joe's sojourn into the Bronx and an alcoholic stupor.

About two hours later, he put up an enlarged email from Scaglionne and then ran the MPEG. Every person in that room was filled with rage and shock. All wanted to make this right and all agreed that the men on their way to Spain had to be stopped. They still were not positive, but since Barney Tunney and Pete Richardson could not be accounted for, it was assumed that the four of them were traveling together. Will had the Binghamton police check on Richardson first thing in the morning and found that his car was gone and the house locked up. He was not at his office either and they said that they would keep checking on him. They would call later if they had any additional information. As far as Will was concerned all four of them, all seasoned retired cops or military men, were together in this justifiable, clandestine, and illegal mission.

Wheelwright, the Attorney General's representative, reminded Schmidt about federal jurisdictions and laws pertaining to acting out of their purview.

Both the CIA and the FBI lacked the necessary assets to man every possible airport. Both agencies had budgetary overload and a severe manpower shortage.

René Starker told the group that she would send the entire file overseas via courier to the Agency office in Spain. So far, it looked like all they would be able to do was monitor El Diablo Rojo hotel and possibly intercede if Donahue showed up. They had a manpower shortage in that area. Most of their agents were in Afghanistan, Pakistan, and Iraq.

Phyllis Lilly, the local office computer pro, said that it seemed like the computer at Donahue Downs was shut down and the cell phones seemed to have been disconnected. She said that maybe they had run out of juice, but either way none of their calls were being answered, even on the main phone line at the hotel. Interestingly enough, she said that a machine was answering Mike McCormick's home phone and we knew that Mrs. McCormick was bouncing back and forth between the hotel and home. Apparently, she was in neither place.

Charlie Beesworth chimed in with the facts about the passports for all four men. It seemed that the four of them updated their passports the day before yesterday and they had gotten all the necessary stamps and medical inoculations needed for international travel. Of interest here, he noted, was the fact that the passports were stamped at the Albany, New York office instead of somewhere down here. This gave rise to the idea that they had already made a plane out of Albany International. The local office was checking into that and would update us when they found out where and when they got on the plane and where they were headed. Schmidt recapped the situation as far as he could see it:

Scaglionne had Mrs. Donahue and her life was in danger.

McCormick, Tunney, Donahue, and Richardson have all had seen the video and read the email.

All four had their passports and all four of them were missing.

They couldn't man all the possible ways out of the country and must assume that they were on their way to Spain right now.

Their only hope was that the CIA could corner them at that hotel in Girona.

According to their sources, assets were spread pretty thin in Spain and those that were not too far away were pretty much involved in major investigations.

So far, to the best of their knowledge, Donahue and crew had not broken any laws, so they really had no reason to arrest or even detain them.

Schmidt asked Mel if he would act as coordinator between all the various offices and agencies for now and Mel nodded his head in agreement but bit his tongue with a smile that no one could see. He knew that Beesworth would do a better job of that job anyway. The meeting came to a close and Schmidt and his boss T.D. Brown went into an inner office for a strategy meeting. Mel waited patiently but was already quietly cleaning out his desk. Forty-five minutes later, Mel's patience had run thin so he knocked on his boss's office door. Brown was in an armchair and the major was at his desk. Lots of papers, pictures, and profiles were scattered around; the desk was a mess of disjointed information and scraps of sticky notes. Mel took a deep breath and caused havoc to both men when he spoke:

"Inspector Brown, Major: I'm really sorry to have to cause a disruption to the case involving this Donahue mess but after twenty-seven years with the Bureau, I'm calling it quits right here and right now. I was going to retire last year after my wife passed away from breast cancer, but I had little else to do with my time so I stayed on the job. Now, things are different; I started to think how many times I have been passed over for promotion and I realize now that every day would be just a repeat of the day before. I'm going full ahead donating my time to charitable organizations and all the papers are already filled out and filed with personnel about ten minutes ago. I have forty-five days accumulated leave time accrued and am starting them today. Like I said, I'm sorry to do this, but this Donahue thing looks like another long case with deep involvement so I had better cut it here and now before I get so deep into this that I find another year has passed me by. I'll be available to testify in any of the ongoing cases that I have been involved with, but that is as far as I want to go. I am leaving this morning and will call this day a wash."

Schmidt paled; he knew that his dislike of blacks had caused this and he knew that Brown and Hairston knew it as well. Brown had asked about Mel's fitness reports over and over as the negatives seemed to be unfounded. On the other hand, Schmidt was just as happy to be rid of him and had always considered him an uppity black and a white-man wannabe. Brown was livid with rage but hid his feelings, safeguarding them for a later time when Schmidt and he were alone for a private talk about his own fitness report.

They had no recourse so they all shook hands and Mel walked out of the FBI offices dropping his gun, badge and ID off at the property clerk's desk. He did not head home; rather he went to the passport office and made ready to prove to himself that he was a righteous human being who would support his friends. He had met Sandy Donahue during that sting op and he too was filled with thoughts of vengeance. Mel was one of the phony bellhops catering to the mobsters in that deal. Back in those days, Mike McCormick and he had worked as a team busting organized crime and Pete Richardson was in charge.

Those were the good days but now with Mike and Pete both gone into retirement, they anchored Mel to a desk and he hated it. Likewise, Joe Donahue and his pal Barney, the New York City cop, were both stand-up guys. He knew that Schmidt would screw up this case big time and if he was ever going to make a stand for an honorable cause, this was it. This was his one chance in a lifetime to prove that his life really made a difference. He knew that there was more to protecting the public than walking on thin ice worrying about the ACLU, meeting schedules, and keeping within budget.

Mel had read all the reports about the apprehension of John Shaft and Herb Philbrick as well. He knew that Santos, the CIA agent in Spain, had helped them pull that off. When he was stateside about five years ago, he and Pete met Santos in a coffee shop to discuss an ongoing mob investigation. He knew that Pete would be in contact with Santos and so would he. Mel figured that Schmidt might figure out where he was going, but what could he do? Every citizen had the right to go where he pleased and for now, this trip pleased Mel. Mel had dinner in his favorite restaurant, forget about the cholesterol, Mel was born again. He went home with a new spring in his step and he knew that he would be calling his travel agent in the morning.

Vito wheeled the unconscious body of Sandy Donahue upstairs into her room and laid her in bed. He did a basic dressing on a few of the more severe wounds but he knew that she had no broken bones and eventually the mess that was her body right now would eventually heal. He called an associate who promised a doctor visit tomorrow, no questions asked. Vito didn't necessarily like Sandy Donahue all that much, but unlike Gert who loved pain, and as crazy as it might sound for a psychopath, Vito couldn't stand the sight of blood. The actual reason that he wanted Sandy alive and well was that he couldn't afford to lose his hostage at this point. Just as he had that thought, he noticed that Sandy had lost a front tooth, probably caused by one of Gertrudes more powerful punches: "Damn that woman; she can get out of hand sometimes, but she's fun to have around."

Sandy awoke a few minutes later to find herself locked in her room. This was OK with her, anyplace but shackled to that wall and at the mercy of Gert. She resolved to find a way to make that leather-clad silver-studded cretin pay for what she did, but her mind could not formulate any kind of plan. She was swimming in a semi-fugue state of borderline unconsciousness and painful coherency. There was a cup of hot tea by her bedside for which she was grateful, but she could only sip it from one side of her mouth. She felt the missing tooth and the warm blood surrounding the area. For a crazy reason unknown even to herself, she thought that her prosthodontist would have some more re-constructive work to do for her.

"Joe, hurry, they will kill me."

Four travel-weary men alit from Swiss International Flight #777 at Orly Airport in Paris. They had forty-five minutes to catch the Iberian jet that would take them to Barcelona. Mike and Pete scanned the waiting area looking for any person that showed even the slightest interest in them but there were none. Pete whispered to Mike, "So far, so good," and Mike shrugged. Barney and Joe were clueless; all they wanted to do was get some guns and find Sandy, dealing with Scaglionne first of course.

None of them had much to say to any of the other men because each of them were wrapped in their own thoughts that ran from doubt to victory, from love for Sandy to hatred for Vito and Gertrude. To a man, the overriding thoughts were: be smart, be strong, be alert, protect your friends, save Sandy, don't get caught by the cops, and win!

Mike and Pete knew that at some point Santos would show and pave the way for a surprise attack on wherever it was that Scaglionne was hiding with the captive Sandy Donahue. What they didn't know was that there were three men waiting for them in Barcelona. They breezed through customs, took the mechanized walkway to Area Two, and easily found the Air Iberia departure gates. Their plane left on time and each took a welcomed two-hour nap. It seemed to each of them that they had gotten on the plane five minutes ago, but all of a sudden the captain was telling the passengers to buckle their seatbelts for the landing at Barcelona.

Excitement and unexpected fear jogged each of them from drowsiness and adrenaline surged through each man. By this time Joe was far from the drunken sot that he had been in the Bronx; now he was a man filled with resolve. By the mercy of God, he had become the man that he always was. Joe had the courage of a lion. He wanted the love of his life back; he would save Sandy, come hell or high water.

Barney, who had given up strong drink right after the hotel fire, knew that if it weren't for Joe and Sandy, he would be just another has-been cop, a lost soul surrounded by thousands of others living a meaningless life in some smoke-filled tavern in the Bronx. In his mind's eye, he could envision himself sitting on a stool, half drunk, re-telling cop stories over and over, and boring whoever was listening to him to tears. To him, he owed his very life to these friends of his and often prayed for each of them and their extended family as well. For the first time in his life, he now had a meaningful relationship with a good woman; he had a new lease on life and was happy to be alive. Barney would not shirk from this task of righteous retribution and prayed to God for his own courage under fire.

Mike had thoughts of his own. He was deeply angered at

Scaglionne's threat against his wife Helen. He knew that if he didn't act now, somehow Scaglionne would find him and Mike knew the mindset of evil men. Mike thought that finally he had retired from police work with the FBI to find a new and more peaceful life when this piece of scum had the balls to threaten not only him and his wife but that he had physically injured his best friend's wife, Sandy. He too would never allow this debt to go unpaid; he wanted to personally handle Scaglionne if the opportunity arose.

When Pete retired from the Bureau, he did so with a clear conscious. He had finally had that one-on-one with Joe Donahue and the ghosts of Vietnam were put to rest. His law practice was boring but he managed to eke out a fairly good living. He stopped his boozing and settled into what he assumed would be a life of leisure until the day that he finally hung up his guns and put away his toys of professionalism. Then this! To Pete this was the price to be paid for his retirement. When this was over, if he lived through it, he would close up shop and go find a warm beach somewhere, maybe even write a book or two. Pete could not turn his back on Mike, his old partner, and he knew Mike's wife Helen as well; he liked her a lot. Mike had saved his life once and Joe had saved his mental sanity. To Pete, he had a debt to both of these men that he could never repay. This surely was the time to end his demon chasing; this was the time to slay them.

Pete thanked whatever spiritual powers were in his mind for the long-standing friendships that he had made while he was with the government service. He recalled Mel Hairston and he felt bad that the incoming boss, Schmidt, had rejected the promotion he had written for him. Mel proved to be a stand-up guy though; his unofficial updates opened up the possibility for them to rescue Sandy and put down this final threat to humanity, Vito Scaglionne. Pete hoped that all was well with his friend.

Vito spent the day on the phone while Gert toyed with his body. "She is an insatiable woman," Vito thought, but allowed her activities to go even further. Gert was thinking of what she would do with Mrs. Donahue strapped to a bed and her excitement rose to fever pitch. She played with her own body while suckling Vito's until both came to release — then she wanted more. Gert took her whip and started to leave the room but Vito yelled after her: "Don't go near the Donahue woman, Gert!" She left the room looking for someone else to play with.

As Gert walked across the lawn toward the wall, she noticed that the parking lot was full of cars. These were vehicles that she had never seen before and wondered what that was all about. She soon found out Vito was building an army of cutthroats to deal with what he assumed would be an all-out attack by Donahue, McCormick, and whoever else they could talk into or hire to come with them. He was right. Gert was a little confused but still determined to allow her passions one more fling of explosive fun and games. She came upon Ramon, who was now in charge of inside security. Gert had her doubts about his commitment to Vito because when she came upon Maria approaching him the other day at the wall; he was smiling, not holding his gun on her as he was supposed to do. She supposed that Ramon wanted a little playtime with Maria then but when the scene got ugly, he quickly became the loyal guard that he was being paid to be.

Gert put on her coquettish face for Ramon and said that there was a small security problem in her room, a wire or something that she didn't know anything about. Ramon stared deep into this woman's eyes, the window of her soul. He knew that he didn't like her and he knew that she could not be trusted. She was a dangerous and evil woman and her eyes were vacant and dead. He was a man of weak passions though and when Gert slowly ran her tongue over her lower lip, Ramon was smitten with desire. How quickly he forgot his wife and child living in the servants' quarters not two hundred feet away. He rationalized that the ploy of a security problem from Gert would be enough of an excuse for him to disappear for a while. He felt the heat in his loins and lost his thoughts of how to get himself and his family away from this place.

A loud noise stopped both of them in their tracks. They turned and stared at the front doors to the main house when all of a sudden a man came crashing through, mortally wounded. Another man came up after him, holding a sawed-off shotgun. He stood over the wounded man and blew off his face with another round from the gun. Ramon drew his pistol and ran to the scene. The man holding the shotgun pointed the weapon to the ground and stood there calm, cool, and collected.

Vito came at the quick. The killer looked at Vito Scaglionne and said, "Mea culpa Padrone, but this man is not your friend. His name is Ignacio Gomes, an underground member of the Basque party separatists. I have met him before and I know him to be a turncoat and traitor loyal only to his party. I do not know why he is here but whatever the reason is, it was not a good one." Ramon looked down at the ruined body of Maria's brother. His name was Tony Remoras. Ramon knew why he was here and he knew that he had good reason to be. Vito had killed his sister, the cook: sweet little Maria with the lovely body, simple mind, and nice smile. Ramon said nothing but ordered two men to get rid of the body and they did so. Ramon liked Tony and Maria; they were neighbors and now he hated his two bloodthirsty employers. He hadda get outta here!

Vito called all the newly hired guns outside for a welcome speech. He now had twenty-eight additional hired killers. Pedro had sent some from Madrid while friends in Italy sent others. Vito knew that he would be paying a king's ransom for these favors. Nothing mattered to him, nothing at all except the capture, torture, and killing of Mike McCormick and Joe Donahue. Vito was consumed with hatred; all he wanted out of life now was the joy of making Sandy Donahue watch the slaughter of her husband and McCormick before he allowed Gert to finish her off slowly.

With a sneer on his lips, he remembered as a youth, he had punched the parish priest who had caught him stealing the ceremonial wine. Vito was not a very good kid and he turned out to be a not-so-nice adult. Padre Macaroni back in Assisi still to this day offered prayers on his behalf — what a colossal waste of time. Oh yes, God heard these pleas on Vito's behalf, but all He would do is shake his Mighty head and let Vito's free will prevail.

Gert lost her zeal to play the whore with Ramon, a man whom she wrote off as a weakling. After seeing the senseless slaughter on the front steps of the house, she now had a new interest. She looked at the man that had just killed the Basque interloper with admiration and lust. Their eyes locked and the slightest hint of a smile crossed both faces; they knew that soon they would be together. For now though, he had to answer Vito's questions. When Vito heard the dead man's last name, he knew why he was here. This was Maria's brother, he told himself. He thanked the hired man from Madrid and with a handshake told him, "Relax for the rest of the day, compadre; you had a long ride to get here and thank you." His name was Fernando Ortiz and he took his leave from Vito, intent on finding that babe in black. She was waiting just outside the door and they whisked away into the woods; it was rutting season. Ramon was sent to town with another guard to buy food supplies for the estate. He made a phone call.

Sandy was upstairs and heard the gunshots. Peering out of the window from behind the safety of the curtains, she saw all of the new faces but was unable to see what had happened. She saw the guns, she saw the cars, and she heard the shouts of "Olé" and "Bravo." Never in her life had she felt so helpless and vulnerable. She prayed with all of her heart for quick and perfect resolution and she prayed for the safety of her husband, Joe. Like Ramon, she hadda get outta there.

Joe, Mike, Barney, and Pete deplaned in Barcelona and walked down the ramp toward the customs desk, single file. Each man took off their shoes and passed through the metal detectors. Passports stamped, they were wished a happy visit in Spain and they were good to go. A bit unsure of where to go or if they should try for a cab right away, they just looked at each other, hoping someone would make a suggestion. They stood there like bumps on a log for a minute then walked over to one of the coffee shops for a quick bite to eat. After that, they would figure out their next move but for now they needed to sit and unwind. They would also need a map so Mike bought one at a concession stand. They were tired and needed sleep so they knew that they would be getting some rooms somewhere, then hire a car tomorrow and head out to Girona. Barney said that he had seen a Holiday Inn sign while landing so he thought they should give them a call. And then the impossible happened:

"Hi, Dad"

Joe almost fell off the chair. Joe Donahue Jr., Steve Manley, and the super-spook Santos eased into the booth. Joe was beside himself; he lost his voice. He wanted to hug these guys, but he was afraid to show any display of emotion in the airport. Barney couldn't contain his surprise and maybe overdid an emotional display of greeting. Pete and Mike maintained stoic attitudes but inwardly the quick response and support from these three brave men overwhelmed them. Joe and his son clasped hands across the table and Steve clasped his over theirs. Barney, Mike, and Pete could not resist the emotional cementing of comradeship and joined their hands into one hodgepodge of clasped hands right there on the table in the little coffee shop in Barcelona International Airport.

The team was coming together. Santos immediately told them that Mel Hairston had gotten hold of him by leaving a cryptic message at his office: "It seems that Mel is on his way guys, and there was nothing I could say that would stop him. He is expected tomorrow around noon right here in this airport. What I suggest is that we get you guys some sleep and food and then tomorrow morning we can have a planning session. By that time, Mel will be here too and we can leave Barcelona but we have got to figure out a good plan. Steve and Joe Jr. are under the jurisdiction of the Uniform Code of Military Justice (UCMJ) and in no way can they be exposed as helping in this venture. We have to protect their identities but we need them with us desperately. As for myself, well, my boss has a hard time keeping tabs on me anyway so let's just not sweat the small stuff."

Seven U.S. citizens had flown in from all over the place on a rescue mission of mercy and retribution. Expecting the eighth man tomorrow, the group was becoming a force with which to be reckoned. Two men, Mike and Pete, were ex-FBI agents. Joe and Pete were older Vietnam combat veteran ex-Marines, and two, Steve and Joe Jr., were active-duty Marines who had both recently faced combat. Barney was a retired cop, Santos was a CIA agent working undercover without U.S. government sanction, and the group was waiting on Mel, who had just quit the FBI two days ago.

Each man was well trained, smart, and courageous.

Pete admitted that he had called Santos and asked him to try to find Steve and Joe Jr., as he knew that they weren't too far away. Both had gotten an emergency ten-day leave from their respective units and the field commanders had no idea that there was any link between them at all.

They were off to the Holiday Inn using a HumVee van that Santos had acquired; nobody asked about it and nobody cared to know. They were all tired but they wanted to do a strategy meeting right then and there. Saner heads prevailed and they all got a well-deserved rest using four rooms at the Inn. Before they hit the sack, Santos told them all that he wasn't all that tired; he worked here, remember? He said that he would pick up Mel in the morning and when he got back to the hotel, they would use one of the small conference rooms at the hotel. "There, over coffee and with full bellies, we will iron this out and come up with some kind of workable plan. You guys can sleep late and have a good breakfast." He told them that he had a pretty good idea where Sandy was and still had a few calls to make.

"You sure about this, Bob?" asked Israel Burns of the Yonkers Police Department. He was talking over coffee with Bob Goodman, Barney's old boss back at the New York City Police Department. "Yeah Burnsy, I have been checking around quietly and there is no trace of any of these guys. They all seem to have disappeared off the face of the earth." Burns said, "Ok, then we'll go," and with that they boarded a United Airlines flight to Madrid. From there they were taking a puddle jumper to Girona, Spain. Barney had called the posse. Both had read Scaglionne's email and seen the video; there was no way that either of these men would be left out of this rescue mission. Both men were putting their careers on the line and in both cases; their wives were worried sick but agreed that they should go to help their friends.

Santos had reserved Conference Room #105 at the Inn for noon. It had a capacity for twelve, plus a dais. Mel was greeted with hugs, handshakes, and introductions. He said that he was proud to be part of the group, had seen the video, and read the email. He was happy to meet Joe Jr. and Steve Manley and was impressed with their credentials and the family involvement in this rescue. Mel knew that the legal ramifications for those two would be a lot worse than for any of the others if things went bad. He gave a report on the plans being initiated by his ex-boss Schmidt:

"Last thing I heard when I was there, they have no idea where you are or how you got out of the country so for now we are safe, but they will try to intercede in Girona at the hotel. Also, they are not positive that you, Pete, or you, Barney, are parts of this crew. For now, to them, you are classified as missing, whereabouts unknown. Needless to say, they haven't thought deep enough to consider that Captain Manley or Lieutenant Donahue here would be contacted at all." Mel was a close friend of both Pete and Mike, but had only briefly met Joe and Barney at Donahue Downs and five years ago he had a meeting with Santos. This was his first introduction to Joe Jr. and Steve Manley.

Santos took the dais and outlined a quickly thrown together plan: "Ok guys, I have loosely come up with an idea of how we can win this, but feel free to interrupt at any time with your concerns or alternative ideas. According to the time frame laid out by Scaglionne, Joe and Mike are a day early so I don't think that he has any way of knowing that you are already here. He would assume that Barney would be with you even though the email said that you two should come alone. I now have an unpaid asset at the Diablo Hotel; don't ask, OK? The reservations have been confirmed and both of your names are in the register for check-in on Thursday. That known, we have to believe everything that Scaglionne told us for the time being. I don't think that Vito will try anything at the hotel because he seems to be so wrapped up in hatred that he would want you hog-tied and dragged to his hideout like dogs. That is where he plans on killing you guys and Sandy too. He will try to grab you at the hotel though and that's where we start.

"First of all, I have amassed a lot of gear for us to use. We have enough artillery to mount a full-frontal assault on his compound, but we would be outnumbered so that isn't the way to go. When we leave here this afternoon, I am taking you to a place where all the tools of our trade have been collected. Early reports tell me that Scaglionne is building an army at the winery estate that he is using. According to my informants, Vito is holed up in his buddy Pedro's winery about fifty miles north of Girona on the southern slopes of the Pyrenees Mountains. That, guys, is where Sandy is right now.

"I gotta admit that my connections around here are extensive so the first flip chart will show a map of the terrain surrounding the estate house on the winery property. As you can see, the house itself sits on the highest ground surrounded by hedgerows of grapevines. The driveway goes right up the middle and I don't think we should just drive up there like lost American tourists; we wouldn't get ten feet past the well-guarded wall around the building. That wall is about two hundred yards from the house in all directions and is manned at every vantage point. Vito has between thirty and fifty guys now, and all are killers, cutthroats, assassins, and villains of every sort. Some are Spanish, others are Italian and, from what I am told, there is at least one female supposedly from the German Baader-Meinhof terrorist organization. That is probably the woman on the video that is called Gertrude. What I propose is the following." Flipping the next chart up on the easel, Santos went on.

347

"Here we see the hotel, El Diablo Rojo and its immediate sur-roundings. The front door is directly across from 855 Rio Del Oro Street. I managed to acquire an empty apartment with a window that faces the hotel entrance. Since Steve has been trained as a Marine sniper, he is stationed in that room. There is a spotter's scope and a Ruger M-77 rifle, which uses a .270 Win cartridge in the room right now. Also, there is a full box of ammunition on the shelf just below the window. I had one of my trusted associates adjust the sights on the weapon and it's a bull's eye at three hundred yards which is just about the distance from the window to the hotel door. The rifle has a Weaver eight power scope and is mounted on a tripod but you can use that or not; it's your call, Steve.

"Vito may be crazy, but he is anything but a fool. We have to assume that whoever he sends to collect Joe and Mike will have pic-tures with them. I would put Joe Jr. in the lobby, but damn Joe, you look too much like your old man and that haircut is a dead giveaway; you look like what you are, a Marine. You and Barney will use the rear entrance to the hotel hours before Joe Sr. gets there with Pete. The reserved room is on the second floor; it is Room 221 and you guys will be in Room 222. As luck would have it, those rooms have an adjoin-ing door that is usually locked. When you get there, the door will not be locked but don't fool with it unless you hear things in 221 getting out of hand. Just so that you all know, the nasty-looking dude at the front desk is on our side. He isn't gonna sound nice or smile even but relax; he is a Basque Separatist who owes me a favor. He also has a big 'pistola' under his counter.

"Pete and I will be in the lobby sipping coffee, reading the paper, and chatting like two tired businessmen. Mel, I think that you should be outside of the hotel in the van ready to do a chase or get-away, if needed. All of us will be armed with military Colt 45s; that was the best I could come up with on such short notice but all have been refurbished, cleaned, and oiled. We each get two additional mag-azines to go with 'em. I also was able to come with a whole bunch of earpiece radio transmitters but they are good for only a half-mile, so let's not get too separated. Later at my little clandestine love-nest in the woods, I have better radio equipment and more formidable weapons.

"The way I see it is that we bust these two or three goons before they are able to disarm Joe and Mike. With guns aimed at their heads, I am sure that they would be most happy to drive us to the compound and through the gates. With luck, most of Vito's troops will be manning the wall or out in the vineyard watching the approach road. We will have mere seconds to pull off the coup of the century, but make no mistake about it, this is one very dangerous mission and we are outnumbered and out-gunned. Joe and Mike will be with Vito's men and we follow in the van. I look like they do and speak the language, so if we are stopped I will just tell the guy that we are more troops sent from the Mafia to help Mr. Scaglionne. I will have a silencer on my sidearm so if we have to pop a guard or two that's the way the mop flops. I know that this plan sounds really hard to pull off, but I have made a few other calls and we may have some assets joining us by the end of the day. I have gotten wind of some information that we may have some help inside Scaglionne's lair as well."

Barney raised his hand and silenced the murmurs coming from all corners of the room. "Fellas, I can't let us go into this thing without all of us knowing all the facts surrounding this deal. Joe, I know you aren't gonna like this, but while you were gone in the Bronx, Bob Goodman and Israel Burns were in constant contact with me. They were as worried about you as the rest of us were. It was Bob who finally got the address where I found you. You know how much you and Sandy mean to both of them and their wives. When I saw that video of what they were doin' to Sandy, my heart broke and I was and still am filled with rage and hatred for this Vito creep. I had gone to my room for a bit to mourn, cry, and think when my cell phone went off. It was Bob asking about you once again. Well guys, I blabbed the whole story to him and he was so damn upset he clicked off the phone telling me to stay right there and that he would call me

349

back." At this point, Joe Jr. and Steve were looking at Joe Sr. with questions and worry but held it for later. "Sure enough, ten minutes later he called me back and asked me to send the email and video to him at his personal email address at home. He had Israel meet him there and they saw it together. Fellas, I couldn't stop them, and they took a flight out of Newark to Madrid early this morning. From there they got a connecting flight to Girona. It looks like they will be somewhere around that hotel waiting for us before we arrive. I have Bob's cell phone number and we should be able to contact them any time we need to. They landed at 9 a.m., so most likely they are in the air on the way to Girona right now."

Pete Richardson stood up and waved everyone to silence. "We can't undo spilt milk, so we use them. What else can we do? Besides, I know both of those guys and if I ever had to go into a dark alley with anybody, I would want those guys with me. As much as I agree that Barney shouldn't have told them, it's done so let's get on with this plan and include them somehow." All Santos could think about was updating the necessary equipment, so he made another phone call. Joe ran the gamut of feelings about what Barney had said, but in the end he understood and walked over to him and shook his hand. He would own up to his son and Steve later with the truth about the Bronx. Mike was happy to have the help and said so. Mel just shrugged his shoulders and said, "Whatever!"

They packed up their non-luggage and checked out of the hotel. Loading the van with eight burly men was almost like a clown show at the circus but it was done, if not with some discomfort. Barney sat facing the back window; he was a little embarrassed but was happy that nobody was cracking on him for his big mouth. Mel sat next to him and both had automatic weapons just to be sure that nobody was tailing them with any crazy ideas. Santos drove out of the city and into wine country, all the while using his cell phone and talking in Spanish. About an hour later, he pulled into a working farm complete with goats, chickens, and little children running around. Santos got out of the van and stood by the front fender. A man was approaching from the house; they greeted with effervescent hugs and the customary kiss on both cheeks. Nobody in the car understood a word, but the conversation ended with the guy shaking Santos' hand, patting him on the back, and pointing to a work shed about a hundred feet to the left of the house.

Santos looked into the van, and told Mike to drive and follow him. He then walked over to the shed and unlocked the doors and Mike drove the van inside. "The last of it was delivered about an hour ago," said our all-accommodating and spooky friend. We looked at a large wooden table full of weaponry of every type. There were hand grenades, automatic "street-sweeper" shotguns, AK-47s with double banana clips, bulletproof vests, knives of all sorts and sizes, and an array of small, walkie-talkie radio transmitters. Santos didn't miss a beat; he opened up one of the boxes and displayed a pile of handcuffs and first aid kits in case we needed them. Another two boxes revealed neatly sorted ammunition for each weapon. He said it was up to us to pick out whichever weapon we were most comfortable with. Mike asked what we should do with the .45s and Santos told him that we should just leave them there on the table with the ammo clips. They would be cleaned of any fingerprints and buried for future use. "Our new sidearm would be an experimental automatic pistol that fires rifle ammunition." Santos conducted a two-minute training exercise, firing one of the pistols into a sack of grain and all we heard was a near-silent poof. He said, "This is a 7.62 Micro-Whisper #308 with a built-in silencer. It's a rifle projectile stuffed into an automatic pistol, a very destructive piece of equipment."

Toying with a pair of night vision binoculars, Santos told us what we didn't need to know. "Courtesy of the Basque Party Separatists, gentlemen: terrorist killers that are on our side for now; so really, for today, they are our terrorist killers. The Spanish Prime Minister, José María Aznar is not all that happy with them and rightfully so, but these dudes now have an issue that involves our mission. It seems that Scaglionne murdered one of their members' sisters and then assassinated the guy like a dog when they caught him infiltrating his ranks."

Santos went on to tell us that since he was an American employee with the CIA, he enjoyed diplomatic immunity but the rest of us didn't. He said that we were dangerously close to creating an international incident so we could not meet with or coordinate in any way with the Basque people. Most important, he said, was that we couldn't afford to be caught and we had to get any wounded or killed member of our group away from the scene when it was over. "We don't want to have to bury any of us out here amidst the grapevines so be careful, don't take too many chances, and aim well. This has to be done neat, clean, and fast, gentlemen, and when the dust settles, the Spanish government can come in and clean up the mess.

"I have a chopper stationed nearby, which will take you across the border into France when we're done. Your passports are already stamped and, from there, you will catch a jumbo jet back to the U.S.. I had an associate meet Bob Goodman and Israel Burns when they got off the plane in Girona to prevent them from walking into a possible ambush. They are safe and waiting for us in a small villa outside of town. Their passports and plane tickets are being arranged for as we speak. Yes, I have a rigged passport for Sandy as well."

Each man broke out in applause for Santos and thanked him for all that he had done for them. We assumed that he would be heading back to Madrid or Barcelona, but that wasn't the case. He said that he had elected himself to be our team leader if that was OK with us. Another round of applause and handshakes even though we were all concerned that this mission may soon become a bloodletting fiasco of monumental proportions.

Major Schmidt kicked the entire debacle upstairs to the Attorney General in one complete yet "open and active" file. René Starker, on orders from T.D. Brown, and George Wheelwright, the Attorney General's aide, sent a complete dossier on the four missing American citizens to the American consulate office in Madrid. The attached memo said that these men were most likely on their way to, or already in, Spain. The file bore a handwritten recommendation that the ambassador should talk to his counterpart in Madrid to try to diffuse this situation in any way possible. Both sets of forwarded files contained Scaglionne's email message, the MPEG video, and a tape of the intercepted and recorded phone call to Mike McCormick.

Charlie Beesworth got a judge to issue a warrant and he had a team of agents combing over every inch of Donahue Downs, Pete Richardson's house, Barney Tunney's residence quarters and Mike McCormick's house. Mrs. McCormick was located at their daughter's house in Cape May and had been placed in protective custody.

Vito Scaglionne was a person who knew his own abilities and limitations. He knew who owed him, who respected him, who hated him, and who would like to see him dead.

At best, he distrusted every person on the face of the globe including his own family. The arrests made at Donahue Downs three years ago drove that thought home for him. The Falcone brothers, once his most trusted allies back in the States, were now in prison singing like canaries trying to avoid the death penalty. They had given Vito up at every turn and Vito knew it was doubtful that he could ever return to the United States. Same thing for Jack "The Lip" Sullivan: he was making a sweetheart deal with the federal prosecutor. He had to be silenced, so Vito had made arrangements for his murder.

At worst, he was forced to put his trust in the greed of the men that he had hired to help him in this cause. This cadre of marauders, rapists, killers, and guerrilla fighters he had assembled were here for one reason only and that was his money. At the drop of a hat they would betray him if they thought that their bosses would believe their story or if it benefited them in any way. He told each man that the pay would be good but dishonor, disrespect, or disobedience would lead to instant death. They all knew the rules of the game and each man had a criminal history that would put Bonnie and Clyde to shame. They were well armed and Ramon, his trusted chief of security, had drawn up a twenty-four hour watch list. Each guard post had communications with Ramon and Scaglionne and to the other guards as well. Nobody could penetrate this armed encampment unannounced.

The dogs, however, would not take to the new men on the wall so they remained with those original local personnel and were not being used in their best capacity. Ramon had confided in Vito that he would tell the guards with the dogs to walk the outermost perimeter of the estate, but he was not sure that they could be trusted. They might just leave and disappear, dogs and all. Vito bought this explanation and trusted Ramon's judgment to a degree but he wasn't totally sure of Ramon either. So far he had done his job very well, but he had yet to be tested. As far as Vito knew, Ramon had not yet killed anyone. Gert never divulged her suspicions about Ramon because at that time she thought him a good playmate. Now that she and Fernando were playing the "touch me, feel me" game, she had put Ramon out of her thoughts. Gert broke security rules for lust; for Ramon, it was a lucky thing she did.

The only local people here were those staff and security people Vito had hired before he even thought of the kidnapping of Mrs. Donahue. He couldn't dismiss them because they knew too much. He wouldn't kill them because he wasn't entirely sure that they couldn't be trusted after all. He also couldn't kill them because they had families out here and some of them were connected to different forces that Vito did not want to have to deal with. When he had found out that the assassin that Fernando had killed was a Basque, it had caused some alarm, but Vito sent a message via his local cop pal to diffuse any thoughts of retribution. When the cook Maria breached security rules, she had to be made an example of in order to drive the message home to the rest of them, Basque or not.

Vito was now sporting a .45-caliber Glock and a bulletproof vest. Although he felt a bit out of character, these protections made him feel good. They also made him feel sexy, so at every opportunity he would take his Gestapo bitch to his room.

Gert wanted to continue her playtime with Sandy Donahue

but found that Fernando Ortiz was a good hump and Vito seemed to be more sexually experimental. Gert had a full regimen of lovers now and the excitement of the impending danger caused her libido to be insatiable. Vito had forbidden her to go near Mrs. Donahue anyway. When Vito told her that, she pouted cutely then laughed. She took off her clothes and romped with Vito one more time. She loved sex more than whipping anyway.

CHAPTER EIGHT

Confusion en Masse

C OMSAT messages flew across the planet in the blink of an eye. Charlie Daniels, who headed up the CIA office in Madrid, owned up to the fact that he did not know where his lead agent Santos was right now. "All he said to me was that he would be undercover for a few days; this is normal for him and I trust him to the max." After reviewing the Donahue file, Charlie had a sick feeling inside; he knew that Santos was involved in this because he was a close friend with both Richardson and Donahue. Charlie liked them as well and made a silent vow to himself that he would cover their tracks and mop up the mess without anyone being the wiser. That is, if he could!

Charlie picked up a large messy file from his desk and put it away; it was the ongoing investigation of some of the recent car-bombings done by local guerrilla fighters. The file was labeled The Basque Party Separatists. "Damn, I hate that kid-killing, ultra-right wing political organization," he muttered. The Basques were Santos' bailiwick and that was what he was supposed to be working on.

Charlie knew Santos well enough to know that he would come to the aid of his friends, especially when it came to the kidnapping and torture of Donahue's wife. Santos had a dangerous job and, although the Basques seemed to like him, others didn't. There had been two or three attempts on his life already and Charlie had him slated for rotation back to the States as soon as possible. Balancing the Basques and the left-wing Catalan separatist party was proving to be more than any one man could do, even as good as Santos was. Busting Carlos and Baum last year had brought other forces into play, and now the Mafia wanted Santos whacked too.

The American consulate's office was concerned and the ambassador had a meeting with his Spanish counterpart. Assured that the U.S. government had not given any kind of permission for any of its citizens to act in an independent manner, the Spaniards were committed to finding Mrs. Donahue before any of their laws were broken and before this issue escalated to major proportions. When rumors filtered down then up about Basque involvement and Charlie Daniels was advised of possible Italian interests as well, all kinds of department heads were called in for meetings and crunch sessions that lasted far into the night.

Governments were doing what governments did best: they held meetings, appointed committees and subcommittees, then ended up doing nothing. The Italian government disavowed any interest in this problem in Spain and felt that if any Italian criminals were involved, they would not try to extradite them, protect them, or even send attorneys on their behalf. The Italian ambassador's representative intimated that his people would be happy to have the Spanish government take care of international crime in any way they deemed appropriate. They said that they did not know of any Italians involved with Vito Scaglionne but he was the only one in whom they had an interest. They said that they did not even know that he was in Spain, but were happy to find out. The others, if there were others, were deemed personas non grata.

And so, Vito was in Spain hiding out in Pedro's estate, holding Sandy Donahue as his captive. Donahue, McCormick, Richardson, Tunney, Hairston, Steve Manley, Joe Donahue Jr., Israel Burns, Santos, and Bob Goodman were coming to rescue her.

Gertrude, from the Baader-Meinhof, was a Nazi-like sadist with an overactive sex drive; her cravings blinded her to details. Ramon was a locally recruited guard who had gained Vito's trust. Fernandez had murdered a Basque Party Separatist who was the cook's brother. Major Schmidt of the FBI was powerless; he filed and filed and filed.

Santos was in to this up to his eyeballs. Sandy was injured and scared beyond comprehension. The Basques wanted retribution for the slaying of one of their best men. The Italian mob leant a hand to Vito by sending men. Pedro, Vito's pal in Madrid, also leant a hand by supplying some of his henchmen.

Charlie Daniels couldn't locate Santos and was worried. Ambassadors from three countries had meetings and argued. Everybody was armed and dangerous.

Santos drove over hill and dale into the rough terrain of northeast Spain. He knew that they were soon to hook up with Mr. Goodman and Mr. Burns who were being "gently" detained by a few friends of his. So far, Santos said, "nobody had ruffled anybody's feathers, but Goodman and Burns ain't too happy about not being informed about why they were whisked away from Girona as soon as they got off the plane." He said it was done easily enough and handled by one of the more intellectual members of his cadre of spooky friends, but the two New York cops wanted some information and it wasn't forthcoming. Bob and Israel were not on solid ground and they knew it; they weren't armed so they bit the bullet and went with their seemingly friendly escort.

As Santos drove onto a dirt-encrusted farm road, he stopped to say hello to the man who looked like he was hunting grouse, pigeons, turkeys, or men! The guy lowered his sawed-off and said, "Buenos dios, amigo." Santos got out of the van and handed his friend a cigar: "Thank you for safeguarding our friends, José. I will remember this kind gesture." With that, he drove to the barn, waving at a few others along the way.

They found Bob and Israel sitting on wine barrels with some goats and chickens running around. They were not happy campers, but super glad to see their friends. They pushed away a bottle of wine, two half-loaves of bread, and a wedge of blue-colored cheese to greet their long-lost pals. Bob actually rushed into the mob and knocked over one of the stools on which they were sitting. Hands were shaken, backs were slapped, hugs were given, and introductions were made all around as Pete, Mike, and Santos brought everyone up to speed. Burns and Goodman had no idea that this mission had escalated to such a high and dangerous degree, but they were here and they knew that this team was the only team in the world that could pull it off. Barney quipped that they were two men short of the dirty dozen. This brought a round of laughs, which aptly served to briefly interrupt the thoughts of possible impending doom.

Santos called the group to order; he was in charge, right? He wanted to outline some changes in the plan now that there were two more men in the group. The only difference from the first plan was that now he had to incorporate Bob and Israel into the mix. He had already asked his friend José for another vehicle: a farm truck, complete with hay, rakes, and shovels. Underneath the hay would be a 3.5 rocket launcher with shells and a tripod mounted 50-caliber machinegun. Bob would drive the truck with Israel next to him but they would park on the opposite end of the hotel front door. Both men would have a sidearm and a shotgun on the floor in case of dire emergency. "No sense taking any chances, right guys?" he asked.

As the discussion progressed, they came to the conclusion that they probably would not need this heavy artillery at the hotel, but it would surely come in handy when the time came to rescue Sandy. Enjoying the hospitality of José, they spent the night on the farm and ate a sumptuous meal of goat meat, bread, and wine.

Joe drank water. Tomorrow was Thursday.

Charlie Daniels and one of his agents, Erik Bronkowski, took seats in the half-empty coffee shop of El Diablo Rojo. Charlie left messages for Santos every place he could think of, but so far he has not heard from him. It was 10:30 a.m.; check-in time was 11. Santos walked up and plopped down at the table just like he was expected. He reintroduced Pete to both men, but he could see that Charlie was really upset with him. He had a lot of explaining to do to his boss, but he avoided this query by telling him, "We have no time boss; I will bring you up to speed later if it's OK with you." Charlie trusted Santos' judgment. They had worked together for years so he agreed but wanted to know what he thought would happen here this morning. Santos told him that he thought that Scaglionne would try to trap Donahue and McCormick and bring them to his hidden compound; he did not tell him where he thought that compound might be. Santos was not surprised to learn that the FBI had forwarded the Vito tapes, video, and email messages to him and apologized for not handling it officially through the office.

There were far more setups going on in this hotel this morning than any of the concerned participants knew. Joe Jr. and Barney were in Room 222. Mel was just outside, sitting in the van with a load of artillery. Bob and Israel were in the work truck parked about a half-block down the street. Both were dressed like peasants, but a close look would reveal that they were anything but. The truck faced the front door of the hotel and they had a clear line of sight. Steve was at the window in the flat across the street and he too had a clear view. All were in communication but committed to silence unless something happened. Santos and Pete were inside having coffee with Charlie and Erik and nobody else there paid them any attention.

What they didn't know was that Ramon and Fernando Ortiz were enjoying coffee not twenty feet from them. They were the only two that Vito actually trusted so they were elected to pull this off for him. In the lobby, two men in suits were reading some documents and chatting over a business deal. They were incognito Basque killers. The front desk manager, Mr. Garcia, was a friend of Santos' and owed him, but he was also a Basque party member who had lots of debts. Everybody was waiting for Joe and Mike to show up and register for their room. The phone rang at the front desk and the manager boringly picked it up.

"Good morning Mr. Garcia, this is Mr. Donahue. You have a room reserved for me which I believe is number 221. Please ask your bell-person to go up and open the room and leave the key on the bed. I will come down in a few minutes to sign your registration forms. For reasons that I think you know, we are coming in through the back door and will use the stairs to get to the room." Garcia listened intently and when Joe was finished speaking, he just said, "Yes sir, it will be done for you."

Joe and Mike waited for the almost silent beep from their phone and they knew that the bellhop had left the lobby with a key. They walked up the back stairs following the path blazed for them by Barney and Joe Jr. It was 10:50 a.m.; they were ten minutes early, just as planned. The door was not locked, the room was empty, and the bellhop was gone. The key was on the bed. Mike opened the adjoining door, and Joe Jr. and Barney were there and ready to take the elevator down to the lobby as a group. All the men were armed and all the guns were loaded; all were on safety but each had a round in the chamber.

A police car pulled up in front of the hotel and parked directly behind Mel's van. Steve watched every move but the cop stayed in his car. Mel also watched him in the rearview mirror. He was thinking that nothing was routine in this scene and that he didn't believe in coincidences. Bob and Israel were parked a bit further from the front door, but they noticed with interest that the cop was using a cell phone and not the normal police radio. They didn't believe in coincidences either.

Sergeant Madera did as Vito had told him on the phone; he sat in the car waiting for Ramon. He wanted to quit this low-pay job; he wanted to become a big time crook instead of the low-life, crooked cop that he had become. He was here to drive the backup car behind Ramon and some other guy. Vito told him that a police car would make what they were doing look official and that there was little danger. Madera knew Ramon well; they had been friends for many years, but he didn't know this Fernando hombre. Supposedly, he would see Ramon and the other guy escorting two men from the hotel. They would get into that Chevy SUV on the corner and drive away. He would follow them to the winery house and that was all there was to it. Both he and Ramon were told not to stop their cars for any reason. Madera was told to make sure of it, even if he had to resort to gunplay. Madera was an order-taking dullard, but he was also a dangerous man with little respect for human life; he would follow his orders to the tee. Besides, Vito promised him fifty Euros ($64.00 plus a few nickels). Sergeant Madera had made the big time!

Joe Jr. and Barney were first off the elevator, followed closely by Joe Sr. and Mike McCormick. To outward appearances, they looked like two groups of two men tending to their own separate business. The coffee shop was not visible from the elevator, so Barney and Joe Jr. stood aside while Joe Sr. and Mike signed in at the desk. Mr. Garcia, the front desk manager, was nervous and said to Joe in plain English, "Señor, be careful. There are at least six men in the coffee shop; I only know one of them," referring to Ramon, "and he is a local hood." The manager paid his debt to Santos with this information; the score was even and he was relieved. Joe nodded and he and Mike walked over to a small table facing the coffee shop. Everybody inside could plainly see them. Pete, Santos, Charlie, and Erik paid them no mind, not a wink nor a nod. Ramon and Fernando rose from their seats and walked across the lobby, looking like they were the most feared individuals in the world. Joe and Mike seemingly didn't see them; Joe Jr. and Barney had their hands in their pockets, ready to do whatever was necessary.

Fernando stood in front of the two seated men and opened the dialogue with a polite greeting: "Mr. Scaglionne sends you greetings, Mr. McCormick and Mr. Donahue. My name is Fernando and my associate here is Ramon. Mr. Scaglionne asks that you accompany us to his home where you will be reunited with Mrs. Donahue."

With that, he asked Joe and Mike to hand him their guns, saying that they would not be needed. As Joe and Mike stood to face the speaker, Ramon remained quiet but moved slightly away from Fernando. Before Joe or Mike could say a word, Ramon said quickly, "They will kill you there." He then drew his pistol and pointed it at Fernando. Fernando was the quintessential hot-blooded Latino; he went for his gun and loudly called Ramon a traitor. Then the shot shattered the quiet of this little hotel on pristine Rio del Oro Street. Fernando fell to the floor dead with a bullet through his heart.

Pete, Santos, Charlie, and Erik saw what had happened and responded in a flash. Ramon had eight guns pointed at him. He nervously smiled and sheepishly holstered his pistol. Santos was on the radio right away; he told everyone outside to remain in place and that all was OK. Sergeant Madera heard the gunshot and got out of his car in a hurry. He ran inside where Mike was waiting for him on the other side of the door. Mike dropped him with one punch reminiscent of the old song, "Big Bad John." Madera never even saw it coming. Disarmed, he was led into the lobby where Barney promptly snapped a pair of handcuffs on him. Madera forgot to call Vito before running into the hotel; he was a brave man, but an oh-so-stupid one. Joe Jr. went to the desk manager and told him to do what he had to do to appease any guests that may have witnessed this scene or heard the shot. Señor Garcia told him that all was well and that he would tend to it. The lobby was cleared and the two men in suits left without a word. They were happy to see that the man who killed their compatriot was dead. Garcia was within earshot of the discussions held by Santos and his crew, and he listened intently.

If our group of heroes is anything, they are truly adaptable to ever-changing conditions. A new plan was formulated on the spot. Ramon told them that he and Fernando were supposed to bring Mr. McCormick and Mr. Donahue to Vito Scaglionne's borrowed villa up in the foothills. Sergeant Madera was supposed to follow in the police car in the event that there were difficulties.

Santos came up with a master plan that seemed workable to all. It went like this: Fernando, the dead hood from Madrid, would be propped up in the Chevy van with Ramon at the wheel. Joe and Mike would ride in the backseat as if Vito's plan was going down just the way he planned it. Sergeant Madera would drive his car with Barney in the back, pointing a gun to his head. He would follow the SUV as planned but if Madera tried to give any sort of signal, he would be shot dead.

Madera was scared to death and was shaking. His friend Ramon did his best to quiet his nerves with a friendly explanation: "Amigo, your friend Mr. Scaglionne murdered Maria Sanchez in cold blood for no reason other than to scare the others into submission. When her brother came to the villa to make this right, this other guy Fernando shot him down like a dog. You and I grew up with these good people and Maria was my wife's cousin; I could not let these things go by and neither should you. I am asking you to change sides right now. It is your best bet to stay alive."

Madera, the "not-to-be-trusted" cowardly cop, nodded his head in agreement. He said, "You are right, Ramon, my friend. I didn't know these things. I will do all that I can to make sure that you and your friends rescue the American lady and that Mr. Scaglionne pays the price for his deeds."

Santos went on outlining his plan. Following closely behind Madera and Barney, he would drive the work truck. Joe Jr. and Steve would be under the hay, manning the rocket launcher and machine gun. Neither they nor the artillery would be visible. Inside the truck with Santos would be Bob and Israel dressed as peasants. Since Santos spoke the language and looked like a Spaniard, he would pass the others off as extra help from Pedro in case a guard stopped them. If the ruse did not go off right, the guard would die on the spot courtesy of the Micro-Whisper #308 with the built-in silencer. He went on to say that the timing for this deal had to be precise because once they were inside the walls, all hell would break loose. Once that happened,

Pete, Erik, Mel, and Charlie would zoom over the hill in the helicopter with guns blazing. The chopper pilot, an old friend named Danny, was a phone call away and was ready to go whenever that they were. Danny was an ex-Army 1st Cavalry chopper jock with Vietnam combat search-and-destroy, as well as rescue mission experience. For his own reasons, he could not go home to the U.S.

Charlie Daniels was not ready for this; he had come to the hotel to intervene in case Donahue was kidnapped. He looked at his associate and said, "Santos, you truly amaze me, man. This may cost us all of our careers but from where I stand right now, I don't see any other way to pull this off. If we do nothing, Vito will know that something's up and if we send Donahue and McCormick inside alone with Ramon, we will be sending them to their deaths. Mrs. Donahue would also be killed so if Erik is in agreement, we go with this."

Erik responded without hesitation, "It's a go; there is no other way out of this."

Santos looked at the others, and then called Steve, Mel, Bob, and Israel and told them to come inside the hotel. He called Danny the chopper pilot as well; he was in a bar right around the corner. Mr. Garcia had emptied the lobby of other guests and had staff on all the floors asking everyone to remain in their rooms for a short while. Santos brought everyone up to speed at the same time. Bob asked for a moment of prayer for this venture and all clasped hands in the circle. Barney did a lot of Amening and they were ready to go in minutes.

Mel drove Danny, Erik, Pete, and Charlie to the chopper, which had a Gatling gun and four AK-47s with loads of ammunition. Ramon and Santos stuffed Fernando in the passenger seat of the Chevy SUV and propped him up quite nicely. Madera was promising Barney that he would not do anything crazy and asked him to please not shoot him. The rest of them got onto and into the truck, ready to rock and roll. Steve asked Joe Jr. how the food was at Leavenworth which elicited the correct response: Joe smiled and said, "We ain't going there brother." They had themselves a convoy of well-armed pseudo-commandos ready to slay a fifty headed dragon of poorly trained killers.

Sandy sat by her window to the world and watched what was going on in the half-circle view that she had of the walled-in villa. From her vantage point, she could see over the wall and out to the hedgerows where armed men were stationed every fifty feet or so. She couldn't believe how gorgeous this day was. Not a breeze in the air, the sun shone brightly, and it wasn't as hot as it had been every other day since her captivity. She watched a wren flying freely, and she wished she too could fly away and put this place behind her.

Watching one of the guards with a dog near the gate, she saw Gert come up to the man with her whip under her arm. It was easy to see that the dog hated Gert; the hair on its back stood straight up and its lips formed a snarl. Gert beat the dog unmercifully with the whip as the guard obediently held the animal at bay. Sandy detected by his face that the guard hated Gert almost as much as the dog did, but he did nothing to protect his animal. "God, I hate that woman," she whispered under her breath. Sandy had to turn away; Vito had entered her room.

"Good afternoon, Mrs. Donahue. It is almost lunchtime and I am happy to tell you that your loving husband and his friend Mr. McCormick are on their way from the local village to take you home. We will have a royal feast for lunch today and I am looking forward to the festivities."

Sandy thought to herself; "God, I hate this man." Sandy was still in pain, but the bandages and minimal medical treatment that she had received seemed to have stopped the bleeding and helped her walk a little better. She could not lie down due to the welts on her back and buttocks nor could she eat very well due to her missing tooth and swollen lips.

Sandy murmured to him, "I hope you die, you snake."

Scaglionne laughed in her face, garlic breath and all. He said that she and her husband would surely be in hell long before he would. His cell phone rang. It was one of the guards on the outer perimeter telling him that vehicles were approaching.

Vito left the room so Sandy went back to her lookout post at the window. In the distance she saw three vehicles coming up the road; one was the Chevy pickup that she had tried to escape in and the next one was a police car followed by a farm truck of some sort. Sandy prayed, "God, if Joe and Mike are being brought here, protect them Lord, and deliver us from all evil."

Ramon drove the Chevy slowly and briefly waved to the guard at the first checkpoint. All was well so far, he thought. In the rearview mirror, he saw that Sergeant Madera also drove by without stopping. But as he made the slow ascent up the circuitous road, he lost his view of the pickup. Santos approached the guard driving the truck slowly, but not willing to stop unless asked to. The guard stepped into the roadway with his automatic weapon pointed directly at the vehicle. As he approached, a shadowy figure came up behind him and neatly slit his throat. The guard fell dead and the man melted back into the foliage without saying hello.

Santos shivered: "Gee guys, it looks like we got us some unsolicited help from the Basques I guess!" They continued up the road and caught up to Madera who was stopped at the second checkpoint. Santos, Bob, and Israel watched as the guard fell to the ground. Their newest ally, Sergeant Madera, had shot him in the face. Santos muttered to himself, "Two down, forty-eight to go." Right on cue, another figure leapt out of the foliage and dragged the dead guard into the bushes. The Basque guy took up the post, radio and all. Santos stopped the truck and thanked their benefactor, who told him that they had just as much at stake here as Donahue did. They too wanted Scaglionne dead.

Santos nodded; there was no time for discussion or plan making and so far this thing was going down OK. Gunshots broke the silence so Santos picked up speed and got directly behind the police car. Other guards at other outposts were engaged in mortal combat with Basque raiders. Vito's men were taken by surprise and were losing this fight to the death quickly. Three of Vito's men were in the roadway trying to stop Sergeant Madera when all hell broke loose. Unseen men hiding in the hedgerows cut them down before they were able to get off even one shot. Madera, who had stopped, drove off quickly and caught up to the SUV. The Chevy entered the gates, followed by Madera and Barney, who was now sitting up straight in the backseat. Barney was shooting in rapid fire, wisely taking advantage of this surprise attack. Hired thugs fell to the left and right and even Madera was shooting. Barney had given him back his gun when they stopped at that last checkpoint. Santos pulled inside the compound as well and he heard the chatter of the .50-caliber machine gun. Steve was mowing down armed men that were in an attack stance. The guard dogs ran out of the gate and into the vineyard, only to be slaughtered by Basque raiders. His hired men surrounded Vito, but he saw to his disgust that some of them were putting up their hands in surrender. He shot two of them in the back, but then he was knocked to the ground and disarmed by another guard who wanted to live.

Sandy had put a chair beneath the doorknob in case Vito or Gert would want to use her as a shield; she would not let that happen. She saw that Gert had her whip in one hand and an automatic weapon in the other. When she saw Vito knocked to the ground, Sandy was shocked to see Gert run toward the entrance of the house. She heard the door slam and hurried footsteps on the staircase. Sandy removed the chair and unlocked the door so Gert could get in easily. Sandy stood by the side of the door with her weapon, a can of Helene Curtis Thermasilk hair spray. Gert kicked open the door and took one step into a blinding mist of stickiness. The automatic sprayed bullets all over the wall and window, but Sandy was uninjured. Sandy blasted Gert in the face with a fist that she had thought she had forgotten how to make. Gert fell and Sandy kicked the gun over to the side. Gert was trying to recompose, but Sandy would not let her up. She jumped on her chest, knees first, and punched her unmercifully about the face. The whip was free and Sandy kicked the door shut. Gert was getting up, snarling and cursing, but Sandy lashed that whip right across her evil face. Sandy grabbed the automatic weapon and fired a volley of shots into Gert's legs, which dropped her on the spot.

The chopper came in flying low and spraying death from the sky. The men on the walls dropped their weapons and raised their hands as quickly as they could. Vito had gotten up only to face Mike McCormick; he sneered in hatred. This mini-devil had raised his fist against good people and now that fist of evil would be shoved where the sun didn't shine. Mike almost took off Vito's head with a round-house pent-up in his emotions for months. Mike hit him again just for general purposes, but Joe stopped him from any further destruction to Vito's body. Joe put his foot on Vito's neck and pressed down as he talked to Mike. Vito was gasping loudly. Charlie Daniels came over and pulled Joe off Vito, telling him and Mike that the chopper was just advised that the Spanish military were on the way: "We gotta get out of here now guys, so get Mrs. Donahue. Let's load the chopper and beat it."

Ramon led Joe into the house; both were armed to the teeth. Joe Jr. and Steve were right behind them, ready to do whatever need-ed to be done to finish this and finish it quickly. Joe saw the kicked-in door and heard Sandy's voice; it was music to his ears. She was a mess, but Joe hugged her and both fell to the floor in a sitting embrace. Gert was moaning, but soon they heard the "death rattle" and she gave up the ghost. She died with a look of disbelief and a sneer of hatred on her face. One of Sandy's shots had hit her in the chest and she was toast.

They walked downstairs and outside amidst the carnage of dead bodies and piled-up weapons. The men left alive were tied together to posts and the Basques wanted to kill them. Santos told them that the military was on the way and that they should disappear quickly. He thanked them profusely for their help, but they said that they were just as happy to have done it; they owed these bad guys for what they had done to Maria and her brother. Most of them got in the truck, covered themselves with hay, and drove off into the hillside. Yes, the machine gun and rocket launcher became their reward.

The group got into the chopper while the Basque raiders disappeared into the foothills like the ghosts that they were. Charlie told Santos and Erik to get Vito Scaglionne on the chopper with them. He didn't care much about the others, but Vito was going to pay for what he had done here. As the chopper lifted off, they flew over a convoy of military vehicles slowly approaching the villa. They noticed that the commander of the militia waved to them from his open-armored vehicle; Danny rocked the chopper in acknowledgement. The convoy drove on without stopping to pick up bodies or even swerving around them.

Danny told them that they had to cross the Pyrenees and hoped that they weren't too overloaded to make the ascent. None of the team was injured except for Sandy, who was overjoyed and filled with love and admiration for these fine men. She could not even think about her pain. Sandy was woman: watch her soar, hear her roar! It just went to show you that you could take the woman out of the Bronx, but you couldn't take the Bronx out of the woman.

The chopper was a Sikorsky HH-60H multi-mission VERTREP; its capacity was four crew members and eight passengers. We were seventeen in total and we had a problem. Danny was chief pilot and Charlie, Pete, and Erik who all had chopper experience, made up his crew. They were the essentials but we knew that we had to lose some weight if we were going to bring this daring venture to a happy close.

Ramon and our dubious new friend, Sergeant Madera, volunteered to be dropped off anywhere on the lower slope to lessen the load. Charlie, Erik, and Santos were all native to this area as well so they too said that we could drop them anywhere. All of them would make their way back home on foot and were in friendly territory. Charlie winked at Joe and Mike, pointed to his cell phone and said, "I ain't walking anywhere." Dropping them just outside Sant Pau de Seguries, we saw that the town was only about a five-mile hike away. We bid adieu to our friends and wished them a good trip. Joe said that he would be in contact with them when they were safely home in the

U.S. Steve jumped into the copilot seat, Joe Jr. plopped into the navigator's chair, and we were good to go.

The three General Electric turbines whined against the load but we lifted off, once again ready to assault the heights of the Pyrenees. We were flying at about two thousand feet when Vito tried to grab a pistol that was lying on the floor. We had literally tossed a lot of gear into the chopper since we were in a rush to split the villa scene. Quite a mess was on the floor of our whirlybird and I guessed that we weren't paying close attention to details. There was a fight and some minor wrestling when all of a sudden the sliding door flew open and Vito escaped. He fell out; he wasn't pushed, was he? Nobody knew, nobody asked and nobody cared, it just happened. He did not have wings, he didn't deserve wings, and he would never have wings. "How did that happen?" somebody asked, but no one could venture a guess. The general consensus was that it was an accident so we all just shrugged our shoulders and said, "Well, that's the way the mop flops. Goodbye, Vito."

Sandy smiled, silently wished Vito a happy landing, and chuckled at the poetry of it all. Joe thought that now Tony and Mario Lorenzo, Tommy McGuinnes, and Bill Grandly would have someone else to swap war stories with as they shoveled coal forever.

Without anyone noticing, Danny hit the button, and the door slid back to its proper place. He jubilantly said that we could now make it over the top with ease.

CHAPTER NINE

Homeward Bound

O ur chopper settled down in a deserted field about twenty miles south of the city of Port-Vendres, France, not far from the Mediterranean Sea. We had no time for sightseeing but our spirits were high. A twelve-seat limousine was waiting for us, parked alongside a Fiat sedan. A friend of Santos greeted us with a big smile and a bottle of French wine. He also had our passports and related paperwork. Joe Jr. and Steve would be taken back to resume their ten-day passes; both were headed to Kandahar, Afghanistan; they left in the Fiat to be driven to the nearest airport. It was a bitter-sweet parting, but it had to be done. Both promised to come home soon and Steve asked Joe to kiss the kids for him.

Danny said that he was taking the helicopter back across the border tonight and in a false tone of voice he said, "My work is never done." He clasped hands with all of us, gave a few genuine hugs and, with a tear in his eye, thanked us for asking for his help. He said that being a spook; he did not always see the good guys win. He went on to say that this deal was the best "shoot-em-up" of his life. He said that he would visit Donahue Downs as soon as he had the chance.

Mike, Sandy, Barney, Pete, Israel, Bob, Mel, and I boarded a puddle-jumper turboprop for the hop to Paris and our connecting flight to New York.

I was Joe Donahue, the frog who had become a prince again and was given a new lease on life. I guess that God really is a God of second chances. I had my wife back and I was the happiest and luckiest man in the world. If any man in the course of history truly had a band of brothers, I had met that lofty plateau with my friends: Barney, Pete, Santos, Charlie, Erik, Mike, Bob, Israel, and Mel. Also, I met that level of brotherhood with Steve, my son-in-law, and Joe Jr., my son. I knew that had I asked, Chris and Rick would have joined this crew as well. I was blessed beyond measure. With these men in my life and Sandy by my side, there was nothing in this life that I could not do. With a clear eye and a clear conscience, I would face whatever came my way. With the truth that always set men free, I would stand tall for honesty, peace, and the American way of life. I guess that I have to tell you that I draw the line about saying anything to the FBI and the U.S. Attorney; they just wouldn't understand. I was sure that the U.S. ambassadors to Spain, France, and Italy would go ballistic if they knew all that went down. I would bite my tongue, plead the Fifth — whatever, they ain't getting this story out of me.

We had no luggage; Danny took all the guns back across the border with him and would turn them over to Santos and Charlie when he got there. We were seven American tourist wannabes and one lady with a missing front tooth and a bruised face. We looked just great. We had a two-hour wait at Orly so we ran our credit cards for all they were worth. We washed up and changed clothes in the men's room, leaving our old clothes in the trash receptacle, shoes and all.

Sandy did wonders with her looks but she was gone for almost the entire two hours. She came out walking a bit slowly, but from outward appearances looked just fine and dandy. The only thing

Sandy wanted to keep was her hairspray; it would be a remembrance of this ordeal for her. She said that she would frame it and put it over the mantle at the hotel. Only those of us who shared in this victory would know the significance of the can of hairspray and why it deserved such a place of honor. I imagine that future guests at the hotel would shake their heads in wonder; some may even think it was pop art. She felt like hell, but her smile and a half-ton of makeup covered the wounds. God, I love this woman.

I called Johnny at Donahue Downs; the confab went like this: "Hi Johnny, everything is OK; I am just touching base with you. Tell me that everything is OK at the hotel and the contractors are ready to submit a building plan to me. Mrs. Donahue and I are anxious to take a look and get this job done already." This was my way of letting Johnny know that we had rescued Sandy. I also knew that Schmidt was listening in and that fact made me chuckle a bit.

Johnny said, "Mr. Donahue, the FBI is all over me. Everyday they ask me questions for which I have no answers. They want to know where you are, what you are doing, when will you be here to talk to them and on and on; it never ends."

I told Johnny that I would not tell him anything; that way, he didn't have to lie to them: "John, you just tell them that you heard from me via cell phone, but you have no idea where I am. Tell them that Mrs. Donahue and I will be home in a couple of days; our vacation is over." I knew that this would cause deep concern for Major Schmidt, who just hadda be monitoring this call.

I closed the call with John by telling him to tell the contractor that I expected a building proposal in three days and if I was not happy with what he had to say, I would put the entire deal out to open bid to all the local contractors. Johnny chuckled and sounded happy with the new authority I had just given him. He said that he would handle the contractor and keep the FBI as happy as he could. He also said that all would be in order by the time we got home. He asked me to call him when we landed in Philly. He wanted to get the new chef working on a suitable welcome home spread for us.

"No problem John, I'll do that. See you soon then, buddy, and by the way, thanks for doing a great job." Click-click, we boarded the plane and we all settled in for a well-deserved nap. Nobody heard the third click on the phone line.

Major Schmidt wanted to find some reason to bust us all but he came up empty-handed on all fronts.

From Spain it was reported that the militia had put down a minor Basque uprising by raiding a small villa just northeast of Girona. Many were slain but no government forces were lost. Massive arrests were made which meant that they valiantly arrested those hired thugs that the Basques had left tied to posts.

In Madrid, a local hood named Pedro was arrested on gun-smuggling charges. An informant at the raided village gave up his name; torture is a compelling argument.

Border patrol from Spain and France, were arguing with each other over a dead Vito Scaglionne: "You take him. No, you take him." Finally, the Italians sent a police representative who identified Scaglionne's body. With no family to claim him, his remains were cremated at Italy's expense. They were glad to do so and were finally able to close a file that they had been working on for years.

None of the men who were in on our deal were even questioned. Charlie Daniels, Erik Bronkowski, and Santos just said, "Huh, whattaya talking about? We got our own problems to deal with; we don't need the extra work."

Major Schmidt was waiting for us at Donahue Downs but the only ones to show were Sandy and I. Bob and Israel grabbed a connecting flight to JFK Airport, and Pete was lucky enough to get a plane that left fifteen minutes later direct to Binghamton. Mel took a cab to his home in Philly and Barney had called ahead to have his lady friend pick him up and take him home with her. He was building his story of a "lost weekend."

Schmidt told us point-blank that he had intercepted Scaglionne's original email with the attached video of Sandy's torture.

He wanted to know just how she had managed to get back home in one piece. I looked at him squarely in the eye and told him that Vito had a change of heart and merely released her in Barcelona, where we picked her up and took her home. Mike was convincing with his off-the-record debriefing and stuck to the same story, word for word.

Later question-and-answer talks with my friends went something like this: Barney said he was with his girlfriend for a week and had no idea that Joe and Mike had even left Pennsylvania. Mel said he was fishing and Pete just said, "Where I have been for the past few days is my business and unless you have a warrant for my arrest, it is none of yours." Pete didn't like Schmidt all that much. He thought that he had done a much better job when he was the boss of that office. He also screwed over Mel, and Pete didn't take that too kindly.

Bob and Israel responded to Schmidt's "courtesy call" up in Yonkers; they faced him together. I knew that Bob wouldn't lie to him because of his strong religious beliefs and wondered how he would handle it. I found out later that Israel did all the talking and Bob just nodded when needed.

None of our stories were believed, but we couldn't be proven wrong; eventually the issue was dropped. Somewhere down deep, I thought that Schmidt was a good guy and really didn't pursue the chase as deeply as he could have. I want to think that he saw the moral justice in what happened and he too wanted to leave it alone. I gave him the benefit of that doubt.

Two weeks after the interviews were over; I got a phone call from an unidentified person. All he said was "Mr. Donahue, I am a representative of our government and I want to assure you and your family and friends, that the issue of your trip to Spain is a closed and forgotten issue. All of the governments involved are happy with the outcome and no person in the employ of any agency of the United States will suffer any consequences."

He closed the call by saying that powerful figures conveyed the following message: "Thank you." With that, the call ended and a chapter of our lives was closed and out of our memory — except for the can of hairspray, that is!

Over the course of the next few weeks, we got Sandy all the medical and dental attention that she needed. Soon she was back to her vibrant, loving, and happy self, but royally upset with the ruination of our hotel. It became her mission to interview interior decorators, restoration experts, and antique dealers with the aim of rebuilding Donahue Downs. Johnny was her right-hand man in this and he turned out to be the guy that I always thought he was. He was a clear-thinking workaholic with a winning personality, coupled with rapt attention to details. Contractors and dealers alike soon found that you could not run a scam by the team of Sandy and John.

CHAPTER TEN

Epilogue

T he hotel was rebuilt in record time and the open-house party was reminiscent of our original opening day affair. Everybody was there: local dignitaries, business owners, cops, and crooks alike. Steve and my son Joe had both been rotated back to the States and they brought their wives and kids. Joe Jr. was now sporting Captain's bars. My other sons, Chris and Rick, showed up with their wives and kids who interacted with each other like a barrel of monkeys. The band played, the drinks flowed (except for me — phooey), the pool was full of kids, and conversations covered the gamut.

Santos had been transferred to Washington and given a sweetheart job piloting a desk and phone bank. He was like a penned-in bull, but smiled and said that soon he would be up and at 'em again. He was pulling strings to go to Mexico and work on the illegal alien problem.

Charlie was on leave and he and Erik managed to both attend our party; we were glad to see them again. They updated us about

Madera, Ramon, and the Basques, but to tell you the truth, I wasn't listening. I was thankful that they were there and did what they did, but they were responsible for their actions and now realized that life was full of choices. Charlie said that to the best of his knowledge, both were walking the straight and narrow now, and neither one went to jail.

Pete filed for licensing in Pennsylvania and was now the attorney of record for Donahue Downs. We were trying to get him to move down here but he said that he couldn't leave his disgruntled divorce clients right then. I asked Mel if he would like to work with us in our security department with his old pal Mike and he jumped at the chance to be busy again.

Barney had an electric-eye motion detector system put in around the maintenance shed and warned even me to stay away from it. My son Joe and Steve didn't have to answer any questions at all, since they were on leave from the Marines at the time and what they did was their business. Nobody except those that were there even knew that they had a hand in the rescue of Sandy and the death of Vito Scaglionne. Danny, the chopper pilot, was still out there shuttling the good guys and bad guys around with a bulletproof vest as his normal attire.

We had a small meeting upstairs with only the A-Team in attendance, including Sandy. Drinks were hoisted, backs were slapped, heartfelt hugs were given all around, and lots of laughs were had too. Bob and I had ginger ale.

Just then a FedEx truck rolled up to the front door and Johnny signed for the delivery. He brought it upstairs, knocked on the office door, and handed me a large bouquet of flowers. The note read "Well done, Mr. Donahue." It was cryptically signed H. Philbrick, #A5-45833 Federal Penitentiary, Allenwood, Pennsylvania.

Printed in the United States
32608LVS00005B/40-153

9 781932 762242